John Griffith London (born **John Griffith Chaney**; January 12, 1876 – November 22, 1916) was an American novelist, journalist, and social activist. A pioneer in the world of commercial magazine fiction, he was one of the first writers to become a worldwide celebrity and earn a large fortune from writing. He was also an innovator in the genre that would later become known as science fiction. His most famous works include The Call of the Wild and White Fang, both set in the Klondike Gold Rush, as well as the short stories "To Build a Fire", "An Odyssey of the North", and "Love of Life". He also wrote about the South Pacific in stories such as "The Pearls of Parlay" and "The Heathen". London was part of the radical literary group "The Crowd" in San Francisco and a passionate advocate of unionization, socialism, and the rights of workers. He wrote several powerful works dealing with these topics, such as his dystopian novel The Iron Heel, his non-fiction exposé The People of the Abyss, and The War of the Classes. (Source: Wikipedia)

Literary works:
The Cruise of the Dazzler (1902)
A Daughter of the Snows (1902)
The Call of the Wild (1903)
The Kempton-Wace Letters (1903)
The Sea-Wolf (1904)
The Game (1905)
White Fang (1906)
Before Adam (1907)
The Iron Heel (1908)
Martin Eden (1909)
Burning Daylight (1910)
Adventure (1911)
The Scarlet Plague (1912)
A Son of the Sun (1912)
The Abysmal Brute (1913)
The Valley of the Moon (1913)

THE
NIGHT–BORN
&
THE STRENGTH OF
THE STRONG

JACK LONDON

PRINCE CLASSICS

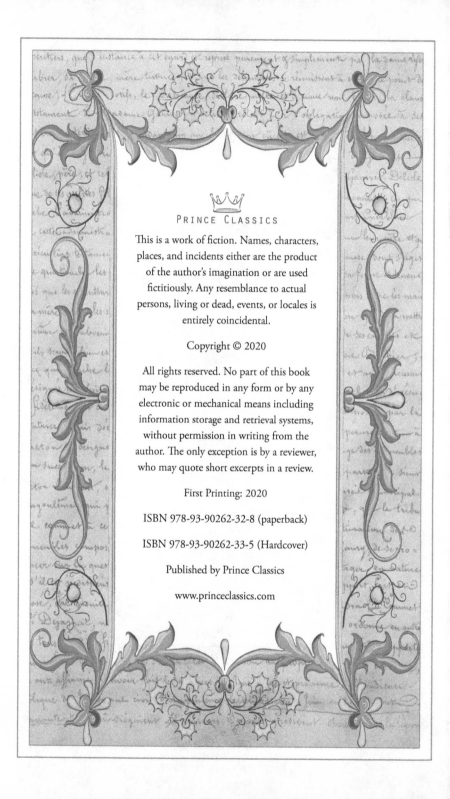

PRINCE CLASSICS

First Printing: 2020

ISBN 978-93-90262-32-8 (paperback)

ISBN 978-93-90262-33-5 (Hardcover)

Published by Prince Classics

www.princeclassics.com

Contents

THE
NIGHT–BORN
&
THE STRENGTH OF
THE STRONG

THE NIGHT-BORN

THE NIGHT-BORN

It was in the old Alta-Inyo Club—a warm night for San Francisco—and through the open windows, hushed and far, came the brawl of the streets. The talk had led on from the Graft Prosecution and the latest signs that the town was to be run wide open, down through all the grotesque sordidness and rottenness of man-hate and man-meanness, until the name of O'Brien was mentioned—O'Brien, the promising young pugilist who had been killed in the prize-ring the night before. At once the air had seemed to freshen. O'Brien had been a clean-living young man with ideals. He neither drank, smoked, nor swore, and his had been the body of a beautiful young god. He had even carried his prayer-book to the ringside. They found it in his coat pocket in the dressing-room... afterward.

Here was Youth, clean and wholesome, unsullied—the thing of glory and wonder for men to conjure with..... after it has been lost to them and they have turned middle-aged. And so well did we conjure, that Romance came and for an hour led us far from the man-city and its snarling roar. Bardwell, in a way, started it by quoting from Thoreau; but it was old Trefethan, bald-headed and dewlapped, who took up the quotation and for the hour to come was romance incarnate. At first we wondered how many Scotches he had consumed since dinner, but very soon all that was forgotten.

"It was in 1898—I was thirty-five then," he said. "Yes, I know you are adding it up. You're right. I'm forty-seven now; look ten years more; and the doctors say—damn the doctors anyway!"

He lifted the long glass to his lips and sipped it slowly to soothe away his irritation.

"But I was young... once. I was young twelve years ago, and I had hair on top of my head, and my stomach was lean as a runner's, and the longest day was none too long for me. I was a husky back there in '98. You remember me, Milner. You knew me then. Wasn't I a pretty good bit of all right?"

Milner nodded and agreed. Like Trefethan, he was another mining engineer who had cleaned up a fortune in the Klondike.

"You certainly were, old man," Milner said. "I'll never forget when you cleaned out those lumberjacks in the M. & M. that night that little newspaper man started the row. Slavin was in the country at the time,"—this to us—"and his manager wanted to get up a match with Trefethan."

"Well, look at me now," Trefethan commanded angrily. "That's what the Goldstead did to me—God knows how many millions, but nothing left in my soul..... nor in my veins. The good red blood is gone. I am a jellyfish, a huge, gross mass of oscillating protoplasm, a—a..."

But language failed him, and he drew solace from the long glass.

"Women looked at me then; and turned their heads to look a second time. Strange that I never married. But the girl. That's what I started to tell you about. I met her a thousand miles from anywhere, and then some. And she quoted to me those very words of Thoreau that Bardwell quoted a moment ago—the ones about the day-born gods and the night-born."

"It was after I had made my locations on Goldstead—and didn't know what a treasure-pot that that trip creek was going to prove—that I made that trip east over the Rockies, angling across to the Great Up North there the Rockies are something more than a back-bone. They are a boundary, a dividing line, a wall impregnable and unscalable. There is no intercourse across them, though, on occasion, from the early days, wandering trappers have crossed them, though more were lost by the way than ever came through. And that was precisely why I tackled the job. It was a traverse any man would be proud to make. I am prouder of it right now than anything else I have ever done.

"It is an unknown land. Great stretches of it have never been explored. There are big valleys there where the white man has never set foot, and Indian tribes as primitive as ten thousand years... almost, for they have had some contact with the whites. Parties of them come out once in a while to trade, and that is all. Even the Hudson Bay Company failed to find them and farm them.

14

"And now the girl. I was coming up a stream—you'd call it a river in California—uncharted—and unnamed. It was a noble valley, now shut in by high canyon walls, and again opening out into beautiful stretches, wide and long, with pasture shoulder-high in the bottoms, meadows dotted with flowers, and with clumps of timberspruce—virgin and magnificent. The dogs were packing on their backs, and were sore-footed and played out; while I was looking for any bunch of Indians to get sleds and drivers from and go on with the first snow. It was late fall, but the way those flowers persisted surprised me. I was supposed to be in sub-arctic America, and high up among the buttresses of the Rockies, and yet there was that everlasting spread of flowers. Some day the white settlers will be in there and growing wheat down all that valley.

"And then I lifted a smoke, and heard the barking of the dogs—Indian dogs—and came into camp. There must have been five hundred of them, proper Indians at that, and I could see by the jerking-frames that the fall hunting had been good. And then I met her—Lucy. That was her name. Sign language—that was all we could talk with, till they led me to a big fly—you know, half a tent, open on the one side where a campfire burned. It was all of moose-skins, this fly—moose-skins, smoke-cured, hand-rubbed, and golden-brown. Under it everything was neat and orderly as no Indian camp ever was. The bed was laid on fresh spruce boughs. There were furs galore, and on top of all was a robe of swanskins—white swan-skins—I have never seen anything like that robe. And on top of it, sitting cross-legged, was Lucy. She was nut-brown. I have called her a girl. But she was not. She was a woman, a nut-brown woman, an Amazon, a full-blooded, full-bodied woman, and royal ripe. And her eyes were blue.

"That's what took me off my feet—her eyes—blue, not China blue, but deep blue, like the sea and sky all melted into one, and very wise. More than that, they had laughter in them—warm laughter, sun-warm and human, very human, and... shall I say feminine? They were. They were a woman's eyes, a proper woman's eyes. You know what that means. Can I say more? Also, in those blue eyes were, at the same time, a wild unrest, a wistful yearning, and a repose, an absolute repose, a sort of all-wise and philosophical calm."

Trefethan broke off abruptly.

"You fellows think I am screwed. I'm not. This is only my fifth since dinner. I am dead sober. I am solemn. I sit here now side by side with my sacred youth. It is not I—'old' Trefethan—that talks; it is my youth, and it is my youth that says those were the most wonderful eyes I have ever seen—so very calm, so very restless; so very wise, so very curious; so very old, so very young; so satisfied and yet yearning so wistfully. Boys, I can't describe them. When I have told you about her, you may know better for yourselves."

"She did not stand up. But she put out her hand."

"'Stranger,' she said, 'I'm real glad to see you.'

"I leave it to you—that sharp, frontier, Western tang of speech. Picture my sensations. It was a woman, a white woman, but that tang! It was amazing that it should be a white woman, here, beyond the last boundary of the world—but the tang. I tell you, it hurt. It was like the stab of a flatted note. And yet, let me tell you, that woman was a poet. You shall see."

"She dismissed the Indians. And, by Jove, they went. They took her orders and followed her blind. She was hi-yu skookam chief. She told the bucks to make a camp for me and to take care of my dogs. And they did, too. And they knew enough not to get away with as much as a moccasin-lace of my outfit. She was a regular She-Who-Must-Be-Obeyed, and I want to tell you it chilled me to the marrow, sent those little thrills Marathoning up and down my spinal column, meeting a white woman out there at the head of a tribe of savages a thousand miles the other side of No Man's Land.

"'Stranger," she said, 'I reckon you're sure the first white that ever set foot in this valley. Set down an' talk a spell, and then we'll have a bite to eat. Which way might you be comin'?'

"There it was, that tang again. But from now to the end of the yarn I want you to forget it. I tell you I forgot it, sitting there on the edge of that swan-skin robe and listening and looking at the most wonderful woman that ever stepped out of the pages of Thoreau or of any other man's book.

"I stayed on there a week. It was on her invitation. She promised to fit me out with dogs and sleds and with Indians that would put me across the best pass of the Rockies in five hundred miles. Her fly was pitched apart from the others, on the high bank by the river, and a couple of Indian girls did her cooking for her and the camp work. And so we talked and talked, while the first snow fell and continued to fall and make a surface for my sleds. And this was her story.

"She was frontier-born, of poor settlers, and you know what that means—work, work, always work, work in plenty and without end.

"'I never seen the glory of the world,' she said. 'I had no time. I knew it was right out there, anywhere, all around the cabin, but there was always the bread to set, the scrubbin' and the washin' and the work that was never done. I used to be plumb sick at times, jes' to get out into it all, especially in the spring when the songs of the birds drove me most clean crazy. I wanted to run out through the long pasture grass, wetting my legs with the dew of it, and to climb the rail fence, and keep on through the timber and up and up over the divide so as to get a look around. Oh, I had all kinds of hankerings—to follow up the canyon beds and slosh around from pool to pool, making friends with the water-dogs and the speckly trout; to peep on the sly and watch the squirrels and rabbits and small furry things and see what they was doing and learn the secrets of their ways. Seemed to me, if I had time, I could crawl among the flowers, and, if I was good and quiet, catch them whispering with themselves, telling all kinds of wise things that mere humans never know.'"

Trefethan paused to see that his glass had been refilled.

"Another time she said: 'I wanted to run nights like a wild thing, just to run through the moonshine and under the stars, to run white and naked in the darkness that I knew must feel like cool velvet, and to run and run and keep on running. One evening, plumb tuckered out—it had been a dreadful hard hot day, and the bread wouldn't raise and the churning had gone wrong, and I was all irritated and jerky—well, that evening I made mention to dad of this wanting to run of mine. He looked at me curious-some and a bit scared. And then he gave me two pills to take. Said to go to bed and get a good sleep and I'd be all hunky-dory in the morning. So I never mentioned my hankerings to him, or any one any more.'

"The mountain home broke up—starved out, I imagine—and the family came to Seattle to live. There she worked in a factory—long hours, you know, and all the rest, deadly work. And after a year of that she became waitress in a cheap restaurant—hash-slinger, she called it. She said to me once, 'Romance I guess was what I wanted. But there wan't no romance floating around in dishpans and washtubs, or in factories and hash-joints.'

"When she was eighteen she married—a man who was going up to Juneau to start a restaurant. He had a few dollars saved, and appeared prosperous. She didn't love him—she was emphatic about that, but she was all tired out, and she wanted to get away from the unending drudgery. Besides, Juneau was in Alaska, and her yearning took the form of a desire to see that wonderland. But little she saw of it. He started the restaurant, a little cheap one, and she quickly learned what he had married her for..... to save paying wages. She came pretty close to running the joint and doing all the work from waiting to dishwashing. She cooked most of the time as well. And she had four years of it.

"Can't you picture her, this wild woods creature, quick with every old primitive instinct, yearning for the free open, and mowed up in a vile little hash-joint and toiling and moiling for four mortal years?

"'There was no meaning in anything,' she said. 'What was it all about! Why was I born! Was that all the meaning of life—just to work and work and be always tired!—to go to bed tired and to wake up tired, with every day like every other day unless it was harder?' She had heard talk of immortal life from the gospel sharps, she said, but she could not reckon that what she was doin' was a likely preparation for her immortality.

"But she still had her dreams, though more rarely. She had read a few books—what, it is pretty hard to imagine, Seaside Library novels most likely; yet they had been food for fancy. 'Sometimes,' she said, 'when I was that dizzy from the heat of the cooking that if I didn't take a breath of fresh air I'd faint, I'd stick my head out of the kitchen window, and close my eyes and see most wonderful things. All of a sudden I'd be traveling down a country road, and everything clean and quiet, no dust, no dirt; just streams ripplin' down sweet meadows, and lambs playing, breezes blowing the breath of flowers, and soft sunshine over everything; and lovely cows lazying knee-deep in quiet pools, and young girls bathing in a curve of stream all white and slim and natural—and I'd know I was in Arcady. I'd read about that country once, in a book. And maybe knights, all flashing in the sun, would come riding around a bend in the road, or a lady on a milk-white mare, and in the distance I could see the towers of a castle rising, or I just knew, on the next turn, that I'd come upon some palace, all white and airy and fairy-like, with fountains playing, and flowers all over everything, and peacocks on the lawn..... and then I'd open my eyes, and the heat of the cooking range would strike on me, and I'd hear Jake sayin'—he was my husband—I'd hear Jake sayin', "Why ain't you served them beans? Think I can wait here all day!" Romance!—I reckon the nearest I ever come to it was when a drunken Armenian cook got the snakes and tried to cut my throat with a potato knife and I got my arm burned on the stove before I could lay him out with the potato stomper.

"'I wanted easy ways, and lovely things, and Romance and all that; but it just seemed I had no luck nohow and was only and expressly born for cooking and dishwashing. There was a wild crowd in Juneau them days, but I looked at the other women, and their way of life didn't excite me. I reckon I wanted to be clean. I don't know why; I just wanted to, I guess; and I reckoned I might as well die dishwashing as die their way.'"

Trefethan halted in his tale for a moment, completing to himself some thread of thought.

"And this is the woman I met up there in the Arctic, running a tribe of wild Indians and a few thousand square miles of hunting territory. And it happened, simply enough, though, for that matter, she might have lived and died among the pots and pans. But 'Came the whisper, came the vision.' That was all she needed, and she got it.

"'I woke up one day,' she said. 'Just happened on it in a scrap of newspaper. I remember every word of it, and I can give it to you.' And then she quoted Thoreau's Cry of the Human:

"'The young pines springing up, in the corn field from year to year are to me a refreshing fact. We talk of civilizing the Indian, but that is not the name for his improvement. By the wary independence and aloofness of his dim forest life he preserves his intercourse with his native gods and is admitted from time to time to a rare and peculiar society with nature. He has glances of starry recognition, to which our saloons are strangers. The steady illumination of his qenius, dim only because distant, is like the faint but satisfying light of the stars compared with the dazzling but ineffectual and short-lived blaze of candles. The Society Islanders had their day-born gods, but they were not supposed to be of equal antiquity with the..... night-born gods.'

"That's what she did, repeated it word for word, and I forgot the tang, for it was solemn, a declaration of religion—pagan, if you will; and clothed in the living garmenture of herself.

"'And the rest of it was torn away,' she added, a great emptiness in her voice. 'It was only a scrap of newspaper. But that Thoreau was a wise man. I wish I knew more about him.' She stopped a moment, and I swear her face was ineffably holy as she said, 'I could have made him a good wife.'

"And then she went on. 'I knew right away, as soon as I read that, what was the matter with me. I was a night-born. I, who had lived all my life with the day-born, was a night-born. That was why I had never been satisfied with cooking and dishwashing; that was why I had hankered to run naked in the moonlight. And I knew that this dirty little Juneau hash-joint was no place for me. And right there and then I said, "I quit." I packed up my few rags of clothes, and started. Jake saw me and tried to stop me.

"'What you doing?" he says.

"'Divorcin' you and me,' I says. 'I'm headin' for tall timber and where I belong.'"

"'No you don't,' he says, reaching for me to stop me. 'The cooking has got on your head. You listen to me talk before you up and do anything brash.'

"But I pulled a gun-a little Colt's forty-four—and says, 'This does my talkin' for me.'

"And I left."

Trefethan emptied his glass and called for another.

"Boys, do you know what that girl did? She was twenty-two. She had spent her life over the dish-pan and she knew no more about the world than I do of the fourth dimension, or the fifth. All roads led to her desire. No; she didn't head for the dance-halls. On the Alaskan Pan-handle it is preferable to travel by water. She went down to the beach. An Indian canoe was starting for Dyea—you know the kind, carved out of a single tree, narrow and deep and sixty feet long. She gave them a couple of dollars and got on board.

"'Romance?' she told me. 'It was Romance from the jump. There were three families altogether in that canoe, and that crowded there wasn't room to turn around, with dogs and Indian babies sprawling over everything, and everybody dipping a paddle and making that canoe go.' And all around the great solemn mountains, and tangled drifts of clouds and sunshine. And oh, the silence! the great wonderful silence! And, once, the smoke of a hunter's camp, away off in the distance, trailing among the trees. It was like a picnic, a grand picnic, and I could see my dreams coming true, and I was ready for something to happen 'most any time. And it did.

"'And that first camp, on the island! And the boys spearing fish in the mouth of the creek, and the big deer one of the bucks shot just around the point. And there were flowers everywhere, and in back from the beach the grass was thick and lush and neck-high. And some of the girls went through this with me, and we climbed the hillside behind and picked berries and roots that tasted sour and were good to eat. And we came upon a big bear in the berries making his supper, and he said "Oof!" and ran away as scared as we were. And then the camp, and the camp smoke, and the smell of fresh venison cooking. It was beautiful. I was with the night-born at last, and I knew that was where I belonged. And for the first time in my life, it seemed to me, I went to bed happy that night, looking out under a corner of the canvas at the stars cut off black by a big shoulder of mountain, and listening to the night-noises, and knowing that the same thing would go on next day and forever and ever, for I wasn't going back. And I never did go back.'

"'Romance! I got it next day. We had to cross a big arm of the ocean—twelve or fifteen miles, at least; and it came on to blow when we were in the middle. That night I was along on shore, with one wolf-dog, and I was the only one left alive.'

"Picture it yourself," Trefethan broke off to say. "The canoe was wrecked and lost, and everybody pounded to death on the rocks except her. She went ashore hanging on to a dog's tail, escaping the rocks and washing up on a tiny beach, the only one in miles.

"'Lucky for me it was the mainland,' she said. 'So I headed right away back, through the woods and over the mountains and straight on anywhere. Seemed I was looking for something and knew I'd find it. I wasn't afraid. I was night-born, and the big timber couldn't kill me. And on the second day I found it. I came upon a small clearing and a tumbledown cabin. Nobody had been there for years and years. The roof had fallen in. Rotted blankets lay in the bunks, and pots and pans were on the stove. But that was not the most curious thing. Outside, along the edge of the trees, you can't guess what I found. The skeletons of eight horses, each tied to a tree. They had starved to death, I reckon, and left only little piles of bones scattered some here and there. And each horse had had a load on its back. There the loads lay, in among the bones—painted canvas sacks, and inside moosehide sacks, and inside the moosehide sacks—what do you think?'"

She stopped, reached under a corner of the bed among the spruce boughs, and pulled out a leather sack. She untied the mouth and ran out into my hand as pretty a stream of gold as I have ever seen—coarse gold, placer gold, some large dust, but mostly nuggets, and it was so fresh and rough that it scarcely showed signs of water-wash.

"'You say you're a mining engineer,' she said, 'and you know this country. Can you name a pay-creek that has the color of that gold!'

"I couldn't! There wasn't a trace of silver. It was almost pure, and I told her so.

22

"'You bet,' she said. 'I sell that for nineteen dollars an ounce. You can't get over seventeen for Eldorado gold, and Minook gold don't fetch quite eighteen. Well, that was what I found among the bones—eight horse-loads of it, one hundred and fifty pounds to the load.'

"'A quarter of a million dollars!' I cried out.

"'That's what I reckoned it roughly,' she answered. 'Talk about Romance! And me a slaving the way I had all the years, when as soon as I ventured out, inside three days, this was what happened. And what became of the men that mined all that gold? Often and often I wonder about it. They left their horses, loaded and tied, and just disappeared off the face of the earth, leaving neither hide nor hair behind them. I never heard tell of them. Nobody knows anything about them. Well, being the night-born, I reckon I was their rightful heir.'"

Trefethan stopped to light a cigar.

"Do you know what that girl did? She cached the gold, saving out thirty pounds, which she carried back to the coast. Then she signaled a passing canoe, made her way to Pat Healy's trading post at Dyea, outfitted, and went over Chilcoot Pass. That was in '88—eight years before the Klondike strike, and the Yukon was a howling wilderness. She was afraid of the bucks, but she took two young squaws with her, crossed the lakes, and went down the river and to all the early camps on the Lower Yukon. She wandered several years over that country and then on in to where I met her. Liked the looks of it, she said, seeing, in her own words, 'a big bull caribou knee-deep in purple iris on the valley-bottom.' She hooked up with the Indians, doctored them, gained their confidence, and gradually took them in charge. She had only left that country once, and then, with a bunch of the young bucks, she went over Chilcoot, cleaned up her gold-cache, and brought it back with her.

"'And here I be, stranger,' she concluded her yarn, 'and here's the most precious thing I own.'

"She pulled out a little pouch of buckskin, worn on her neck like a locket, and opened it. And inside, wrapped in oiled silk, yellowed with age and worn and thumbed, was the original scrap of newspaper containing the quotation from Thoreau.

"'And are you happy... satisfied?' I asked her. 'With a quarter of a million you wouldn't have to work down in the States. You must miss a lot.'

"'Not much,' she answered. 'I wouldn't swop places with any woman down in the States. These are my people; this is where I belong. But there are times—and in her eyes smoldered up that hungry yearning I've mentioned—'there are times when I wish most awful bad for that Thoreau man to happen along.'

"'Why?' I asked.

"'So as I could marry him. I do get mighty lonesome at spells. I'm just a woman—a real woman. I've heard tell of the other kind of women that gallivanted off like me and did queer things—the sort that become soldiers in armies, and sailors on ships. But those women are queer themselves. They're more like men than women; they look like men and they don't have ordinary women's needs. They don't want love, nor little children in their arms and around their knees. I'm not that sort. I leave it to you, stranger. Do I look like a man?'

"She didn't. She was a woman, a beautiful, nut-brown woman, with a sturdy, health-rounded woman's body and with wonderful deep-blue woman's eyes.

"'Ain't I woman?' she demanded. 'I am. I'm 'most all woman, and then some. And the funny thing is, though I'm night-born in everything else, I'm not when it comes to mating. I reckon that kind likes its own kind best. That's the way it is with me, anyway, and has been all these years.'

"'You mean to tell me—' I began.

"'Never,' she said, and her eyes looked into mine with the straightness of truth. 'I had one husband, only—him I call the Ox; and I reckon he's still down in Juneau running the hash-joint. Look him up, if you ever get back, and you'll find he's rightly named.'

"And look him up I did, two years afterward. He was all she said—solid and stolid, the Ox—shuffling around and waiting on the tables.

"'You need a wife to help you,' I said.

"'I had one once,' was his answer.

"'Widower?'

"'Yep. She went loco. She always said the heat of the cooking would get her, and it did. Pulled a gun on me one day and ran away with some Siwashes in a canoe. Caught a blow up the coast and all hands drowned.'"

Trefethan devoted himself to his glass and remained silent.

"But the girl?" Milner reminded him.

"You left your story just as it was getting interesting, tender. Did it?"

"It did," Trefethan replied. "As she said herself, she was savage in everything except mating, and then she wanted her own kind. She was very nice about it, but she was straight to the point. She wanted to marry me.

"'Stranger,' she said, 'I want you bad. You like this sort of life or you wouldn't be here trying to cross the Rockies in fall weather. It's a likely spot. You'll find few likelier. Why not settle down! I'll make you a good wife.'

"And then it was up to me. And she waited. I don't mind confessing that I was sorely tempted. I was half in love with her as it was. You know I have never married. And I don't mind adding, looking back over my life, that she is the only woman that ever affected me that way. But it was too preposterous, the whole thing, and I lied like a gentleman. I told her I was already married.

"'Is your wife waiting for you?' she asked.

"I said yes.

"'And she loves you?'

"I said yes.

"And that was all. She never pressed her point... except once, and then she showed a bit of fire.

"'All I've got to do,' she said, 'is to give the word, and you don't get away from here. If I give the word, you stay on... But I ain't going to give it. I wouldn't want you if you didn't want to be wanted... and if you didn't want me.'

"She went ahead and outfitted me and started me on my way.

"'It's a darned shame, stranger,' she said, at parting. 'I like your looks, and I like you. If you ever change your mind, come back.'

"Now there was one thing I wanted to do, and that was to kiss her good-bye, but I didn't know how to go about it nor how she would take it.—I tell you I was half in love with her. But she settled it herself.

"'Kiss me,' she said. 'Just something to go on and remember.'

"And we kissed, there in the snow, in that valley by the Rockies, and I left her standing by the trail and went on after my dogs. I was six weeks in crossing over the pass and coming down to the first post on Great Slave Lake."

The brawl of the streets came up to us like a distant surf. A steward, moving noiselessly, brought fresh siphons. And in the silence Trefethan's voice fell like a funeral bell:

"It would have been better had I stayed. Look at me."

We saw his grizzled mustache, the bald spot on his head, the puff-sacks under his eyes, the sagging cheeks, the heavy dewlap, the general tiredness and staleness and fatness, all the collapse and ruin of a man who had once been strong but who had lived too easily and too well.

"It's not too late, old man," Bardwell said, almost in a whisper.

"By God! I wish I weren't a coward!" was Trefethan's answering cry. "I could go back to her. She's there, now. I could shape up and live many a long year... with her... up there. To remain here is to commit suicide. But I am an old man—forty-seven—look at me. The trouble is," he lifted his glass and glanced at it, "the trouble is that suicide of this sort is so easy. I am soft and tender. The thought of the long day's travel with the dogs appalls me; the thought of the keen frost in the morning and of the frozen sled-lashings frightens me—"

Automatically the glass was creeping toward his lips. With a swift surge of anger he made as if to crash it down upon the floor. Next came hesitancy and second thought. The glass moved upward to his lips and paused. He laughed harshly and bitterly, but his words were solemn:

"Well, here's to the Night-Born. She WAS a wonder."

THE MADNESS OF JOHN HARNED

I

TELL this for a fact. It happened in the bull-ring at Quito. I sat in the box with John Harned, and with Maria Valenzuela, and with Luis Cervallos. I saw it happen. I saw it all from first to last. I was on the steamer Ecuadore from Panama to Guayaquil. Maria Valenzuela is my cousin. I have known her always. She is very beautiful. I am a Spaniard—an Ecuadoriano, true, but I am descended from Pedro Patino, who was one of Pizarro's captains. They were brave men. They were heroes. Did not Pizarro lead three hundred and fifty Spanish cavaliers and four thousand Indians into the far Cordilleras in search of treasure? And did not all the four thousand Indians and three hundred of the brave cavaliers die on that vain quest? But Pedro Patino did not die. He it was that lived to found the family of the Patino. I am Ecuadoriano, true, but I am Spanish. I am Manuel de Jesus Patino. I own many haciendas, and ten thousand Indians are my slaves, though the law says they are free men who work by freedom of contract. The law is a funny thing. We Ecuadorianos laugh at it. It is our law. We make it for ourselves. I am Manuel de Jesus Patino. Remember that name. It will be written some day in history. There are revolutions in Ecuador. We call them elections. It is a good joke is it not?—what you call a pun?

John Harned was an American. I met him first at the Tivoli hotel in Panama. He had much money—this I have heard. He was going to Lima, but he met Maria Valenzuela in the Tivoli hotel. Maria Valenzuela is my cousin, and she is beautiful. It is true, she is the most beautiful woman in Ecuador. But also is she most beautiful in every country—in Paris, in Madrid, in New York, in Vienna. Always do all men look at her, and John Harned looked long at her at Panama. He loved her, that I know for a fact. She was Ecuadoriano, true—but she was of all countries; she was of all the world. She spoke many languages. She sang—ah! like an artiste. Her smile—wonderful, divine. Her eyes—ah! have I not seen men look in her eyes? They were what you English call amazing. They were promises of paradise. Men drowned themselves in her eyes.

Maria Valenzuela was rich—richer than I, who am accounted very rich in Ecuador. But John Harned did not care for her money. He had a heart—a funny heart. He was a fool. He did not go to Lima. He left the steamer at Guayaquil and followed her to Quito. She was coming home from Europe and other places. I do not see what she found in him, but she liked him. This I know for a fact, else he would not have followed her to Quito. She asked him to come. Well do I remember the occasion. She said:

"Come to Quito and I will show you the bullfight—brave, clever, magnificent!"

But he said: "I go to Lima, not Quito. Such is my passage engaged on the steamer."

"You travel for pleasure—no?" said Maria Valenzuela; and she looked at him as only Maria Valenzuela could look, her eyes warm with the promise.

And he came. No; he did not come for the bull-fight. He came because of what he had seen in her eyes. Women like Maria Valenzuela are born once in a hundred years. They are of no country and no time. They are what you call goddesses. Men fall down at their feet. They play with men and run them through their pretty fingers like sand. Cleopatra was such a woman they say; and so was Circe. She turned men into swine. Ha! ha! It is true—no?

It all came about because Maria Valenzuela said:

"You English people are—what shall I say?—savage—no? You prize-fight. Two men each hit the other with their fists till their eyes are blinded and their noses are broken. Hideous! And the other men who look on cry out loudly and are made glad. It is barbarous—no?"

"But they are men," said John Harned; "and they prize-fight out of desire. No one makes them prize-fight. They do it because they desire it more than anything else in the world."

Maria Valenzuela—there was scorn in her smile as she said: "They kill each other often—is it not so? I have read it in the papers."

"But the bull," said John Harned.

"The bull is killed many times in the bull-fight, and the bull does not come into the the ring out of desire. It is not fair to the bull. He is compelled to fight. But the man in the prize-fight—no; he is not compelled."

"He is the more brute therefore," said Maria Valenzuela.

"He is savage. He is primitive. He is animal. He strikes with his paws like a bear from a cave, and he is ferocious. But the bull-fight—ah! You have not seen the bullfight—no? The toreador is clever. He must have skill. He is modern. He is romantic. He is only a man, soft and tender, and he faces the wild bull in conflict. And he kills with a sword, a slender sword, with one thrust, so, to the heart of the great beast. It is delicious. It makes the heart beat to behold—the small man, the great beast, the wide level sand, the thousands that look on without breath; the great beast rushes to the attack, the small man stands like a statue; he does not move, he is unafraid, and in his hand is the slender sword flashing like silver in the sun; nearer and nearer rushes the great beast with its sharp horns, the man does not move, and then—so—the sword flashes, the thrust is made, to the heart, to the hilt, the bull falls to the sand and is dead, and the man is unhurt. It is brave. It is magnificent! Ah!—I could love the toreador. But the man of the prize-fight—he is the brute, the human beast, the savage primitive, the maniac that receives many blows in his stupid face and rejoices. Come to Quito and I will show you the brave sport of men, the toreador and the bull."

But John Harned did not go to Quito for the bull-fight. He went because of Maria Valenzuela. He was a large man, more broad of shoulder than we Ecuadorianos, more tall, more heavy of limb and bone. True, he was larger of his own race. His eyes were blue, though I have seen them gray, and, sometimes, like cold steel. His features were large, too—not delicate like ours, and his jaw was very strong to look at. Also, his face was smooth-shaven like a priest's. Why should a man feel shame for the hair on his face? Did not God put it there? Yes, I believe in God—I am not a pagan like many of you English. God is good. He made me an Ecuadoriano with ten thousand slaves. And when I die I shall go to God. Yes, the priests are right.

But John Harned. He was a quiet man. He talked always in a low voice, and he never moved his hands when he talked. One would have thought his heart was a piece of ice; yet did he have a streak of warm in his blood, for he followed Maria Valenzuela to Quito. Also, and for all that he talked low without moving his hands, he was an animal, as you shall see—the beast primitive, the stupid, ferocious savage of the long ago that dressed in wild skins and lived in the caves along with the bears and wolves.

Luis Cervallos is my friend, the best of Ecuadorianos. He owns three cacao plantations at Naranjito and Chobo. At Milagro is his big sugar plantation. He has large haciendas at Ambato and Latacunga, and down the coast is he interested in oil-wells. Also has he spent much money in planting rubber along the Guayas. He is modern, like the Yankee; and, like the Yankee, full of business. He has much money, but it is in many ventures, and ever he needs more money for new ventures and for the old ones. He has been everywhere and seen everything. When he was a very young man he was in the Yankee military academy what you call West Point. There was trouble. He was made to resign. He does not like Americans. But he did like Maria Valenzuela, who was of his own country. Also, he needed her money for his ventures and for his gold mine in Eastern Ecuador where the painted Indians live. I was his friend. It was my desire that he should marry Maria Valenzuela. Further, much of my money had I invested in his ventures, more so in his gold mine which was very rich but which first required the expense of much money before it would yield forth its riches. If Luis Cervallos married Maria Valenzuela I should have more money very immediately.

But John Harned followed Maria Valenzuela to Quito, and it was quickly clear to us—to Luis Cervallos and me that she looked upon John Harned with great kindness. It is said that a woman will have her will, but this is a case not in point, for Maria Valenzuela did not have her will—at least not with John Harned. Perhaps it would all have happened as it did, even if Luis Cervallos and I had not sat in the box that day at the bull-ring in Quito. But this I know: we DID sit in the box that day. And I shall tell you what happened.

The four of us were in the one box, guests of Luis Cervallos. I was next to the Presidente's box. On the other side was the box of General Jose Eliceo Salazar. With him were Joaquin Endara and Urcisino Castillo, both generals, and Colonel Jacinto Fierro and Captain Baltazar de Echeverria. Only Luis Cervallos had the position and the influence to get that box next to the Presidente. I know for a fact that the Presidente himself expressed the desire to the management that Luis Cervallos should have that box.

The band finished playing the national hymn of Ecuador. The procession of the toreadors was over. The Presidente nodded to begin. The bugles blew, and the bull dashed in—you know the way, excited, bewildered, the darts in its shoulder burning like fire, itself seeking madly whatever enemy to destroy. The toreadors hid behind their shelters and waited. Suddenly they appeared forth, the capadores, five of them, from every side, their colored capes flinging wide. The bull paused at sight of such a generosity of enemies, unable in his own mind to know which to attack. Then advanced one of the capadors alone to meet the bull. The bull was very angry. With its fore-legs it pawed the sand of the arena till the dust rose all about it. Then it charged, with lowered head, straight for the lone capador.

It is always of interest, the first charge of the first bull. After a time it is natural that one should grow tired, trifle, that the keenness should lose its edge. But that first charge of the first bull! John Harned was seeing it for the first time, and he could not escape the excitement—the sight of the man, armed only with a piece of cloth, and of the bull rushing upon him across the sand with sharp horns, widespreading.

"See!" cried Maria Valenzuela. "Is it not superb?"

John Harned nodded, but did not look at her. His eyes were sparkling, and they were only for the bull-ring. The capador stepped to the side, with a twirl of the cape eluding the bull and spreading the cape on his own shoulders.

"What do you think?" asked Maria Venzuela. "Is it not a—what-you-call—sporting proposition—no?"

"It is certainly," said John Harned. "It is very clever."

She clapped her hands with delight. They were little hands. The audience applauded. The bull turned and came back. Again the capadore eluded him, throwing the cape on his shoulders, and again the audience applauded. Three times did this happen. The capadore was very excellent. Then he retired, and the other capadore played with the bull. After that they placed the banderillos in the bull, in the shoulders, on each side of the back-bone, two at a time. Then stepped forward Ordonez, the chief matador, with the long sword and the scarlet cape. The bugles blew for the death. He is not so good as Matestini. Still he is good, and with one thrust he drove the sword to the heart, and the bull doubled his legs under him and lay down and died. It was a pretty thrust, clean and sure; and there was much applause, and many of the common people threw their hats into the ring. Maria Valenzuela clapped her hands with the rest, and John Harned, whose cold heart was not touched by the event, looked at her with curiosity.

"You like it?" he asked.

"Always," she said, still clapping her hands.

"From a little girl," said Luis Cervallos. "I remember her first fight. She was four years old. She sat with her mother, and just like now she clapped her hands. She is a proper Spanish woman.

"You have seen it," said Maria Valenzuela to John Harned, as they fastened the mules to the dead bull and dragged it out. "You have seen the bull-fight and you like it—no? What do you think?

"I think the bull had no chance," he said. "The bull was doomed from the first. The issue was not in doubt. Every one knew, before the bull entered the ring, that it was to die. To be a sporting proposition, the issue must be in doubt. It was one stupid bull who had never fought a man against five wise men who had fought many bulls. It would be possibly a little bit fair if it were one man against one bull."

"Or one man against five bulls," said Maria Valenzuela; and we all laughed, and Luis Ceryallos laughed loudest.

33

"Yes," said John Harned, "against five bulls, and the man, like the bulls, never in the bull ring before—a man like yourself, Senor Crevallos."

"Yet we Spanish like the bull-fight," said Luis Cervallos; and I swear the devil was whispering then in his ear, telling him to do that which I shall relate.

"Then must it be a cultivated taste," John Harned made answer. "We kill bulls by the thousand every day in Chicago, yet no one cares to pay admittance to see."

"That is butchery," said I; "but this—ah, this is an art. It is delicate. It is fine. It is rare."

"Not always," said Luis Cervallos. "I have seen clumsy matadors, and I tell you it is not nice."

He shuddered, and his face betrayed such what-you-call disgust, that I knew, then, that the devil was whispering and that he was beginning to play a part.

"Senor Harned may be right," said Luis Cervallos. "It may not be fair to the bull. For is it not known to all of us that for twenty-four hours the bull is given no water, and that immediately before the fight he is permitted to drink his fill?"

"And he comes into the ring heavy with water?" said John Harned quickly; and I saw that his eyes were very gray and very sharp and very cold.

"It is necessary for the sport," said Luis Cervallos. "Would you have the bull so strong that he would kill the toreadors?"

"I would that he had a fighting chance," said John Harned, facing the ring to see the second bull come in.

It was not a good bull. It was frightened. It ran around the ring in search of a way to get out. The capadors stepped forth and flared their capes, but he refused to charge upon them.

"It is a stupid bull," said Maria Valenzuela.

"I beg pardon," said John Harned; "but it would seem to me a wise bull. He knows he must not fight man. See! He smells death there in the ring."

True. The bull, pausing where the last one had died, was smelling the wet sand and snorting. Again he ran around the ring, with raised head, looking at the faces of the thousands that hissed him, that threw orange-peel at him and called him names. But the smell of blood decided him, and he charged a capador, so without warning that the man just escaped. He dropped his cape and dodged into the shelter. The bull struck the wall of the ring with a crash. And John Harned said, in a quiet voice, as though he talked to himself:

"I will give one thousand sucres to the lazar-house of Quito if a bull kills a man this day."

"You like bulls?" said Maria Valenzuela with a smile.

"I like such men less," said John Harned. "A toreador is not a brave man. He surely cannot be a brave man. See, the bull's tongue is already out. He is tired and he has not yet begun."

"It is the water," said Luis Cervallos.

"Yes, it is the water," said John Harned. "Would it not be safer to hamstring the bull before he comes on?"

Maria Valenzuela was made angry by this sneer in John Harned's words. But Luis Cervallos smiled so that only I could see him, and then it broke upon my mind surely the game he was playing. He and I were to be banderilleros. The big American bull was there in the box with us. We were to stick the darts in him till he became angry, and then there might be no marriage with Maria Valenzuela. It was a good sport. And the spirit of bull-fighters was in our blood.

The bull was now angry and excited. The capadors had great game with him. He was very quick, and sometimes he turned with such sharpness that his hind legs lost their footing and he plowed the sand with his quarter. But he charged always the flung capes and committed no harm.

"He has no chance," said John Harned. "He is fighting wind."

"He thinks the cape is his enemy," explained Maria Valenzuela. "See how cleverly the capador deceives him."

"It is his nature to be deceived," said John Harned. "Wherefore he is doomed to fight wind. The toreadors know it, you know it, I know it—we all know from the first that he will fight wind. He only does not know it. It is his stupid beast-nature. He has no chance."

"It is very simple," said Luis Cervallos. "The bull shuts his eyes when he charges. Therefore—"

"The man steps, out of the way and the bull rushes by," Harned interrupted.

"Yes," said Luis Cervallos; "that is it. The bull shuts his eyes, and the man knows it."

"But cows do not shut their eyes," said John Harned. "I know a cow at home that is a Jersey and gives milk, that would whip the whole gang of them."

"But the toreadors do not fight cows," said I.

"They are afraid to fight cows," said John Harned.

"Yes," said Luis Cervallos, "they are afraid to fight cows. There would be no sport in killing toreadors."

"There would be some sport," said John Harned, "if a toreador were killed once in a while. When I become an old man, and mayhap a cripple, and should I need to make a living and be unable to do hard work, then would I become a bull-fighter. It is a light vocation for elderly gentlemen and pensioners."

"But see!" said Maria Valenzuela, as the bull charged bravely and the capador eluded it with a fling of his cape. "It requires skill so to avoid the beast."

"True," said John Harned. "But believe me, it requires a thousand times more skill to avoid the many and quick punches of a prize-fighter who keeps his eyes open and strikes with intelligence. Furthermore, this bull does not want to fight. Behold, he runs away."

It was not a good bull, for again it ran around the ring, seeking to find a way out.

"Yet these bulls are sometimes the most dangerous," said Luis Cervallos. "It can never be known what they will do next. They are wise. They are half cow. The bull-fighters never like them.—See! He has turned!"

Once again, baffled and made angry by the walls of the ring that would not let him out, the bull was attacking his enemies valiantly.

"His tongue is hanging out," said John Harned. "First, they fill him with water. Then they tire him out, one man and then another, persuading him to exhaust himself by fighting wind. While some tire him, others rest. But the bull they never let rest. Afterward, when he is quite tired and no longer quick, the matador sticks the sword into him."

The time had now come for the banderillos. Three times one of the fighters endeavored to place the darts, and three times did he fail. He but stung the bull and maddened it. The banderillos must go in, you know, two at a time, into the shoulders, on each side the backbone and close to it. If but one be placed, it is a failure. The crowd hissed and called for Ordonez. And then Ordonez did a great thing. Four times he stood forth, and four times, at the first attempt, he stuck in the banderillos, so that eight of them, well placed, stood out of the back of the bull at one time. The crowd went mad, and a rain of hats and money fell on the sand of the ring.

And just then the bull charged unexpectedly one of the capadors. The man slipped and lost his head. The bull caught him—fortunately, between his wide horns. And while the audience watched, breathless and silent, John Harned stood up and yelled with gladness. Alone, in that hush of all of us, John Harned yelled. And he yelled for the bull. As you see yourself, John Harned wanted the man killed. His was a brutal heart. This bad conduct made those angry that sat in the box of General Salazar, and they cried out against John Harned. And Urcisino Castillo told him to his face that he was a dog of a Gringo and other things. Only it was in Spanish, and John Harned did not understand. He stood and yelled, perhaps for the time of ten seconds, when the bull was enticed into charging the other capadors and the man arose unhurt.

"The bull has no chance," John Harned said with sadness as he sat down. "The man was uninjured. They fooled the bull away from him." Then he turned to Maria Valenzuela and said: "I beg your pardon. I was excited."

She smiled and in reproof tapped his arm with her fan.

"It is your first bull-fight," she said. "After you have seen more you will not cry for the death of the man. You Americans, you see, are more brutal than we. It is because of your prize-fighting. We come only to see the bull killed."

"But I would the bull had some chance," he answered. "Doubtless, in time, I shall cease to be annoyed by the men who take advantage of the bull."

The bugles blew for the death of the bull. Ordonez stood forth with the sword and the scarlet cloth. But the bull had changed again, and did not want to fight. Ordonez stamped his foot in the sand, and cried out, and waved the scarlet cloth. Then the bull charged, but without heart. There was no weight to the charge. It was a poor thrust. The sword struck a bone and bent. Ordonez took a fresh sword. The bull, again stung to fight, charged once more. Five times Ordonez essayed the thrust, and each time the sword went but part way in or struck bone. The sixth time, the sword went in to the hilt. But it was a bad thrust. The sword missed the heart and stuck out half a yard through the ribs on the opposite side. The audience hissed the matador. I glanced at John Harned. He sat silent, without movement; but I could see his teeth were set, and his hands were clenched tight on the railing of the box.

All fight was now out of the bull, and, though it was no vital thrust, he trotted lamely what of the sword that stuck through him, in one side and out the other. He ran away from the matador and the capadors, and circled the edge of the ring, looking up at the many faces.

"He is saying: 'For God's sake let me out of this; I don't want to fight,'" said John Harned.

That was all. He said no more, but sat and watched, though sometimes he looked sideways at Maria Valenzuela to see how she took it. She was angry with the matador. He was awkward, and she had desired a clever exhibition.

The bull was now very tired, and weak from loss of blood, though far from dying. He walked slowly around the wall of the ring, seeking a way out. He would not charge. He had had enough. But he must be killed. There is a place, in the neck of a bull behind the horns, where the cord of the spine is unprotected and where a short stab will immediately kill. Ordonez stepped in front of the bull and lowered his scarlet cloth to the ground. The bull would not charge. He stood still and smelled the cloth, lowering his head to do so. Ordonez stabbed between the horns at the spot in the neck. The bull jerked his head up. The stab had missed. Then the bull watched the sword. When Ordonez moved the cloth on the ground, the bull forgot the sword and lowered his head to smell the cloth. Again Ordonez stabbed, and again he failed. He tried many times. It was stupid. And John Harned said nothing. At last a stab went home, and the bull fell to the sand, dead immediately, and the mules were made fast and he was dragged out.

"The Gringos say it is a cruel sport—no?" said Luis Cervallos. "That it is not humane. That it is bad for the bull. No?"

"No," said John Harned. "The bull does not count for much. It is bad for those that look on. It is degrading to those that look on. It teaches them to delight in animal suffering. It is cowardly for five men to fight one stupid bull. Therefore those that look on learn to be cowards. The bull dies, but those that look on live and the lesson is learned. The bravery of men is not nourished by scenes of cowardice."

Maria Valenzuela said nothing. Neither did she look at him. But she heard every word and her cheeks were white with anger. She looked out across the ring and fanned herself, but I saw that her hand trembled. Nor did John Harned look at her. He went on as though she were not there. He, too, was angry, coldly angry.

"It is the cowardly sport of a cowardly people," he said.

"Ah," said Luis Cervallos softly, "you think you understand us."

"I understand now the Spanish Inquisition," said John Harned. "It must have been more delightful than bull-fighting."

Luis Cervallos smiled but said nothing. He glanced at Maria Valenzuela, and knew that the bull-fight in the box was won. Never would she have further to do with the Gringo who spoke such words. But neither Luis Cervallos nor I was prepared for the outcome of the day. I fear we do not understand the Gringos. How were we to know that John Harned, who was so coldly angry, should go suddenly mad! But mad he did go, as you shall see. The bull did not count for much—he said so himself. Then why should the horse count for so much? That I cannot understand. The mind of John Harned lacked logic. That is the only explanation.

"It is not usual to have horses in the bull-ring at Quito," said Luis Cervallos, looking up from the program. "In Spain they always have them. But to-day, by special permission we shall have them. When the next bull comes on there will be horses and picadors-you know, the men who carry lances and ride the horses."

"The bull is doomed from the first," said John Harned. "Are the horses then likewise doomed!"

"They are blindfolded so that they may not see the bull," said Luis Cervallos. "I have seen many horses killed. It is a brave sight."

"I have seen the bull slaughtered," said John Harned "I will now see the horse slaughtered, so that I may understand more fully the fine points of this noble sport."

"They are old horses," said Luis Cervallos, "that are not good for anything else."

"I see," said John Harned.

The third bull came on, and soon against it were both capadors and picadors. One picador took his stand directly below us. I agree, it was a thin and aged horse he rode, a bag of bones covered with mangy hide.

"It is a marvel that the poor brute can hold up the weight of the rider," said John Harned. "And now that the horse fights the bull, what weapons has it?"

"The horse does not fight the bull," said Luis Cervallos.

"Oh," said John Harned, "then is the horse there to be gored? That must be why it is blindfolded, so that it shall not see the bull coming to gore it."

"Not quite so," said I. "The lance of the picador is to keep the bull from goring the horse."

"Then are horses rarely gored?" asked John Harned.

"No," said Luis Cervallos. "I have seen, at Seville, eighteen horses killed in one day, and the people clamored for more horses."

"Were they blindfolded like this horse?" asked John Harned.

"Yes," said Luis Cervallos.

After that we talked no more, but watched the fight. And John Harned was going mad all the time, and we did not know. The bull refused to charge the horse. And the horse stood still, and because it could not see it did not know that the capadors were trying to make the bull charge upon it. The capadors teased the bull their capes, and when it charged them they ran toward the horse and into their shelters. At last the bull was angry, and it saw the horse before it.

"The horse does not know, the horse does not know," John Harned whispered to himself, unaware that he voiced his thought aloud.

The bull charged, and of course the horse knew nothing till the picador failed and the horse found himself impaled on the bull's horns from beneath. The bull was magnificently strong. The sight of its strength was splendid to see. It lifted the horse clear into the air; and as the horse fell to its side on on the ground the picador landed on his feet and escaped, while the capadors lured the bull away. The horse was emptied of its essential organs. Yet did it rise to its feet screaming. It was the scream of the horse that did it, that made John Harned completely mad; for he, too, started to rise to his feet, I heard him curse low and deep. He never took his eyes from the horse, which, screaming, strove to run, but fell down instead and rolled on its back so that all its four legs were kicking in the air. Then the bull charged it and gored it again and again until it was dead.

John Harned was now on his feet. His eyes were no longer cold like steel. They were blue flames. He looked at Maria Valenzuela, and she looked at him, and in his face was a great loathing. The moment of his madness was upon him. Everybody was looking, now that the horse was dead; and John Harned was a large man and easy to be seen.

"Sit down," said Luis Cervallos, "or you will make a fool of yourself."

John Harned replied nothing. He struck out his fist. He smote Luis Cervallos in the face so that he fell like a dead man across the chairs and did not rise again. He saw nothing of what followed. But I saw much. Urcisino Castillo, leaning forward from the next box, with his cane struck John Harned full across the face. And John Harned smote him with his fist so that in falling he overthrew General Salazar. John Harned was now in what-you-call Berserker rage—no? The beast primitive in him was loose and roaring—the beast primitive of the holes and caves of the long ago.

"You came for a bull-fight," I heard him say, "And by God I'll show you a man-fight!"

It was a fight. The soldiers guarding the Presidente's box leaped across, but from one of them he took a rifle and beat them on their heads with it. From the other box Colonel Jacinto Fierro was shooting at him with a revolver. The first shot killed a soldier. This I know for a fact. I saw it. But the second shot struck John Harned in the side. Whereupon he swore, and with a lunge drove the bayonet of his rifle into Colonel Jacinto Fierro's body. It was horrible to behold. The Americans and the English are a brutal race. They sneer at our bull-fighting, yet do they delight in the shedding of blood. More men were killed that day because of John Harned than were ever killed in all the history of the bull-ring of Quito, yes, and of Guayaquil and all Ecuador.

It was the scream of the horse that did it, yet why did not John Harned go mad when the bull was killed? A beast is a beast, be it bull or horse. John Harned was mad. There is no other explanation. He was blood-mad, a beast himself. I leave it to your judgment. Which is worse—the goring of the horse by the bull, or the goring of Colonel Jacinto Fierro by the bayonet in the hands of John Harned! And John Harned gored others with that bayonet. He was full of devils. He fought with many bullets in him, and he was hard to kill. And Maria Valenzuela was a brave woman. Unlike the other women, she did not cry out nor faint. She sat still in her box, gazing out across the bull-ring. Her face was white and she fanned herself, but she never looked around.

From all sides came the soldiers and officers and the common people bravely to subdue the mad Gringo. It is true—the cry went up from the crowd to kill all the Gringos. It is an old cry in Latin-American countries, what of the dislike for the Gringos and their uncouth ways. It is true, the cry went up. But the brave Ecuadorianos killed only John Harned, and first he killed seven of them. Besides, there were many hurt. I have seen many bull-fights, but never have I seen anything so abominable as the scene in the boxes when the fight was over. It was like a field of battle. The dead lay around everywhere, while the wounded sobbed and groaned and some of them died. One man, whom John Harned had thrust through the belly with the bayonet, clutched at himself with both his hands and screamed. I tell you for a fact it was more terrible than the screaming of a thousand horses.

No, Maria Valenzuela did not marry Luis Cervallos. I am sorry for that. He was my friend, and much of my money was invested in his ventures. It was five weeks before the surgeons took the bandages from his face. And there is a scar there to this day, on the cheek, under the eye. Yet John Harned struck him but once and struck him only with his naked fist. Maria Valenzuela is in Austria now. It is said she is to marry an Arch-Duke or some high nobleman. I do not know. I think she liked John Harned before he followed her to Quito to see the bull-fight. But why the horse? That is what I desire to know. Why should he watch the bull and say that it did not count, and then go immediately and most horribly mad because a horse screamed? There is no understanding the Gringos. They are barbarians.

WHEN THE WORLD WAS YOUNG

HE was a very quiet, self-possessed sort of man, sitting a moment on top of the wall to sound the damp darkness for warnings of the dangers it might conceal. But the plummet of his hearing brought nothing to him save the moaning of wind through invisible trees and the rustling of leaves on swaying branches. A heavy fog drifted and drove before the wind, and though he could not see this fog, the wet of it blew upon his face, and the wall on which he sat was wet.

Without noise he had climbed to the top of the wall from the outside, and without noise he dropped to the ground on the inside. From his pocket he drew an electric night-stick, but he did not use it. Dark as the way was, he was not anxious for light. Carrying the night-stick in his hand, his finger on the button, he advanced through the darkness. The ground was velvety and springy to his feet, being carpeted with dead pine-needles and leaves and mold which evidently had been undisturbed for years. Leaves and branches brushed against his body, but so dark was it that he could not avoid them. Soon he walked with his hand stretched out gropingly before him, and more than once the hand fetched up against the solid trunks of massive trees. All about him he knew were these trees; he sensed the loom of them everywhere; and he experienced a strange feeling of microscopic smallness in the midst of great bulks leaning toward him to crush him. Beyond, he knew, was the house, and he expected to find some trail or winding path that would lead easily to it.

Once, he found himself trapped. On every side he groped against trees and branches, or blundered into thickets of underbrush, until there seemed no way out. Then he turned on his light, circumspectly, directing its rays to the ground at his feet. Slowly and carefully he moved it about him, the white brightness showing in sharp detail all the obstacles to his progress. He saw, an opening between huge-trunked trees, and advanced through it, putting out the light and treading on dry footing as yet protected from the drip of the fog by the dense foliage overhead. His sense of direction was good, and he knew he was going toward the house.

And then the thing happened—the thing unthinkable and unexpected. His descending foot came down upon something that was soft and alive, and that arose with a snort under the weight of his body. He sprang clear, and crouched for another spring, anywhere, tense and expectant, keyed for the onslaught of the unknown. He waited a moment, wondering what manner of animal it was that had arisen from under his foot and that now made no sound nor movement and that must be crouching and waiting just as tensely and expectantly as he. The strain became unbearable. Holding the night-stick before him, he pressed the button, saw, and screamed aloud in terror. He was prepared for anything, from a frightened calf or fawn to a belligerent lion, but he was not prepared for what he saw. In that instant his tiny searchlight, sharp and white, had shown him what a thousand years would not enable him to forget—a man, huge and blond, yellow-haired and yellow-bearded, naked except for soft-tanned moccasins and what seemed a goat-skin about his middle. Arms and legs were bare, as were his shoulders and most of his chest. The skin was smooth and hairless, but browned by sun and wind, while under it heavy muscles were knotted like fat snakes. Still, this alone, unexpected as it well was, was not what had made the man scream out. What had caused his terror was the unspeakable ferocity of the face, the wild-animal glare of the blue eyes scarcely dazzled by the light, the pine-needles matted and clinging in the beard and hair, and the whole formidable body crouched and in the act of springing at him. Practically in the instant he saw all this, and while his scream still rang, the thing leaped, he flung his night-stick full at it, and threw himself to the ground. He felt its feet and shins strike against his ribs, and he bounded up and away while the thing itself hurled onward in a heavy crashing fall into the underbrush.

As the noise of the fall ceased, the man stopped and on hands and knees waited. He could hear the thing moving about, searching for him, and he was afraid to advertise his location by attempting further flight. He knew that inevitably he would crackle the underbrush and be pursued. Once he drew out his revolver, then changed his mind. He had recovered his composure and hoped to get away without noise. Several times he heard the thing beating up the thickets for him, and there were moments when it, too, remained still and listened. This gave an idea to the man. One of his hands was resting on a chunk of dead wood. Carefully, first feeling about him in the darkness to know that the full swing of his arm was clear, he raised the chunk of wood and threw it. It was not a large piece, and it went far, landing noisily in a bush. He heard the thing bound into the bush, and at the same time himself crawled steadily away. And on hands and knees, slowly and cautiously, he crawled on, till his knees were wet on the soggy mold, When he listened he heard naught but the moaning wind and the drip-drip of the fog from the branches. Never abating his caution, he stood erect and went on to the stone wall, over which he climbed and dropped down to the road outside.

Feeling his way in a clump of bushes, he drew out a bicycle and prepared to mount. He was in the act of driving the gear around with his foot for the purpose of getting the opposite pedal in position, when he heard the thud of a heavy body that landed lightly and evidently on its feet. He did not wait for more, but ran, with hands on the handles of his bicycle, until he was able to vault astride the saddle, catch the pedals, and start a spurt. Behind he could hear the quick thud-thud of feet on the dust of the road, but he drew away from it and lost it. Unfortunately, he had started away from the direction of town and was heading higher up into the hills. He knew that on this particular road there were no cross roads. The only way back was past that terror, and he could not steel himself to face it. At the end of half an hour, finding himself on an ever increasing grade, he dismounted. For still greater safety, leaving the wheel by the roadside, he climbed through a fence into what he decided was a hillside pasture, spread a newspaper on the ground, and sat down.

"Gosh!" he said aloud, mopping the sweat and fog from his face.

And "Gosh!" he said once again, while rolling a cigarette and as he pondered the problem of getting back.

But he made no attempt to go back. He was resolved not to face that road in the dark, and with head bowed on knees, he dozed, waiting for daylight.

46

How long afterward he did not know, he was awakened by the yapping bark of a young coyote. As he looked about and located it on the brow of the hill behind him, he noted the change that had come over the face of the night. The fog was gone; the stars and moon were out; even the wind had died down. It had transformed into a balmy California summer night. He tried to doze again, but the yap of the coyote disturbed him. Half asleep, he heard a wild and eery chant. Looking about him, he noticed that the coyote had ceased its noise and was running away along the crest of the hill, and behind it, in full pursuit, no longer chanting, ran the naked creature he had encountered in the garden. It was a young coyote, and it was being overtaken when the chase passed from view. The man trembled as with a chill as he started to his feet, clambered over the fence, and mounted his wheel. But it was his chance and he knew it. The terror was no longer between him and Mill Valley.

He sped at a breakneck rate down the hill, but in the turn at the bottom, in the deep shadows, he encountered a chuck-hole and pitched headlong over the handle bar.

"It's sure not my night," he muttered, as he examined the broken fork of the machine.

Shouldering the useless wheel, he trudged on. In time he came to the stone wall, and, half disbelieving his experience, he sought in the road for tracks, and found them—moccasin tracks, large ones, deep-bitten into the dust at the toes. It was while bending over them, examining, that again he heard the eery chant. He had seen the thing pursue the coyote, and he knew he had no chance on a straight run. He did not attempt it, contenting himself with hiding in the shadows on the off side of the road.

And again he saw the thing that was like a naked man, running swiftly and lightly and singing as it ran. Opposite him it paused, and his heart stood still. But instead of coming toward his hiding-place, it leaped into the air, caught the branch of a roadside tree, and swung swiftly upward, from limb to limb, like an ape. It swung across the wall, and a dozen feet above the top, into the branches of another tree, and dropped out of sight to the ground. The man waited a few wondering minutes, then started on.

II

Dave Slotter leaned belligerently against the desk that barred the way to the private office of James Ward, senior partner of the firm of Ward, Knowles & Co. Dave was angry. Every one in the outer office had looked him over suspiciously, and the man who faced him was excessively suspicious.

"You just tell Mr. Ward it's important," he urged.

"I tell you he is dictating and cannot be disturbed," was the answer. "Come to-morrow."

"To-morrow will be too late. You just trot along and tell Mr. Ward it's a matter of life and death."

The secretary hesitated and Dave seized the advantage.

"You just tell him I was across the bay in Mill Valley last night, and that I want to put him wise to something."

"What name?" was the query.

"Never mind the name. He don't know me."

When Dave was shown into the private office, he was still in the belligerent frame of mind, but when he saw a large fair man whirl in a revolving chair from dictating to a stenographer to face him, Dave's demeanor abruptly changed. He did not know why it changed, and he was secretly angry with himself.

"You are Mr. Ward?" Dave asked with a fatuousness that still further irritated him. He had never intended it at all.

"Yes," came the answer.

"And who are you?"

"Harry Bancroft," Dave lied. "You don't know me, and my name don't matter."

"You sent in word that you were in Mill Valley last night?"

"You live there, don't you?" Dave countered, looking suspiciously at the stenographer.

"Yes. What do you mean to see me about? I am very busy."

"I'd like to see you alone, sir."

Mr. Ward gave him a quick, penetrating look, hesitated, then made up his mind.

"That will do for a few minutes, Miss Potter."

The girl arose, gathered her notes together, and passed out. Dave looked at Mr. James Ward wonderingly, until that gentleman broke his train of inchoate thought.

"Well?"

"I was over in Mill Valley last night," Dave began confusedly.

"I've heard that before. What do you want?"

And Dave proceeded in the face of a growing conviction that was unbelievable. "I was at your house, or in the grounds, I mean."

"What were you doing there?"

"I came to break in," Dave answered in all frankness.

"I heard you lived all alone with a Chinaman for cook, and it looked good to me. Only I didn't break in. Something happened that prevented. That's why I'm here. I come to warn you. I found a wild man loose in your grounds—a regular devil. He could pull a guy like me to pieces. He gave me the run of my life. He don't wear any clothes to speak of, he climbs trees like a monkey, and he runs like a deer. I saw him chasing a coyote, and the last I saw of it, by God, he was gaining on it."

Dave paused and looked for the effect that would follow his words. But no effect came. James Ward was quietly curious, and that was all.

"Very remarkable, very remarkable," he murmured. "A wild man, you say. Why have you come to tell me?"

"To warn you of your danger. I'm something of a hard proposition myself, but I don't believe in killing people... that is, unnecessarily. I realized that you was in danger. I thought I'd warn you. Honest, that's the game. Of course, if you wanted to give me anything for my trouble, I'd take it. That was in my mind, too. But I don't care whether you give me anything or not. I've warned you any way, and done my duty."

Mr. Ward meditated and drummed on the surface of his desk. Dave noticed they were large, powerful hands, withal well-cared for despite their dark sunburn. Also, he noted what had already caught his eye before—a tiny strip of flesh-colored courtplaster on the forehead over one eye. And still the thought that forced itself into his mind was unbelievable.

Mr. Ward took a wallet from his inside coat pocket, drew out a greenback, and passed it to Dave, who noted as he pocketed it that it was for twenty dollars.

"Thank you," said Mr. Ward, indicating that the interview was at an end.

"I shall have the matter investigated. A wild man running loose IS dangerous."

But so quiet a man was Mr. Ward, that Dave's courage returned. Besides, a new theory had suggested itself. The wild man was evidently Mr. Ward's brother, a lunatic privately confined. Dave had heard of such things. Perhaps Mr. Ward wanted it kept quiet. That was why he had given him the twenty dollars.

"Say," Dave began, "now I come to think of it that wild man looked a lot like you—"

That was as far as Dave got, for at that moment he witnessed a transformation and found himself gazing into the same unspeakably ferocious blue eyes of the night before, at the same clutching talon-like hands, and at

50

the same formidable bulk in the act of springing upon him. But this time Dave had no night-stick to throw, and he was caught by the biceps of both arms in a grip so terrific that it made him groan with pain. He saw the large white teeth exposed, for all the world as a dog's about to bite. Mr. Ward's beard brushed his face as the teeth went in for the grip on his throat. But the bite was not given. Instead, Dave felt the other's body stiffen as with an iron restraint, and then he was flung aside, without effort but with such force that only the wall stopped his momentum and dropped him gasping to the floor.

"What do you mean by coming here and trying to blackmail me?" Mr. Ward was snarling at him. "Here, give me back that money."

Dave passed the bill back without a word.

"I thought you came here with good intentions. I know you now. Let me see and hear no more of you, or I'll put you in prison where you belong. Do you understand?"

"Yes, sir," Dave gasped.

"Then go."

And Dave went, without further word, both his biceps aching intolerably from the bruise of that tremendous grip. As his hand rested on the door knob, he was stopped.

"You were lucky," Mr. Ward was saying, and Dave noted that his face and eyes were cruel and gloating and proud.

"You were lucky. Had I wanted, I could have torn your muscles out of your arms and thrown them in the waste basket there."

"Yes, sir," said Dave; and absolute conviction vibrated in his voice.

He opened the door and passed out. The secretary looked at him interrogatively.

"Gosh!" was all Dave vouchsafed, and with this utterance passed out of the offices and the story.

III

James G. Ward was forty years of age, a successful business man, and very unhappy. For forty years he had vainly tried to solve a problem that was really himself and that with increasing years became more and more a woeful affliction. In himself he was two men, and, chronologically speaking, these men were several thousand years or so apart. He had studied the question of dual personality probably more profoundly than any half dozen of the leading specialists in that intricate and mysterious psychological field. In himself he was a different case from any that had been recorded. Even the most fanciful flights of the fiction-writers had not quite hit upon him. He was not a Dr. Jekyll and Mr. Hyde, nor was he like the unfortunate young man in Kipling's "Greatest Story in the World." His two personalities were so mixed that they were practically aware of themselves and of each other all the time.

His other self he had located as a savage and a barbarian living under the primitive conditions of several thousand years before. But which self was he, and which was the other, he could never tell. For he was both selves, and both selves all the time. Very rarely indeed did it happen that one self did not know what the other was doing. Another thing was that he had no visions nor memories of the past in which that early self had lived. That early self lived in the present; but while it lived in the present, it was under the compulsion to live the way of life that must have been in that distant past.

In his childhood he had been a problem to his father and mother, and to the family doctors, though never had they come within a thousand miles of hitting upon the clue to his erratic, conduct. Thus, they could not understand his excessive somnolence in the forenoon, nor his excessive activity at night. When they found him wandering along the hallways at night, or climbing over giddy roofs, or running in the hills, they decided he was a somnambulist. In reality he was wide-eyed awake and merely under the nightroaming compulsion of his early self. Questioned by an obtuse medico, he once told the truth and suffered the ignominy of having the revelation contemptuously labeled and dismissed as "dreams."

The point was, that as twilight and evening came on he became wakeful. The four walls of a room were an irk and a restraint. He heard a thousand voices whispering to him through the darkness. The night called to him, for he was, for that period of the twenty-four hours, essentially a night-prowler. But nobody understood, and never again did he attempt to explain. They classified him as a sleep-walker and took precautions accordingly—precautions that very often were futile. As his childhood advanced, he grew more cunning, so that the major portion of all his nights were spent in the open at realizing his other self. As a result, he slept in the forenoons. Morning studies and schools were impossible, and it was discovered that only in the afternoons, under private teachers, could he be taught anything. Thus was his modern self educated and developed.

But a problem, as a child, he ever remained. He was known as a little demon, of insensate cruelty and viciousness. The family medicos privately adjudged him a mental monstrosity and degenerate. Such few boy companions as he had, hailed him as a wonder, though they were all afraid of him. He could outclimb, outswim, outrun, outdevil any of them; while none dared fight with him. He was too terribly strong, madly furious.

When nine years of age he ran away to the hills, where he flourished, night-prowling, for seven weeks before he was discovered and brought home. The marvel was how he had managed to subsist and keep in condition during that time. They did not know, and he never told them, of the rabbits he had killed, of the quail, young and old, he had captured and devoured, of the farmers' chicken-roosts he had raided, nor of the cave-lair he had made and carpeted with dry leaves and grasses and in which he had slept in warmth and comfort through the forenoons of many days.

At college he was notorious for his sleepiness and stupidity during the morning lectures and for his brilliance in the afternoon. By collateral reading and by borrowing the notebook of his fellow students he managed to scrape through the detestable morning courses, while his afternoon courses were triumphs. In football he proved a giant and a terror, and, in almost every form of track athletics, save for strange Berserker rages that were sometimes displayed, he could be depended upon to win. But his fellows were afraid to box with him, and he signalized his last wrestling bout by sinking his teeth into the shoulder of his opponent.

After college, his father, in despair, sent him among the cow-punchers of a Wyoming ranch. Three months later the doughty cowmen confessed he was too much for them and telegraphed his father to come and take the wild man away. Also, when the father arrived to take him away, the cowmen allowed that they would vastly prefer chumming with howling cannibals, gibbering lunatics, cavorting gorillas, grizzly bears, and man-eating tigers than with this particular Young college product with hair parted in the middle.

There was one exception to the lack of memory of the life of his early self, and that was language. By some quirk of atavism, a certain portion of that early self's language had come down to him as a racial memory. In moments of happiness, exaltation, or battle, he was prone to burst out in wild barbaric songs or chants. It was by this means that he located in time and space that strayed half of him who should have been dead and dust for thousands of years. He sang, once, and deliberately, several of the ancient chants in the presence of Professor Wertz, who gave courses in old Saxon and who was a philologist of repute and passion. At the first one, the professor pricked up his ears and demanded to know what mongrel tongue or hog-German it was. When the second chant was rendered, the professor was highly excited. James Ward then concluded the performance by giving a song that always irresistibly rushed to his lips when he was engaged in fierce struggling or fighting. Then it was that Professor Wertz proclaimed it no hog-German, but early German, or early Teuton, of a date that must far precede anything that had ever been discovered and handed down by the scholars. So early was it that it was beyond him; yet it was filled with haunting reminiscences of word-forms he knew and which his trained intuition told him were true and real. He demanded the source of the songs, and asked to borrow the precious book that contained them. Also, he demanded to know why young Ward had always posed as being profoundly ignorant of the German language. And Ward could neither explain his ignorance nor lend the book. Whereupon, after pleadings and entreaties that extended through weeks, Professor Wert took a dislike to the young man, believed him a liar, and classified him as a man of monstrous selfishness for not giving him a glimpse of this wonderful screed that was older than the oldest any philologist had ever known or dreamed.

But little good did it do this much-mixed young man to know that half of him was late American and the other half early Teuton. Nevertheless, the late American in him was no weakling, and he (if he were a he and had a shred of existence outside of these two) compelled an adjustment or compromise between his one self that was a nightprowling savage that kept his other self sleepy of mornings, and that other self that was cultured and refined and that wanted to be normal and live and love and prosecute business like other people. The afternoons and early evenings he gave to the one, the nights to the other; the forenoons and parts of the nights were devoted to sleep for the twain. But in the mornings he slept in bed like a civilized man. In the night time he slept like a wild animal, as he had slept Dave Slotter stepped on him in the woods.

Persuading his father to advance the capital, he went into business and keen and successful business he made of it, devoting his afternoons whole-souled to it, while his partner devoted the mornings. The early evenings he spent socially, but, as the hour grew to nine or ten, an irresistible restlessness overcame him and he disappeared from the haunts of men until the next afternoon. Friends and acquaintances thought that he spent much of his time in sport. And they were right, though they never would have dreamed of the nature of the sport, even if they had seen him running coyotes in night-chases over the hills of Mill Valley. Neither were the schooner captains believed when they reported seeing, on cold winter mornings, a man swimming in the tide-rips of Raccoon Straits or in the swift currents between Goat island and Angel Island miles from shore.

In the bungalow at Mill Valley he lived alone, save for Lee Sing, the Chinese cook and factotum, who knew much about the strangeness of his master, who was paid well for saying nothing, and who never did say anything. After the satisfaction of his nights, a morning's sleep, and a breakfast of Lee Sing's, James Ward crossed the bay to San Francisco on a midday ferryboat and went to the club and on to his office, as normal and conventional a man of business as could be found in the city. But as the evening lengthened, the night called to him. There came a quickening of all his perceptions and a restlessness. His hearing was suddenly acute; the myriad night-noises told him a luring and familiar story; and, if alone, he would begin to pace up and down the narrow room like any caged animal from the wild.

Once, he ventured to fall in love. He never permitted himself that diversion again. He was afraid. And for many a day the young lady, scared at least out of a portion of her young ladyhood, bore on her arms and shoulders and wrists divers black-and-blue bruises—tokens of caresses which he had bestowed in all fond gentleness but too late at night. There was the mistake. Had he ventured love-making in the afternoon, all would have been well, for it would have been as the quiet gentleman that he would have made love— but at night it was the uncouth, wife-stealing savage of the dark German forests. Out of his wisdom, he decided that afternoon love-making could be prosecuted successfully; but out of the same wisdom he was convinced that marriage as would prove a ghastly failure. He found it appalling to imagine being married and encountering his wife after dark.

So he had eschewed all love-making, regulated his dual life, cleaned up a million in business, fought shy of match-making mamas and bright-eyed and eager young ladies of various ages, met Lilian Gersdale and made it a rigid observance never to see her later than eight o'clock in the evening, run of nights after his coyotes, and slept in forest lairs—and through it all had kept his secret safe save Lee Sing... and now, Dave Slotter. It was the latter's discovery of both his selves that frightened him. In spite of the counter fright he had given the burglar, the latter might talk. And even if he did not, sooner or later he would be found out by some one else.

Thus it was that James Ward made a fresh and heroic effort to control the Teutonic barbarian that was half of him. So well did he make it a point to see Lilian in the afternoons, that the time came when she accepted him for better or worse, and when he prayed privily and fervently that it was not for worse. During this period no prize-fighter ever trained more harshly and faithfully for a contest than he trained to subdue the wild savage in him. Among other things, he strove to exhaust himself during the day, so that sleep would render him deaf to the call of the night. He took a vacation from the office and went on long hunting trips, following the deer through the most inaccessible and rugged country he could find—and always in the daytime. Night found him indoors and tired. At home he installed a score of exercise machines, and where other men might go through a particular movement ten times, he went hundreds. Also, as a compromise, he built a sleeping porch on the second story. Here he at least breathed the blessed night air. Double screens prevented him from escaping into the woods, and each night Lee Sing locked him in and each morning let him out.

The time came, in the month of August, when he engaged additional servants to assist Lee Sing and dared a house party in his Mill Valley bungalow. Lilian, her mother and brother, and half a dozen mutual friends, were the guests. For two days and nights all went well. And on the third night, playing bridge till eleven o'clock, he had reason to be proud of himself. His restlessness fully hid, but as luck would have it, Lilian Gersdale was his opponent on his right. She was a frail delicate flower of a woman, and in his night-mood her very frailty incensed him. Not that he loved her less, but that he felt almost irresistibly impelled to reach out and paw and maul her. Especially was this true when she was engaged in playing a winning hand against him.

He had one of the deer-hounds brought in and, when it seemed he must fly to pieces with the tension, a caressing hand laid on the animal brought him relief. These contacts with the hairy coat gave him instant easement and enabled him to play out the evening. Nor did anyone guess the while terrible struggle their host was making, the while he laughed so carelessly and played so keenly and deliberately.

When they separated for the night, he saw to it that he parted from Lilian in the presence or the others. Once on his sleeping porch and safely locked in, he doubled and tripled and even quadrupled his exercises until, exhausted, he lay down on the couch to woo sleep and to ponder two problems that especially troubled him. One was this matter of exercise. It was a paradox. The more he exercised in this excessive fashion, the stronger he became. While it was true that he thus quite tired out his night-running Teutonic self, it seemed that he was merely setting back the fatal day when his strength would be too much for him and overpower him, and then it would be a strength more terrible than he had yet known. The other problem was that of his marriage and of the stratagems he must employ in order to avoid his wife after dark. And thus, fruitlessly pondering, he fell asleep.

Now, where the huge grizzly bear came from that night was long a mystery, while the people of the Springs Brothers' Circus, showing at Sausalito, searched long and vainly for "Big Ben, the Biggest Grizzly in Captivity." But Big Ben escaped, and, out of the mazes of half a thousand bungalows and country estates, selected the grounds of James J. Ward for visitation. The self first Mr. Ward knew was when he found him on his feet, quivering and tense, a surge of battle in his breast and on his lips the old war-chant. From without came a wild baying and bellowing of the hounds. And sharp as a knife-thrust through the pandemonium came the agony of a stricken dog—his dog, he knew.

Not stopping for slippers, pajama-clad, he burst through the door Lee Sing had so carefully locked, and sped down the stairs and out into the night. As his naked feet struck the graveled driveway, he stopped abruptly, reached under the steps to a hiding-place he knew well, and pulled forth a huge knotty club—his old companion on many a mad night adventure on the hills. The frantic hullabaloo of the dogs was coming nearer, and, swinging the club, he sprang straight into the thickets to meet it.

The aroused household assembled on the wide veranda. Somebody turned on the electric lights, but they could see nothing but one another's frightened faces. Beyond the brightly illuminated driveway the trees formed a wall of impenetrable blackness. Yet somewhere in that blackness a terrible struggle was going on. There was an infernal outcry of animals, a great snarling and growling, the sound of blows being struck and a smashing and crashing of underbrush by heavy bodies.

The tide of battle swept out from among the trees and upon the driveway just beneath the onlookers. Then they saw. Mrs. Gersdale cried out and clung fainting to her son. Lilian, clutching the railing so spasmodically that a bruising hurt was left in her finger-ends for days, gazed horror-stricken at a yellow-haired, wild-eyed giant whom she recognized as the man who was to be her husband. He was swinging a great club, and fighting furiously and calmly with a shaggy monster that was bigger than any bear she had ever seen. One rip of the beast's claws had dragged away Ward's pajama-coat and streaked his flesh with blood.

While most of Lilian Gersdale's fright was for the man beloved, there was a large portion of it due to the man himself. Never had she dreamed so formidable and magnificent a savage lurked under the starched shirt and conventional garb of her betrothed. And never had she had any conception of how a man battled. Such a battle was certainly not modern; nor was she there beholding a modern man, though she did not know it. For this was not Mr. James J. Ward, the San Francisco business man, but one, unnamed and unknown, a crude, rude savage creature who, by some freak of chance, lived again after thrice a thousand years.

The hounds, ever maintaining their mad uproar, circled about the fight, or dashed in and out, distracting the bear. When the animal turned to meet such flanking assaults, the man leaped in and the club came down. Angered afresh by every such blow, the bear would rush, and the man, leaping and skipping, avoiding the dogs, went backwards or circled to one side or the other. Whereupon the dogs, taking advantage of the opening, would again spring in and draw the animal's wrath to them.

The end came suddenly. Whirling, the grizzly caught a hound with a wide sweeping cuff that sent the brute, its ribs caved in and its back broken, hurtling twenty feet. Then the human brute went mad. A foaming rage flecked the lips that parted with a wild inarticulate cry, as it sprang in, swung the club mightily in both hands, and brought it down full on the head of the uprearing grizzly. Not even the skull of a grizzly could withstand the crushing force of such a blow, and the animal went down to meet the worrying of the hounds. And through their scurrying leaped the man, squarely upon the body, where, in the white electric light, resting on his club, he chanted a triumph in an unknown tongue—a song so ancient that Professor Wertz would have given ten years of his life for it.

His guests rushed to possess him and acclaim him, but James Ward, suddenly looking out of the eyes of the early Teuton, saw the fair frail Twentieth Century girl he loved, and felt something snap in his brain. He staggered weakly toward her, dropped the club, and nearly fell. Something had gone wrong with him. Inside his brain was an intolerable agony. It seemed as if the soul of him were flying asunder. Following the excited gaze of the others, he glanced back and saw the carcass of the bear. The sight filled him with fear. He uttered a cry and would have fled, had they not restrained him and led him into the bungalow.

James J. Ward is still at the head of the firm of Ward, Knowles & Co. But he no longer lives in the country; nor does he run of nights after the coyotes under the moon. The early Teuton in him died the night of the Mill Valley fight with the bear. James J. Ward is now wholly James J. Ward, and he shares no part of his being with any vagabond anachronism from the younger world. And so wholly is James J. Ward modern, that he knows in all its bitter fullness the curse of civilized fear. He is now afraid of the dark, and night in the forest is to him a thing of abysmal terror. His city house is of the spick and span order, and he evinces a great interest in burglarproof devices. His home is a tangle of electric wires, and after bed-time a guest can scarcely breathe without setting off an alarm. Also, he had invented a combination keyless door-lock that travelers may carry in their vest pockets and apply immediately and successfully under all circumstances. But his wife does not deem him a coward. She knows better. And, like any hero, he is content to rest on his laurels. His bravery is never questioned by those friends who are aware of the Mill Valley episode.

THE BENEFIT OF THE DOUBT

CARTER WATSON, a current magazine under his arm, strolled slowly along, gazing about him curiously. Twenty years had elapsed since he had been on this particular street, and the changes were great and stupefying. This Western city of three hundred thousand souls had contained but thirty thousand, when, as a boy, he had been wont to ramble along its streets. In those days the street he was now on had been a quiet residence street in the respectable workingclass quarter. On this late afternoon he found that it had been submerged by a vast and vicious tenderloin. Chinese and Japanese shops and dens abounded, all confusedly intermingled with low white resorts and boozing dens. This quiet street of his youth had become the toughest quarter of the city.

He looked at his watch. It was half-past five. It was the slack time of the day in such a region, as he well knew, yet he was curious to see. In all his score of years of wandering and studying social conditions over the world, he had carried with him the memory of his old town as a sweet and wholesome place. The metamorphosis he now beheld was startling. He certainly must continue his stroll and glimpse the infamy to which his town had descended.

Another thing: Carter Watson had a keen social and civic consciousness. Independently wealthy, he had been loath to dissipate his energies in the pink teas and freak dinners of society, while actresses, race-horses, and kindred diversions had left him cold. He had the ethical bee in his bonnet and was a reformer of no mean pretension, though his work had been mainly in the line of contributions to the heavier reviews and quarterlies and to the publication over his name of brightly, cleverly written books on the working classes and the slum-dwellers. Among the twenty-seven to his credit occurred titles such as, "If Christ Came to New Orleans," "The Worked-out Worker," "Tenement Reform in Berlin," "The Rural Slums of England," "The people of the East Side," "Reform Versus Revolution," "The University Settlement as a Hot Bed of Radicalism" and "The Cave Man of Civilization."

But Carter Watson was neither morbid nor fanatic. He did not lose his head over the horrors he encountered, studied, and exposed. No hair brained enthusiasm branded him. His humor saved him, as did his wide experience and his conservative philosophic temperament. Nor did he have any patience with lightning change reform theories. As he saw it, society would grow better only through the painfully slow and arduously painful processes of evolution. There were no short cuts, no sudden regenerations. The betterment of mankind must be worked out in agony and misery just as all past social betterments had been worked out.

But on this late summer afternoon, Carter Watson was curious. As he moved along he paused before a gaudy drinking place. The sign above read, "The Vendome." There were two entrances. One evidently led to the bar. This he did not explore. The other was a narrow hallway. Passing through this he found himself in a huge room, filled with chair-encircled tables and quite deserted. In the dim light he made out a piano in the distance. Making a mental note that he would come back some time and study the class of persons that must sit and drink at those multitudinous tables, he proceeded to circumnavigate the room.

Now, at the rear, a short hallway led off to a small kitchen, and here, at a table, alone, sat Patsy Horan, proprietor of the Vendome, consuming a hasty supper ere the evening rush of business. Also, Patsy Horan was angry with the world. He had got out of the wrong side of bed that morning, and nothing had gone right all day. Had his barkeepers been asked, they would have described his mental condition as a grouch. But Carter Watson did not know this. As he passed the little hallway, Patsy Horan's sullen eyes lighted on the magazine he carried under his arm. Patsy did not know Carter Watson, nor did he know that what he carried under his arm was a magazine. Patsy, out of the depths of his grouch, decided that this stranger was one of those pests who marred and scarred the walls of his back rooms by tacking up or pasting up advertisements. The color on the front cover of the magazine convinced him that it was such an advertisement. Thus the trouble began. Knife and fork in hand, Patsy leaped for Carter Watson.

"Out wid yeh!" Patsy bellowed. "I know yer game!"

Carter Watson was startled. The man had come upon him like the eruption of a jack-in-the-box.

"A defacin' me walls," cried Patsy, at the same time emitting a string of vivid and vile, rather than virile, epithets of opprobrium.

"If I have given any offense I did not mean to—"

But that was as far as the visitor got. Patsy interrupted.

"Get out wid yeh; yeh talk too much wid yer mouth," quoted Patsy, emphasizing his remarks with flourishes of the knife and fork.

Carter Watson caught a quick vision of that eating-fork inserted uncomfortably between his ribs, knew that it would be rash to talk further with his mouth, and promptly turned to go. The sight of his meekly retreating back must have further enraged Patsy Horan, for that worthy, dropping the table implements, sprang upon him.

Patsy weighed one hundred and eighty pounds. So did Watson. In this they were equal. But Patsy was a rushing, rough-and-tumble saloon-fighter, while Watson was a boxer. In this the latter had the advantage, for Patsy came in wide open, swinging his right in a perilous sweep. All Watson had to do was to straight-left him and escape. But Watson had another advantage. His boxing, and his experience in the slums and ghettos of the world, had taught him restraint.

He pivoted on his feet, and, instead of striking, ducked the other's swinging blow and went into a clinch. But Patsy, charging like a bull, had the momentum of his rush, while Watson, whirling to meet him, had no momentum. As a result, the pair of them went down, with all their three hundred and sixty pounds of weight, in a long crashing fall, Watson underneath. He lay with his head touching the rear wall of the large room. The street was a hundred and fifty feet away, and he did some quick thinking. His first thought was to avoid trouble. He had no wish to get into the papers of this, his childhood town, where many of his relatives and family friends still lived.

So it was that he locked his arms around the man on top of him, held him close, and waited for the help to come that must come in response to the crash of the fall. The help came—that is, six men ran in from the bar and formed about in a semi-circle.

"Take him off, fellows," Watson said. "I haven't struck him, and I don't want any fight."

But the semi-circle remained silent. Watson held on and waited. Patsy, after various vain efforts to inflict damage, made an overture.

"Leggo o' me an' I'll get off o' yeh," said he.

Watson let go, but when Patsy scrambled to his feet he stood over his recumbent foe, ready to strike.

"Get up," Patsy commanded.

His voice was stern and implacable, like the voice of God calling to judgment, and Watson knew there was no mercy there.

"Stand back and I'll get up," he countered.

"If yer a gentleman, get up," quoth Patsy, his pale blue eyes aflame with wrath, his fist ready for a crushing blow.

At the same moment he drew his foot back to kick the other in the face. Watson blocked the kick with his crossed arms and sprang to his feet so quickly that he was in a clinch with his antagonist before the latter could strike. Holding him, Watson spoke to the onlookers:

"Take him away from me, fellows. You see I am not striking him. I don't want to fight. I want to get out of here."

The circle did not move nor speak. Its silence was ominous and sent a chill to Watson's heart.

Patsy made an effort to throw him, which culminated in his putting Patsy on his back. Tearing loose from him, Watson sprang to his feet and made for the door. But the circle of men was interposed a wall. He noticed the white, pasty faces, the kind that never see the sun, and knew that the men who barred his way were the nightprowlers and preying beasts of the city jungle. By them he was thrust back upon the pursuing, bull-rushing Patsy.

Again it was a clinch, in which, in momentary safety, Watson appealed to the gang. And again his words fell on deaf ears. Then it was that he knew of many similar knew fear. For he had known of many similar situations, in low dens like this, when solitary men were man-handled, their ribs and features caved in, themselves beaten and kicked to death. And he knew, further, that if he were to escape he must neither strike his assailant nor any of the men who opposed him.

Yet in him was righteous indignation. Under no circumstances could seven to one be fair. Also, he was angry, and there stirred in him the fighting beast that is in all men. But he remembered his wife and children, his unfinished book, the ten thousand rolling acres of the up-country ranch he loved so well. He even saw in flashing visions the blue of the sky, the golden sun pouring down on his flower-spangled meadows, the lazy cattle knee-deep in the brooks, and the flash of trout in the riffles. Life was good-too good for him to risk it for a moment's sway of the beast. In short, Carter Watson was cool and scared.

His opponent, locked by his masterly clinch, was striving to throw him. Again Watson put him on the floor, broke away, and was thrust back by the pasty-faced circle to duck Patsy's swinging right and effect another clinch. This happened many times. And Watson grew even cooler, while the baffled Patsy, unable to inflict punishment, raged wildly and more wildly. He took to batting with his head in the clinches. The first time, he landed his forehead flush on Watson's nose. After that, the latter, in the clinches, buried his face in Patsy's breast. But the enraged Patsy batted on, striking his own eye and nose and cheek on the top of the other's head. The more he was thus injured, the more and the harder did Patsy bat.

This one-sided contest continued for twelve or fifteen minutes. Watson never struck a blow, and strove only to escape. Sometimes, in the free moments, circling about among the tables as he tried to win the door, the pasty-faced men gripped his coat-tails and flung him back at the swinging right of the on-rushing Patsy. Time upon time, and times without end, he clinched and put Patsy on his back, each time first whirling him around and putting him down in the direction of the door and gaining toward that goal by the length of the fall.

In the end, hatless, disheveled, with streaming nose and one eye closed, Watson won to the sidewalk and into the arms of a policeman.

"Arrest that man," Watson panted.

"Hello, Patsy," said the policeman. "What's the mix-up?"

"Hello, Charley," was the answer. "This guy comes in—"

"Arrest that man, officer," Watson repeated.

"G'wan! Beat it!" said Patsy.

"Beat it!" added the policeman. "If you don't, I'll pull you in."

"Not unless you arrest that man. He has committed a violent and unprovoked assault on me."

"Is it so, Patsy?" was the officer's query.

"Nah. Lemme tell you, Charley, an' I got the witnesses to prove it, so help me God. I was settin' in me kitchen eatin' a bowl of soup, when this guy comes in an' gets gay wid me. I never seen him in me born days before. He was drunk—"

"Look at me, officer," protested the indignant sociologist. "Am I drunk?"

The officer looked at him with sullen, menacing eyes and nodded to Patsy to continue.

"This guy gets gay wid me. 'I'm Tim McGrath,' says he, 'an' I can do the like to you,' says he. 'Put up yer hands.' I smiles, an' wid that, biff biff, he lands me twice an' spills me soup. Look at me eye. I'm fair murdered."

"What are you going to do, officer?" Watson demanded.

"Go on, beat it," was the answer, "or I'll pull you sure."

The civic righteousness of Carter Watson flamed up.

"Mr. Officer, I protest—"

But at that moment the policeman grabbed his arm with a savage jerk that nearly overthrew him.

"Come on, you're pulled."

"Arrest him, too," Watson demanded.

"Nix on that play," was the reply.

"What did you assault him for, him a peacefully eatin' his soup?"

II

Carter Watson was genuinely angry. Not only had he been wantonly assaulted, badly battered, and arrested, but the morning papers without exception came out with lurid accounts of his drunken brawl with the proprietor of the notorious Vendome. Not one accurate or truthful line was published. Patsy Horan and his satellites described the battle in detail. The one incontestable thing was that Carter Watson had been drunk. Thrice he had been thrown out of the place and into the gutter, and thrice he had come back, breathing blood and fire and announcing that he was going to clean out the place. "EMINENT SOCIOLOGIST JAGGED AND JUGGED," was the first head-line he read, on the front page, accompanied by a large portrait of himself. Other headlines were: "CARTER WATSON ASPIRED TO CHAMPIONSHIP HONORS"; "CARTER WATSON GETS HIS"; "NOTED SOCIOLOGIST ATTEMPTS TO CLEAN OUT A TENDERLOIN CAFE"; and "CARTER WATSON KNOCKED OUT BY PATSY HORAN IN THREE ROUNDS."

At the police court, next morning, under bail, appeared Carter Watson to answer the complaint of the People Versus Carter Watson, for the latter's assault and battery on one Patsy Horan. But first, the Prosecuting Attorney, who was paid to prosecute all offenders against the People, drew him aside and talked with him privately.

"Why not let it drop!" said the Prosecuting Attorney. "I tell you what you do, Mr. Watson: Shake hands with Mr. Horan and make it up, and we'll drop the case right here. A word to the Judge, and the case against you will be dismissed."

"But I don't want it dismissed," was the answer. "Your office being what it is, you should be prosecuting me instead of asking me to make up with this—this fellow."

"Oh, I'll prosecute you all right," retorted the Prosecuting Attorney.

"Also you will have to prosecute this Patsy Horan," Watson advised; "for I shall now have him arrested for assault and battery."

"You'd better shake and make up," the Prosecuting Attorney repeated, and this time there was almost a threat in his voice.

The trials of both men were set for a week later, on the same morning, in Police Judge Witberg's court.

"You have no chance," Watson was told by an old friend of his boyhood, the retired manager of the biggest paper in the city. "Everybody knows you were beaten up by this man. His reputation is most unsavory. But it won't help you in the least. Both cases will be dismissed. This will be because you are you. Any ordinary man would be convicted."

"But I do not understand," objected the perplexed sociologist. "Without warning I was attacked by this man; and badly beaten. I did not strike a blow. I—"

"That has nothing to do with it," the other cut him off.

"Then what is there that has anything to do with it?"

"I'll tell you. You are now up against the local police and political machine. Who are you? You are not even a legal resident in this town. You live up in the country. You haven't a vote of your own here. Much less do you swing any votes. This dive proprietor swings a string of votes in his precincts—a mighty long string."

"Do you mean to tell me that this Judge Witberg will violate the sacredness of his office and oath by letting this brute off?" Watson demanded.

"Watch him," was the grim reply. "Oh, he'll do it nicely enough. He will give an extra-legal, extra-judicial decision, abounding in every word in the dictionary that stands for fairness and right."

"But there are the newspapers," Watson cried.

"They are not fighting the administration at present. They'll give it to you hard. You see what they have already done to you."

"Then these snips of boys on the police detail won't write the truth?"

"They will write something so near like the truth that the public will believe it. They write their stories under instruction, you know. They have their orders to twist and color, and there won't be much left of you when they get done. Better drop the whole thing right now. You are in bad."

"But the trials are set."

"Give the word and they'll drop them now. A man can't fight a machine unless he has a machine behind him."

III

But Carter Watson was stubborn. He was convinced that the machine would beat him, but all his days he had sought social experience, and this was certainly something new.

The morning of the trial the Prosecuting Attorney made another attempt to patch up the affair.

"If you feel that way, I should like to get a lawyer to prosecute the case," said Watson.

"No, you don't," said the Prosecuting Attorney. "I am paid by the People to prosecute, and prosecute I will. But let me tell you. You have no chance. We shall lump both cases into one, and you watch out."

Judge Witberg looked good to Watson. A fairly young man, short, comfortably stout, smooth-shaven and with an intelligent face, he seemed a very nice man indeed. This good impression was added to by the smiling lips and the wrinkles of laughter in the corners of his black eyes. Looking at him and studying him, Watson felt almost sure that his old friend's prognostication was wrong.

But Watson was soon to learn. Patsy Horan and two of his satellites testified to a most colossal aggregation of perjuries. Watson could not have believed it possible without having experienced it. They denied the existence of the other four men. And of the two that testified, one claimed to have been in the kitchen, a witness to Watson's unprovoked assault on Patsy, while the other, remaining in the bar, had witnessed Watson's second and third rushes into the place as he attempted to annihilate the unoffending Patsy. The vile language ascribed to Watson was so voluminously and unspeakably vile, that he felt they were injuring their own case. It was so impossible that he should utter such things. But when they described the brutal blows he had rained on poor Patsy's face, and the chair he demolished when he vainly attempted to kick Patsy, Watson waxed secretly hilarious and at the same time sad. The trial was a farce, but such lowness of life was depressing to contemplate when he considered the long upward climb humanity must make.

Watson could not recognize himself, nor could his worst enemy have recognized him, in the swashbuckling, rough-housing picture that was painted of him. But, as in all cases of complicated perjury, rifts and contradictions in the various stories appeared. The Judge somehow failed to notice them, while the Prosecuting Attorney and Patsy's attorney shied off from them gracefully. Watson had not bothered to get a lawyer for himself, and he was now glad that he had not.

Still, he retained a semblance of faith in Judge Witberg when he went himself on the stand and started to tell his story.

"I was strolling casually along the street, your Honor," Watson began, but was interrupted by the Judge.

"We are not here to consider your previous actions," bellowed Judge Witberg. "Who struck the first blow?"

"Your Honor," Watson pleaded, "I have no witnesses of the actual fray, and the truth of my story can only be brought out by telling the story fully—"

Again he was interrupted.

"We do not care to publish any magazines here," Judge Witberg roared, looking at him so fiercely and malevolently that Watson could scarcely bring himself to believe that this was same man he had studied a few minutes previously.

"Who struck the first blow?" Patsy's attorney asked.

The Prosecuting Attorney interposed, demanding to know which of the two cases lumped together was, and by what right Patsy's lawyer, at that stage of the proceedings, should take the witness. Patsy's attorney fought back. Judge Witberg interfered, professing no knowledge of any two cases being lumped together. All this had to be explained. Battle royal raged, terminating in both attorneys apologizing to the Court and to each other. And so it went, and to Watson it had the seeming of a group of pickpockets ruffling and bustling an honest man as they took his purse. The machine was working, that was all.

"Why did you enter this place of unsavory reputations?" was asked him.

"It has been my custom for many years, as a student of economics and sociology, to acquaint myself—"

But this was as far as Watson got.

"We want none of your ologies here," snarled Judge Witberg. "It is a plain question. Answer it plainly. Is it true or not true that you were drunk? That is the gist of the question."

When Watson attempted to tell how Patsy had injured his face in his attempts to bat with his head, Watson was openly scouted and flouted, and Judge Witberg again took him in hand.

"Are you aware of the solemnity of the oath you took to testify to nothing but the truth on this witness stand?" the Judge demanded. "This is a fairy story you are telling. It is not reasonable that a man would so injure himself, and continue to injure himself, by striking the soft and sensitive parts of his face against your head. You are a sensible man. It is unreasonable, is it not?"

"Men are unreasonable when they are angry," Watson answered meekly.

Then it was that Judge Witberg was deeply outraged and righteously wrathful.

"What right have you to say that?" he cried. "It is gratuitous. It has no bearing on the case. You are here as a witness, sir, of events that have transpired. The Court does not wish to hear any expressions of opinion from you at all."

"I but answered your question, your Honor," Watson protested humbly.

"You did nothing of the sort," was the next blast. "And let me warn you, sir, let me warn you, that you are laying yourself liable to contempt by such insolence. And I will have you know that we know how to observe the law and the rules of courtesy down here in this little courtroom. I am ashamed of you."

And, while the next punctilious legal wrangle between the attorneys interrupted his tale of what happened in the Vendome, Carter Watson, without bitterness, amused and at the same time sad, saw rise before him the machine, large and small, that dominated his country, the unpunished and shameless grafts of a thousand cities perpetrated by the spidery and vermin-like creatures of the machines. Here it was before him, a courtroom and a judge, bowed down in subservience by the machine to a dive-keeper who swung a string of votes. Petty and sordid as it was, it was one face of the many-faced machine that loomed colossally, in every city and state, in a thousand guises overshadowing the land.

A familiar phrase rang in his ears: "It is to laugh." At the height of the wrangle, he giggled, once, aloud, and earned a sullen frown from Judge Witberg. Worse, a myriad times, he decided, were these bullying lawyers and this bullying judge then the bucko mates in first quality hell-ships, who not only did their own bullying but protected themselves as well. These petty rapscallions, on the other hand, sought protection behind the majesty of the law. They struck, but no one was permitted to strike back, for behind them were the prison cells and the clubs of the stupid policemen—paid and professional fighters and beaters-up of men. Yet he was not bitter. The grossness and the sliminess of it was forgotten in the simple grotesqueness of it, and he had the saving sense of humor.

Nevertheless, hectored and heckled though he was, he managed in the end to give a simple, straightforward version of the affair, and, despite a belligerent cross-examination, his story was not shaken in any particular. Quite different it was from the perjuries that had shouted aloud from the perjuries of Patsy and his two witnesses.

Both Patsy's attorney and the Prosecuting Attorney rested their cases, letting everything go before the Court without argument. Watson protested against this, but was silenced when the Prosecuting Attorney told him that Public Prosecutor and knew his business.

"Patrick Horan has testified that he was in danger of his life and that he was compelled to defend himself," Judge Witberg's verdict began. "Mr. Watson has testified to the same thing. Each has sworn that the other struck the first blow; each has sworn that the other made an unprovoked assault on him. It is an axiom of the law that the defendant should be given the benefit of the doubt. A very reasonable doubt exists. Therefore, in the case of the People Versus Carter Watson the benefit of the doubt is given to said Carter Watson and he is herewith ordered discharged from custody. The same reasoning applies to the case of the People Versus Patrick Horan. He is given the benefit of the doubt and discharged from custody. My recommendation is that both defendants shake hands and make up."

In the afternoon papers the first headline that caught Watson's eye was: "CARTER WATSON ACQUITTED." In the second paper it was: "CARTER WATSON ESCAPES A FINE." But what capped everything was the one beginning: "CARTER WATSON A GOOD FELLOW." In the text he read how Judge Witberg had advised both fighters to shake hands, which they promptly did. Further, he read:

"'Let's have a nip on it,' said Patsy Horan.

"'Sure,' said Carter Watson.

"And, arm in arm, they ambled for the nearest saloon."

IV

Now, from the whole adventure, Watson carried away no bitterness. It was a social experience of a new order, and it led to the writing of another book, which he entitled, "POLICE COURT PROCEDURE: A Tentative Analysis."

One summer morning a year later, on his ranch, he left his horse and himself clambered on through a miniature canyon to inspect some rock ferns he had planted the previous winter. Emerging from the upper end of the canyon, he came out on one of his flower-spangled meadows, a delightful isolated spot, screened from the world by low hills and clumps of trees. And here he found a man, evidently on a stroll from the summer hotel down at the little town a mile away. They met face to face and the recognition was mutual. It was Judge Witberg. Also, it was a clear case of trespass, for Watson had trespass signs upon his boundaries, though he never enforced them.

Judge Witberg held out his hand, which Watson refused to see.

"Politics is a dirty trade, isn't it, Judge?" he remarked. "Oh, yes, I see your hand, but I don't care to take it. The papers said I shook hands with Patsy Horan after the trial. You know I did not, but let me tell you that I'd a thousand times rather shake hands with him and his vile following of curs, than with you."

Judge Witberg was painfully flustered, and as he hemmed and hawed and essayed to speak, Watson, looking at him, was struck by a sudden whim, and he determined on a grim and facetious antic.

"I should scarcely expect any animus from a man of your acquirements and knowledge of the world," the Judge was saying.

"Animus?" Watson replied. "Certainly not. I haven't such a thing in my nature. And to prove it, let me show you something curious, something you have never seen before." Casting about him, Watson picked up a rough stone the size of his fist. "See this. Watch me."

So saying, Carter Watson tapped himself a sharp blow on the cheek. The stone laid the flesh open to the bone and the blood spurted forth.

"The stone was too sharp," he announced to the astounded police judge, who thought he had gone mad.

"I must bruise it a trifle. There is nothing like being realistic in such matters."

Whereupon Carter Watson found a smooth stone and with it pounded his cheek nicely several times.

"Ah," he cooed. "That will turn beautifully green and black in a few hours. It will be most convincing."

"You are insane," Judge Witberg quavered.

"Don't use such vile language to me," said Watson. "You see my bruised and bleeding face? You did that, with that right hand of yours. You hit me twice—biff, biff. It is a brutal and unprovoked assault. I am in danger of my life. I must protect myself."

Judge Witberg backed away in alarm before the menacing fists of the other.

"If you strike me I'll have you arrested," Judge Witberg threatened.

"That is what I told Patsy," was the answer. "And do you know what he did when I told him that?"

"No."

"That!"

And at the same moment Watson's right fist landed flush on Judge Witberg's nose, putting that legal gentleman over on his back on the grass.

"Get up!" commanded Watson. "If you are a gentleman, get up—that's what Patsy told me, you know."

Judge Witberg declined to rise, and was dragged to his feet by the coat-collar, only to have one eye blacked and be put on his back again. After that it was a red Indian massacre. Judge Witberg was humanely and scientifically beaten up. His checks were boxed, his ears cuffed, and his face was rubbed in the turf. And all the time Watson exposed the way Patsy Horan had done it. Occasionally, and very carefully, the facetious sociologist administered a real bruising blow. Once, dragging the poor Judge to his feet, he deliberately bumped his own nose on the gentleman's head. The nose promptly bled.

"See that!" cried Watson, stepping back and deftly shedding his blood all down his own shirt front. "You did it. With your fist you did it. It is awful. I am fair murdered. I must again defend myself."

And once more Judge Witberg impacted his features on a fist and was sent to grass.

"I will have you arrested," he sobbed as he lay.

"That's what Patsy said."

"A brutal—-sniff, sniff,—and unprovoked—sniff, sniff—assault."

"That's what Patsy said."

"I will surely have you arrested."

"Speaking slangily, not if I can beat you to it."

And with that, Carter Watson departed down the canyon, mounted his horse, and rode to town.

An hour later, as Judge Witberg limped up the grounds to his hotel, he was arrested by a village constable on a charge of assault and battery preferred by Carter Watson.

V

"Your Honor," Watson said next day to the village Justice, a well to do farmer and graduate, thirty years before, from a cow college, "since this Sol Witberg has seen fit to charge me with battery, following upon my charge of battery against him, I would suggest that both cases be lumped together. The testimony and the facts are the same in both cases."

To this the Justice agreed, and the double case proceeded. Watson, as prosecuting witness, first took the stand and told his story.

"I was picking flowers," he testified. "Picking flowers on my own land, never dreaming of danger. Suddenly this man rushed upon me from behind the trees. 'I am the Dodo,' he says, 'and I can do you to a frazzle. Put up your hands.' I smiled, but with that, biff, biff, he struck me, knocking me down and spilling my flowers. The language he used was frightful. It was an unprovoked and brutal assault. Look at my cheek. Look at my nose—I could not understand it. He must have been drunk. Before I recovered from my surprise he had administered this beating. I was in danger of my life and was compelled to defend himself. That is all, Your Honor, though I must say, in conclusion, that I cannot get over my perplexity. Why did he say he was the Dodo? Why did he so wantonly attack me?"

And thus was Sol Witberg given a liberal education in the art of perjury. Often, from his high seat, he had listened indulgently to police court perjuries in cooked-up cases; but for the first time perjury was directed against him, and he no longer sat above the court, with the bailiffs, the Policemen's clubs, and the prison cells behind him.

"Your Honor," he cried, "never have I heard such a pack of lies told by so bare-faced a liar—!"

Watson here sprang to his feet.

"Your Honor, I protest. It is for your Honor to decide truth or falsehood. The witness is on the stand to testify to actual events that have transpired. His personal opinion upon things in general, and upon me, has no bearing on the case whatever."

The Justice scratched his head and waxed phlegmatically indignant.

"The point is well taken," he decided. "I am surprised at you, Mr. Witberg, claiming to be a judge and skilled in the practice of the law, and yet being guilty of such unlawyerlike conduct. Your manner, sir, and your methods, remind me of a shyster. This is a simple case of assault and battery. We are here to determine who struck the first blow, and we are not interested in your estimates of Mr. Watson's personal character. Proceed with your story."

Sol Witberg would have bitten his bruised and swollen lip in chagrin, had it not hurt so much. But he contained himself and told a simple, straightforward, truthful story.

"Your Honor," Watson said, "I would suggest that you ask him what he was doing on my premises."

"A very good question. What were you doing, sir, on Mr. Watson's premises?"

"I did not know they were his premises."

"It was a trespass, your Honor," Watson cried. "The warnings are posted conspicuously."

"I saw no warnings," said Sol Witberg.

"I have seen them myself," snapped the Justice. "They are very conspicuous. And I would warn you, sir, that if you palter with the truth in such little matters you may darken your more important statements with suspicion. Why did you strike Mr. Watson?"

"Your Honor, as I have testified, I did not strike a blow."

The Justice looked at Carter Watson's bruised and swollen visage, and turned to glare at Sol Witberg.

"Look at that man's cheek!" he thundered. "If you did not strike a blow how comes it that he is so disfigured and injured?"

"As I testified—"

"Be careful," the Justice warned.

"I will be careful, sir. I will say nothing but the truth. He struck himself with a rock. He struck himself with two different rocks."

"Does it stand to reason that a man, any man not a lunatic, would so injure himself, and continue to injure himself, by striking the soft and sensitive parts of his face with a stone?" Carter Watson demanded

"It sounds like a fairy story," was the Justice's comment.

"Mr. Witberg, had you been drinking?"

"No, sir."

"Do you never drink?"

"On occasion."

The Justice meditated on this answer with an air of astute profundity.

Watson took advantage of the opportunity to wink at Sol Witberg, but that much-abused gentleman saw nothing humorous in the situation.

"A very peculiar case, a very peculiar case," the Justice announced, as he began his verdict. "The evidence of the two parties is flatly contradictory. There are no witnesses outside the two principals. Each claims the other committed the assault, and I have no legal way of determining the truth. But I have my private opinion, Mr. Witberg, and I would recommend that henceforth you keep off of Mr. Watson's premises and keep away from this section of the country—"

"This is an outrage!" Sol Witberg blurted out.

"Sit down, sir!" was the Justice's thundered command. "If you interrupt the Court in this manner again, I shall fine you for contempt. And I warn you I shall fine you heavily—you, a judge yourself, who should be conversant with the courtesy and dignity of courts. I shall now give my verdict:

"It is a rule of law that the defendant shall be given the benefit of the doubt. As I have said, and I repeat, there is no legal way for me to determine who struck the first blow. Therefore, and much to my regret,"—here he paused and glared at Sol Witberg—"in each of these cases I am compelled to give the defendant the benefit of the doubt. Gentlemen, you are both dismissed."

"Let us have a nip on it," Watson said to Witberg, as they left the courtroom; but that outraged person refused to lock arms and amble to the nearest saloon.

WINGED BLACKMAIL

PETER WINN lay back comfortably in a library chair, with closed eyes, deep in the cogitation of a scheme of campaign destined in the near future to make a certain coterie of hostile financiers sit up. The central idea had come to him the night before, and he was now reveling in the planning of the remoter, minor details. By obtaining control of a certain up-country bank, two general stores, and several logging camps, he could come into control of a certain dinky jerkwater line which shall here be nameless, but which, in his hands, would prove the key to a vastly larger situation involving more main-line mileage almost than there were spikes in the aforesaid dinky jerkwater. It was so simple that he had almost laughed aloud when it came to him. No wonder those astute and ancient enemies of his had passed it by.

The library door opened, and a slender, middle-aged man, weak-eyed and eye glassed, entered. In his hands was an envelope and an open letter. As Peter Winn's secretary it was his task to weed out, sort, and classify his employer's mail.

"This came in the morning post," he ventured apologetically and with the hint of a titter. "Of course it doesn't amount to anything, but I thought you would like to see it."

"Read it," Peter Winn commanded, without opening his eyes.

The secretary cleared his throat.

"It is dated July seventeenth, but is without address. Postmark San Francisco. It is also quite illiterate. The spelling is atrocious. Here it is:

"Mr. Peter Winn, SIR: I send you respectfully by express a pigeon worth good money. She's a loo-loo—"

"What is a loo-loo?" Peter Winn interrupted.

The secretary tittered.

"I'm sure I don't know, except that it must be a superlative of some sort. The letter continues:

"Please freight it with a couple of thousand-dollar bills and let it go. If you do I wont never annoy you no more. If you dont you will be sorry.

"That is all. It is unsigned. I thought it would amuse you."

"Has the pigeon come?" Peter Winn demanded.

"I'm sure I never thought to enquire."

"Then do so."

In five minutes the secretary was back.

"Yes, sir. It came this morning."

"Then bring it in."

The secretary was inclined to take the affair as a practical joke, but Peter Winn, after an examination of the pigeon, thought otherwise.

"Look at it," he said, stroking and handling it. "See the length of the body and that elongated neck. A proper carrier. I doubt if I've ever seen a finer specimen. Powerfully winged and muscled. As our unknown correspondent remarked, she is a loo-loo. It's a temptation to keep her."

The secretary tittered.

"Why not? Surely you will not let it go back to the writer of that letter."

Peter Winn shook his head.

"I'll answer. No man can threaten me, even anonymously or in foolery."

On a slip of paper he wrote the succinct message, "Go to hell," signed it, and placed it in the carrying apparatus with which the bird had been thoughtfully supplied.

"Now we'll let her loose. Where's my son? I'd like him to see the flight."

"He's down in the workshop. He slept there last night, and had his breakfast sent down this morning."

"He'll break his neck yet," Peter Winn remarked, half-fiercely, half-proudly, as he led the way to the veranda.

Standing at the head of the broad steps, he tossed the pretty creature outward and upward. She caught herself with a quick beat of wings, fluttered about undecidedly for a space, then rose in the air.

Again, high up, there seemed indecision; then, apparently getting her bearings, she headed east, over the oak-trees that dotted the park-like grounds.

"Beautiful, beautiful," Peter Winn murmured. "I almost wish I had her back."

But Peter Winn was a very busy man, with such large plans in his head and with so many reins in his hands that he quickly forgot the incident. Three nights later the left wing of his country house was blown up. It was not a heavy explosion, and nobody was hurt, though the wing itself was ruined. Most of the windows of the rest of the house were broken, and there was a deal of general damage. By the first ferry boat of the morning half a dozen San Francisco detectives arrived, and several hours later the secretary, in high excitement, erupted on Peter Winn.

"It's come!" the secretary gasped, the sweat beading his forehead and his eyes bulging behind their glasses.

"What has come?" Peter demanded. "It—the—the loo-loo bird."

Then the financier understood.

"Have you gone over the mail yet?"

"I was just going over it, sir."

"Then continue, and see if you can find another letter from our mysterious friend, the pigeon fancier."

The letter came to light. It read:

Mr. Peter Winn, HONORABLE SIR: Now dont be a fool. If youd came through, your shack would not have blew up—I beg to inform you respectfully, am sending same pigeon. Take good care of same, thank you. Put five one thousand dollar bills on her and let her go. Dont feed her. Dont try to follow bird. She is wise to the way now and makes better time. If you dont come through, watch out.

Peter Winn was genuinely angry. This time he indited no message for the pigeon to carry. Instead, he called in the detectives, and, under their advice, weighted the pigeon heavily with shot. Her previous flight having been eastward toward the bay, the fastest motor-boat in Tiburon was commissioned to take up the chase if it led out over the water.

But too much shot had been put on the carrier, and she was exhausted before the shore was reached. Then the mistake was made of putting too little shot on her, and she rose high in the air, got her bearings and started eastward across San Francisco Bay. She flew straight over Angel Island, and here the motor-boat lost her, for it had to go around the island.

That night, armed guards patrolled the grounds. But there was no explosion. Yet, in the early morning Peter Winn learned by telephone that his sister's home in Alameda had been burned to the ground.

Two days later the pigeon was back again, coming this time by freight in what had seemed a barrel of potatoes. Also came another letter:

Mr. Peter Winn, RESPECTABLE SIR: It was me that fixed yr sisters house. You have raised hell, aint you. Send ten thousand now. Going up all the time. Dont put any more handicap weights on that bird. You sure cant follow her, and its cruelty to animals.

Peter Winn was ready to acknowledge himself beaten. The detectives were powerless, and Peter did not know where next the man would strike— perhaps at the lives of those near and dear to him. He even telephoned to San Francisco for ten thousand dollars in bills of large denomination. But Peter had a son, Peter Winn, Junior, with the same firm-set jaw as his fathers, and the same knitted, brooding determination in his eyes. He was only twenty-six, but he was all man, a secret terror and delight to the financier, who alternated between pride in his son's aeroplane feats and fear for an untimely and terrible end.

"Hold on, father, don't send that money," said Peter Winn, Junior. "Number Eight is ready, and I know I've at last got that reefing down fine. It will work, and it will revolutionize flying. Speed—that's what's needed, and so are the large sustaining surfaces for getting started and for altitude. I've got them both. Once I'm up I reef down. There it is. The smaller the sustaining surface, the higher the speed. That was the law discovered by Langley. And I've applied it. I can rise when the air is calm and full of holes, and I can rise when its boiling, and by my control of my plane areas I can come pretty close to making any speed I want. Especially with that new Sangster-Endholm engine."

"You'll come pretty close to breaking your neck one of these days," was his father's encouraging remark.

"Dad, I'll tell you what I'll come pretty close to-ninety miles an hour—Yes, and a hundred. Now listen! I was going to make a trial tomorrow. But it won't take two hours to start today. I'll tackle it this afternoon. Keep that money. Give me the pigeon and I'll follow her to her loft where ever it is. Hold on, let me talk to the mechanics."

He called up the workshop, and in crisp, terse sentences gave his orders in a way that went to the older man's heart. Truly, his one son was a chip off the old block, and Peter Winn had no meek notions concerning the intrinsic value of said old block.

Timed to the minute, the young man, two hours later, was ready for the start. In a holster at his hip, for instant use, cocked and with the safety on, was a large-caliber automatic pistol. With a final inspection and overhauling he took his seat in the aeroplane. He started the engine, and with a wild burr of gas explosions the beautiful fabric darted down the launching ways and lifted into the air. Circling, as he rose, to the west, he wheeled about and jockeyed and maneuvered for the real start of the race.

This start depended on the pigeon. Peter Winn held it. Nor was it weighted with shot this time. Instead, half a yard of bright ribbon was firmly attached to its leg—this the more easily to enable its flight being followed. Peter Winn released it, and it arose easily enough despite the slight drag of the ribbon. There was no uncertainty about its movements. This was the third time it had made particular homing passage, and it knew the course.

At an altitude of several hundred feet it straightened out and went due east. The aeroplane swerved into a straight course from its last curve and followed. The race was on. Peter Winn, looking up, saw that the pigeon was outdistancing the machine. Then he saw something else. The aeroplane suddenly and instantly became smaller. It had reefed. Its high-speed plane-design was now revealed. Instead of the generous spread of surface with which it had taken the air, it was now a lean and hawklike monoplane balanced on long and exceedingly narrow wings.

When young Winn reefed down so suddenly, he received a surprise. It was his first trial of the new device, and while he was prepared for increased speed he was not prepared for such an astonishing increase. It was better than he dreamed, and, before he knew it, he was hard upon the pigeon. That little creature, frightened by this, the most monstrous hawk it had ever seen, immediately darted upward, after the manner of pigeons that strive always to rise above a hawk.

In great curves the monoplane followed upward, higher and higher into the blue. It was difficult, from underneath to see the pigeon, and young Winn dared not lose it from his sight. He even shook out his reefs in order to rise more quickly. Up, up they went, until the pigeon, true to its instinct, dropped and struck at what it thought to be the back of its pursuing enemy. Once was enough, for, evidently finding no life in the smooth cloth surface of the machine, it ceased soaring and straightened out on its eastward course.

A carrier pigeon on a passage can achieve a high rate of speed, and Winn reefed again. And again, to his satisfaction, he found that he was beating the pigeon. But this time he quickly shook out a portion of his reefed sustaining surface and slowed down in time. From then on he knew he had the chase safely in hand, and from then on a chant rose to his lips which he continued to sing at intervals, and unconsciously, for the rest of the passage. It was: "Going some; going some; what did I tell you!—going some."

Even so, it was not all plain sailing. The air is an unstable medium at best, and quite without warning, at an acute angle, he entered an aerial tide which he recognized as the gulf stream of wind that poured through the drafty-mouthed Golden Gate. His right wing caught it first—a sudden, sharp puff that lifted and tilted the monoplane and threatened to capsize it. But he rode with a sensitive "loose curb," and quickly, but not too quickly, he shifted the angles of his wing-tips, depressed the front horizontal rudder, and swung over the rear vertical rudder to meet the tilting thrust of the wind. As the machine came back to an even keel, and he knew that he was now wholly in the invisible stream, he readjusted the wing-tips, rapidly away from him during the several moments of his discomfiture.

The pigeon drove straight on for the Alameda County shore, and it was near this shore that Winn had another experience. He fell into an air-hole. He had fallen into air-holes before, in previous flights, but this was a far larger one than he had ever encountered. With his eyes strained on the ribbon attached to the pigeon, by that fluttering bit of color he marked his fall. Down he went, at the pit of his stomach that old sink sensation which he had known as a boy he first negotiated quick-starting elevators. But Winn, among other secrets of aviation, had learned that to go up it was sometimes necessary first to go down. The air had refused to hold him. Instead of struggling futilely and perilously against this lack of sustension, he yielded to it. With steady head and hand, he depressed the forward horizontal rudder—just recklessly enough and not a fraction more—and the monoplane dived head foremost and sharply down the void. It was falling with the keenness of a knife-blade. Every instant the speed accelerated frightfully. Thus he accumulated the momentum that would save him. But few instants were required, when, abruptly shifting the double horizontal rudders forward and astern, he shot upward on the tense and straining plane and out of the pit.

At an altitude of five hundred feet, the pigeon drove on over the town of Berkeley and lifted its flight to the Contra Costa hills. Young Winn noted the campus and buildings of the University of California—his university—as he rose after the pigeon.

Once more, on these Contra Costa hills, he early came to grief. The pigeon was now flying low, and where a grove of eucalyptus presented a solid front to the wind, the bird was suddenly sent fluttering wildly upward for a distance of a hundred feet. Winn knew what it meant. It had been caught in an air-surf that beat upward hundreds of feet where the fresh west wind smote the upstanding wall of the grove. He reefed hastily to the uttermost, and at the same time depressed the angle of his flight to meet that upward surge. Nevertheless, the monoplane was tossed fully three hundred feet before the danger was left astern.

Two or more ranges of hills the pigeon crossed, and then Winn saw it dropping down to a landing where a small cabin stood in a hillside clearing. He blessed that clearing. Not only was it good for alighting, but, on account of the steepness of the slope, it was just the thing for rising again into the air.

A man, reading a newspaper, had just started up at the sight of the returning pigeon, when he heard the burr of Winn's engine and saw the huge monoplane, with all surfaces set, drop down upon him, stop suddenly on an air-cushion manufactured on the spur of the moment by a shift of the horizontal rudders, glide a few yards, strike ground, and come to rest not a score of feet away from him. But when he saw a young man, calmly sitting in the machine and leveling a pistol at him, the man turned to run. Before he could make the corner of the cabin, a bullet through the leg brought him down in a sprawling fall.

"What do you want!" he demanded sullenly, as the other stood over him.

"I want to take you for a ride in my new machine," Winn answered. "Believe me, she is a loo-loo."

The man did not argue long, for this strange visitor had most convincing ways. Under Winn's instructions, covered all the time by the pistol, the man improvised a tourniquet and applied it to his wounded leg. Winn helped him to a seat in the machine, then went to the pigeon-loft and took possession of the bird with the ribbon still fast to its leg.

A very tractable prisoner, the man proved. Once up in the air, he sat close, in an ecstasy of fear. An adept at winged blackmail, he had no aptitude for wings himself, and when he gazed down at the flying land and water far beneath him, he did not feel moved to attack his captor, now defenseless, both hands occupied with flight.

Instead, the only way the man felt moved was to sit closer.

Peter Winn, Senior, scanning the heavens with powerful glasses, saw the monoplane leap into view and grow large over the rugged backbone of Angel Island. Several minutes later he cried out to the waiting detectives that the machine carried a passenger. Dropping swiftly and piling up an abrupt air-cushion, the monoplane landed.

"That reefing device is a winner!" young Winn cried, as he climbed out. "Did you see me at the start? I almost ran over the pigeon. Going some, dad! Going some! What did I tell you? Going some!"

"But who is that with you?" his father demanded.

The young man looked back at his prisoner and remembered.

"Why, that's the pigeon-fancier," he said. "I guess the officers can take care of him."

Peter Winn gripped his son's hand in grim silence, and fondled the pigeon which his son had passed to him. Again he fondled the pretty creature. Then he spoke.

"Exhibit A, for the People," he said.

BUNCHES OF KNUCKLES

ARRANGEMENTS quite extensive had been made for the celebration of Christmas on the yacht Samoset. Not having been in any civilized port for months, the stock of provisions boasted few delicacies; yet Minnie Duncan had managed to devise real feasts for cabin and forecastle.

"Listen, Boyd," she told her husband. "Here are the menus. For the cabin, raw bonita native style, turtle soup, omelette a la Samoset—"

"What the dickens?" Boyd Duncan interrupted.

"Well, if you must know, I found a tin of mushrooms and a package of egg-powder which had fallen down behind the locker, and there are other things as well that will go into it. But don't interrupt. Boiled yam, fried taro, alligator pear salad—there, you've got me all mixed, Then I found a last delectable half-pound of dried squid. There will be baked beans Mexican, if I can hammer it into Toyama's head; also, baked papaia with Marquesan honey, and, lastly, a wonderful pie the secret of which Toyama refuses to divulge."

"I wonder if it is possible to concoct a punch or a cocktail out of trade rum?" Duncan muttered gloomily.

"Oh! I forgot! Come with me."

His wife caught his hand and led him through the small connecting door to her tiny stateroom. Still holding his hand, she fished in the depths of a hat-locker and brought forth a pint bottle of champagne.

"The dinner is complete!" he cried.

"Wait."

She fished again, and was rewarded with a silver-mounted whisky flask. She held it to the light of a port-hole, and the liquor showed a quarter of the distance from the bottom.

"I've been saving it for weeks," she explained. "And there's enough for you and Captain Dettmar."

"Two mighty small drinks," Duncan complained.

"There would have been more, but I gave a drink to Lorenzo when he was sick."

Duncan growled, "Might have given him rum," facetiously.

"The nasty stuff! For a sick man? Don't be greedy, Boyd. And I'm glad there isn't any more, for Captain Dettmar's sake. Drinking always makes him irritable. And now for the men's dinner. Soda crackers, sweet cakes, candy—"

"Substantial, I must say."

"Do hush. Rice, and curry, yam, taro, bonita, of course, a big cake Toyama is making, young pig—"

"Oh, I say," he protested.

"It is all right, Boyd. We'll be in Attu-Attu in three days. Besides, it's my pig. That old chief what-ever-his-name distinctly presented it to me. You saw him yourself. And then two tins of bullamacow. That's their dinner. And now about the presents. Shall we wait until tomorrow, or give them this evening?"

"Christmas Eve, by all means," was the man's judgment. "We'll call all hands at eight bells; I'll give them a tot of rum all around, and then you give the presents. Come on up on deck. It's stifling down here. I hope Lorenzo has better luck with the dynamo; without the fans there won't be much sleeping to-night if we're driven below."

They passed through the small main-cabin, climbed a steep companion ladder, and emerged on deck. The sun was setting, and the promise was for a clear tropic night. The Samoset, with fore- and main-sail winged out on either side, was slipping a lazy four-knots through the smooth sea. Through the engine-room skylight came a sound of hammering. They strolled aft to where Captain Dettmar, one foot on the rail, was oiling the gear of the patent log. At the wheel stood a tall South Sea Islander, clad in white undershirt and scarlet hip-cloth.

Boyd Duncan was an original. At least that was the belief of his friends. Of comfortable fortune, with no need to do anything but take his comfort, he elected to travel about the world in outlandish and most uncomfortable ways. Incidentally, he had ideas about coral-reefs, disagreed profoundly with Darwin on that subject, had voiced his opinion in several monographs and one book, and was now back at his hobby, cruising the South Seas in a tiny, thirty-ton yacht and studying reef-formations.

His wife, Minnie Duncan, was also declared an original, inasmuch as she joyfully shared his vagabond wanderings. Among other things, in the six exciting years of their marriage she had climbed Chimborazo with him, made a three-thousand-mile winter journey with dogs and sleds in Alaska, ridden a horse from Canada to Mexico, cruised the Mediterranean in a ten-ton yawl, and canoed from Germany to the Black Sea across the heart of Europe. They were a royal pair of wanderlusters, he, big and broad-shouldered, she a small, brunette, and happy woman, whose one hundred and fifteen pounds were all grit and endurance, and withal, pleasing to look upon.

The Samoset had been a trading schooner, when Duncan bought her in San Francisco and made alterations. Her interior was wholly rebuilt, so that the hold became main-cabin and staterooms, while abaft amidships were installed engines, a dynamo, an ice machine, storage batteries, and, far in the stern, gasoline tanks. Necessarily, she carried a small crew. Boyd, Minnie, and Captain Dettmar were the only whites on board, though Lorenzo, the small and greasy engineer, laid a part claim to white, being a Portuguese half-caste. A Japanese served as cook, and a Chinese as cabin boy. Four white sailors had constituted the original crew for'ard, but one by one they had yielded to the charms of palm-waving South Sea isles and been replaced by islanders. Thus, one of the dusky sailors hailed from Easter Island, a second from the Carolines, a third from the Paumotus, while the fourth was a gigantic Samoan. At sea, Boyd Duncan, himself a navigator, stood a mate's watch with Captain Dettmar, and both of them took a wheel or lookout occasionally. On a pinch, Minnie herself could take a wheel, and it was on pinches that she proved herself more dependable at steering than did the native sailors.

At eight bells, all hands assembled at the wheel, and Boyd Duncan appeared with a black bottle and a mug. The rum he served out himself, half a mug of it to each man. They gulped the stuff down with many facial expressions of delight, followed by loud lip-smackings of approval, though the liquor was raw enough and corrosive enough to burn their mucous membranes. All drank except Lee Goom, the abstemious cabin boy. This rite accomplished, they waited for the next, the present-giving. Generously molded on Polynesian lines, huge-bodied and heavy-muscled, they were nevertheless like so many children, laughing merrily at little things, their eager black eyes flashing in the lantern light as their big bodies swayed to the heave and roll of the ship.

Calling each by name, Minnie gave the presents out, accompanying each presentation with some happy remark that added to the glee. There were trade watches, clasp knives, amazing assortments of fish-hooks in packages, plug tobacco, matches, and gorgeous strips of cotton for loincloths all around. That Boyd Duncan was liked by them was evidenced by the roars of laughter with which they greeted his slightest joking allusion.

Captain Dettmar, white-faced, smiling only when his employer chanced to glance at him, leaned against the wheel-box, looking on. Twice, he left the group and went below, remaining there but a minute each time. Later, in the main cabin, when Lorenzo, Lee Goom and Toyama received their presents, he disappeared into his stateroom twice again. For of all times, the devil that slumbered in Captain Dettmar's soul chose this particular time of good cheer to awaken. Perhaps it was not entirely the devil's fault, for Captain Dettmar, privily cherishing a quart of whisky for many weeks, had selected Christmas Eve for broaching it.

It was still early in the evening—two bells had just gone—when Duncan and his wife stood by the cabin companionway, gazing to windward and canvassing the possibility of spreading their beds on deck. A small, dark blot of cloud, slowly forming on the horizon, carried the threat of a rain-squall, and it was this they were discussing when Captain Dettmar, coming from aft and about to go below, glanced at them with sudden suspicion. He paused, his face working spasmodically. Then he spoke:

"You are talking about me."

His voice was hoarse, and there was an excited vibration in it. Minnie Duncan started, then glanced at her husband's immobile face, took the cue, and remained silent.

"I say you were talking about me," Captain Dettmar repeated, this time with almost a snarl.

He did not lurch nor betray the liquor on him in any way save by the convulsive working of his face.

"Minnie, you'd better go down," Duncan said gently. "Tell Lee Goom we'll sleep below. It won't be long before that squall is drenching things."

She took the hint and left, delaying just long enough to give one anxious glance at the dim faces of the two men.

Duncan puffed at his cigar and waited till his wife's voice, in talk with the cabin-boy, came up through the open skylight.

"Well?" Duncan demanded in a low voice, but sharply.

"I said you were talking about me. I say it again. Oh, I haven't been blind. Day after day I've seen the two of you talking about me. Why don't you come out and say it to my face! I know you know. And I know your mind's made up to discharge me at Attu-Attu."

"I am sorry you are making such a mess of everything," was Duncan's quiet reply.

But Captain Dettmar's mind was set on trouble.

"You know you are going to discharge me. You think you are too good to associate with the likes of me—you and your wife."

"Kindly keep her out of this," Duncan warned. "What do you want?"

"I want to know what you are going to do!"

"Discharge you, after this, at Attu-Attu."

"You intended to, all along."

"On the contrary. It is your present conduct that compels me."

"You can't give me that sort of talk."

"I can't retain a captain who calls me a liar."

Captain Dettmar for the moment was taken aback. His face and lips worked, but he could say nothing. Duncan coolly pulled at his cigar and glanced aft at the rising cloud of squall.

"Lee Goom brought the mail aboard at Tahiti," Captain Dettmar began.

"We were hove short then and leaving. You didn't look at your letters until we were outside, and then it was too late. That's why you didn't discharge me at Tahiti. Oh, I know. I saw the long envelope when Lee Goom came over the side. It was from the Governor of California, printed on the corner for any one to see. You'd been working behind my back. Some beachcomber in Honolulu had whispered to you, and you'd written to the Governor to find out. And that was his answer Lee Goom carried out to you. Why didn't you come to me like a man! No, you must play underhand with me, knowing that this billet was the one chance for me to get on my feet again. And as soon as you read the Governor's letter your mind was made up to get rid of me. I've seen it on your face ever since for all these months.. I've seen the two of you, polite as hell to me all the time, and getting away in corners and talking about me and that affair in 'Frisco."

"Are you done?" Duncan asked, his voice low, and tense. "Quite done?"

Captain Dettmar made no answer.

"Then I'll tell you a few things. It was precisely because of that affair in 'Frisco that I did not discharge you in Tahiti. God knows you gave me sufficient provocation. I thought that if ever a man needed a chance to rehabilitate himself, you were that man. Had there been no black mark against you, I would have discharged you when I learned how you were robbing me."

Captain Dettmar showed surprise, started to interrupt, then changed his mind.

"There was that matter of the deck-calking, the bronze rudder-irons, the overhauling of the engine, the new spinnaker boom, the new davits, and the repairs to the whale-boat. You OKd the shipyard bill. It was four thousand one hundred and twenty-two francs. By the regular shipyard charges it ought not to have been a centime over twenty-five hundred francs-"

"If you take the word of those alongshore sharks against mine—' the other began thickly.

"Save yourself the trouble of further lying," Duncan went on coldly. "I looked it up. I got Flaubin before the Governor himself, and the old rascal confessed to sixteen hundred overcharge. Said you'd stuck him up for it. Twelve hundred went to you, and his share was four hundred and the job. Don't interrupt. I've got his affidavit below. Then was when I would have put you ashore, except for the cloud you were under. You had to have this one chance or go clean to hell. I gave you the chance. And what have you got to say about it?"

"What did the Governor say?" Captain Dettmar demanded truculently.

"Which governor?"

"Of California. Did he lie to you like all the rest?"

"I'll tell you what he said. He said that you had been convicted on circumstantial evidence; that was why you had got life imprisonment instead of hanging; that you had always stoutly maintained your innocence; that you were the black sheep of the Maryland Dettmars; that they moved heaven and earth for your pardon; that your prison conduct was most exemplary; that he was prosecuting attorney at the time you were convicted; that after you had served seven years he yielded to your family's plea and pardoned you; and that in his own mind existed a doubt that you had killed McSweeny."

There was a pause, during which Duncan went on studying the rising squall, while Captain Dettmar's face worked terribly.

"Well, the Governor was wrong," he announced, with a short laugh. "I did kill McSweeny. I did get the watchman drunk that night. I beat

96

McSweeny to death in his bunk. I used the iron belaying pin that appeared in the evidence. He never had a chance. I beat him to a jelly. Do you want the details?"

Duncan looked at him in the curious way one looks at any monstrosity, but made no reply.

"Oh, I'm not afraid to tell you," Captain Dettmar blustered on. "There are no witnesses. Besides, I am a free man now. I am pardoned, and by God they can never put me back in that hole again. I broke McSweeny's jaw with the first blow. He was lying on his back asleep. He said, 'My God, Jim! My God!' It was funny to see his broken jaw wabble as he said it. Then I smashed him... I say, do you want the rest of the details?"

"Is that all you have to say?" was the answer.

"Isn't it enough?" Captain Dettmar retorted.

"It is enough."

"What are you going to do about it?"

"Put you ashore at Attu-Attu."

"And in the meantime?"

"In the meantime..." Duncan paused. An increase of weight in the wind rippled his hair. The stars overhead vanished, and the Samoset swung four points off her course in the careless steersman's hands. "In the meantime throw your halyards down on deck and look to your wheel. I'll call the men."

The next moment the squall burst upon them. Captain Dettmar, springing aft, lifted the coiled mainsail halyards from their pins and threw them, ready to run, on the deck. The three islanders swarmed from the tiny forecastle, two of them leaping to the halyards and holding by a single turn, while the third fastened down the engineroom, companion and swung the ventilators around. Below, Lee Goom and Toyama were lowering skylight covers and screwing up deadeyes. Duncan pulled shut the cover of the companion scuttle, and held on, waiting, the first drops of rain pelting his face, while the Samoset leaped violently ahead, at the same time heeling first to starboard then to port as the gusty pressures caught her winged-out sails.

All waited. But there was no need to lower away on the run. The power went out of the wind, and the tropic rain poured a deluge over everything. Then it was, the danger past, and as the Kanakas began to coil the halyards back on the pins, that Boyd Duncan went below.

"All right," he called in cheerily to his wife. "Only a puff."

"And Captain Dettmar?" she queried.

"Has been drinking, that is all. I shall get rid of him at Attu-Attu."

But before Duncan climbed into his bunk, he strapped around himself, against the skin and under his pajama coat, a heavy automatic pistol.

He fell asleep almost immediately, for his was the gift of perfect relaxation. He did things tensely, in the way savages do, but the instant the need passed he relaxed, mind and body. So it was that he slept, while the rain still poured on deck and the yacht plunged and rolled in the brief, sharp sea caused by the squall.

He awoke with a feeling of suffocation and heaviness. The electric fans had stopped, and the air was thick and stifling. Mentally cursing all Lorenzos and storage batteries, he heard his wife moving in the adjoining stateroom and pass out into the main cabin. Evidently heading for the fresher air on deck, he thought, and decided it was a good example to imitate. Putting on his slippers and tucking a pillow and a blanket under his arm, he followed her. As he was about to emerge from the companionway, the ship's clock in the cabin began to strike and he stopped to listen. Four bells sounded. It was two in the morning. From without came the creaking of the gaff-jaw against the mast. The Samoset rolled and righted on a sea, and in the light breeze her canvas gave forth a hollow thrum.

He was just putting his foot out on the damp deck when he heard his wife scream. It was a startled frightened scream that ended in a splash overside. He leaped out and ran aft. In the dim starlight he could make out her head and shoulders disappearing astern in the lazy wake.

"What was it?" Captain Dettmar, who was at the wheel, asked.

"Mrs. Duncan," was Duncan's reply, as he tore the life-buoy from its hook and flung it aft. "Jibe over to starboard and come up on the wind!" he commanded.

And then Boyd Duncan made a mistake. He dived overboard.

When he came up, he glimpsed the blue-light on the buoy, which had ignited automatically when it struck the water. He swam for it, and found Minnie had reached it first.

"Hello," he said. "Just trying to keep cool?"

"Oh, Boyd!" was her answer, and one wet hand reached out and touched his.

The blue light, through deterioration or damage, flickered out. As they lifted on the smooth crest of a wave, Duncan turned to look where the Samoset made a vague blur in the darkness. No lights showed, but there was noise of confusion. He could hear Captain Dettmar's shouting above the cries of the others.

"I must say he's taking his time," Duncan grumbled. "Why doesn't he jibe? There she goes now."

They could hear the rattle of the boom tackle blocks as the sail was eased across.

"That was the mainsail," he muttered. "Jibed to port when I told him starboard."

Again they lifted on a wave, and again and again, ere they could make out the distant green of the Samoset's starboard light. But instead of remaining stationary, in token that the yacht was coming toward them, it began moving across their field of vision. Duncan swore.

"What's the lubber holding over there for!" he demanded. "He's got his compass. He knows our bearing."

But the green light, which was all they could see, and which they could see only when they were on top of a wave, moved steadily away from them, withal it was working up to windward, and grew dim and dimmer. Duncan called out loudly and repeatedly, and each time, in the intervals, they could hear, very faintly, the voice of Captain Dettmar shouting orders.

"How can he hear me with such a racket?" Duncan complained.

"He's doing it so the crew won't hear you," was Minnie's answer.

There was something in the quiet way she said it that caught her husband's attention.

"What do you mean?"

"I mean that he is not trying to pick us up," she went on in the same composed voice. "He threw me overboard."

"You are not making a mistake?"

"How could I? I was at the main rigging, looking to see if any more rain threatened. He must have left the wheel and crept behind me. I was holding on to a stay with one hand. He gripped my hand free from behind and threw me over. It's too bad you didn't know, or else you would have staid aboard."

Duncan groaned, but said nothing for several minutes. The green light changed the direction of its course.

"She's gone about," he announced. "You are right. He's deliberately working around us and to windward. Up wind they can never hear me. But here goes."

He called at minute intervals for a long time. The green light disappeared, being replaced by the red, showing that the yacht had gone about again.

"Minnie," he said finally, "it pains me to tell you, but you married a fool. Only a fool would have gone overboard as I did."

"What chance have we of being picked up... by some other vessel, I mean?" she asked.

"About one in ten thousand, or ten thousand million. Not a steamer route nor trade route crosses this stretch of ocean. And there aren't any whalers knocking about the South Seas. There might be a stray trading schooner running across from Tutuwanga. But I happen to know that island is visited only once a year. A chance in a million is ours."

"And we'll play that chance," she rejoined stoutly.

"You ARE a joy!" His hand lifted hers to his lips. "And Aunt Elizabeth always wondered what I saw in you. Of course we'll play that chance. And we'll win it, too. To happen otherwise would be unthinkable. Here goes."

He slipped the heavy pistol from his belt and let it sink into the sea. The belt, however, he retained.

"Now you get inside the buoy and get some sleep. Duck under."

She ducked obediently, and came up inside the floating circle. He fastened the straps for her, then, with the pistol belt, buckled himself across one shoulder to the outside of the buoy.

"We're good for all day to-morrow," he said. "Thank God the water's warm. It won't be a hardship for the first twenty-hour hours, anyway. And if we're not picked up by nightfall, we've just got to hang on for another day, that's all."

For half an hour they maintained silence, Duncan, his head resting on the arm that was on the buoy, seemed asleep.

"Boyd?" Minnie said softly.

"Thought you were asleep," he growled.

"Boyd, if we don't come through this—"

"Stow that!" he broke in ungallantly. "Of course we're coming through. There is isn't a doubt of it. Somewhere on this ocean is a ship that's heading right for us. You wait and see. Just the same I wish my brain were equipped with wireless. Now I'm going to sleep, if you don't."

But for once, sleep baffled him. An hour later he heard Minnie stir and knew she was awake.

"Say, do you know what I've been thinking!" she asked.

"No; what?"

"That I'll wish you a Merry Christmas."

"By George, I never thought of it. Of course it's Christmas Day. We'll have many more of them, too. And do you know what I've been thinking? What a confounded shame we're done out of our Christmas dinner. Wait till I lay hands on Dettmar. I'll take it out of him. And it won't be with an iron belaying pin either, Just two bunches of naked knuckles, that's all."

Despite his facetiousness, Boyd Duncan had little hope. He knew well enough the meaning of one chance in a million, and was calmly certain that his wife and he had entered upon their last few living hours—hours that were inevitably bound to be black and terrible with tragedy.

The tropic sun rose in a cloudless sky. Nothing was to be seen. The Samoset was beyond the sea-rim. As the sun rose higher, Duncan ripped his pajama trousers in halves and fashioned them into two rude turbans. Soaked in sea-water they offset the heat-rays.

"When I think of that dinner, I'm really angry," he complained, as he noted an anxious expression threatening to set on his wife's face. "And I want you to be with me when I settle with Dettmar. I've always been opposed to women witnessing scenes of blood, but this is different. It will be a beating."

"I hope I don't break my knuckles on him," he added, after a pause.

Midday came and went, and they floated on, the center of a narrow sea-circle. A gentle breath of the dying trade-wind fanned them, and they rose and fell monotonously on the smooth swells of a perfect summer sea. Once, a gunie spied them, and for half an hour circled about them with majestic sweeps. And, once, a huge rayfish, measuring a score of feet across the tips, passed within a few yards.

By sunset, Minnie began to rave, softly, babblingly, like a child. Duncan's face grew haggard as he watched and listened, while in his mind he revolved plans of how best to end the hours of agony that were coming. And, so planning, as they rose on a larger swell than usual, he swept the circle of the sea with his eyes, and saw, what made him cry out.

"Minnie!" She did not answer, and he shouted her name again in her ear, with all the voice he could command. Her eyes opened, in them fluttered commingled consciousness and delirium. He slapped her hands and wrists till the sting of the blows roused her.

"There she is, the chance in a million!" he cried.

"A steamer at that, heading straight for us! By George, it's a cruiser! I have it!—the Annapolis, returning with those astronomers from Tutuwanga."

United States Consul Lingford was a fussy, elderly gentleman, and in the two years of his service at Attu-Attu had never encountered so unprecedented a case as that laid before him by Boyd Duncan. The latter, with his wife, had been landed there by the Annapolis, which had promptly gone on with its cargo of astronomers to Fiji.

"It was cold-blooded, deliberate attempt to murder," said Consul Lingford. "The law shall take its course. I don't know how precisely to deal with this Captain Dettmar, but if he comes to Attu-Attu, depend upon it he shall be dealt with, he—ah—shall be dealt with. In the meantime, I shall read up the law. And now, won't you and your good lady stop for lunch!"

As Duncan accepted the invitation, Minnie, who had been glancing out of the window at the harbor, suddenly leaned forward and touched her husband's arm. He followed her gaze, and saw the Samoset, flag at half mast, rounding up and dropping anchor scarcely a hundred yards away.

"There's my boat now," Duncan said to the Consul. "And there's the launch over the side, and Captain Dettmar dropping into it. If I don't miss my guess, he's coming to report our deaths to you."

The launch landed on the white beach, and leaving Lorenzo tinkering with the engine, Captain Dettmar strode across the beach and up the path to the Consulate.

"Let him make his report," Duncan said. "We'll just step into this next room and listen."

And through the partly open door, he and his wife heard Captain Dettmar, with tears in his voice, describe the loss of his owners.

"I jibed over and went back across the very spot," he concluded. "There was not a sign of them. I called and called, but there was never an answer. I tacked back and forth and wore for two solid hours, then hove to till daybreak, and cruised back and forth all day, two men at the mastheads. It is terrible. I am heartbroken. Mr. Duncan was a splendid man, and I shall never..."

But he never completed the sentence, for at that moment his splendid employer strode out upon him, leaving Minnie standing in the doorway. Captain Dettmar's white face blanched even whiter.

"I did my best to pick you up, sir," he began.

Boyd Duncan's answer was couched in terms of bunched knuckles, two bunches of them, that landed right and left on Captain Dettmar's face.

Captain Dettmar staggered backward, recovered, and rushed with swinging arms at his employer, only to be met with a blow squarely between the eyes. This time the Captain went down, bearing the typewriter under him as he crashed to the floor.

"This is not permissible," Consul Lingford spluttered. "I beg of you, I beg of you, to desist."

"I'll pay the damages to office furniture," Duncan answered, and at the same time landing more bunched knuckles on the eyes and nose of Dettmar.

Consul Lingford bobbed around in the turmoil like a wet hen, while his office furniture went to ruin. Once, he caught Duncan by the arm, but was flung back, gasping, half-across the room. Another time he appealed to Minnie.

104

"Mrs. Duncan, won't you, please, please, restrain your husband?"

But she, white-faced and trembling, resolutely shook her head and watched the fray with all her eyes.

"It is outrageous," Consul Lingford cried, dodging the hurtling bodies of the two men. "It is an affront to the Government, to the United States Government. Nor will it be overlooked, I warn you. Oh, do pray desist, Mr. Duncan. You will kill the man. I beg of you. I beg, I beg..."

But the crash of a tall vase filled with crimson hibiscus blossoms left him speechless.

The time came when Captain Dettmar could no longer get up. He got as far as hands and knees, struggled vainly to rise further, then collapsed. Duncan stirred the groaning wreck with his foot.

"He's all right," he announced. "I've only given him what he has given many a sailor and worse."

"Great heavens, sir!" Consul Lingford exploded, staring horror-stricken at the man whom he had invited to lunch.

Duncan giggled involuntarily, then controlled himself.

"I apologize, Mr. Lingford, I most heartily apologize. I fear I was slightly carried away by my feelings."

Consul Lingford gulped and sawed the air speechlessly with his arms.

"Slightly, sir? Slightly?" he managed to articulate.

"Boyd," Minnie called softly from the doorway.

He turned and looked.

"You ARE a joy," she said.

"And now, Mr. Lingford, I am done with him," Duncan said. "I turn over what is left to you and the law."

"That?" Consul Lingford queried, in accent of horror.

"That," Boyd Duncan replied, looking ruefully at his battered knuckles.

WAR

HE was a young man, not more than twenty-four or five, and he might have sat his horse with the careless grace of his youth had he not been so catlike and tense. His black eyes roved everywhere, catching the movements of twigs and branches where small birds hopped, questing ever onward through the changing vistas of trees and brush, and returning always to the clumps of undergrowth on either side. And as he watched, so did he listen, though he rode on in silence, save for the boom of heavy guns from far to the west. This had been sounding monotonously in his ears for hours, and only its cessation could have aroused his notice. For he had business closer to hand. Across his saddle-bow was balanced a carbine.

So tensely was he strung, that a bunch of quail, exploding into flight from under his horse's nose, startled him to such an extent that automatically, instantly, he had reined in and fetched the carbine halfway to his shoulder. He grinned sheepishly, recovered himself, and rode on. So tense was he, so bent upon the work he had to do, that the sweat stung his eyes unwiped, and unheeded rolled down his nose and spattered his saddle pommel. The band of his cavalryman's hat was fresh-stained with sweat. The roan horse under him was likewise wet. It was high noon of a breathless day of heat. Even the birds and squirrels did not dare the sun, but sheltered in shady hiding places among the trees.

Man and horse were littered with leaves and dusted with yellow pollen, for the open was ventured no more than was compulsory. They kept to the brush and trees, and invariably the man halted and peered out before crossing a dry glade or naked stretch of upland pasturage. He worked always to the north, though his way was devious, and it was from the north that he seemed most to apprehend that for which he was looking. He was no coward, but his courage was only that of the average civilized man, and he was looking to live, not die.

Up a small hillside he followed a cowpath through such dense scrub that he was forced to dismount and lead his horse. But when the path swung around to the west, he abandoned it and headed to the north again along the oak-covered top of the ridge.

The ridge ended in a steep descent-so steep that he zigzagged back and forth across the face of the slope, sliding and stumbling among the dead leaves and matted vines and keeping a watchful eye on the horse above that threatened to fall down upon him. The sweat ran from him, and the pollen-dust, settling pungently in mouth and nostrils, increased his thirst. Try as he would, nevertheless the descent was noisy, and frequently he stopped, panting in the dry heat and listening for any warning from beneath.

At the bottom he came out on a flat, so densely forested that he could not make out its extent. Here the character of the woods changed, and he was able to remount. Instead of the twisted hillside oaks, tall straight trees, big-trunked and prosperous, rose from the damp fat soil. Only here and there were thickets, easily avoided, while he encountered winding, park-like glades where the cattle had pastured in the days before war had run them off.

His progress was more rapid now, as he came down into the valley, and at the end of half an hour he halted at an ancient rail fence on the edge of a clearing. He did not like the openness of it, yet his path lay across to the fringe of trees that marked the banks of the stream. It was a mere quarter of a mile across that open, but the thought of venturing out in it was repugnant. A rifle, a score of them, a thousand, might lurk in that fringe by the stream.

Twice he essayed to start, and twice he paused. He was appalled by his own loneliness. The pulse of war that beat from the West suggested the companionship of battling thousands; here was naught but silence, and himself, and possible death-dealing bullets from a myriad ambushes. And yet his task was to find what he feared to find. He must on, and on, till somewhere, some time, he encountered another man, or other men, from the other side, scouting, as he was scouting, to make report, as he must make report, of having come in touch.

Changing his mind, he skirted inside the woods for a distance, and again peeped forth. This time, in the middle of the clearing, he saw a small farmhouse. There were no signs of life. No smoke curled from the chimney, not a barnyard fowl clucked and strutted. The kitchen door stood open, and he gazed so long and hard into the black aperture that it seemed almost that a farmer's wife must emerge at any moment.

He licked the pollen and dust from his dry lips, stiffened himself, mind and body, and rode out into the blazing sunshine. Nothing stirred. He went on past the house, and approached the wall of trees and bushes by the river's bank. One thought persisted maddeningly. It was of the crash into his body of a high-velocity bullet. It made him feel very fragile and defenseless, and he crouched lower in the saddle.

Tethering his horse in the edge of the wood, he continued a hundred yards on foot till he came to the stream. Twenty feet wide it was, without perceptible current, cool and inviting, and he was very thirsty. But he waited inside his screen of leafage, his eyes fixed on the screen on the opposite side. To make the wait endurable, he sat down, his carbine resting on his knees. The minutes passed, and slowly his tenseness relaxed. At last he decided there was no danger; but just as he prepared to part the bushes and bend down to the water, a movement among the opposite bushes caught his eye.

It might be a bird. But he waited. Again there was an agitation of the bushes, and then, so suddenly that it almost startled a cry from him, the bushes parted and a face peered out. It was a face covered with several weeks' growth of ginger-colored beard. The eyes were blue and wide apart, with laughter-wrinkles in the comers that showed despite the tired and anxious expression of the whole face.

All this he could see with microscopic clearness, for the distance was no more than twenty feet. And all this he saw in such brief time, that he saw it as he lifted his carbine to his shoulder. He glanced along the sights, and knew that he was gazing upon a man who was as good as dead. It was impossible to miss at such point blank range.

But he did not shoot. Slowly he lowered the carbine and watched. A hand, clutching a water-bottle, became visible and the ginger beard bent downward to fill the bottle. He could hear the gurgle of the water. Then arm and bottle and ginger beard disappeared behind the closing bushes. A long time he waited, when, with thirst unslaked, he crept back to his horse, rode slowly across the sun-washed clearing, and passed into the shelter of the woods beyond.

II

Another day, hot and breathless. A deserted farmhouse, large, with many outbuildings and an orchard, standing in a clearing. From the Woods, on a roan horse, carbine across pommel, rode the young man with the quick black eyes. He breathed with relief as he gained the house. That a fight had taken place here earlier in the season was evident. Clips and empty cartridges, tarnished with verdigris, lay on the ground, which, while wet, had been torn up by the hoofs of horses. Hard by the kitchen garden were graves, tagged and numbered. From the oak tree by the kitchen door, in tattered, weatherbeaten garments, hung the bodies of two men. The faces, shriveled and defaced, bore no likeness to the faces of men. The roan horse snorted beneath them, and the rider caressed and soothed it and tied it farther away.

Entering the house, he found the interior a wreck. He trod on empty cartridges as he walked from room to room to reconnoiter from the windows. Men had camped and slept everywhere, and on the floor of one room he came upon stains unmistakable where the wounded had been laid down.

Again outside, he led the horse around behind the barn and invaded the orchard. A dozen trees were burdened with ripe apples. He filled his pockets, eating while he picked. Then a thought came to him, and he glanced at the sun, calculating the time of his return to camp. He pulled off his shirt, tying the sleeves and making a bag. This he proceeded to fill with apples.

As he was about to mount his horse, the animal suddenly pricked up its ears. The man, too, listened, and heard, faintly, the thud of hoofs on soft earth. He crept to the corner of the barn and peered out. A dozen mounted men, strung out loosely, approaching from the opposite side of the clearing, were only a matter of a hundred yards or so away. They rode on to the house. Some dismounted, while others remained in the saddle as an earnest that their stay would be short. They seemed to be holding a council, for he could hear them talking excitedly in the detested tongue of the alien invader. The time passed, but they seemed unable to reach a decision. He put the carbine away in its boot, mounted, and waited impatiently, balancing the shirt of apples on the pommel.

He heard footsteps approaching, and drove his spurs so fiercely into the roan as to force a surprised groan from the animal as it leaped forward. At the corner of the barn he saw the intruder, a mere boy of nineteen or twenty for all of his uniform jump back to escape being run down. At the same moment the roan swerved and its rider caught a glimpse of the aroused men by the house. Some were springing from their horses, and he could see the rifles going to their shoulders. He passed the kitchen door and the dried corpses swinging in the shade, compelling his foes to run around the front of the house. A rifle cracked, and a second, but he was going fast, leaning forward, low in the saddle, one hand clutching the shirt of apples, the other guiding the horse.

The top bar of the fence was four feet high, but he knew his roan and leaped it at full career to the accompaniment of several scattered shots. Eight hundred yards straight away were the woods, and the roan was covering the distance with mighty strides. Every man was now firing. pumping their guns so rapidly that he no longer heard individual shots. A bullet went through his hat, but he was unaware, though he did know when another tore through the apples on the pommel. And he winced and ducked even lower when a third bullet, fired low, struck a stone between his horse's legs and ricochetted off through the air, buzzing and humming like some incredible insect.

The shots died down as the magazines were emptied, until, quickly, there was no more shooting. The young man was elated. Through that astonishing fusillade he had come unscathed. He glanced back. Yes, they had emptied their magazines. He could see several reloading. Others were running back behind the house for their horses. As he looked, two already mounted, came back into view around the corner, riding hard. And at the same moment, he saw the man with the unmistakable ginger beard kneel down on the ground, level his gun, and coolly take his time for the long shot.

The young man threw his spurs into the horse, crouched very low, and swerved in his flight in order to distract the other's aim. And still the shot did not come. With each jump of the horse, the woods sprang nearer. They were only two hundred yards away and still the shot was delayed.

And then he heard it, the last thing he was to hear, for he was dead ere he hit the ground in the long crashing fall from the saddle. And they, watching at the house, saw him fall, saw his body bounce when it struck the earth, and saw the burst of red-cheeked apples that rolled about him. They laughed at the unexpected eruption of apples, and clapped their hands in applause of the long shot by the man with the ginger beard.

UNDER THE DECK AWNINGS

"CAN any man—a gentleman, I mean—call a woman a pig?"

The little man flung this challenge forth to the whole group, then leaned back in his deck chair, sipping lemonade with an air commingled of certitude and watchful belligerence. Nobody made answer. They were used to the little man and his sudden passions and high elevations.

"I repeat, it was in my presence that he said a certain lady, whom none of you knows, was a pig. He did not say swine. He grossly said that she was a pig. And I hold that no man who is a man could possibly make such a remark about any woman."

Dr. Dawson puffed stolidly at his black pipe. Matthews, with knees hunched up and clasped by his arms, was absorbed in the flight of a gunie. Sweet, finishing his Scotch and soda, was questing about with his eyes for a deck steward.

"I ask you, Mr. Treloar, can any man call any woman a pig?"

Treloar, who happened to be sitting next to him, was startled by the abruptness of the attack, and wondered what grounds he had ever given the little man to believe that he could call a woman a pig.

"I should say," he began his hesitant answer, "that it—er—depends on the—er—the lady."

The little man was aghast.

"You mean...?" he quavered.

"That I have seen female humans who were as bad as pigs—and worse."

There was a long pained silence. The little man seemed withered by the coarse brutality of the reply. In his face was unutterable hurt and woe.

"You have told of a man who made a not nice remark and you have classified him," Treloar said in cold, even tones. "I shall now tell you about a woman—I beg your pardon—a lady, and when I have finished I shall ask you to classify her. Miss Caruthers I shall call her, principally for the reason that it is not her name. It was on a P. & O. boat, and it occurred neither more nor less than several years ago.

"Miss Caruthers was charming. No; that is not the word. She was amazing. She was a young woman, and a lady. Her father was a certain high official whose name, if I mentioned it, would be immediately recognized by all of you. She was with her mother and two maids at the time, going out to join the old gentleman wherever you like to wish in the East.

"She, and pardon me for repeating, was amazing. It is the one adequate word. Even the most minor adjectives applicable to her are bound to be sheer superlatives. There was nothing she could not do better than any woman and than most men. Sing, play—bah!—as some rhetorician once said of old Nap, competition fled from her. Swim! She could have made a fortune and a name as a public performer. She was one of those rare women who can strip off all the frills of dress, and in simple swimming suit be more satisfying beautiful. Dress! She was an artist.

"But her swimming. Physically, she was the perfect woman—you know what I mean, not in the gross, muscular way of acrobats, but in all the delicacy of line and fragility of frame and texture. And combined with this, strength. How she could do it was the marvel. You know the wonder of a woman's arm—the fore arm, I mean; the sweet fading away from rounded biceps and hint of muscle, down through small elbow and firm soft swell to the wrist, small, unthinkably small and round and strong. This was hers. And yet, to see her swimming the sharp quick English overhand stroke, and getting somewhere with it, too, was—well, I understand anatomy and athletics and such things, and yet it was a mystery to me how she could do it.

"She could stay under water for two minutes. I have timed her. No man on board, except Dennitson, could capture as many coins as she with a single dive. On the forward main-deck was a big canvas tank with six feet of

113

sea-water. We used to toss small coins into it. I have seen her dive from the bridge deck—no mean feat in itself—into that six-feet of water, and fetch up no less than forty-seven coins, scattered willy-nilly over the whole bottom of the tank. Dennitson, a quiet young Englishman, never exceeded her in this, though he made it a point always to tie her score.

"She was a sea-woman, true. But she was a land-woman, a horsewoman—a—she was the universal woman. To see her, all softness of soft dress, surrounded by half a dozen eager men, languidly careless of them all or flashing brightness and wit on them and at them and through them, one would fancy she was good for nothing else in the world. At such moments I have compelled myself to remember her score of forty-seven coins from the bottom of the swimming tank. But that was she, the everlasting, wonder of a woman who did all things well.

"She fascinated every betrousered human around her. She had me—and I don't mind confessing it—she bad me to heel along with the rest. Young puppies and old gray dogs who ought to have known better—oh, they all came up and crawled around her skirts and whined and fawned when she whistled. They were all guilty, from young Ardmore, a pink cherub of nineteen outward bound for some clerkship in the Consular Service, to old Captain Bentley, grizzled and sea-worn, and as emotional, to look at, as a Chinese joss. There was a nice middle-aged chap, Perkins, I believe, who forgot his wife was on board until Miss Caruthers sent him to the right about and back where he belonged.

"Men were wax in her hands. She melted them, or softly molded them, or incinerated them, as she pleased. There wasn't a steward, even, grand and remote as she was, who, at her bidding, would have hesitated to souse the Old Man himself with a plate of soup. You have all seen such women—a sort of world's desire to all men. As a man-conqueror she was supreme. She was a whip-lash, a sting and a flame, an electric spark. Oh, believe me, at times there were flashes of will that scorched through her beauty and seduction and smote a victim into blank and shivering idiocy and fear.

"And don't fail to mark, in the light of what is to come, that she was a prideful woman. Pride of race, pride of caste, pride of sex, pride of power—she had it all, a pride strange and wilful and terrible.

"She ran the ship, she ran the voyage, she ran everything, and she ran Dennitson. That he had outdistanced the pack even the least wise of us admitted. That she liked him, and that this feeling was growing, there was not a doubt. I am certain that she looked on him with kinder eyes than she had ever looked with on man before. We still worshiped, and were always hanging about waiting to be whistled up, though we knew that Dennitson was laps and laps ahead of us. What might have happened we shall never know, for we came to Colombo and something else happened.

"You know Colombo, and how the native boys dive for coins in the shark-infested bay. Of course, it is only among the ground sharks and fish sharks that they venture. It is almost uncanny the way they know sharks and can sense the presence of a real killer—a tiger shark, for instance, or a gray nurse strayed up from Australian waters. Let such a shark appear, and, long before the passengers can guess, every mother's son of them is out of the water in a wild scramble for safety.

"It was after tiffin, and Miss Caruthers was holding her usual court under the deck-awnings. Old Captain Bentley had just been whistled up, and had granted her what he never granted before... nor since—permission for the boys to come up on the promenade deck. You see, Miss Caruthers was a swimmer, and she was interested. She took up a collection of all our small change, and herself tossed it overside, singly and in handfuls, arranging the terms of the contests, chiding a miss, giving extra rewards to clever wins, in short, managing the whole exhibition.

"She was especially keen on their jumping. You know, jumping feet-first from a height, it is very difficult to hold the body perpendicularly while in the air. The center of gravity of the male body is high, and the tendency is to overtopple. But the little beggars employed a method which she declared was new to her and which she desired to learn. Leaping from the davits of the boat-deck above, they plunged downward, their faces and shoulders bowed forward, looking at the water. And only at the last moment did they abruptly straighten up and enter the water erect and true.

115

"It was a pretty sight. Their diving was not so good, though there was one of them who was excellent at it, as he was in all the other stunts. Some white man must have taught him, for he made the proper swan dive and did it as beautifully as I have ever seen it. You know, headfirst into the water, from a great height, the problem is to enter the water at the perfect angle. Miss the angle and it means at the least a twisted back and injury for life. Also, it has meant death for many a bungler. But this boy could do it—seventy feet I know he cleared in one dive from the rigging—clenched hands on chest, head thrown back, sailing more like a bird, upward and out, and out and down, body flat on the air so that if it struck the surface in that position it would be split in half like a herring. But the moment before the water is reached, the head drops forward, the hands go out and lock the arms in an arch in advance of the head, and the body curves gracefully downward and enters the water just right.

"This the boy did, again and again, to the delight of all of us, but particularly of Miss Caruthers. He could not have been a moment over twelve or thirteen, yet he was by far the cleverest of the gang. He was the favorite of his crowd, and its leader. Though there were a number older than he, they acknowledged his chieftaincy. He was a beautiful boy, a lithe young god in breathing bronze, eyes wide apart, intelligent and daring, a bubble, a mote, a beautiful flash and sparkle of life. You have seen wonderful glorious creatures—animals, anything, a leopard, a horse-restless, eager, too much alive ever to be still, silken of muscle, each slightest movement a benediction of grace, every action wild, untrammeled, and over all spilling out that intense vitality, that sheen and luster of living light. The boy had it. Life poured out of him almost in an effulgence. His skin glowed with it. It burned in his eyes. I swear I could almost hear it crackle from him. Looking at him, it was as if a whiff of ozone came to one's nostrils—so fresh and young was he, so resplendent with health, so wildly wild.

"This was the boy. And it was he who gave the alarm in the midst of the sport. The boys made a dash of it for the gangway platform, swimming the fastest strokes they knew, pellmell, floundering and splashing, fright in their faces, clambering out with jumps and surges, any way to get out, lending one another a hand to safety, till all were strung along the gangway and peering down into the water.

"'What is the matter?' asked Miss Caruthers.

"'A shark, I fancy,' Captain Bentley answered. 'Lucky little beggars that he didn't get one of them.'

"'Are they afraid of sharks?' she asked.

"'Aren't you?' he asked back."

She shuddered, looked overside at the water, and made a move.

"'Not for the world would I venture where a shark might be,' she said, and shuddered again. 'They are horrible! Horrible!'

"The boys came up on the promenade deck, clustering close to the rail and worshiping Miss Caruthers who had flung them such a wealth of backsheesh. The performance being over, Captain Bentley motioned to them to clear out. But she stopped him.

"'One moment, please, Captain. I have always understood that the natives are not afraid of sharks.'

"She beckoned the boy of the swan dive nearer to her, and signed to him to dive over again. He shook his head, and along with all his crew behind him laughed as if it were a good joke.

"'Shark,' he volunteered, pointing to the water.

"'No,' she said. 'There is no shark.'

"But he nodded his head positively, and the boys behind him nodded with equal positiveness.

"'No, no, no,' she cried. And then to us, 'Who'll lend me a half-crown and a sovereign!'

"Immediately the half dozen of us were presenting her with crowns and sovereigns, and she accepted the two coins from young Ardmore.

"She held up the half-crown for the boys to see. But there was no eager rush to the rail preparatory to leaping. They stood there grinning sheepishly.

She offered the coin to each one individually, and each, as his turn came, rubbed his foot against his calf, shook his head, and grinned. Then she tossed the half-crown overboard. With wistful, regretful faces they watched its silver flight through the air, but not one moved to follow it.

"'Don't do it with the sovereign,' Dennitson said to her in a low voice.

"She took no notice, but held up the gold coin before the eyes of the boy of the swan dive.

"'Don't,' said Captain Bentley. 'I wouldn't throw a sick cat overside with a shark around.'

"But she laughed, bent on her purpose, and continued to dazzle the boy.

"'Don't tempt him,' Dennitson urged. 'It is a fortune to him, and he might go over after it.'

"'Wouldn't YOU?' she flared at him. 'If I threw it?'"

This last more softly.

Dennitson shook his head.

"'Your price is high,' she said. 'For how many sovereigns would you go?'

"'There are not enough coined to get me overside,' was his answer.

"She debated a moment, the boy forgotten in her tilt with Dennitson.

"'For me?' she said very softly.

"'To save your life—yes. But not otherwise.'

"She turned back to the boy. Again she held the coin before his eyes, dazzling him with the vastness of its value. Then she made as to toss it out, and, involuntarily, he made a half-movement toward the rail, but was checked by sharp cries of reproof from his companions. There was anger in their voices as well.

"'I know it is only fooling,' Dennitson said. 'Carry it as far as you like, but for heaven's sake don't throw it.'

"Whether it was that strange wilfulness of hers, or whether she doubted the boy could be persuaded, there is no telling. It was unexpected to all of us. Out from the shade of the awning the coin flashed golden in the blaze of sunshine and fell toward the sea in a glittering arch. Before a hand could stay him, the boy was over the rail and curving beautifully downward after the coin. Both were in the air at the same time. It was a pretty sight. The sovereign cut the water sharply, and at the very spot, almost at the same instant, with scarcely a splash, the boy entered.

"From the quicker-eyed black boys watching, came an exclamation. We were all at the railing. Don't tell me it is necessary for a shark to turn on its back. That one did not. In the clear water, from the height we were above it, we saw everything. The shark was a big brute, and with one drive he cut the boy squarely in half.

"There was a murmur or something from among us—who made it I did not know; it might have been I. And then there was silence. Miss Caruthers was the first to speak. Her face was deathly white.

"'I never dreamed,' she said, and laughed a short, hysterical laugh.

"All her pride was at work to give her control. She turned weakly toward Dennitson, and then, on from one to another of us. In her eyes was a terrible sickness, and her lips were trembling. We were brutes—oh, I know it, now that I look back upon it. But we did nothing.

"'Mr. Dennitson,' she said, 'Tom, won't you take me below!'

"He never changed the direction of his gaze, which was the bleakest I have ever seen in a man's face, nor did he move an eyelid. He took a cigarette from his case and lighted it. Captain Bentley made a nasty sound in his throat and spat overboard. That was all; that and the silence.

"She turned away and started to walk firmly down the deck. Twenty feet away, she swayed and thrust a hand against the wall to save herself. And so she went on, supporting herself against the cabins and walking very slowly." Treloar ceased. He turned his head and favored the little man with a look of cold inquiry.

"Well," he said finally. "Classify her."

The little man gulped and swallowed.

"I have nothing to say," he said. "I have nothing whatever to say."

TO KILL A MAN

THOUGH dim night-lights burned, she moved familiarly through the big rooms and wide halls, seeking vainly the half-finished book of verse she had mislaid and only now remembered. When she turned on the lights in the drawing-room, she disclosed herself clad in a sweeping negligee gown of soft rose-colored stuff, throat and shoulders smothered in lace. Her rings were still on her fingers, her massed yellow hair had not yet been taken down. She was delicately, gracefully beautiful, with slender, oval face, red lips, a faint color in the cheeks, and blue eyes of the chameleon sort that at will stare wide with the innocence of childhood, go hard and gray and brilliantly cold, or flame up in hot wilfulness and mastery.

She turned the lights off and passed out and down the hall toward the morning room. At the entrance she paused and listened. From farther on had come, not a noise, but an impression of movement. She could have sworn she had not heard anything, yet something had been different. The atmosphere of night quietude had been disturbed. She wondered what servant could be prowling about. Not the butler, who was notorious for retiring early save on special occasion. Nor could it be her maid, whom she had permitted to go that evening.

Passing on to the dining-room, she found the door closed. Why she opened it and went on in, she did not know, except for the feeling that the disturbing factor, whatever it might be, was there. The room was in darkness, and she felt her way to the button and pressed. As the blaze of light flashed on, she stepped back and cried out. It was a mere "Oh!" and it was not loud.

Facing her, alongside the button, flat against the wall, was a man. In his hand, pointed toward her, was a revolver. She noticed, even in the shock of seeing him, that the weapon was black and exceedingly long-barreled. She knew black and exceedingly long it for what it was, a Colt's. He was a medium-sized man, roughly clad, brown-eyed, and swarthy with sunburn. He seemed very cool. There was no wabble to the revolver and it was directed toward her stomach, not from an outstretched arm, but from the hip, against which the forearm rested.

"Oh," she said. "I beg your pardon. You startled me. What do you want?"

"I reckon I want to get out," he answered, with a humorous twitch to the lips. "I've kind of lost my way in this here shebang, and if you'll kindly show me the door I'll cause no trouble and sure vamoose."

"But what are you doing here?" she demanded, her voice touched with the sharpness of one used to authority.

"Plain robbing, Miss, that's all. I came snooping around to see what I could gather up. I thought you wan't to home, seein' as I saw you pull out with your old man in an auto. I reckon that must a ben your pa, and you're Miss Setliffe."

Mrs. Setliffe saw his mistake, appreciated the naive compliment, and decided not to undeceive him.

"How do you know I am Miss Setliffe?" she asked.

"This is old Setliffe's house, ain't it?"

She nodded.

"I didn't know he had a daughter, but I reckon you must be her. And now, if it ain't botherin' you too much, I'd sure be obliged if you'd show me the way out."

"But why should I? You are a robber, a burglar."

"If I wan't an ornery shorthorn at the business, I'd be accumulatin' them rings on your fingers instead of being polite," he retorted.

"I come to make a raise outa old Setliffe, and not to be robbing women-folks. If you get outa the way, I reckon I can find my own way out."

Mrs. Setliffe was a keen woman, and she felt that from such a man there was little to fear. That he was not a typical criminal, she was certain. From his speech she knew he was not of the cities, and she seemed to sense the wider, homelier air of large spaces.

"Suppose I screamed?" she queried curiously. "Suppose I made an outcry for help? You couldn't shoot me?... a woman?"

She noted the fleeting bafflement in his brown eyes. He answered slowly and thoughtfully, as if working out a difficult problem. "I reckon, then, I'd have to choke you and maul you some bad."

"A woman?"

"I'd sure have to," he answered, and she saw his mouth set grimly.

"You're only a soft woman, but you see, Miss, I can't afford to go to jail. No, Miss, I sure can't. There's a friend of mine waitin' for me out West. He's in a hole, and I've got to help him out." The mouth shaped even more grimly. "I guess I could choke you without hurting you much to speak of."

Her eyes took on a baby stare of innocent incredulity as she watched him.

"I never met a burglar before," she assured him, "and I can't begin to tell you how interested I am."

"I'm not a burglar, Miss. Not a real one," he hastened to add as she looked her amused unbelief. "It looks like it, me being here in your house. But it's the first time I ever tackled such a job. I needed the money bad. Besides, I kind of look on it like collecting what's coming to me."

"I don't understand," she smiled encouragingly. "You came here to rob, and to rob is to take what is not yours."

"Yes, and no, in this here particular case. But I reckon I'd better be going now."

He started for the door of the dining-room, but she interposed, and a very beautiful obstacle she made of herself. His left hand went out as if to grip her, then hesitated. He was patently awed by her soft womanhood.

"There!" she cried triumphantly. "I knew you wouldn't."

The man was embarrassed.

"I ain't never manhandled a woman yet," he explained, "and it don't come easy. But I sure will, if you set to screaming."

"Won't you stay a few minutes and talk?" she urged. "I'm so interested. I should like to hear you explain how burglary is collecting what is coming to you."

He looked at her admiringly.

"I always thought women-folks were scairt of robbers," he confessed. "But you don't seem none."

She laughed gaily.

"There are robbers and robbers, you know. I am not afraid of you, because I am confident you are not the sort of creature that would harm a woman. Come, talk with me a while. Nobody will disturb us. I am all alone. My—father caught the night train to New York. The servants are all asleep. I should like to give you something to eat—women always prepare midnight suppers for the burglars they catch, at least they do in the magazine stories. But I don't know where to find the food. Perhaps you will have something to drink?"

He hesitated, and did not reply; but she could see the admiration for her growing in his eyes.

"You're not afraid?" she queried. "I won't poison you, I promise. I'll drink with you to show you it is all right."

"You sure are a surprise package of all right," he declared, for the first time lowering the weapon and letting it hang at his side. "No one don't need to tell me ever again that women-folks in cities is afraid. You ain't much—just a little soft pretty thing. But you've sure got the spunk. And you're trustful on top of it. There ain't many women, or men either, who'd treat a man with a gun the way you're treating me."

She smiled her pleasure in the compliment, and her face, was very earnest as she said:

"That is because I like your appearance. You are too decent-looking a man to be a robber. You oughtn't to do such things. If you are in bad luck you should go to work. Come, put away that nasty revolver and let us talk it over. The thing for you to do is to work."

"Not in this burg," he commented bitterly. "I've walked two inches off the bottom of my legs trying to find a job. Honest, I was a fine large man once... before I started looking for a job."

The merry laughter with which she greeted his sally obviously pleased him, and she was quick to note and take advantage of it. She moved directly away from the door and toward the sideboard.

"Come, you must tell me all about it while I get that drink for you. What will it be? Whisky?"

"Yes, ma'am," he said, as he followed her, though he still carried the big revolver at his side, and though he glanced reluctantly at the unguarded open door.

She filled a glass for him at the sideboard.

"I promised to drink with you," she said hesitatingly. "But I don't like whisky. I... I prefer sherry."

She lifted the sherry bottle tentatively for his consent.

"Sure," he answered, with a nod. "Whisky's a man's drink. I never like to see women at it. Wine's more their stuff."

She raised her glass to his, her eyes meltingly sympathetic.

"Here's to finding you a good position—"

But she broke off at sight of the expression of surprised disgust on his face. The glass, barely touched, was removed from his wry lips.

"What is the matter!" she asked anxiously. "Don't you like it? Have I made a mistake?"

"It's sure funny whisky. Tastes like it got burned and smoked in the making."

"Oh! How silly of me! I gave you Scotch. Of course you are accustomed to rye. Let me change it."

She was almost solicitiously maternal, as she replaced the glass with another and sought and found the proper bottle.

"Better?" she asked.

"Yes, ma'am. No smoke in it. It's sure the real good stuff. I ain't had a drink in a week. Kind of slick, that; oily, you know; not made in a chemical factory."

"You are a drinking man?" It was half a question, half a challenge.

"No, ma'am, not to speak of. I HAVE rared up and ripsnorted at spells, but most unfrequent. But there is times when a good stiff jolt lands on the right spot kerchunk, and this is sure one of them. And now, thanking you for your kindness, ma'am, I'll just be a pulling along."

But Mrs. Setliffe did not want to lose her burglar. She was too poised a woman to possess much romance, but there was a thrill about the present situation that delighted her. Besides, she knew there was no danger. The man, despite his jaw and the steady brown eyes, was eminently tractable. Also, farther back in her consciousness glimmered the thought of an audience of admiring friends. It was too bad not to have that audience.

"You haven't explained how burglary, in your case, is merely collecting what is your own," she said. "Come, sit down, and tell me about it here at the table."

She maneuvered for her own seat, and placed him across the corner from her. His alertness had not deserted him, as she noted, and his eyes roved sharply about, returning always with smoldering admiration to hers, but never resting long. And she noted likewise that while she spoke he was intent on listening for other sounds than those of her voice. Nor had he relinquished the revolver, which lay at the corner of the table between them, the butt close to his right hand.

But he was in a new habitat which he did not know. This man from the West, cunning in woodcraft and plainscraft, with eyes and ears open, tense and suspicious, did not know that under the table, close to her foot, was the push button of an electric bell. He had never heard of such a contrivance, and his keenness and wariness went for naught.

"It's like this, Miss," he began, in response to her urging. "Old Setliffe done me up in a little deal once. It was raw, but it worked. Anything will work full and legal when it's got few hundred million behind it. I'm not squealin', and I ain't taking a slam at your pa. He don't know me from Adam, and I reckon he don't know he done me outa anything. He's too big, thinking and dealing in millions, to ever hear of a small potato like me. He's an operator. He's got all kinds of experts thinking and planning and working for him, some of them, I hear, getting more cash salary than the President of the United States. I'm only one of thousands that have been done up by your pa, that's all.

"You see, ma'am, I had a little hole in the ground—a dinky, hydraulic, one-horse outfit of a mine. And when the Setliffe crowd shook down Idaho, and reorganized the smelter trust, and roped in the rest of the landscape, and put through the big hydraulic scheme at Twin Pines, why I sure got squeezed. I never had a run for my money. I was scratched off the card before the first heat. And so, to-night, being broke and my friend needing me bad, I just dropped around to make a raise outa your pa. Seeing as I needed it, it kinda was coming to me."

"Granting all that you say is so," she said, "nevertheless it does not make house-breaking any the less house-breaking. You couldn't make such a defense in a court of law."

"I know that," he confessed meekly. "What's right ain't always legal. And that's why I am so uncomfortable a-settin' here and talking with you. Not that I ain't enjoying your company—I sure do enjoy it—but I just can't afford to be caught. I know what they'd do to me in this here city. There was a young fellow that got fifty years only last week for holding a man up on the street for two dollars and eighty-five cents. I read about it in the paper. When times is hard and they ain't no work, men get desperate. And then the other men who've got something to be robbed of get desperate, too, and they just sure soak it to the other fellows. If I got caught, I reckon I wouldn't get a mite less than ten years. That's why I'm hankering to be on my way."

"No; wait." She lifted a detaining hand, at the same time removing her foot from the bell, which she had been pressing intermittently. "You haven't told me your name yet."

He hesitated.

"Call me Dave."

"Then... Dave," she laughed with pretty confusion. "Something must be done for you. You are a young man, and you are just at the beginning of a bad start. If you begin by attempting to collect what you think is coming to you, later on you will be collecting what you are perfectly sure isn't coming to you. And you know what the end will be. Instead of this, we must find something honorable for you to do."

"I need the money, and I need it now," he replied doggedly. "It's not for myself, but for that friend I told you about. He's in a peck of trouble, and he's got to get his lift now or not at all."

"I can find you a position," she said quickly. "And—yes, the very thing!—I'll lend you the money you want to send to your friend. This you can pay back out of your salary."

"About three hundred would do," he said slowly. "Three hundred would pull him through. I'd work my fingers off for a year for that, and my keep, and a few cents to buy Bull Durham with."

"Ah! You smoke! I never thought of it."

Her hand went out over the revolver toward his hand, as she pointed to the tell-tale yellow stain on his fingers. At the same time her eyes measured the nearness of her own hand and of his to the weapon. She ached to grip it in one swift movement. She was sure she could do it, and yet she was not sure; and so it was that she refrained as she withdrew her hand.

"Won't you smoke?" she invited.

"I'm 'most dying to."

"Then do so. I don't mind. I really like it—cigarettes, I mean."

With his left band he dipped into his side pocket, brought out a loose wheat-straw paper and shifted it to his right hand close by the revolver. Again he dipped, transferring to the paper a pinch of brown, flaky tobacco. Then he proceeded, both hands just over the revolver, to roll the cigarette.

"From the way you hover close to that nasty weapon, you seem to be afraid of me," she challenged.

"Not exactly afraid of you, ma'am, but, under the circumstances, just a mite timid."

"But I've not been afraid of you."

"You've got nothing to lose."

"My life," she retorted.

"That's right," he acknowledged promptly, "and you ain't been scairt of me. Mebbe I am over anxious."

"I wouldn't cause you any harm."

Even as she spoke, her slipper felt for the bell and pressed it. At the same time her eyes were earnest with a plea of honesty.

"You are a judge of men. I know it. And of women. Surely, when I am trying to persuade you from a criminal life and to get you honest work to do....?"

He was immediately contrite.

"I sure beg your pardon, ma'am," he said. "I reckon my nervousness ain't complimentary."

As he spoke, he drew his right hand from the table, and after lighting the cigarette, dropped it by his side.

"Thank you for your confidence," she breathed softly, resolutely keeping her eyes from measuring the distance to the revolver, and keeping her foot pressed firmly on the bell.

"About that three hundred," he began. "I can telegraph it West to-night. And I'll agree to work a year for it and my keep."

"You will earn more than that. I can promise seventy-five dollars a month at the least. Do you know horses?"

His face lighted up and his eyes sparkled.

"Then go to work for me—or for my father, rather, though I engage all the servants. I need a second coachman—"

"And wear a uniform?" he interrupted sharply, the sneer of the free-born West in his voice and on his lips.

She smiled tolerantly.

"Evidently that won't do. Let me think. Yes. Can you break and handle colts?"

He nodded.

"We have a stock farm, and there's room for just such a man as you. Will you take it?"

"Will I, ma'am?" His voice was rich with gratitude and enthusiasm. "Show me to it. I'll dig right in to-morrow. And I can sure promise you one thing, ma'am. You'll never be sorry for lending Hughie Luke a hand in his trouble—"

"I thought you said to call you Dave," she chided forgivingly.

"I did, ma'am. I did. And I sure beg your pardon. It was just plain bluff. My real name is Hughie Luke. And if you'll give me the address of that stock farm of yours, and the railroad fare, I head for it first thing in the morning."

Throughout the conversation she had never relaxed her attempts on the bell. She had pressed it in every alarming way—three shorts and a long, two

130

and a long, and five. She had tried long series of shorts, and, once, she had held the button down for a solid three minutes. And she had been divided between objurgation of the stupid, heavy-sleeping butler and doubt if the bell were in order.

"I am so glad," she said; "so glad that you are willing. There won't be much to arrange. But you will first have to trust me while I go upstairs for my purse."

She saw the doubt flicker momentarily in his eyes, and added hastily, "But you see I am trusting you with the three hundred dollars."

"I believe you, ma'am," he came back gallantly. "Though I just can't help this nervousness."

"Shall I go and get it?"

But before she could receive consent, a slight muffled jar from the distance came to her ear. She knew it for the swing-door of the butler's pantry. But so slight was it—more a faint vibration than a sound—that she would not have heard had not her ears been keyed and listening for it. Yet the man had heard. He was startled in his composed way.

"What was that?" he demanded.

For answer, her left hand flashed out to the revolver and brought it back. She had had the start of him, and she needed it, for the next instant his hand leaped up from his side, clutching emptiness where the revolver had been.

"Sit down!" she commanded sharply, in a voice new to him. "Don't move. Keep your hands on the table."

She had taken a lesson from him. Instead of holding the heavy weapon extended, the butt of it and her forearm rested on the table, the muzzle pointed, not at his head, but his chest. And he, looking coolly and obeying her commands, knew there was no chance of the kick-up of the recoil producing a miss. Also, he saw that the revolver did not wabble, nor the hand shake, and he was thoroughly conversant with the size of hole the soft-nosed bullets could make. He had eyes, not for her, but for the hammer, which had risen under the pressure of her forefinger on the trigger.

"I reckon I'd best warn you that there trigger-pull is filed dreadful fine. Don't press too hard, or I'll have a hole in me the size of a walnut."

She slacked the hammer partly down.

"That's better," he commented. "You'd best put it down all the way. You see how easy it works. If you want to, a quick light pull will jiffy her up and back and make a pretty mess all over your nice floor."

A door opened behind him, and he heard somebody enter the room. But he did not turn his bead. He was looking at her, and he found it the face of another woman—hard, cold, pitiless yet brilliant in its beauty. The eyes, too, were hard, though blazing with a cold light.

"Thomas," she commanded, "go to the telephone and call the police. Why were you so long in answering?"

"I came as soon as I heard the bell, madam," was the answer.

The robber never took his eyes from hers, nor did she from his, but at mention of the bell she noticed that his eyes were puzzled for the moment.

"Beg your pardon," said the butler from behind, "but wouldn't it be better for me to get a weapon and arouse the servants?"

"No; ring for the police. I can hold this man. Go and do it—quickly."

The butler slippered out of the room, and the man and the woman sat on, gazing into each other's eyes. To her it was an experience keen with enjoyment, and in her mind was the gossip of her crowd, and she saw notes in the society weeklies of the beautiful young Mrs. Setliffe capturing an armed robber single-handed. It would create a sensation, she was sure.

"When you get that sentence you mentioned," she said coldly, "you will have time to meditate upon what a fool you have been, taking other persons' property and threatening women with revolvers. You will have time to learn your lesson thoroughly. Now tell the truth. You haven't any friend in trouble. All that you told me was lies."

He did not reply. Though his eyes were upon her, they seemed blank. In truth, for the instant she was veiled to him, and what he saw was the wide sunwashed spaces of the West, where men and women were bigger than the rotten denizens, as he had encountered them, of the thrice rotten cities of the East.

"Go on. Why don't you speak? Why don't you lie some more? Why don't you beg to be let off?"

"I might," he answered, licking his dry lips. "I might ask to be let off if..."

"If what?" she demanded peremptorily, as he paused.

"I was trying to think of a word you reminded me of. As I was saying, I might if you was a decent woman."

Her face paled.

"Be careful," she warned.

"You don't dast kill me," he sneered. "The world's a pretty low down place to have a thing like you prowling around in it, but it ain't so plumb low down, I reckon, as to let you put a hole in me. You're sure bad, but the trouble with you is that you're weak in your badness. It ain't much to kill a man, but you ain't got it in you. There's where you lose out."

"Be careful of what you say," she repeated. "Or else, I warn you, it will go hard with you. It can be seen to whether your sentence is light or heavy."

"Something's the matter with God," he remarked irrelevantly, "to be letting you around loose. It's clean beyond me what he's up to, playing such-like tricks on poor humanity. Now if I was God—"

His further opinion was interrupted by the entrance of the butler.

"Something is wrong with the telephone, madam," he announced. "The wires are crossed or something, because I can't get Central."

"Go and call one of the servants," she ordered. "Send him out for an officer, and then return here."

Again the pair was left alone.

"Will you kindly answer one question, ma'am?" the man said. "That servant fellow said something about a bell. I watched you like a cat, and you sure rung no bell."

"It was under the table, you poor fool. I pressed it with my foot."

"Thank you, ma'am. I reckoned I'd seen your kind before, and now I sure know I have. I spoke to you true and trusting, and all the time you was lying like hell to me."

She laughed mockingly.

"Go on. Say what you wish. It is very interesting."

"You made eyes at me, looking soft and kind, playing up all the time the fact that you wore skirts instead of pants—and all the time with your foot on the bell under the table. Well, there's some consolation. I'd sooner be poor Hughie Luke, doing his ten years, than be in your skin. Ma'am, hell is full of women like you."

There was silence for a space, in which the man, never taking his eyes from her, studying her, was making up his mind.

"Go on," she urged. "Say something."

"Yes, ma'am, I'll say something. I'll sure say something. Do you know what I'm going to do? I'm going to get right up from this chair and walk out that door. I'd take the gun from you, only you might turn foolish and let it go off. You can have the gun. It's a good one. As I was saying, I am going right out that door. And you ain't going to pull that gun off either. It takes guts to shoot a man, and you sure ain't got them. Now get ready and see if you can pull that trigger. I ain't going to harm you. I'm going out that door, and I'm starting."

Keeping his eyes fixed on her, he pushed back the chair and slowly stood erect. The hammer rose halfway. She watched it. So did he.

"Pull harder," he advised. "It ain't half up yet. Go on and pull it and kill a man. That's what I said, kill a man, spatter his brains out on the floor, or slap a hole into him the size of your fist. That's what killing a man means."

The hammer lowered jerkily but gently. The man turned his back and walked slowly to the door. She swung the revolver around so that it bore on his back. Twice again the hammer came up halfway and was reluctantly eased down.

At the door the man turned for a moment before passing on. A sneer was on his lips. He spoke to her in a low voice, almost drawling, but in it was the quintessence of all loathing, as he called her a name unspeakable and vile.

THE MEXICAN

NOBODY knew his history—they of the Junta least of all. He was their "little mystery," their "big patriot," and in his way he worked as hard for the coming Mexican Revolution as did they. They were tardy in recognizing this, for not one of the Junta liked him. The day he first drifted into their crowded, busy rooms, they all suspected him of being a spy—one of the bought tools of the Diaz secret service. Too many of the comrades were in civil an military prisons scattered over the United States, and others of them, in irons, were even then being taken across the border to be lined up against adobe walls and shot.

At the first sight the boy did not impress them favorably. Boy he was, not more than eighteen and not over large for his years. He announced that he was Felipe Rivera, and that it was his wish to work for the Revolution. That was all—not a wasted word, no further explanation. He stood waiting. There was no smile on his lips, no geniality in his eyes. Big dashing Paulino Vera felt an inward shudder. Here was something forbidding, terrible, inscrutable. There was something venomous and snakelike in the boy's black eyes. They burned like cold fire, as with a vast, concentrated bitterness. He flashed them from the faces of the conspirators to the typewriter which little Mrs. Sethby was industriously operating. His eyes rested on hers but an instant—she had chanced to look up—and she, too, sensed the nameless something that made her pause. She was compelled to read back in order to regain the swing of the letter she was writing.

Paulino Vera looked questioningly at Arrellano and Ramos, and questioningly they looked back and to each other. The indecision of doubt brooded in their eyes. This slender boy was the Unknown, vested with all the menace of the Unknown. He was unrecognizable, something quite beyond the ken of honest, ordinary revolutionists whose fiercest hatred for Diaz and his tyranny after all was only that of honest and ordinary patriots. Here was something else, they knew not what. But Vera, always the most impulsive, the quickest to act, stepped into the breach.

"Very well," he said coldly. "You say you want to work for the Revolution. Take off your coat. Hang it over there. I will show you, come—where are the buckets and cloths. The floor is dirty. You will begin by scrubbing it, and by scrubbing the floors of the other rooms. The spittoons need to be cleaned. Then there are the windows."

"Is it for the Revolution?" the boy asked.

"It is for the Revolution," Vera answered.

Rivera looked cold suspicion at all of them, then proceeded to take off his coat.

"It is well," he said.

And nothing more. Day after day he came to his work—sweeping, scrubbing, cleaning. He emptied the ashes from the stoves, brought up the coal and kindling, and lighted the fires before the most energetic one of them was at his desk.

"Can I sleep here?" he asked once.

Ah, ha! So that was it—the hand of Diaz showing through! To sleep in the rooms of the Junta meant access to their secrets, to the lists of names, to the addresses of comrades down on Mexican soil. The request was denied, and Rivera never spoke of it again. He slept they knew not where, and ate they knew not where nor how. Once, Arrellano offered him a couple of dollars. Rivera declined the money with a shake of the head. When Vera joined in and tried to press it upon him, he said:

"I am working for the Revolution."

It takes money to raise a modern revolution, and always the Junta was pressed. The members starved and toiled, and the longest day was none too long, and yet there were times when it appeared as if the Revolution stood or fell on no more than the matter of a few dollars. Once, the first time, when the rent of the house was two months behind and the landlord was threatening dispossession, it was Felipe Rivera, the scrub-boy in the poor, cheap clothes, worn and threadbare, who laid sixty dollars in gold on May

Sethby's desk. There were other times. Three hundred letters, clicked out on the busy typewriters (appeals for assistance, for sanctions from the organized labor groups, requests for square news deals to the editors of newspapers, protests against the high-handed treatment of revolutionists by the United States courts), lay unmailed, awaiting postage. Vera's watch had disappeared— the old-fashioned gold repeater that had been his father's. Likewise had gone the plain gold band from May Setbby's third finger. Things were desperate. Ramos and Arrellano pulled their long mustaches in despair. The letters must go off, and the Post Office allowed no credit to purchasers of stamps. Then it was that Rivera put on his hat and went out. When he came back he laid a thousand two-cent stamps on May Sethby's desk.

"I wonder if it is the cursed gold of Diaz?" said Vera to the comrades.

They elevated their brows and could not decide. And Felipe Rivera, the scrubber for the Revolution, continued, as occasion arose, to lay down gold and silver for the Junta's use.

And still they could not bring themselves to like him. They did not know him. His ways were not theirs. He gave no confidences. He repelled all probing. Youth that he was, they could never nerve themselves to dare to question him.

"A great and lonely spirit, perhaps, I do not know, I do not know," Arrellano said helplessly.

"He is not human," said Ramos.

"His soul has been seared," said May Sethby. "Light and laughter have been burned out of him. He is like one dead, and yet he is fearfully alive."

"He has been through hell," said Vera. "No man could look like that who has not been through hell—and he is only a boy."

Yet they could not like him. He never talked, never inquired, never suggested. He would stand listening, expressionless, a thing dead, save for his eyes, coldly burning, while their talk of the Revolution ran high and warm. From face to face and speaker to speaker his eyes would turn, boring like gimlets of incandescent ice, disconcerting and perturbing.

"He is no spy," Vera confided to May Sethby. "He is a patriot—mark me, the greatest patriot of us all. I know it, I feel it, here in my heart and head I feel it. But him I know not at all."

"He has a bad temper," said May Sethby.

"I know," said Vera, with a shudder. "He has looked at me with those eyes of his. They do not love; they threaten; they are savage as a wild tiger's. I know, if I should prove unfaithful to the Cause, that he would kill me. He has no heart. He is pitiless as steel, keen and cold as frost. He is like moonshine in a winter night when a man freezes to death on some lonely mountain top. I am not afraid of Diaz and all his killers; but this boy, of him am I afraid. I tell you true. I am afraid. He is the breath of death."

Yet Vera it was who persuaded the others to give the first trust to Rivera. The line of communication between Los Angeles and Lower California had broken down. Three of the comrades had dug their own graves and been shot into them. Two more were United States prisoners in Los Angeles. Juan Alvarado, the Federal commander, was a monster. All their plans did he checkmate. They could no longer gain access to the active revolutionists, and the incipient ones, in Lower California.

Young Rivera was given his instructions and dispatched south. When he returned, the line of communication was reestablished, and Juan Alvarado was dead. He had been found in bed, a knife hilt-deep in his breast. This had exceeded Rivera's instructions, but they of the Junta knew the times of his movements. They did not ask him. He said nothing. But they looked at one another and conjectured.

"I have told you," said Vera. "Diaz has more to fear from this youth than from any man. He is implacable. He is the hand of God."

The bad temper, mentioned by May Sethby, and sensed by them all, was evidenced by physical proofs. Now he appeared with a cut lip, a blackened cheek, or a swollen ear. It was patent that he brawled, somewhere in that outside world where he ate and slept, gained money, and moved in ways unknown to them. As the time passed, he had come to set type for the little revolutionary sheet they published weekly. There were occasions when he was unable to set type, when his knuckles were bruised and battered, when his thumbs were injured and helpless, when one arm or the other hung wearily at his side while his face was drawn with unspoken pain.

"A wastrel," said Arrellano.

"A frequenter of low places," said Ramos.

"But where does he get the money?" Vera demanded. "Only to-day, just now, have I learned that he paid the bill for white paper—one hundred and forty dollars."

"There are his absences," said May Sethby. "He never explains them."

"We should set a spy upon him," Ramos propounded.

"I should not care to be that spy," said Vera. "I fear you would never see me again, save to bury me. He has a terrible passion. Not even God would he permit to stand between him and the way of his passion."

"I feel like a child before him," Ramos confessed.

"To me he is power—he is the primitive, the wild wolf, the striking rattlesnake, the stinging centipede," said Arrellano.

"He is the Revolution incarnate," said Vera. "He is the flame and the spirit of it, the insatiable cry for vengeance that makes no cry but that slays noiselessly. He is a destroying angel in moving through the still watches of the night."

"I could weep over him," said May Sethby. "He knows nobody. He hates all people. Us he tolerates, for we are the way of his desire. He is alone.... lonely." Her voice broke in a half sob and there was dimness in her eyes.

Rivera's ways and times were truly mysterious. There were periods when they did not see him for a week at a time. Once, he was away a month. These occasions were always capped by his return, when, without advertisement or speech, he laid gold coins on May Sethby's desk. Again, for days and weeks, he spent all his time with the Junta. And yet again, for irregular periods, he would disappear through the heart of each day, from early morning until late afternoon. At such times he came early and remained late. Arrellano had found him at midnight, setting type with fresh swollen knuckles, or mayhap it was his lip, new-split, that still bled.

II

The time of the crisis approached. Whether or not the Revolution would be depended upon the Junta, and the Junta was hard-pressed. The need for money was greater than ever before, while money was harder to get. Patriots had given their last cent and now could give no more. Section gang laborers-fugitive peons from Mexico—were contributing half their scanty wages. But more than that was needed. The heart-breaking, conspiring, undermining toil of years approached fruition. The time was ripe. The Revolution hung on the balance. One shove more, one last heroic effort, and it would tremble across the scales to victory. They knew their Mexico. Once started, the Revolution would take care of itself. The whole Diaz machine would go down like a house of cards. The border was ready to rise. One Yankee, with a hundred I.W.W. men, waited the word to cross over the border and begin the conquest of Lower California. But he needed guns. And clear across to the Atlantic, the Junta in touch with them all and all of them needing guns, mere adventurers, soldiers of fortune, bandits, disgruntled American union men, socialists, anarchists, rough-necks, Mexican exiles, peons escaped from bondage, whipped miners from the bull-pens of Coeur d'Alene and Colorado who desired only the more vindictively to fight—all the flotsam and jetsam of wild spirits from the madly complicated modern world. And it was guns and ammunition, ammunition and guns—the unceasing and eternal cry.

Fling this heterogeneous, bankrupt, vindictive mass across the border, and the Revolution was on. The custom house, the northern ports of entry, would be captured. Diaz could not resist. He dared not throw the weight of his armies against them, for he must hold the south. And through the south the flame would spread despite. The people would rise. The defenses of city after city would crumple up. State after state would totter down. And at last, from every side, the victorious armies of the Revolution would close in on the City of Mexico itself, Diaz's last stronghold.

But the money. They had the men, impatient and urgent, who would use the guns. They knew the traders who would sell and deliver the guns. But to culture the Revolution thus far had exhausted the Junta. The last dollar had been spent, the last resource and the last starving patriot milked dry, and the great adventure still trembled on the scales. Guns and ammunition! The ragged battalions must be armed. But how? Ramos lamented his confiscated estates. Arrellano wailed the spendthriftness of his youth. May Sethby wondered if it would have been different had they of the Junta been more economical in the past.

"To think that the freedom of Mexico should stand or fall on a few paltry thousands of dollars," said Paulino Vera.

Despair was in all their faces. Jose Amarillo, their last hope, a recent convert, who had promised money, had been apprehended at his hacienda in Chihuahua and shot against his own stable wall. The news had just come through.

Rivera, on his knees, scrubbing, looked up, with suspended brush, his bare arms flecked with soapy, dirty water.

"Will five thousand do it?" he asked.

They looked their amazement. Vera nodded and swallowed. He could not speak, but he was on the instant invested with a vast faith.

"Order the guns," Rivera said, and thereupon was guilty of the longest flow of words they had ever heard him utter. "The time is short. In three weeks I shall bring you the five thousand. It is well. The weather will be warmer for those who fight. Also, it is the best I can do."

Vera fought his faith. It was incredible. Too many fond hopes had been shattered since he had begun to play the revolution game. He believed this threadbare scrubber of the Revolution, and yet he dared not believe.

"You are crazy," he said.

"In three weeks," said Rivera. "Order the guns."

142

He got up, rolled down his sleeves, and put on his coat.

"Order the guns," he said.

"I am going now."

III

After hurrying and scurrying, much telephoning and bad language, a night session was held in Kelly's office. Kelly was rushed with business; also, he was unlucky. He had brought Danny Ward out from New York, arranged the fight for him with Billy Carthey, the date was three weeks away, and for two days now, carefully concealed from the sporting writers, Carthey had been lying up, badly injured. There was no one to take his place. Kelly had been burning the wires East to every eligible lightweight, but they were tied up with dates and contracts. And now hope had revived, though faintly.

"You've got a hell of a nerve," Kelly addressed Rivera, after one look, as soon as they got together.

Hate that was malignant was in Rivera's eyes, but his face remained impassive.

"I can lick Ward," was all he said.

"How do you know? Ever see him fight?"

Rivera shook his head.

"He can beat you up with one hand and both eyes closed."

Rivera shrugged his shoulders.

"Haven't you got anything to say?" the fight promoter snarled.

"I can lick him."

"Who'd you ever fight, anyway!" Michael Kelly demanded. Michael was the promotor's brother, and ran the Yellowstone pool rooms where he made goodly sums on the fight game.

Rivera favored him with a bitter, unanswering stare.

The promoter's secretary, a distinctively sporty young man, sneered audibly.

"Well, you know Roberts," Kelly broke the hostile silence. "He ought to be here. I've sent for him. Sit down and wait, though from the looks of you, you haven't got a chance. I can't throw the public down with a bum fight. Ringside seats are selling at fifteen dollars, you know that."

When Roberts arrived, it was patent that he was mildly drunk. He was a tall, lean, slack-jointed individual, and his walk, like his talk, was a smooth and languid drawl.

Kelly went straight to the point.

"Look here, Roberts, you've been bragging you discovered this little Mexican. You know Carthey's broke his arm. Well, this little yellow streak has the gall to blow in to-day and say he'll take Carthey's place. What about it?"

"It's all right, Kelly," came the slow response. "He can put up a fight."

"I suppose you'll be sayin' next that he can lick Ward," Kelly snapped.

Roberts considered judicially.

"No, I won't say that. Ward's a top-notcher and a ring general. But he can't hashhouse Rivera in short order. I know Rivera. Nobody can get his goat. He ain't got a goat that I could ever discover. And he's a two-handed fighter. He can throw in the sleep-makers from any position."

"Never mind that. What kind of a show can he put up? You've been conditioning and training fighters all your life. I take off my hat to your judgment. Can he give the public a run for its money?"

"He sure can, and he'll worry Ward a mighty heap on top of it. You don't know that boy. I do. I discovered him. He ain't got a goat. He's a devil. He's a wizzy-wooz if anybody should ask you. He'll make Ward sit up with a show of local talent that'll make the rest of you sit up. I won't say he'll lick Ward, but he'll put up such a show that you'll all know he's a comer."

144

"All right." Kelly turned to his secretary. "Ring up Ward. I warned him to show up if I thought it worth while. He's right across at the Yellowstone, throwin' chests and doing the popular."

Kelly turned back to the conditioner. "Have a drink?"

Roberts sipped his highball and unburdened himself.

"Never told you how I discovered the little cuss. It was a couple of years ago he showed up out at the quarters. I was getting Prayne ready for his fight with Delaney. Prayne's wicked. He ain't got a tickle of mercy in his make-up. I chopped up his pardner's something cruel, and I couldn't find a willing boy that'd work with him. I'd noticed this little starved Mexican kid hanging around, and I was desperate. So I grabbed him, shoved on the gloves and put him in. He was tougher'n rawhide, but weak. And he didn't know the first letter in the alphabet of boxing. Prayne chopped him to ribbons. But he hung on for two sickening rounds, when he fainted. Starvation, that was all. Battered! You couldn't have recognized him. I gave him half a dollar and a square meal. You oughta seen him wolf it down. He hadn't had the end of a bite for a couple of days. That's the end of him, thinks I. But next day he showed up, stiff an' sore, ready for another half and a square meal. And he done better as time went by. Just a born fighter, and tough beyond belief. He hasn't a heart. He's a piece of ice. And he never talked eleven words in a string since I know him. He saws wood and does his work."

"I've seen 'm," the secretary said. "He's worked a lot for you."

"All the big little fellows has tried out on him," Roberts answered. "And he's learned from 'em. I've seen some of them he could lick. But his heart wasn't in it. I reckoned he never liked the game. He seemed to act that way."

"He's been fighting some before the little clubs the last few months," Kelly said.

"Sure. But I don't know what struck 'm. All of a sudden his heart got into it. He just went out like a streak and cleaned up all the little local fellows. Seemed to want the money, and he's won a bit, though his clothes don't look it. He's peculiar. Nobody knows his business. Nobody knows how he spends his time. Even when he's on the job, he plumb up and disappears most of each day soon as his work is done. Sometimes he just blows away for weeks at a time. But he don't take advice. There's a fortune in it for the fellow that gets the job of managin' him, only he won't consider it. And you watch him hold out for the cash money when you get down to terms."

It was at this stage that Danny Ward arrived. Quite a party it was. His manager and trainer were with him, and he breezed in like a gusty draught of geniality, good-nature, and all-conqueringness. Greetings flew about, a joke here, a retort there, a smile or a laugh for everybody. Yet it was his way, and only partly sincere. He was a good actor, and he had found geniality a most valuable asset in the game of getting on in the world. But down underneath he was the deliberate, cold-blooded fighter and business man. The rest was a mask. Those who knew him or trafficked with him said that when it came to brass tacks he was Danny-on-the-Spot. He was invariably present at all business discussions, and it was urged by some that his manager was a blind whose only function was to serve as Danny's mouth-piece.

Rivera's way was different. Indian blood, as well as Spanish, was in his veins, and he sat back in a corner, silent, immobile, only his black eyes passing from face to face and noting everything.

"So that's the guy," Danny said, running an appraising eye over his proposed antagonist. "How de do, old chap."

Rivera's eyes burned venomously, but he made no sign of acknowledgment. He disliked all Gringos, but this Gringo he hated with an immediacy that was unusual even in him.

"Gawd!" Danny protested facetiously to the promoter. "You ain't expectin' me to fight a deef mute." When the laughter subsided, he made another hit. "Los Angeles must be on the dink when this is the best you can scare up. What kindergarten did you get 'm from?"

"He's a good little boy, Danny, take it from me," Roberts defended. "Not as easy as he looks."

"And half the house is sold already," Kelly pleaded. "You'll have to take 'm on, Danny. It is the best we can do."

146

Danny ran another careless and unflattering glance over Rivera and sighed.

"I gotta be easy with 'm, I guess. If only he don't blow up."

Roberts snorted.

"You gotta be careful," Danny's manager warned. "No taking chances with a dub that's likely to sneak a lucky one across."

"Oh, I'll be careful all right, all right," Danny smiled. "I'll get in at the start an' nurse 'im along for the dear public's sake. What d' ye say to fifteen rounds, Kelly—an' then the hay for him?"

"That'll do," was the answer. "As long as you make it realistic."

"Then let's get down to biz." Danny paused and calculated. "Of course, sixty-five per cent of the gate receipts, same as with Carthey. But the split'll be different. Eighty will just about suit me." And to his manager, "That right?"

The manager nodded.

"Here, you, did you get that?" Kelly asked Rivera.

Rivera shook his head.

"Well, it is this way," Kelly exposited. "The purse'll be sixty-five per cent of the gate receipts. You're a dub, and an unknown. You and Danny split, twenty per cent goin' to you, an' eighty to Danny. That's fair, isn't it, Roberts?"

"Very fair, Rivera," Roberts agreed.

"You see, you ain't got a reputation yet."

"What will sixty-five per cent of the gate receipts be?" Rivera demanded.

"Oh, maybe five thousand, maybe as high as eight thousand," Danny broke in to explain. "Something like that. Your share'll come to something like a thousand or sixteen hundred. Pretty good for takin' a licking from a guy with my reputation. What d' ye say?"

Then Rivera took their breaths away. "Winner takes all," he said with finality.

147

A dead silence prevailed.

"It's like candy from a baby," Danny's manager proclaimed.

Danny shook his head.

"I've been in the game too long," he explained.

"I'm not casting reflections on the referee, or the present company. I'm not sayin' nothing about book-makers an' frame-ups that sometimes happen. But what I do say is that it's poor business for a fighter like me. I play safe. There's no tellin'. Mebbe I break my arm, eh? Or some guy slips me a bunch of dope?" He shook his head solemnly. "Win or lose, eighty is my split. What d' ye say, Mexican?"

Rivera shook his head.

Danny exploded. He was getting down to brass tacks now.

"Why, you dirty little greaser! I've a mind to knock your block off right now."

Roberts drawled his body to interposition between hostilities.

"Winner takes all," Rivera repeated sullenly.

"Why do you stand out that way?" Danny asked.

"I can lick you," was the straight answer.

Danny half started to take off his coat. But, as his manager knew, it was a grand stand play. The coat did not come off, and Danny allowed himself to be placated by the group. Everybody sympathized with him. Rivera stood alone.

"Look here, you little fool," Kelly took up the argument. "You're nobody. We know what you've been doing the last few months—putting away little local fighters. But Danny is class. His next fight after this will be for the championship. And you're unknown. Nobody ever heard of you out of Los Angeles."

148

"They will," Rivera answered with a shrug, "after this fight."

"You think for a second you can lick me?" Danny blurted in.

Rivera nodded.

"Oh, come; listen to reason," Kelly pleaded. "Think of the advertising."

"I want the money," was Rivera's answer.

"You couldn't win from me in a thousand years," Danny assured him.

"Then what are you holdin' out for?" Rivera countered. "If the money's that easy, why don't you go after it?"

"I will, so help me!" Danny cried with abrupt conviction. "I'll beat you to death in the ring, my boy—you monkeyin' with me this way. Make out the articles, Kelly. Winner take all. Play it up in the sportin' columns. Tell 'em it's a grudge fight. I'll show this fresh kid a few."

Kelly's secretary had begun to write, when Danny interrupted.

"Hold on!" He turned to Rivera.

"Weights?"

"Ringside," came the answer.

"Not on your life, Fresh Kid. If winner takes all, we weigh in at ten A.M."

"And winner takes all?" Rivera queried.

Danny nodded. That settled it. He would enter the ring in his full ripeness of strength.

"Weigh in at ten," Rivera said.

The secretary's pen went on scratching.

"It means five pounds," Roberts complained to Rivera.

"You've given too much away. You've thrown the fight right there. Danny'll lick you sure. He'll be as strong as a bull. You're a fool. You ain't got the chance of a dewdrop in hell."

Rivera's answer was a calculated look of hatred. Even this Gringo he despised, and him had he found the whitest Gringo of them all.

IV

Barely noticed was Rivera as he entered the ring. Only a very slight and very scattering ripple of half-hearted hand-clapping greeted him. The house did not believe in him. He was the lamb led to slaughter at the hands of the great Danny. Besides, the house was disappointed. It had expected a rushing battle between Danny Ward and Billy Carthey, and here it must put up with this poor little tyro. Still further, it had manifested its disapproval of the change by betting two, and even three, to one on Danny. And where a betting audience's money is, there is its heart.

The Mexican boy sat down in his corner and waited. The slow minutes lagged by. Danny was making him wait. It was an old trick, but ever it worked on the young, new fighters. They grew frightened, sitting thus and facing their own apprehensions and a callous, tobacco-smoking audience. But for once the trick failed. Roberts was right. Rivera had no goat. He, who was more delicately coordinated, more finely nerved and strung than any of them, had no nerves of this sort. The atmosphere of foredoomed defeat in his own corner had no effect on him. His handlers were Gringos and strangers. Also they were scrubs—the dirty driftage of the fight game, without honor, without efficiency. And they were chilled, as well, with certitude that theirs was the losing corner.

"Now you gotta be careful," Spider Hagerty warned him. Spider was his chief second. "Make it last as long as you can—them's my instructions from Kelly. If you don't, the papers'll call it another bum fight and give the game a bigger black eye in Los Angeles."

All of which was not encouraging. But Rivera took no notice. He despised prize fighting. It was the hated game of the hated Gringo. He had taken up with it, as a chopping block for others in the training quarters, solely because he was starving. The fact that he was marvelously made for it had meant nothing. He hated it. Not until he had come in to the Junta, had he fought for money, and he had found the money easy. Not first among the sons of men had he been to find himself successful at a despised vocation.

He did not analyze. He merely knew that he must win this fight. There could be no other outcome. For behind him, nerving him to this belief, were profounder forces than any the crowded house dreamed. Danny Ward fought for money, and for the easy ways of life that money would bring. But the things Rivera fought for burned in his brain—blazing and terrible visions, that, with eyes wide open, sitting lonely in the corner of the ring and waiting for his tricky antagonist, he saw as clearly as he had lived them.

He saw the white-walled, water-power factories of Rio Blanco. He saw the six thousand workers, starved and wan, and the little children, seven and eight years of age, who toiled long shifts for ten cents a day. He saw the perambulating corpses, the ghastly death's heads of men who labored in the dye-rooms. He remembered that he had heard his father call the dye-rooms the "suicide-holes," where a year was death. He saw the little patio, and his mother cooking and moiling at crude housekeeping and finding time to caress and love him. And his father he saw, large, big-moustached and deep-chested, kindly above all men, who loved all men and whose heart was so large that there was love to overflowing still left for the mother and the little muchacho playing in the corner of the patio. In those days his name had not been Felipe Rivera. It had been Fernandez, his father's and mother's name. Him had they called Juan. Later, he had changed it himself, for he had found the name of Fernandez hated by prefects of police, jefes politicos, and rurales.

Big, hearty Joaquin Fernandez! A large place he occupied in Rivera's visions. He had not understood at the time, but looking back he could understand. He could see him setting type in the little printery, or scribbling endless hasty, nervous lines on the much-cluttered desk. And he could see the strange evenings, when workmen, coming secretly in the dark like men who did ill deeds, met with his father and talked long hours where he, the muchacho, lay not always asleep in the corner.

As from a remote distance he could hear Spider Hagerty saying to him: "No layin' down at the start. Them's instructions. Take a beatin' and earn your dough."

Ten minutes had passed, and he still sat in his corner. There were no signs of Danny, who was evidently playing the trick to the limit.

But more visions burned before the eye of Rivera's memory. The strike, or, rather, the lockout, because the workers of Rio Blanco had helped their striking brothers of Puebla. The hunger, the expeditions in the hills for berries, the roots and herbs that all ate and that twisted and pained the stomachs of all of them. And then, the nightmare; the waste of ground before the company's store; the thousands of starving workers; General Rosalio Martinez and the soldiers of Porfirio Diaz, and the death-spitting rifles that seemed never to cease spitting, while the workers' wrongs were washed and washed again in their own blood. And that night! He saw the flat cars, piled high with the bodies of the slain, consigned to Vera Cruz, food for the sharks of the bay. Again he crawled over the grisly heaps, seeking and finding, stripped and mangled, his father and his mother. His mother he especially remembered— only her face projecting, her body burdened by the weight of dozens of bodies. Again the rifles of the soldiers of Porfirio Diaz cracked, and again he dropped to the ground and slunk away like some hunted coyote of the hills.

To his ears came a great roar, as of the sea, and he saw Danny Ward, leading his retinue of trainers and seconds, coming down the center aisle. The house was in wild uproar for the popular hero who was bound to win. Everybody proclaimed him. Everybody was for him. Even Rivera's own seconds warmed to something akin to cheerfulness when Danny ducked jauntily through the ropes and entered the ring. His face continually spread to an unending succession of smiles, and when Danny smiled he smiled in every feature, even to the laughter-wrinkles of the corners of the eyes and into the depths of the eyes themselves. Never was there so genial a fighter. His face was a running advertisement of good feeling, of good fellowship. He knew everybody. He joked, and laughed, and greeted his friends through the ropes. Those farther away, unable to suppress their admiration, cried loudly: "Oh, you Danny!" It was a joyous ovation of affection that lasted a full five minutes.

Rivera was disregarded. For all that the audience noticed, he did not exist. Spider Lagerty's bloated face bent down close to his.

"No gettin' scared," the Spider warned.

"An' remember instructions. You gotta last. No layin' down. If you lay down, we got instructions to beat you up in the dressing rooms. Savve? You just gotta fight."

The house began to applaud. Danny was crossing the ring to him. Danny bent over, caught Rivera's right hand in both his own and shook it with impulsive heartiness. Danny's smile-wreathed face was close to his. The audience yelled its appreciation of Danny's display of sporting spirit. He was greeting his opponent with the fondness of a brother. Danny's lips moved, and the audience, interpreting the unheard words to be those of a kindly-natured sport, yelled again. Only Rivera heard the low words.

"You little Mexican rat," hissed from between Danny's gaily smiling lips, "I'll fetch the yellow outa you."

Rivera made no move. He did not rise. He merely hated with his eyes.

"Get up, you dog!" some man yelled through the ropes from behind.

The crowd began to hiss and boo him for his unsportsmanlike conduct, but he sat unmoved. Another great outburst of applause was Danny's as he walked back across the ring.

When Danny stripped, there was ohs! and ahs! of delight. His body was perfect, alive with easy suppleness and health and strength. The skin was white as a woman's, and as smooth. All grace, and resilience, and power resided therein. He had proved it in scores of battles. His photographs were in all the physical culture magazines.

153

A groan went up as Spider Hagerty peeled Rivera's sweater over his head. His body seemed leaner, because of the swarthiness of the skin. He had muscles, but they made no display like his opponent's. What the audience neglected to see was the deep chest. Nor could it guess the toughness of the fiber of the flesh, the instantaneousness of the cell explosions of the muscles, the fineness of the nerves that wired every part of him into a splendid fighting mechanism. All the audience saw was a brown-skinned boy of eighteen with what seemed the body of a boy. With Danny it was different. Danny was a man of twenty-four, and his body was a man's body. The contrast was still more striking as they stood together in the center of the ring receiving the referee's last instructions.

Rivera noticed Roberts sitting directly behind the newspaper men. He was drunker than usual, and his speech was correspondingly slower.

"Take it easy, Rivera," Roberts drawled.

"He can't kill you, remember that. He'll rush you at the go-off, but don't get rattled. You just and stall, and clinch. He can't hurt cover up, much. Just make believe to yourself that he's choppin' out on you at the trainin' quarters."

Rivera made no sign that he had heard.

"Sullen little devil," Roberts muttered to the man next to him. "He always was that way."

But Rivera forgot to look his usual hatred. A vision of countless rifles blinded his eyes. Every face in the audience, far as he could see, to the high dollar-seats, was transformed into a rifle. And he saw the long Mexican border arid and sun-washed and aching, and along it he saw the ragged bands that delayed only for the guns.

Back in his corner he waited, standing up. His seconds had crawled out through the ropes, taking the canvas stool with them. Diagonally across the squared ring, Danny faced him. The gong struck, and the battle was on. The audience howled its delight. Never had it seen a battle open more convincingly. The papers were right. It was a grudge fight. Three-quarters of the distance Danny covered in the rush to get together, his intention to eat up

154

the Mexican lad plainly advertised. He assailed with not one blow, nor two, nor a dozen. He was a gyroscope of blows, a whirlwind of destruction. Rivera was nowhere. He was overwhelmed, buried beneath avalanches of punches delivered from every angle and position by a past master in the art. He was overborne, swept back against the ropes, separated by the referee, and swept back against the ropes again.

It was not a fight. It was a slaughter, a massacre. Any audience, save a prize fighting one, would have exhausted its emotions in that first minute. Danny was certainly showing what he could do—a splendid exhibition. Such was the certainty of the audience, as well as its excitement and favoritism, that it failed to take notice that the Mexican still stayed on his feet. It forgot Rivera. It rarely saw him, so closely was he enveloped in Danny's man-eating attack. A minute of this went by, and two minutes. Then, in a separation, it caught a clear glimpse of the Mexican. His lip was cut, his nose was bleeding. As he turned and staggered into a clinch, the welts of oozing blood, from his contacts with the ropes, showed in red bars across his back. But what the audience did not notice was that his chest was not heaving and that his eyes were coldly burning as ever. Too many aspiring champions, in the cruel welter of the training camps, had practiced this man-eating attack on him. He had learned to live through for a compensation of from half a dollar a go up to fifteen dollars a week—a hard school, and he was schooled hard.

Then happened the amazing thing. The whirling, blurring mix-up ceased suddenly. Rivera stood alone. Danny, the redoubtable Danny, lay on his back. His body quivered as consciousness strove to return to it. He had not staggered and sunk down, nor had he gone over in a long slumping fall. The right hook of Rivera had dropped him in midair with the abruptness of death. The referee shoved Rivera back with one hand, and stood over the fallen gladiator counting the seconds. It is the custom of prize-fighting audiences to cheer a clean knock-down blow. But this audience did not cheer. The thing had been too unexpected. It watched the toll of the seconds in tense silence, and through this silence the voice of Roberts rose exultantly:

"I told you he was a two-handed fighter!"

By the fifth second, Danny was rolling over on his face, and when seven was counted, he rested on one knee, ready to rise after the count of nine and before the count of ten. If his knee still touched the floor at "ten," he was considered "down," and also "out." The instant his knee left the floor, he was considered "up," and in that instant it was Rivera's right to try and put him down again. Rivera took no chances. The moment that knee left the floor he would strike again. He circled around, but the referee circled in between, and Rivera knew that the seconds he counted were very slow. All Gringos were against him, even the referee.

At "nine" the referee gave Rivera a sharp thrust back. It was unfair, but it enabled Danny to rise, the smile back on his lips. Doubled partly over, with arms wrapped about face and abdomen, he cleverly stumbled into a clinch. By all the rules of the game the referee should have broken it, but he did not, and Danny clung on like a surf-battered barnacle and moment by moment recuperated. The last minute of the round was going fast. If he could live to the end, he would have a full minute in his corner to revive. And live to the end he did, smiling through all desperateness and extremity.

"The smile that won't come off!" somebody yelled, and the audience laughed loudly in its relief.

"The kick that Greaser's got is something God-awful," Danny gasped in his corner to his adviser while his handlers worked frantically over him.

The second and third rounds were tame. Danny, a tricky and consummate ring general, stalled and blocked and held on, devoting himself to recovering from that dazing first-round blow. In the fourth round he was himself again. Jarred and shaken, nevertheless his good condition had enabled him to regain his vigor. But he tried no man-eating tactics. The Mexican had proved a tartar. Instead, he brought to bear his best fighting powers. In tricks and skill and experience he was the master, and though he could land nothing vital, he proceeded scientifically to chop and wear down his opponent. He landed three blows to Rivera's one, but they were punishing blows only, and not deadly. It was the sum of many of them that constituted deadliness. He was respectful of this two-handed dub with the amazing short-arm kicks in both his fists.

In defense, Rivera developed a disconcerting straight-left. Again and again, attack after attack he straight-lefted away from him with accumulated damage to Danny's mouth and nose. But Danny was protean. That was why he was the coming champion. He could change from style to style of fighting at will. He now devoted himself to infighting. In this he was particularly wicked, and it enabled him to avoid the other's straight-left. Here he set the house wild repeatedly, capping it with a marvelous lockbreak and lift of an inside upper-cut that raised the Mexican in the air and dropped him to the mat. Rivera rested on one knee, making the most of the count, and in the soul of him he knew the referee was counting short seconds on him.

Again, in the seventh, Danny achieved the diabolical inside uppercut. He succeeded only in staggering Rivera, but, in the ensuing moment of defenseless helplessness, he smashed him with another blow through the ropes. Rivera's body bounced on the heads of the newspaper men below, and they boosted him back to the edge of the platform outside the ropes. Here he rested on one knee, while the referee raced off the seconds. Inside the ropes, through which he must duck to enter the ring, Danny waited for him. Nor did the referee intervene or thrust Danny back.

The house was beside itself with delight.

"Kill'm, Danny, kill'm!" was the cry.

Scores of voices took it up until it was like a war-chant of wolves.

Danny did his best, but Rivera, at the count of eight, instead of nine, came unexpectedly through the ropes and safely into a clinch. Now the referee worked, tearing him away so that he could be hit, giving Danny every advantage that an unfair referee can give.

But Rivera lived, and the daze cleared from his brain. It was all of a piece. They were the hated Gringos and they were all unfair. And in the worst of it visions continued to flash and sparkle in his brain—long lines of railroad track that simmered across the desert; rurales and American constables, prisons and calabooses; tramps at water tanks—all the squalid and painful panorama of his odyssey after Rio Blanca and the strike. And, resplendent and glorious, he saw the great, red Revolution sweeping across his land. The guns were there before him. Every hated face was a gun. It was for the guns he fought. He was the guns. He was the Revolution. He fought for all Mexico.

The audience began to grow incensed with Rivera. Why didn't he take the licking that was appointed him? Of course he was going to be licked, but why should he be so obstinate about it? Very few were interested in him, and they were the certain, definite percentage of a gambling crowd that plays long shots. Believing Danny to be the winner, nevertheless they had put their money on the Mexican at four to ten and one to three. More than a trifle was up on the point of how many rounds Rivera could last. Wild money had appeared at the ringside proclaiming that he could not last seven rounds, or even six. The winners of this, now that their cash risk was happily settled, had joined in cheering on the favorite.

Rivera refused to be licked. Through the eighth round his opponent strove vainly to repeat the uppercut. In the ninth, Rivera stunned the house again. In the midst of a clinch he broke the lock with a quick, lithe movement, and in the narrow space between their bodies his right lifted from the waist. Danny went to the floor and took the safety of the count. The crowd was appalled. He was being bested at his own game. His famous right-uppercut had been worked back on him. Rivera made no attempt to catch him as he arose at "nine." The referee was openly blocking that play, though he stood clear when the situation was reversed and it was Rivera who desired to rise.

Twice in the tenth, Rivera put through the right-uppercut, lifted from waist to opponent's chin. Danny grew desperate. The smile never left his face, but he went back to his man-eating rushes. Whirlwind as he would, he could not damage Rivera, while Rivera through the blur and whirl, dropped him to the mat three times in succession. Danny did not recuperate so quickly now, and by the eleventh round he was in a serious way. But from then till the fourteenth he put up the gamest exhibition of his career. He stalled and blocked, fought parsimoniously, and strove to gather strength. Also, he fought as foully as a successful fighter knows how. Every trick and device he employed, butting in the clinches with the seeming of accident, pinioning

Rivera's glove between arm and body, heeling his glove on Rivera's mouth to clog his breathing. Often, in the clinches, through his cut and smiling lips he snarled insults unspeakable and vile in Rivera's ear. Everybody, from the referee to the house, was with Danny and was helping Danny. And they knew what he had in mind. Bested by this surprise-box of an unknown, he was pinning all on a single punch. He offered himself for punishment, fished, and feinted, and drew, for that one opening that would enable him to whip a blow through with all his strength and turn the tide. As another and greater fighter had done before him, he might do a right and left, to solar plexus and across the jaw. He could do it, for he was noted for the strength of punch that remained in his arms as long as he could keep his feet.

Rivera's seconds were not half-caring for him in the intervals between rounds. Their towels made a showing, but drove little air into his panting lungs. Spider Hagerty talked advice to him, but Rivera knew it was wrong advice. Everybody was against him. He was surrounded by treachery. In the fourteenth round he put Danny down again, and himself stood resting, hands dropped at side, while the referee counted. In the other corner Rivera had been noting suspicious whisperings. He saw Michael Kelly make his way to Roberts and bend and whisper. Rivera's ears were a cat's, desert-trained, and he caught snatches of what was said. He wanted to hear more, and when his opponent arose he maneuvered the fight into a clinch over against the ropes.

"Got to," he could hear Michael, while Roberts nodded. "Danny's got to win—I stand to lose a mint—I've got a ton of money covered—my own. If he lasts the fifteenth I'm bust—the boy'll mind you. Put something across."

And thereafter Rivera saw no more visions. They were trying to job him. Once again he dropped Danny and stood resting, his hands at his slide. Roberts stood up.

"That settled him," he said.

"Go to your corner."

He spoke with authority, as he had often spoken to Rivera at the training quarters. But Rivera looked hatred at him and waited for Danny to rise. Back

159

in his corner in the minute interval, Kelly, the promoter, came and talked to Rivera.

"Throw it, damn you," he rasped in, a harsh low voice. "You gotta lay down, Rivera. Stick with me and I'll make your future. I'll let you lick Danny next time. But here's where you lay down."

Rivera showed with his eyes that he heard, but he made neither sign of assent nor dissent.

"Why don't you speak?" Kelly demanded angrily.

"You lose, anyway," Spider Hagerty supplemented. "The referee'll take it away from you. Listen to Kelly, and lay down."

"Lay down, kid," Kelly pleaded, "and I'll help you to the championship."

Rivera did not answer.

"I will, so help me, kid."

At the strike of the gong Rivera sensed something impending. The house did not. Whatever it was it was there inside the ring with him and very close. Danny's earlier surety seemed returned to him. The confidence of his advance frightened Rivera. Some trick was about to be worked. Danny rushed, but Rivera refused the encounter. He side-stepped away into safety. What the other wanted was a clinch. It was in some way necessary to the trick. Rivera backed and circled away, yet he knew, sooner or later, the clinch and the trick would come. Desperately he resolved to draw it. He made as if to effect the clinch with Danny's next rush. Instead, at the last instant, just as their bodies should have come together, Rivera darted nimbly back. And in the same instant Danny's corner raised a cry of foul. Rivera had fooled them. The referee paused irresolutely. The decision that trembled on his lips was never uttered, for a shrill, boy's voice from the gallery piped, "Raw work!"

Danny cursed Rivera openly, and forced him, while Rivera danced away. Also, Rivera made up his mind to strike no more blows at the body. In this he threw away half his chance of winning, but he knew if he was to win at all it was with the outfighting that remained to him. Given the least opportunity, they would lie a foul on him. Danny threw all caution to the winds. For two rounds he tore after and into the boy who dared not meet him at close quarters. Rivera was struck again and again; he took blows by the dozens to avoid the perilous clinch. During this supreme final rally of Danny's the audience rose to its feet and went mad. It did not understand. All it could see was that its favorite was winning, after all.

"Why don't you fight?" it demanded wrathfully of Rivera.

"You're yellow! You're yellow!" "Open up, you cur! Open up!" "Kill'm, Danny! Kill 'm!" "You sure got 'm! Kill 'm!"

In all the house, bar none, Rivera was the only cold man. By temperament and blood he was the hottest-passioned there; but he had gone through such vastly greater heats that this collective passion of ten thousand throats, rising surge on surge, was to his brain no more than the velvet cool of a summer twilight.

Into the seventeenth round Danny carried his rally. Rivera, under a heavy blow, drooped and sagged. His hands dropped helplessly as he reeled backward. Danny thought it was his chance. The boy was at, his mercy. Thus Rivera, feigning, caught him off his guard, lashing out a clean drive to the mouth. Danny went down. When he arose, Rivera felled him with a down-chop of the right on neck and jaw. Three times he repeated this. It was impossible for any referee to call these blows foul.

"Oh, Bill! Bill!" Kelly pleaded to the referee.

"I can't," that official lamented back. "He won't give me a chance."

Danny, battered and heroic, still kept coming up. Kelly and others near to the ring began to cry out to the police to stop it, though Danny's corner refused to throw in the towel. Rivera saw the fat police captain starting awkwardly to climb through the ropes, and was not sure what it meant. There were so many ways of cheating in this game of the Gringos. Danny, on his feet, tottered groggily and helplessly before him. The referee and the captain were both reaching for Rivera when he struck the last blow. There was no need to stop the fight, for Danny did not rise.

"Count!" Rivera cried hoarsely to the referee.

And when the count was finished, Danny's seconds gathered him up and carried him to his corner.

"Who wins?" Rivera demanded.

Reluctantly, the referee caught his gloved hand and held it aloft.

There were no congratulations for Rivera. He walked to his corner unattended, where his seconds had not yet placed his stool. He leaned backward on the ropes and looked his hatred at them, swept it on and about him till the whole ten thousand Gringos were included. His knees trembled under him, and he was sobbing from exhaustion. Before his eyes the hated faces swayed back and forth in the giddiness of nausea. Then he remembered they were the guns. The guns were his. The Revolution could go on.

THE STRENGTH OF THE STRONG

THE STRENGTH OF THE STRONG

Parables don't lie, but liars will parable.

—*Lip-King.*

Old Long-Beard paused in his narrative, licked his greasy fingers, and wiped them on his naked sides where his one piece of ragged bearskin failed to cover him. Crouched around him, on their hams, were three young men, his grandsons, Deer-Runner, Yellow-Head, and Afraid-of-the-Dark. In appearance they were much the same. Skins of wild animals partly covered them. They were lean and meagre of build, narrow-hipped and crooked-legged, and at the same time deep-chested, with heavy arms and enormous hands. There was much hair on their chests and shoulders, and on the outsides of their arms and legs. Their heads were matted with uncut hair, long locks of which often strayed before their eyes, beady and black and glittering like the eyes of birds. They were narrow between the eyes and broad between the cheeks, while their lower jaws were projecting and massive.

It was a night of clear starlight, and below them, stretching away remotely, lay range on range of forest-covered hills. In the distance the heavens were red from the glow of a volcano. At their backs yawned the black mouth of a cave, out of which, from time to time, blew draughty gusts of wind. Immediately in front of them blazed a fire. At one side, partly devoured, lay the carcass of a bear, with about it, at a respectable distance, several large dogs, shaggy and wolf-like. Beside each man lay his bow and arrows and a huge club. In the cave-mouth a number of rude spears leaned against the rock.

"So that was how we moved from the cave to the tree," old Long-Beard spoke up.

They laughed boisterously, like big children, at recollection of a previous story his words called up. Long-Beard laughed, too, the five-inch bodkin of bone, thrust midway through the cartilage of his nose, leaping and dancing and adding to his ferocious appearance. He did not exactly say the words recorded, but he made animal-like sounds with his mouth that meant the same thing.

"And that is the first I remember of the Sea Valley," Long-Beard went on. "We were a very foolish crowd. We did not know the secret of strength. For, behold, each family lived by itself, and took care of itself. There were thirty families, but we got no strength from one another. We were in fear of each other all the time. No one ever paid visits. In the top of our tree we built a grass house, and on the platform outside was a pile of rocks, which were for the heads of any that might chance to try to visit us. Also, we had our spears and arrows. We never walked under the trees of the other families, either. My brother did, once, under old Boo-oogh's tree, and he got his head broken and that was the end of him.

"Old Boo-oogh was very strong. It was said he could pull a grown man's head right off. I never heard of him doing it, because no man would give him a chance. Father wouldn't. One day, when father was down on the beach, Boo-oogh took after mother. She couldn't run fast, for the day before she had got her leg clawed by a bear when she was up on the mountain gathering berries. So Boo-oogh caught her and carried her up into his tree. Father never got her back. He was afraid. Old Boo-oogh made faces at him.

"But father did not mind. Strong-Arm was another strong man. He was one of the best fishermen. But one day, climbing after sea-gull eggs, he had a fall from the cliff. He was never strong after that. He coughed a great deal, and his shoulders drew near to each other. So father took Strong-Arm's wife. When he came around and coughed under our tree, father laughed at him and threw rocks at him. It was our way in those days. We did not know how to add strength together and become strong."

"Would a brother take a brother's wife?" Deer-Runner demanded.

"Yes, if he had gone to live in another tree by himself."

"But we do not do such things now," Afraid-of-the-Dark objected.

"It is because I have taught your fathers better." Long-Beard thrust his hairy paw into the bear meat and drew out a handful of suet, which he sucked with a meditative air. Again he wiped his hands on his naked sides and went on. "What I am telling you happened in the long ago, before we knew any better."

"You must have been fools not to know better," was Deer-Runner's comment, Yellow-Head grunting approval.

"So we were, but we became bigger fools, as you shall see. Still, we did learn better, and this was the way of it. We Fish-Eaters had not learned to add our strength until our strength was the strength of all of us. But the Meat-Eaters, who lived across the divide in the Big Valley, stood together, hunted together, fished together, and fought together. One day they came into our valley. Each family of us got into its own cave and tree. There were only ten Meat-Eaters, but they fought together, and we fought, each family by itself."

Long-Beard counted long and perplexedly on his fingers.

"There were sixty men of us," was what he managed to say with fingers and lips combined. "And we were very strong, only we did not know it. So we watched the ten men attack Boo-oogh's tree. He made a good fight, but he had no chance. We looked on. When some of the Meat-Eaters tried to climb the tree, Boo-oogh had to show himself in order to drop stones on their heads, whereupon the other Meat-Eaters, who were waiting for that very thing, shot him full of arrows. And that was the end of Boo-oogh.

"Next, the Meat-Eaters got One-Eye and his family in his cave. They built a fire in the mouth and smoked him out, like we smoked out the bear there to-day. Then they went after Six-Fingers, up his tree, and, while they were killing him and his grown son, the rest of us ran away. They caught some of our women, and killed two old men who could not run fast and several children. The women they carried away with them to the Big Valley.

"After that the rest of us crept back, and, somehow, perhaps because we were in fear and felt the need for one another, we talked the thing over. It was our first council—our first real council. And in that council we formed our first tribe. For we had learned the lesson. Of the ten Meat-Eaters, each man had had the strength of ten, for the ten had fought as one man. They had added their strength together. But of the thirty families and the sixty men of us, we had had the strength of but one man, for each had fought alone.

"It was a great talk we had, and it was hard talk, for we did not have the words then as now with which to talk. The Bug made some of the words long afterward, and so did others of us make words from time to time. But in the end we agreed to add our strength together and to be as one man when the Meat-Eaters came over the divide to steal our women. And that was the tribe.

"We set two men on the divide, one for the day and one for the night, to watch if the Meat-Eaters came. These were the eyes of the tribe. Then, also, day and night, there were to be ten men awake with their clubs and spears and arrows in their hands, ready to fight. Before, when a man went after fish, or clams, or gull-eggs, he carried his weapons with him, and half the time he was getting food and half the time watching for fear some other man would get him. Now that was all changed. The men went out without their weapons and spent all their time getting food. Likewise, when the women went into the mountains after roots and berries, five of the ten men went with them to guard them. While all the time, day and night, the eyes of the tribe watched from the top of the divide.

"But troubles came. As usual, it was about the women. Men without wives wanted other men's wives, and there was much fighting between men, and now and again one got his head smashed or a spear through his body. While one of the watchers was on top of the divide, another man stole his wife, and he came down to fight. Then the other watcher was in fear that some one would take his wife, and he came down likewise. Also, there was trouble among the ten men who carried always their weapons, and they fought five against five, till some ran away down the coast and the others ran after them.

"So it was that the tribe was left without eyes or guards. We had not the strength of sixty. We had no strength at all. So we held a council and made our first laws. I was but a cub at the time, but I remember. We said that, in order to be strong, we must not fight one another, and we made a law that when a man killed another him would the tribe kill. We made another law that whoso stole another man's wife him would the tribe kill. We said that whatever man had too great strength, and by that strength hurt his brothers in the tribe, him would we kill that his strength might hurt no more. For, if we let his strength hurt, the brothers would become afraid and the tribe would fall apart, and we would be as weak as when the Meat-Eaters first came upon us and killed Boo-oogh.

"Knuckle-Bone was a strong man, a very strong man, and he knew not law. He knew only his own strength, and in the fullness thereof he went forth and took the wife of Three-Clams. Three-Clams tried to fight, but Knuckle-Bone clubbed out his brains. Yet had Knuckle-Bone forgotten that all the men of us had added our strength to keep the law among us, and him we killed, at the foot of his tree, and hung his body on a branch as a warning that the law was stronger than any man. For we were the law, all of us, and no man was greater than the law.

"Then there were other troubles, for know, O Deer-Runner, and Yellow-Head, and Afraid-of-the-Dark, that it is not easy to make a tribe. There were many things, little things, that it was a great trouble to call all the men together to have a council about. We were having councils morning, noon, and night, and in the middle of the night. We could find little time to go out and get food, because of the councils, for there was always some little thing to be settled, such as naming two new watchers to take the place of the old ones on the hill, or naming how much food should fall to the share of the men who kept their weapons always in their hands and got no food for themselves.

"We stood in need of a chief man to do these things, who would be the voice of the council, and who would account to the council for the things he did. So we named Fith-Fith the chief man. He was a strong man, too, and very cunning, and when he was angry he made noises just like that, *fith-fith*, like a wild-cat.

"The ten men who guarded the tribe were set to work making a wall of stones across the narrow part of the valley. The women and large children helped, as did other men, until the wall was strong. After that, all the families came down out of their caves and trees and built grass houses behind the shelter of the wall. These houses were large and much better than the caves

171

and trees, and everybody had a better time of it because the men had added their strength together and become a tribe. Because of the wall and the guards and the watchers, there was more time to hunt and fish and pick roots and berries; there was more food, and better food, and no one went hungry. And Three-Legs, so named because his legs had been smashed when a boy and who walked with a stick—Three-Legs got the seed of the wild corn and planted it in the ground in the valley near his house. Also, he tried planting fat roots and other things he found in the mountain valleys.

"Because of the safety in the Sea Valley, which was because of the wall and the watchers and the guards, and because there was food in plenty for all without having to fight for it, many families came in from the coast valleys on both sides and from the high back mountains where they had lived more like wild animals than men. And it was not long before the Sea Valley filled up, and in it were countless families. But, before this happened, the land, which had been free to all and belonged to all, was divided up. Three-Legs began it when he planted corn. But most of us did not care about the land. We thought the marking of the boundaries with fences of stone was a foolishness. We had plenty to eat, and what more did we want? I remember that my father and I built stone fences for Three-Legs and were given corn in return.

"So only a few got all the land, and Three-Legs got most of it. Also, others that had taken land gave it to the few that held on, being paid in return with corn and fat roots, and bear-skins, and fishes which the farmers got from the fishermen in exchange for corn. And, the first thing we knew, all the land was gone.

"It was about this time that Fith-Fith died and Dog-Tooth, his son, was made chief. He demanded to be made chief anyway, because his father had been chief before him. Also, he looked upon himself as a greater chief than his father. He was a good chief at first, and worked hard, so that the council had less and less to do. Then arose a new voice in the Sea Valley. It was Twisted-Lip. We had never thought much of him, until he began to talk with the spirits of the dead. Later we called him Big-Fat, because he ate over-much, and did no work, and grew round and large. One day Big-Fat told us that the secrets of the dead were his, and that he was the voice of God. He became great friends with Dog-Tooth, who commanded that we should build Big-Fat a grass house. And Big-Fat put taboos all around this house and kept God inside.

"More and more Dog-Tooth became greater than the council, and when the council grumbled and said it would name a new chief, Big-Fat spoke with the voice of God and said no. Also, Three-Legs and the others who held the land stood behind Dog-Tooth. Moreover, the strongest man in the council was Sea-Lion, and him the land-owners gave land to secretly, along with many bearskins and baskets of corn. So Sea-Lion said that Big-Fat's voice was truly the voice of God and must be obeyed. And soon afterward Sea-Lion was named the voice of Dog-Tooth and did most of his talking for him.

"Then there was Little-Belly, a little man, so thin in the middle that he looked as if he had never had enough to eat. Inside the mouth of the river, after the sand-bar had combed the strength of the breakers, he built a big fish-trap. No man had ever seen or dreamed a fish-trap before. He worked weeks on it, with his son and his wife, while the rest of us laughed at their labours. But, when it was done, the first day he caught more fish in it than could the whole tribe in a week, whereat there was great rejoicing. There was only one other place in the river for a fish-trap, but, when my father and I and a dozen other men started to make a very large trap, the guards came from the big grass-house we had built for Dog-Tooth. And the guards poked us with their spears and told us begone, because Little-Belly was going to build a trap there himself on the word of Sea-Lion, who was the voice of Dog-Tooth.

"There was much grumbling, and my father called a council. But, when he rose to speak, him the Sea-Lion thrust through the throat with a spear and he died. And Dog-Tooth and Little-Belly, and Three-Legs and all that held land said it was good. And Big-Fat said it was the will of God. And after that all men were afraid to stand up in the council, and there was no more council.

"Another man, Pig-Jaw, began to keep goats. He had heard about it as among the Meat-Eaters, and it was not long before he had many flocks. Other men, who had no land and no fish-traps, and who else would have gone hungry, were glad to work for Pig-Jaw, caring for his goats, guarding them from wild dogs and tigers, and driving them to the feeding pastures in the mountains. In return, Pig-Jaw gave them goat-meat to eat and goat-skins to wear, and sometimes they traded the goat-meat for fish and corn and fat roots.

"It was this time that money came to be. Sea-Lion was the man who first thought of it, and he talked it over with Dog-Tooth and Big-Fat. You see, these three were the ones that got a share of everything in the Sea Valley. One basket out of every three of corn was theirs, one fish out of every three, one goat out of every three. In return, they fed the guards and the watchers, and kept the rest for themselves. Sometimes, when a big haul of fish was made they did not know what to do with all their share. So Sea-Lion set the women to making money out of shell—little round pieces, with a hole in each one, and all made smooth and fine. These were strung on strings, and the strings were called money.

"Each string was of the value of thirty fish, or forty fish, but the women, who made a string a day, were given two fish each. The fish came out of the shares of Dog-Tooth, Big-Fat, and Sea-Lion, which they three did not eat. So all the money belonged to them. Then they told Three-Legs and the other land-owners that they would take their share of corn and roots in money, Little-Belly that they would take their share of fish in money, Pig-Jaw that they would take their share of goats and cheese in money. Thus, a man who had nothing, worked for one who had, and was paid in money. With this money he bought corn, and fish, and meat, and cheese. And Three-Legs and all owners of things paid Dog-Tooth and Sea-Lion and Big-Fat their share in money. And they paid the guards and watchers in money, and the guards and watchers bought their food with the money. And, because money was cheap, Dog-Tooth made many more men into guards. And, because money was cheap to make, a number of men began to make money out of shell themselves. But the guards stuck spears in them and shot them full of arrows, because they were trying to break up the tribe. It was bad to break up the tribe, for then the Meat-Eaters would come over the divide and kill them all.

"Big-Fat was the voice of God, but he took Broken-Rib and made him into a priest, so that he became the voice of Big-Fat and did most of his talking for him. And both had other men to be servants to them. So, also, did Little-Belly and Three-Legs and Pig-Jaw have other men to lie in the sun about their grass houses and carry messages for them and give commands. And more and more were men taken away from work, so that those that were left worked harder than ever before. It seemed that men desired to do no work and strove to seek out other ways whereby men should work for them. Crooked-Eyes found such a way. He made the first fire-brew out of corn. And thereafter he worked no more, for he talked secretly with Dog-Tooth and Big-Fat and the other masters, and it was agreed that he should be the only one to make fire-brew. But Crooked-Eyes did no work himself. Men made the brew for him, and he paid them in money. Then he sold the fire-brew for money, and all men bought. And many strings of money did he give Dog-Tooth and Sea-Lion and all of them.

"Big-Fat and Broken-Rib stood by Dog-Tooth when he took his second wife, and his third wife. They said Dog-Tooth was different from other men and second only to God that Big-Fat kept in his taboo house, and Dog-Tooth said so, too, and wanted to know who were they to grumble about how many wives he took. Dog-Tooth had a big canoe made, and, many more men he took from work, who did nothing and lay in the sun, save only when Dog-Tooth went in the canoe, when they paddled for him. And he made Tiger-Face head man over all the guards, so that Tiger-Face became his right arm, and when he did not like a man Tiger-Face killed that man for him. And Tiger-Face, also, made another man to be his right arm, and to give commands, and to kill for him.

"But this was the strange thing: as the days went by we who were left worked harder and harder, and yet did we get less and less to eat."

"But what of the goats and the corn and the fat roots and the fish-trap?" spoke up Afraid-of-the-Dark, "what of all this? Was there not more food to be gained by man's work?"

"It is so," Long-Beard agreed. "Three men on the fish-trap got more fish than the whole tribe before there was a fish-trap. But have I not said we were fools? The more food we were able to get, the less food did we have to eat."

"But was it not plain that the many men who did not work ate it all up?" Yellow-Head demanded.

Long-Beard nodded his head sadly.

"Dog-Tooth's dogs were stuffed with meat, and the men who lay in the sun and did no work were rolling in fat, and, at the same time, there were little children crying themselves to sleep with hunger biting them with every wail."

Deer-Runner was spurred by the recital of famine to tear out a chunk of bear-meat and broil it on a stick over the coals. This he devoured with smacking lips, while Long-Beard went on:

"When we grumbled Big-Fat arose, and with the voice of God said that God had chosen the wise men to own the land and the goats and the fish-trap, and the fire-brew, and that without these wise men we would all be animals, as in the days when we lived in trees.

"And there arose one who became a singer of songs for the king. Him they called the Bug, because he was small and ungainly of face and limb and excelled not in work or deed. He loved the fattest marrow bones, the choicest fish, the milk warm from the goats, the first corn that was ripe, and the snug place by the fire. And thus, becoming singer of songs to the king, he found a way to do nothing and be fat. And when the people grumbled more and more, and some threw stones at the king's grass house, the Bug sang a song of how good it was to be a Fish-Eater. In his song he told that the Fish-Eaters were the chosen of God and the finest men God had made. He sang of the Meat-Eaters as pigs and crows, and sang how fine and good it was for the Fish-Eaters to fight and die doing God's work, which was the killing of Meat-Eaters. The words of his song were like fire in us, and we clamoured to be led against the Meat-Eaters. And we forgot that we were hungry, and why we had grumbled, and were glad to be led by Tiger-Face over the divide, where we killed many Meat-Eaters and were content.

"But things were no better in the Sea Valley. The only way to get food was to work for Three-Legs or Little-Belly or Pig-Jaw; for there was no land that a man might plant with corn for himself. And often there were more men than Three-Legs and the others had work for. So these men went hungry, and so did their wives and children and their old mothers. Tiger-Face said they could become guards if they wanted to, and many of them did, and thereafter they did no work except to poke spears in the men who did work and who grumbled at feeding so many idlers.

"And when we grumbled, ever the Bug sang new songs. He said that Three-Legs and Pig-Jaw and the rest were strong men, and that that was why they had so much. He said that we should be glad to have strong men with us, else would we perish of our own worthlessness and the Meat-Eaters. Therefore, we should be glad to let such strong men have all they could lay hands on. And Big-Fat and Pig-Jaw and Tiger-Face and all the rest said it was true.

"'All right,' said Long-Fang, 'then will I, too, be a strong man.' And he got himself corn, and began to make fire-brew and sell it for strings of money. And, when Crooked-Eyes complained, Long-Fang said that he was himself a strong man, and that if Crooked-Eyes made any more noise he would bash his brains out for him. Whereat Crooked-Eyes was afraid and went and talked with Three-Legs and Pig-Jaw. And all three went and talked to Dog-Tooth. And Dog-Tooth spoke to Sea-Lion, and Sea-Lion sent a runner with a message to Tiger-Face. And Tiger-Face sent his guards, who burned Long-Fang's house along with the fire-brew he had made. Also, they killed him and all his family. And Big-Fat said it was good, and the Bug sang another song about how good it was to observe the law, and what a fine land the Sea Valley was, and how every man who loved the Sea Valley should go forth and kill the bad Meat-Eaters. And again his song was as fire to us, and we forgot to grumble.

"It was very strange. When Little-Belly caught too many fish, so that it took a great many to sell for a little money, he threw many of the fish back into the sea, so that more money would be paid for what was left. And Three-Legs often let many large fields lie idle so as to get more money for his corn. And the women, making so much money out of shell that much money was needed to buy with, Dog-Tooth stopped the making of money. And the women had no work, so they took the places of the men. I worked on the fish-trap, getting a string of money every five days. But my sister now did my work, getting a string of money for every ten days. The women worked cheaper, and there was less food, and Tiger-Face said we should become guards. Only I could not become a guard because I was lame of one leg and Tiger-Face would not have me. And there were many like me. We were broken men and only fit to beg for work or to take care of the babies while the women worked."

Yellow-Head, too, was made hungry by the recital and broiled a piece of bear-meat on the coals.

"But why didn't you rise up, all of you, and kill Three-Legs and Pig-Jaw and Big-Fat and the rest and get enough to eat?" Afraid-in-the-Dark demanded.

"Because we could not understand," Long-Beard answered. "There was too much to think about, and, also, there were the guards sticking spears into us, and Big-Fat talking about God, and the Bug singing new songs. And when any man did think right, and said so, Tiger-Face and the guards got him, and he was tied out to the rocks at low tide so that the rising waters drowned him.

"It was a strange thing—the money. It was like the Bug's songs. It seemed all right, but it wasn't, and we were slow to understand. Dog-Tooth began to gather the money in. He put it in a big pile, in a grass house, with guards to watch it day and night. And the more money he piled in the house the dearer money became, so that a man worked a longer time for a string of money than before. Then, too, there was always talk of war with the Meat-Eaters, and Dog-Tooth and Tiger-Face filled many houses with corn, and dried fish, and smoked goat-meat, and cheese. And with the food, piled there in mountains the people had not enough to eat. But what did it matter? Whenever the people grumbled too loudly the Bug sang a new song, and Big-Fat said it was God's word that we should kill Meat-Eaters, and Tiger-Face led us over the divide to kill and be killed. I was not good enough to be a guard and lie fat in the sun, but, when we made war, Tiger-Face was glad to take me along. And when we had eaten, all the food stored in the houses we stopped fighting and went back to work to pile up more food."

"Then were you all crazy," commented Deer-Runner.

"Then were we indeed all crazy," Long-Beard agreed. "It was strange, all of it. There was Split-Nose. He said everything was wrong. He said it was true that we grew strong by adding our strength together. And he said that, when we first formed the tribe, it was right that the men whose strength hurt the tribe should be shorn of their strength—men who bashed their brothers' heads and stole their brothers' wives. And now, he said, the tribe was not getting stronger, but was getting weaker, because there were men with another kind of strength that were hurting the tribe—men who had the strength of the land, like Three-Legs; who had the strength of the fish-trap, like Little-Belly; who had the strength of all the goat-meat, like Pig-Jaw. The thing to do, Split-Nose said, was to shear these men of their evil strength; to make them go to work, all of them, and to let no man eat who did not work.

"And the Bug sang another song about men like Split-Nose, who wanted to go back, and live in trees.

"Yet Split-Nose said no; that he did not want to go back, but ahead; that they grew strong only as they added their strength together; and that, if the Fish-Eaters would add their strength to the Meat-Eaters, there would be no more fighting and no more watchers and no more guards, and that, with all men working, there would be so much food that each man would have to work not more than two hours a day.

"Then the Bug sang again, and he sang that Split-Nose was lazy, and he sang also the 'Song of the Bees.' It was a strange song, and those who listened were made mad, as from the drinking of strong fire-brew. The song was of a swarm of bees, and of a robber wasp who had come in to live with the bees and who was stealing all their honey. The wasp was lazy and told them there was no need to work; also, he told them to make friends with the bears, who were not honey-stealers but only very good friends. And the Bug sang in crooked words, so that those who listened knew that the swarm was the Sea Valley tribe, that the bears were the Meat-Eaters, and that the lazy wasp was

Split-Nose. And when the Bug sang that the bees listened to the wasp till the swarm was near to perishing, the people growled and snarled, and when the Bug sang that at last the good bees arose and stung the wasp to death, the people picked up stones from the ground and stoned Split-Nose to death till there was naught to be seen of him but the heap of stones they had flung on top of him. And there were many poor people who worked long and hard and had not enough to eat that helped throw the stones on Split-Nose.

"And, after the death of Split-Nose, there was but one other man that dared rise up and speak his mind, and that man was Hair-Face. 'Where is the strength of the strong?' he asked. 'We are the strong, all of us, and we are stronger than Dog-Tooth and Tiger-Face and Three-Legs and Pig-Jaw and all the rest who do nothing and eat much and weaken us by the hurt of their strength which is bad strength. Men who are slaves are not strong. If the man who first found the virtue and use of fire had used his strength we would have been his slaves, as we are the slaves to-day of Little-Belly, who found the virtue and use of the fish-trap; and of the men who found the virtue and use of the land, and the goats, and the fire-brew. Before, we lived in trees, my brothers, and no man was safe. But we fight no more with one another. We have added our strength together. Then let us fight no more with the Meat-Eaters. Let us add our strength and their strength together. Then will we be indeed strong. And then we will go out together, the Fish-Eaters and the Meat-Eaters, and we will kill the tigers and the lions and the wolves and the wild dogs, and we will pasture our goats on all the hill-sides and plant our corn and fat roots in all the high mountain valleys. In that day we will be so strong that all the wild animals will flee before us and perish. And nothing will withstand us, for the strength of each man will be the strength of all men in the world.'

"So said Hair-Face, and they killed him, because, they said, he was a wild man and wanted to go back and live in a tree. It was very strange. Whenever a man arose and wanted to go forward all those that stood still said he went backward and should be killed. And the poor people helped stone him, and were fools. We were all fools, except those who were fat and did no work. The fools were called wise, and the wise were stoned. Men who worked did not get enough to eat, and the men who did not work ate too much.

"And the tribe went on losing strength. The children were weak and sickly. And, because we ate not enough, strange sicknesses came among us and we died like flies. And then the Meat-Eaters came upon us. We had followed Tiger-Face too often over the divide and killed them. And now they came to repay in blood. We were too weak and sick to man the big wall. And they killed us, all of us, except some of the women, which they took away with them. The Bug and I escaped, and I hid in the wildest places, and became a hunter of meat and went hungry no more. I stole a wife from the Meat-Eaters, and went to live in the caves of the high mountains where they could not find me. And we had three sons, and each son stole a wife from the Meat-Eaters. And the rest you know, for are you not the sons of my sons?"

"But the Bug?" queried Deer-Runner. "What became of him?"

"He went to live with the Meat-Eaters and to be a singer of songs to the king. He is an old man now, but he sings the same old songs; and, when a man rises up to go forward, he sings that that man is walking backward to live in a tree."

Long-Beard dipped into the bear-carcass and sucked with toothless gums at a fist of suet.

"Some day," he said, wiping his hands on his sides, "all the fools will be dead and then all live men will go forward. The strength of the strong will be theirs, and they will add their strength together, so that, of all the men in the world, not one will fight with another. There will be no guards nor watchers on the walls. And all the hunting animals will be killed, and, as Hair-Face said, all the hill-sides will be pastured with goats and all the high mountain valleys will be planted with corn and fat roots. And all men will be brothers, and no man will lie idle in the sun and be fed by his fellows. And all that will come to pass in the time when the fools are dead, and when there will be no more singers to stand still and sing the 'Song of the Bees.' Bees are not men."

SOUTH OF THE SLOT

Old San Francisco, which is the San Francisco of only the other day, the day before the Earthquake, was divided midway by the Slot. The Slot was an iron crack that ran along the centre of Market Street, and from the Slot arose the burr of the ceaseless, endless cable that was hitched at will to the cars it dragged up and down. In truth, there were two slots, but in the quick grammar of the West time was saved by calling them, and much more that they stood for, "The Slot." North of the Slot were the theatres, hotels, and shopping district, the banks and the staid, respectable business houses. South of the Slot were the factories, slums, laundries, machine-shops, boiler works, and the abodes of the working class.

The Slot was the metaphor that expressed the class cleavage of Society, and no man crossed this metaphor, back and forth, more successfully than Freddie Drummond. He made a practice of living in both worlds, and in both worlds he lived signally well. Freddie Drummond was a professor in the Sociology Department of the University of California, and it was as a professor of sociology that he first crossed over the Slot, lived for six mouths in the great labour-ghetto, and wrote *The Unskilled Labourer*—a book that was hailed everywhere as an able contribution to the literature of progress, and as a splendid reply to the literature of discontent. Politically and economically it was nothing if not orthodox. Presidents of great railway systems bought whole editions of it to give to their employees. The Manufacturers' Association alone distributed fifty thousand copies of it. In a way, it was almost as immoral as the far-famed and notorious *Message to Garcia*, while in its pernicious preachment of thrift and content it ran Mr. *Wiggs of the Cabbage Patch* a close second.

At first, Freddie Drummond found it monstrously difficult to get along among the working people. He was not used to their ways, and they certainly were not used to his. They were suspicious. He had no antecedents. He could talk of no previous jobs. His hands were soft. His extraordinary politeness was ominous. His first idea of the rôle he would play was that of a free and independent American who chose to work with his hands and no explanations given. But it wouldn't do, as he quickly discovered. At the beginning they accepted him, very provisionally, as a freak. A little later, as he began to know his way about better, he insensibly drifted into the rôle that would work—namely, he was a man who had seen better days, very much better days, but who was down on his luck, though, to be sure, only temporarily.

He learned many things, and generalized much and often erroneously, all of which can be found in the pages of *The Unskilled Labourer*. He saved himself, however, after the sane and conservative manner of his kind, by labelling his generalizations as "tentative." One of his first experiences was in the great Wilmax Cannery, where he was put on piece-work making small packing cases. A box factory supplied the parts, and all Freddie Drummond had to do was to fit the parts into a form and drive in the wire nails with a light hammer.

It was not skilled labour, but it was piece-work. The ordinary labourers in the cannery got a dollar and a half per day. Freddie Drummond found the other men on the same job with him jogging along and earning a dollar and seventy-five cents a day. By the third day he was able to earn the same. But he was ambitious. He did not care to jog along and, being unusually able and fit, on the fourth day earned two dollars.

The next day, having keyed himself up to an exhausting high-tension, he earned two dollars and a half. His fellow workers favoured him with scowls and black looks, and made remarks, slangily witty and which he did not understand, about sucking up to the boss and pace-making and holding her down, when the rains set in. He was astonished at their malingering on piece-work, generalized about the inherent laziness of *the unskilled labourer*, and proceeded next day to hammer out three dollars' worth of boxes.

And that night, coming out of the cannery, he was interviewed by his fellow workmen, who were very angry and incoherently slangy. He failed to comprehend the motive behind their action. The action itself was strenuous.

When he refused to ease down his pace and bleated about freedom of contract, independent Americanism, and the dignity of toil, they proceeded to spoil his pace-making ability. It was a fierce battle, for Drummond was a large man and an athlete, but the crowd finally jumped on his ribs, walked on his face, and stamped on his fingers, so that it was only after lying in bed for a week that he was able to get up and look for another job. All of which is duly narrated in that first book of his, in the chapter entitled "The Tyranny of Labour."

A little later, in another department of the Wilmax Cannery, lumping as a fruit-distributor among the women, he essayed to carry two boxes of fruit at a time, and was promptly reproached by the other fruit-lumpers. It was palpable malingering; but he was there, he decided, not to change conditions, but to observe. So he lumped one box thereafter, and so well did he study the art of shirking that he wrote a special chapter on it, with the last several paragraphs devoted to tentative generalizations.

In those six months he worked at many jobs and developed into a very good imitation of a genuine worker. He was a natural linguist, and he kept notebooks, making a scientific study of the workers' slang or argot, until he could talk quite intelligibly. This language also enabled him more intimately to follow their mental processes, and thereby to gather much data for a projected chapter in some future book which he planned to entitle *Synthesis of Working-Class Psychology*.

Before he arose to the surface from that first plunge into the underworld he discovered that he was a good actor and demonstrated the plasticity of his nature. He was himself astonished at his own fluidity. Once having mastered the language and conquered numerous fastidious qualms, he found that he could flow into any nook of working-class life and fit it so snugly as to feel comfortably at home. As he said, in the preface to his second book, *The Toiler*, he endeavoured really to know the working people, and the only possible way to achieve this was to work beside them, eat their food, sleep in their beds, be amused with their amusements, think their thoughts, and feel their feeling.

He was not a deep thinker. He had no faith in new theories. All his norms and criteria were conventional. His Thesis on the French Revolution was noteworthy in college annals, not merely for its painstaking and voluminous accuracy, but for the fact that it was the dryest, deadest, most formal, and most orthodox screed ever written on the subject. He was a very reserved man, and his natural inhibition was large in quantity and steel-like in quality. He had but few friends. He was too undemonstrative, too frigid. He had no vices, nor had any one ever discovered any temptations. Tobacco he detested, beer he abhorred, and he was never known to drink anything stronger than an occasional light wine at dinner.

When a freshman he had been baptized "Ice-Box" by his warmer-blooded fellows. As a member of the faculty he was known as "Cold-Storage." He had but one grief, and that was "Freddie." He had earned it when he played full-back in the 'Varsity eleven, and his formal soul had never succeeded in living it down. "Freddie" he would ever be, except officially, and through nightmare vistas he looked into a future when his world would speak of him as "Old Freddie."

For he was very young to be a doctor of sociology, only twenty-seven, and he looked younger. In appearance and atmosphere he was a strapping big college man, smooth-faced and easy-mannered, clean and simple and wholesome, with a known record of being a splendid athlete and an implied vast possession of cold culture of the inhibited sort. He never talked shop out of class and committee rooms, except later on, when his books showered him with distasteful public notice and he yielded to the extent of reading occasional papers before certain literary and economic societies.

He did everything right—too right; and in dress and comportment was inevitably correct. Not that he was a dandy. Far from it. He was a college man, in dress and carriage as like as a pea to the type that of late years is being so generously turned out of our institutions of higher learning. His handshake was satisfyingly strong and stiff. His blue eyes were coldly blue and convincingly sincere. His voice, firm and masculine, clean and crisp of enunciation, was pleasant to the ear. The one drawback to Freddie Drummond was his inhibition. He never unbent. In his football days, the higher the tension of the game, the cooler he grew. He was noted as a boxer, but he was regarded as an automaton, with the inhuman precision of a machine judging distance and timing blows, guarding, blocking, and stalling. He was rarely punished himself, while he rarely punished an opponent. He was too clever and too controlled to permit himself to put a pound more weight into a punch than he intended. With him it was a matter of exercise. It kept him fit.

As time went by, Freddie Drummond found himself more frequently crossing the Slot and losing himself in South of Market. His summer and winter holidays were spent there, and, whether it was a week or a week-end, he found the time spent there to be valuable and enjoyable. And there was so much material to be gathered. His third book, *Mass and Master*, became a text-book in the American universities; and almost before he knew it, he was at work on a fourth one, *The Fallacy of the Inefficient*.

Somewhere in his make-up there was a strange twist or quirk. Perhaps it was a recoil from his environment and training, or from the tempered seed of his ancestors, who had been book-men generation preceding generation; but at any rate, he found enjoyment in being down in the working-class world. In his own world he was "Cold-Storage," but down below he was "Big" Bill Totts, who could drink and smoke, and slang and fight, and be an all-round favourite. Everybody liked Bill, and more than one working girl made love to him. At first he had been merely a good actor, but as time went on, simulation became second nature. He no longer played a part, and he loved sausages, sausages and bacon, than which, in his own proper sphere, there was nothing more loathsome in the way of food.

From doing the thing for the need's sake, he came to doing the thing for the thing's sake. He found himself regretting as the time drew near for him to go back to his lecture-room and his inhibition. And he often found himself waiting with anticipation for the dreamy time to pass when he could cross the Slot and cut loose and play the devil. He was not wicked, but as "Big" Bill Totts he did a myriad things that Freddie Drummond would never have been permitted to do. Moreover, Freddie Drummond never would have wanted to do them. That was the strangest part of his discovery. Freddie

Drummond and Bill Totts were two totally different creatures. The desires and tastes and impulses of each ran counter to the other's. Bill Totts could shirk at a job with clear conscience, while Freddie Drummond condemned shirking as vicious, criminal, and un-American, and devoted whole chapters to condemnation of the vice. Freddie Drummond did not care for dancing, but Bill Totts never missed the nights at the various dancing clubs, such as The Magnolia, The Western Star, and The Elite; while he won a massive silver cup, standing thirty inches high, for being the best-sustained character at the Butchers and Meat Workers' annual grand masked ball. And Bill Totts liked the girls and the girls liked him, while Freddie Drummond enjoyed playing the ascetic in this particular, was open in his opposition to equal suffrage, and cynically bitter in his secret condemnation of coeducation.

Freddie Drummond changed his manners with his dress, and without effort. When he entered the obscure little room used for his transformation scenes, he carried himself just a bit too stiffly. He was too erect, his shoulders were an inch too far back, while his face was grave, almost harsh, and practically expressionless. But when he emerged in Bill Totts' clothes he was another creature. Bill Totts did not slouch, but somehow his whole form limbered up and became graceful. The very sound of the voice was changed, and the laugh was loud and hearty, while loose speech and an occasional oath were as a matter of course on his lips. Also, Bill Totts was a trifle inclined to late hours, and at times, in saloons, to be good-naturedly bellicose with other workmen. Then, too, at Sunday picnics or when coming home from the show, either arm betrayed a practised familiarity in stealing around girls' waists, while he displayed a wit keen and delightful in the flirtatious badinage that was expected of a good fellow in his class.

So thoroughly was Bill Totts himself, so thoroughly a workman, a genuine denizen of South of the Slot, that he was as class-conscious as the average of his kind, and his hatred for a scab even exceeded that of the average loyal union man. During the Water Front Strike, Freddie Drummond was somehow able to stand apart from the unique combination, and, coldly critical, watch Bill Totts hilariously slug scab longshoremen. For Bill Totts was a dues-paying member of the Longshoremen Union and had a right to be indignant with the usurpers of his job. "Big" Bill Totts was so very big, and so very able, that it was "Big" Bill to the front when trouble was brewing. From acting outraged feelings, Freddie Drummond, in the rôle of his other self, came to experience genuine outrage, and it was only when he returned to the classic atmosphere of the university that he was able, sanely and conservatively, to generalize upon his underworld experiences and put them down on paper as a trained sociologist should. That Bill Totts lacked the perspective to raise him above class-consciousness Freddie Drummond clearly saw. But Bill Totts could not see it. When he saw a scab taking his job away, he saw red at the same time, and little else did he see. It was Freddie Drummond, irreproachably clothed and comported, seated at his study desk or facing his class in *Sociology* 17, who saw Bill Totts, and all around Bill Totts, and all around the whole scab and union-labour problem and its relation to the economic welfare of the United States in the struggle for the world market. Bill Totts really wasn't able to see beyond the next meal and the prize-fight the following night at the Gaiety Athletic Club.

It was while gathering material for *Women and Work* that Freddie received his first warning of the danger he was in. He was too successful at living in both worlds. This strange dualism he had developed was after all very unstable, and, as he sat in his study and meditated, he saw that it could not endure. It was really a transition stage, and if he persisted he saw that he would inevitably have to drop one world or the other. He could not continue in both. And as he looked at the row of volumes that graced the upper shelf of his revolving book-case, his volumes, beginning with his Thesis and ending with *Women and Work*, he decided that that was the world he would hold to and stick by. Bill Totts had served his purpose, but he had become a too dangerous accomplice. Bill Totts would have to cease.

Freddie Drummond's fright was due to Mary Condon, President of the International Glove Workers' Union No. 974. He had seen her, first, from the spectators' gallery, at the annual convention of the Northwest Federation of Labour, and he had seen her through Bill Totts' eyes, and that individual had been most favourably impressed by her. She was not Freddie Drummond's sort at all. What if she were a royal-bodied woman, graceful and sinewy as a panther, with amazing black eyes that could fill with fire or laughter-love, as the mood might dictate? He detested women with a too exuberant vitality and a lack of . . . well, of inhibition. Freddie Drummond accepted the doctrine of evolution because it was quite universally accepted by college men, and he flatly believed that man had climbed up the ladder of life out of the weltering muck and mess of lower and monstrous organic things. But he was a trifle ashamed of this genealogy, and preferred not to think of it. Wherefore, probably, he practised his iron inhibition and preached it to others, and preferred women of his own type, who could shake free of this bestial and regrettable ancestral line and by discipline and control emphasize the wideness of the gulf that separated them from what their dim forbears had been.

Bill Totts had none of these considerations. He had liked Mary Condon from the moment his eyes first rested on her in the convention hall, and he had made it a point, then and there, to find out who she was. The next time he met her, and quite by accident, was when he was driving an express waggon for Pat Morrissey. It was in a lodging-house in Mission Street, where he had been called to take a trunk into storage. The landlady's daughter had called him and led him to the little bedroom, the occupant of which, a glove-maker, had just been removed to hospital. But Bill did not know this. He stooped, up-ended the trunk, which was a large one, got it on his shoulder, and struggled to his feet with his back toward the open door. At that moment he heard a woman's voice.

"Belong to the union?" was the question asked.

"Aw, what's it to you?" he retorted. "Run along now, an' git outa my way. I wanta turn round."

The next he know, big as he was, he was whirled half around and sent reeling backward, the trunk overbalancing him, till he fetched up with a crash against the wall. He started to swear, but at the same instant found himself looking into Mary Condon's flashing, angry eyes.

"Of course I b'long to the union," he said. "I was only kiddin' you."

189

"Where's your card?" she demanded in businesslike tones.

"In my pocket. But I can't git it out now. This trunk's too damn heavy. Come on down to the waggon an' I'll show it to you."

"Put that trunk down," was the command.

"What for? I got a card, I'm tellin' you."

"Put it down, that's all. No scab's going to handle that trunk. You ought to be ashamed of yourself, you big coward, scabbing on honest men. Why don't you join the union and be a man?"

Mary Condon's colour had left her face, and it was apparent that she was in a rage.

"To think of a big man like you turning traitor to his class. I suppose you're aching to join the militia for a chance to shoot down union drivers the next strike. You may belong to the militia already, for that matter. You're the sort—"

"Hold on, now, that's too much!" Bill dropped the trunk to the floor with a bang, straightened up, and thrust his hand into his inside coat pocket. "I told you I was only kiddin'. There, look at that."

It was a union card properly enough.

"All right, take it along," Mary Condon said. "And the next time don't kid."

Her face relaxed as she noticed the ease with which he got the big trunk to his shoulder, and her eyes glowed as they glanced over the graceful massiveness of the man. But Bill did not see that. He was too busy with the trunk.

The next time he saw Mary Condon was during the Laundry Strike. The Laundry Workers, but recently organized, were green at the business, and had petitioned Mary Condon to engineer the strike. Freddie Drummond had had an inkling of what was coming, and had sent Bill Totts to join the union and investigate. Bill's job was in the wash-room, and the men had been called out first, that morning, in order to stiffen the courage of the girls; and Bill chanced to be near the door to the mangle-room when Mary Condon started to enter. The superintendent, who was both large and stout, barred her way. He wasn't going to have his girls called out, and he'd teach her a lesson to mind her own business. And as Mary tried to squeeze past him he thrust her back with a fat hand on her shoulder. She glanced around and saw Bill.

"Here you, Mr. Totts," she called. "Lend a hand. I want to get in."

Bill experienced a startle of warm surprise. She had remembered his name from his union card. The next moment the superintendent had been plucked from the doorway raving about rights under the law, and the girls were deserting their machines. During the rest of that short and successful strike, Bill constituted himself Mary Condon's henchman and messenger, and when it was over returned to the University to be Freddie Drummond and to wonder what Bill Totts could see in such a woman.

Freddie Drummond was entirely safe, but Bill had fallen in love. There was no getting away from the fact of it, and it was this fact that had given Freddie Drummond his warning. Well, he had done his work, and his adventures could cease. There was no need for him to cross the Slot again. All but the last three chapters of his latest, *Labour Tactics and Strategy*, was finished, and he had sufficient material on hand adequately to supply those chapters.

Another conclusion he arrived at, was that in order to sheet-anchor himself as Freddie Drummond, closer ties and relations in his own social nook were necessary. It was time that he was married, anyway, and he was fully aware that if Freddie Drummond didn't get married, Bill Totts assuredly would, and the complications were too awful to contemplate. And so, enters Catherine Van Vorst. She was a college woman herself, and her father, the one wealthy member of the faculty, was the head of the Philosophy Department as well. It would be a wise marriage from every standpoint, Freddie Drummond concluded when the engagement was consummated and announced. In appearance cold and reserved, aristocratic and wholesomely conservative, Catherine Van Vorst, though warm in her way, possessed an inhibition equal to Drummond's.

All seemed well with him, but Freddie Drummond could not quite shake off the call of the underworld, the lure of the free and open, of the unhampered, irresponsible life South of the Slot. As the time of his marriage approached, he felt that he had indeed sowed wild oats, and he felt, moreover, what a good thing it would be if he could have but one wild fling more, play the good fellow and the wastrel one last time, ere he settled down to grey lecture-rooms and sober matrimony. And, further to tempt him, the very last chapter of *Labour Tactics and Strategy* remained unwritten for lack of a trifle more of essential data which he had neglected to gather.

So Freddie Drummond went down for the last time as Bill Totts, got his data, and, unfortunately, encountered Mary Condon. Once more installed in his study, it was not a pleasant thing to look back upon. It made his warning doubly imperative. Bill Totts had behaved abominably. Not only had he met Mary Condon at the Central Labour Council, but he had stopped at a chop-house with her, on the way home, and treated her to oysters. And before they parted at her door, his arms had been about her, and he had kissed her on the lips and kissed her repeatedly. And her last words in his ear, words uttered softly with a catchy sob in the throat that was nothing more nor less than a love cry, were "Bill . . . dear, dear Bill."

Freddie Drummond shuddered at the recollection. He saw the pit yawning for him. He was not by nature a polygamist, and he was appalled at the possibilities of the situation. It would have to be put an end to, and it would end in one only of two ways: either he must become wholly Bill Totts and be married to Mary Condon, or he must remain wholly Freddie Drummond and be married to Catherine Van Vorst. Otherwise, his conduct would be beneath contempt and horrible.

In the several months that followed, San Francisco was torn with labour strife. The unions and the employers' associations had locked horns with a determination that looked as if they intended to settle the matter, one way or the other, for all time. But Freddie Drummond corrected proofs, lectured classes, and did not budge. He devoted himself to Catherine Van Vorst, and day by day found more to respect and admire in her—nay, even to love in her. The Street Car Strike tempted him, but not so severely as he would have expected; and the great Meat Strike came on and left him cold. The ghost of Bill Totts had been successfully laid, and Freddie Drummond with rejuvenescent zeal tackled a brochure, long-planned, on the topic of "diminishing returns."

The wedding was two weeks off, when, one afternoon, in San Francisco, Catherine Van Vorst picked him up and whisked him away to see a Boys' Club, recently instituted by the settlement workers in whom she was interested. It was her brother's machine, but they were alone with the exception of the chauffeur. At the junction with Kearny Street, Market and Geary Streets intersect like the sides of a sharp-angled letter "V." They, in the auto, were coming down Market with the intention of negotiating the sharp apex and going up Geary. But they did not know what was coming down Geary, timed by fate to meet them at the apex. While aware from the papers that the Meat Strike was on and that it was an exceedingly bitter one, all thought of it at that moment was farthest from Freddie Drummond's mind. Was he not seated beside Catherine? And besides, he was carefully expositing to her his views on settlement work—views that Bill Totts' adventures had played a part in formulating.

Coming down Geary Street were six meat waggons. Beside each scab driver sat a policeman. Front and rear, and along each side of this procession, marched a protecting escort of one hundred police. Behind the police rearguard, at a respectful distance, was an orderly but vociferous mob, several blocks in length, that congested the street from sidewalk to sidewalk. The Beef Trust was making an effort to supply the hotels, and, incidentally, to begin the breaking of the strike. The St. Francis had already been supplied, at a cost of many broken windows and broken heads, and the expedition was marching to the relief of the Palace Hotel.

All unwitting, Drummond sat beside Catherine, talking settlement work, as the auto, honking methodically and dodging traffic, swung in a wide curve to get around the apex. A big coal waggon, loaded with lump coal and drawn by four huge horses, just debouching from Kearny Street as though to turn down Market, blocked their way. The driver of the waggon seemed undecided, and the chauffeur, running slow but disregarding some shouted warning from the crossing policemen, swerved the auto to the left, violating the traffic rules, in order to pass in front of the waggon.

At that moment Freddie Drummond discontinued his conversation. Nor did he resume it again, for the situation was developing with the rapidity of a transformation scene. He heard the roar of the mob at the rear, and caught a glimpse of the helmeted police and the lurching meat waggons. At the same moment, laying on his whip, and standing up to his task, the coal driver rushed horses and waggon squarely in front of the advancing procession, pulled the horses up sharply, and put on the big brake. Then he made his lines fast to the brake-handle and sat down with the air of one who had stopped to stay. The auto had been brought to a stop, too, by his big panting leaders which had jammed against it.

Before the chauffeur could back clear, an old Irishman, driving a rickety express waggon and lashing his one horse to a gallop, had locked wheels with the auto. Drummond recognized both horse and waggon, for he had driven them often himself. The Irishman was Pat Morrissey. On the other side a brewery waggon was locking with the coal waggon, and an east-bound Kearny Street car, wildly clanging its gong, the motorman shouting defiance at the crossing policeman, was dashing forward to complete the blockade. And waggon after waggon was locking and blocking and adding to the confusion. The meat waggons halted. The police were trapped. The roar at the rear increased as the mob came on to the attack, while the vanguard of the police charged the obstructing waggons.

"We're in for it," Drummond remarked coolly to Catherine.

"Yes," she nodded, with equal coolness. "What savages they are."

His admiration for her doubled on itself. She was indeed his sort. He would have been satisfied with her even if she had screamed, and clung to him, but this—this was magnificent. She sat in that storm centre as calmly as if it had been no more than a block of carriages at the opera.

The police were struggling to clear a passage. The driver of the coal waggon, a big man in shirt sleeves, lighted a pipe and sat smoking. He glanced down complacently at a captain of police who was raving and cursing at him, and his only acknowledgment was a shrug of the shoulders. From the rear arose the rat-rat-tat of clubs on heads and a pandemonium of cursing, yelling, and shouting. A violent accession of noise proclaimed that the mob had broken through and was dragging a scab from a waggon. The police captain reinforced from his vanguard, and the mob at the rear was repelled. Meanwhile, window after window in the high office building on the right had been opened, and the class-conscious clerks were raining a shower of office furniture down on the heads of police and scabs. Waste-baskets, ink-bottles, paper-weights, type-writers—anything and everything that came to hand was filling the air.

A policeman, under orders from his captain, clambered to the lofty seat of the coal waggon to arrest the driver. And the driver, rising leisurely and peacefully to meet him, suddenly crumpled him in his arms and threw him down on top of the captain. The driver was a young giant, and when he climbed on his load and poised a lump of coal in both hands, a policeman, who was just scaling the waggon from the side, let go and dropped back to earth. The captain ordered half-a-dozen of his men to take the waggon. The teamster, scrambling over the load from side to side, beat them down with huge lumps of coal.

The crowd on the sidewalks and the teamsters on the locked waggons roared encouragement and their own delight. The motorman, smashing helmets with his controller bar, was beaten into insensibility and dragged from his platform. The captain of police, beside himself at the repulse of his men, led the next assault on the coal waggon. A score of police were swarming up the tall-sided fortress. But the teamster multiplied himself. At times there were six or eight policemen rolling on the pavement and under the waggon. Engaged in repulsing an attack on the rear end of his fortress, the teamster turned about to see the captain just in the act of stepping on to the seat from the front end. He was still in the air and in most unstable equilibrium, when the teamster hurled a thirty-pound lump of coal. It caught the captain fairly on the chest, and he went over backward, striking on a wheeler's back, tumbling on to the ground, and jamming against the rear wheel of the auto.

Catherine thought he was dead, but he picked himself up and charged back. She reached out her gloved hand and patted the flank of the snorting, quivering horse. But Drummond did not notice the action. He had eyes for nothing save the battle of the coal waggon, while somewhere in his complicated psychology, one Bill Totts was heaving and straining in an effort to come to life. Drummond believed in law and order and the maintenance of the established, but this riotous savage within him would have none of it. Then, if ever, did Freddie Drummond call upon his iron inhibition to save him. But it is written that the house divided against itself must fall. And Freddie Drummond found that he had divided all the will and force of him with Bill Totts, and between them the entity that constituted the pair of them was being wrenched in twain.

Freddie Drummond sat in the auto, quite composed, alongside Catherine Van Vorst; but looking out of Freddie Drummond's eyes was Bill Totts, and somewhere behind those eyes, battling for the control of their mutual body, were Freddie Drummond the sane and conservative sociologist, and Bill Totts, the class-conscious and bellicose union working man. It was Bill Totts, looking out of those eyes, who saw the inevitable end of the battle on the coal waggon. He saw a policeman gain the top of the load, a second, and a third. They lurched clumsily on the loose footing, but their long riot-clubs were out and swinging. One blow caught the teamster on the head. A second he dodged, receiving it on the shoulder. For him the game was plainly up. He dashed in suddenly, clutched two policemen in his arms, and hurled himself a prisoner to the pavement, his hold never relaxing on his two captors.

Catherine Van Vorst was sick and faint at sight of the blood and brutal fighting. But her qualms were vanquished by the sensational and most unexpected happening that followed. The man beside her emitted an unearthly and uncultured yell and rose to his feet. She saw him spring over the front seat, leap to the broad rump of the wheeler, and from there gain the waggon. His onslaught was like a whirlwind. Before the bewildered officer on the load could guess the errand of this conventionally clad but excited-seeming gentleman, he was the recipient of a punch that arched him back through the air to the pavement. A kick in the face led an ascending policeman to follow his example. A rush of three more gained the top and locked with Bill Totts in a gigantic clinch, during which his scalp was opened up by a club, and coat, vest, and half his starched shirt were torn from him. But the three policemen were flung far and wide, and Bill Totts, raining down lumps of coal, held the fort.

The captain led gallantly to the attack, but was bowled over by a chunk of coal that burst on his head in black baptism. The need of the police was to break the blockade in front before the mob could break in at the rear, and Bill Totts' need was to hold the waggon till the mob did break through. So the battle of the coal went on.

The crowd had recognized its champion. "Big" Bill, as usual, had come to the front, and Catherine Van Vorst was bewildered by the cries of "Bill! O you Bill!" that arose on every hand. Pat Morrissey, on his waggon seat, was jumping and screaming in an ecstasy, "Eat 'em, Bill! Eat 'em! Eat 'em alive!" From the sidewalk she heard a woman's voice cry out, "Look out, Bill—front end!" Bill took the warning and with well-directed coal cleared the front end of the waggon of assailants. Catherine Van Vorst turned her head and saw on the curb of the sidewalk a woman with vivid colouring and flashing black eyes who was staring with all her soul at the man who had been Freddie Drummond a few minutes before.

The windows of the office building became vociferous with applause. A fresh shower of office chairs and filing cabinets descended. The mob had broken through on one side the line of waggons, and was advancing, each segregated policeman the centre of a fighting group. The scabs were torn from their seats, the traces of the horses cut, and the frightened animals put in flight. Many policemen crawled under the coal waggon for safety, while the loose horses, with here and there a policeman on their backs or struggling at their heads to hold them, surged across the sidewalk opposite the jam and broke into Market Street.

Catherine Van Vorst heard the woman's voice calling in warning. She was back on the curb again, and crying out—

"Beat it, Bill! Now's your time! Beat it!"

The police for the moment had been swept away. Bill Totts leaped to the pavement and made his way to the woman on the sidewalk. Catherine Van Vorst saw her throw her arms around him and kiss him on the lips; and Catherine Van Vorst watched him curiously as he went on down the sidewalk, one arm around the woman, both talking and laughing, and he with a volubility and abandon she could never have dreamed possible.

The police were back again and clearing the jam while waiting for reinforcements and new drivers and horses. The mob had done its work and was scattering, and Catherine Van Vorst, still watching, could see the man she had known as Freddie Drummond. He towered a head above the crowd. His arm was still about the woman. And she in the motor-car, watching, saw the pair cross Market Street, cross the Slot, and disappear down Third Street into the labour ghetto.

In the years that followed no more lectures were given in the University of California by one Freddie Drummond, and no more books on economics and the labour question appeared over the name of Frederick A. Drummond. On the other hand there arose a new labour leader, William Totts by name. He it was who married Mary Condon, President of the International Glove Workers' Union No. 974; and he it was who called the notorious Cooks and Waiters' Strike, which, before its successful termination, brought out with it scores of other unions, among which, of the more remotely allied, were the Chicken Pickers and the Undertakers.

198

THE UNPARALLELED INVASION

It was in the year 1976 that the trouble between the world and China reached its culmination. It was because of this that the celebration of the Second Centennial of American Liberty was deferred. Many other plans of the nations of the earth were twisted and tangled and postponed for the same reason. The world awoke rather abruptly to its danger; but for over seventy years, unperceived, affairs had been shaping toward this very end.

The year 1904 logically marks the beginning of the development that, seventy years later, was to bring consternation to the whole world. The Japanese-Russian War took place in 1904, and the historians of the time gravely noted it down that that event marked the entrance of Japan into the comity of nations. What it really did mark was the awakening of China. This awakening, long expected, had finally been given up. The Western nations had tried to arouse China, and they had failed. Out of their native optimism and race-egotism they had therefore concluded that the task was impossible, that China would never awaken.

What they had failed to take into account was this: *that between them and China was no common psychological speech.* Their thought-processes were radically dissimilar. There was no intimate vocabulary. The Western mind penetrated the Chinese mind but a short distance when it found itself in a fathomless maze. The Chinese mind penetrated the Western mind an equally short distance when it fetched up against a blank, incomprehensible wall. It was all a matter of language. There was no way to communicate Western ideas to the Chinese mind. China remained asleep. The material achievement and progress of the West was a closed book to her; nor could the West open the book. Back and deep down on the tie-ribs of consciousness, in the mind, say, of the English-speaking race, was a capacity to thrill to short, Saxon words; back and deep down on the tie-ribs of consciousness of the Chinese mind was a capacity to thrill to its own hieroglyphics; but the Chinese mind could not thrill to short, Saxon words; nor could the English-speaking mind thrill to hieroglyphics. The fabrics of their minds were woven from totally different stuffs. They were mental aliens. And so it was that Western material achievement and progress made no dent on the rounded sleep of China.

Came Japan and her victory over Russia in 1904. Now the Japanese race was the freak and paradox among Eastern peoples. In some strange way Japan was receptive to all the West had to offer. Japan swiftly assimilated the Western ideas, and digested them, and so capably applied them that she suddenly burst forth, full-panoplied, a world-power. There is no explaining this peculiar openness of Japan to the alien culture of the West. As well might be explained any biological sport in the animal kingdom.

Having decisively thrashed the great Russian Empire, Japan promptly set about dreaming a colossal dream of empire for herself. Korea she had made into a granary and a colony; treaty privileges and vulpine diplomacy gave her the monopoly of Manchuria. But Japan was not satisfied. She turned her eyes upon China. There lay a vast territory, and in that territory were the hugest deposits in the world of iron and coal—the backbone of industrial civilization. Given natural resources, the other great factor in industry is labour. In that territory was a population of 400,000,000 souls— one quarter of the then total population of the earth. Furthermore, the Chinese were excellent workers, while their fatalistic philosophy (or religion) and their stolid nervous organization constituted them splendid soldiers—if they were properly managed. Needless to say, Japan was prepared to furnish that management.

But best of all, from the standpoint of Japan, the Chinese was a kindred race. The baffling enigma of the Chinese character to the West was no baffling enigma to the Japanese. The Japanese understood as we could never school ourselves or hope to understand. Their mental processes were the same. The Japanese thought with the same thought-symbols as did the Chinese, and they thought in the same peculiar grooves. Into the Chinese mind the Japanese went on where we were balked by the obstacle of incomprehension. They took the turning which we could not perceive, twisted around the obstacle, and were out of sight in the ramifications of the Chinese mind where we could not follow. They were brothers. Long ago one had borrowed the other's written language, and, untold generations before that, they had diverged from the common Mongol stock. There had been changes, differentiations brought about by diverse conditions and infusions of other blood; but down at the bottom of their beings, twisted into the fibres of them, was a heritage in common, a sameness in kind that time had not obliterated.

And so Japan took upon herself the management of China. In the years immediately following the war with Russia, her agents swarmed over the Chinese Empire. A thousand miles beyond the last mission station toiled her engineers and spies, clad as coolies, under the guise of itinerant merchants or proselytizing Buddhist priests, noting down the horse-power of every waterfall, the likely sites for factories, the heights of mountains and passes, the strategic advantages and weaknesses, the wealth of the farming valleys, the number of bullocks in a district or the number of labourers that could be collected by forced levies. Never was there such a census, and it could have been taken by no other people than the dogged, patient, patriotic Japanese.

But in a short time secrecy was thrown to the winds. Japan's officers reorganized the Chinese army; her drill sergeants made the mediæval warriors over into twentieth century soldiers, accustomed to all the modern machinery of war and with a higher average of marksmanship than the soldiers of any Western nation. The engineers of Japan deepened and widened the intricate system of canals, built factories and foundries, netted the empire with telegraphs and telephones, and inaugurated the era of railroad-building. It was these same protagonists of machine-civilization that discovered the great oil deposits of Chunsan, the iron mountains of Whang-Sing, the copper ranges of Chinchi, and they sank the gas wells of Wow-Wee, that most marvellous reservoir of natural gas in all the world.

In China's councils of empire were the Japanese emissaries. In the ears of the statesmen whispered the Japanese statesmen. The political reconstruction of the Empire was due to them. They evicted the scholar class, which was violently reactionary, and put into office progressive officials. And in every town and city of the Empire newspapers were started. Of course, Japanese editors ran the policy of these papers, which policy they got direct from Tokio. It was these papers that educated and made progressive the great mass of the population.

China was at last awake. Where the West had failed, Japan succeeded. She had transmuted Western culture and achievement into terms that were intelligible to the Chinese understanding. Japan herself, when she so suddenly awakened, had astounded the world. But at the time she was only forty millions strong. China's awakening, with her four hundred millions and the scientific advance of the world, was frightfully astounding. She was the colossus of the nations, and swiftly her voice was heard in no uncertain tones in the affairs and councils of the nations. Japan egged her on, and the proud Western peoples listened with respectful ears.

China's swift and remarkable rise was due, perhaps more than to anything else, to the superlative quality of her labour. The Chinese was the perfect type of industry. He had always been that. For sheer ability to work no worker in the world could compare with him. Work was the breath of his nostrils. It was to him what wandering and fighting in far lands and spiritual adventure had been to other peoples. Liberty, to him, epitomized itself in access to the means of toil. To till the soil and labour interminably was all he asked of life and the powers that be. And the awakening of China had given its vast population not merely free and unlimited access to the means of toil, but access to the highest and most scientific machine-means of toil.

China rejuvenescent! It was but a step to China rampant. She discovered a new pride in herself and a will of her own. She began to chafe under the guidance of Japan, but she did not chafe long. On Japan's advice, in the beginning, she had expelled from the Empire all Western missionaries, engineers, drill sergeants, merchants, and teachers. She now began to expel the similar representatives of Japan. The latter's advisory statesmen were showered with honours and decorations, and sent home. The West had awakened Japan, and, as Japan had then requited the West, Japan was not requited by China. Japan was thanked for her kindly aid and flung out bag and baggage by her gigantic protégé. The Western nations chuckled. Japan's rainbow dream had gone glimmering. She grew angry. China laughed at her. The blood and the swords of the Samurai would out, and Japan rashly went to war. This occurred in 1922, and in seven bloody months Manchuria, Korea, and Formosa were taken away from her and she was hurled back, bankrupt, to stifle in her tiny, crowded islands. Exit Japan from the world drama. Thereafter she devoted herself to art, and her task became to please the world greatly with her creations of wonder and beauty.

Contrary to expectation, China did not prove warlike. She had no Napoleonic dream, and was content to devote herself to the arts of peace. After a time of disquiet, the idea was accepted that China was to be feared, not in war, but in commerce. It will be seen that the real danger was not apprehended. China went on consummating her machine-civilization. Instead of a large standing army, she developed an immensely larger and splendidly efficient militia. Her navy was so small that it was the laughing stock of the world; nor did she attempt to strengthen her navy. The treaty ports of the world were never entered by her visiting battleships.

The real danger lay in the fecundity of her loins, and it was in 1970 that the first cry of alarm was raised. For some time all territories adjacent to China had been grumbling at Chinese immigration; but now it suddenly came home to the world that China's population was 500,000,000. She had increased by a hundred millions since her awakening. Burchaldter called attention to the fact that there were more Chinese in existence than white-skinned people. He performed a simple sum in arithmetic. He added together the populations of the United States, Canada, New Zealand, Australia, South Africa, England, France, Germany, Italy, Austria, European Russia, and all Scandinavia. The result was 495,000,000. And the population of China overtopped this tremendous total by 5,000,000. Burchaldter's figures went round the world, and the world shivered.

For many centuries China's population had been constant. Her territory had been saturated with population; that is to say, her territory, with the primitive method of production, had supported the maximum limit of population. But when she awoke and inaugurated the machine-civilization, her productive power had been enormously increased. Thus, on the same territory, she was able to support a far larger population. At once the birth rate began to rise and the death rate to fall. Before, when population pressed against the means of subsistence, the excess population had been swept away by famine. But now, thanks to the machine-civilization, China's means of subsistence had been enormously extended, and there were no famines; her population followed on the heels of the increase in the means of subsistence.

During this time of transition and development of power, China had entertained no dreams of conquest. The Chinese was not an imperial race. It was industrious, thrifty, and peace-loving. War was looked upon as an unpleasant but necessary task that at times must be performed. And so, while the Western races had squabbled and fought, and world-adventured against one another, China had calmly gone on working at her machines and growing. Now she was spilling over the boundaries of her Empire—that was all, just spilling over into the adjacent territories with all the certainty and terrifying slow momentum of a glacier.

Following upon the alarm raised by Burchaldter's figures, in 1970 France made a long-threatened stand. French Indo-China had been overrun, filled up, by Chinese immigrants. France called a halt. The Chinese wave flowed on. France assembled a force of a hundred thousand on the boundary between her unfortunate colony and China, and China sent down an army of militia-soldiers a million strong. Behind came the wives and sons and daughters and relatives, with their personal household luggage, in a second army. The French force was brushed aside like a fly. The Chinese militia-soldiers, along with their families, over five millions all told, coolly took possession of French Indo-China and settled down to stay for a few thousand years.

Outraged France was in arms. She hurled fleet after fleet against the coast of China, and nearly bankrupted herself by the effort. China had no navy. She withdrew like a turtle into her shell. For a year the French fleets blockaded the coast and bombarded exposed towns and villages. China did not mind. She did not depend upon the rest of the world for anything. She calmly kept out of range of the French guns and went on working. France wept and wailed, wrung her impotent hands and appealed to the dumfounded nations. Then she landed a punitive expedition to march to Peking. It was two hundred and fifty thousand strong, and it was the flower of France. It landed without opposition and marched into the interior. And that was the last ever seen of it. The line of communication was snapped on the second day. Not a survivor came back to tell what had happened. It had been swallowed up in China's cavernous maw, that was all.

In the five years that followed, China's expansion, in all land directions, went on apace. Siam was made part of the Empire, and, in spite of all that England could do, Burma and the Malay Peninsula were overrun; while all along the long south boundary of Siberia, Russia was pressed severely by China's advancing hordes. The process was simple. First came the Chinese immigration (or, rather, it was already there, having come there slowly and insidiously during the previous years). Next came the clash of arms and the brushing away of all opposition by a monster army of militia-soldiers, followed by their families and household baggage. And finally came their settling down as colonists in the conquered territory. Never was there so strange and effective a method of world conquest.

Napal and Bhutan were overrun, and the whole northern boundary of India pressed against by this fearful tide of life. To the west, Bokhara, and, even to the south and west, Afghanistan, were swallowed up. Persia, Turkestan, and all Central Asia felt the pressure of the flood. It was at this time that Burchaldter revised his figures. He had been mistaken. China's population must be seven hundred millions, eight hundred millions, nobody knew how many millions, but at any rate it would soon be a billion. There were two Chinese for every white-skinned human in the world, Burchaldter announced, and the world trembled. China's increase must have begun immediately, in 1904. It was remembered that since that date there had not been a single famine. At 5,000,000 a year increase, her total increase in the intervening seventy years must be 350,000,000. But who was to know? It might be more. Who was to know anything of this strange new menace of the twentieth century—China, old China, rejuvenescent, fruitful, and militant!

The Convention of 1975 was called at Philadelphia. All the Western nations, and some few of the Eastern, were represented. Nothing was accomplished. There was talk of all countries putting bounties on children to increase the birth rate, but it was laughed to scorn by the arithmeticians, who pointed out that China was too far in the lead in that direction. No feasible way of coping with China was suggested. China was appealed to and threatened by the United Powers, and that was all the Convention of Philadelphia came to; and the Convention and the Powers were laughed at by China. Li Tang Fwung, the power behind the Dragon Throne, deigned to reply.

"What does China care for the comity of nations?" said Li Tang Fwung. "We are the most ancient, honourable, and royal of races. We have our own destiny to accomplish. It is unpleasant that our destiny does not tally with the destiny of the rest of the world, but what would you? You have talked windily about the royal races and the heritage of the earth, and we can only reply that that remains to be seen. You cannot invade us. Never mind about your navies. Don't shout. We know our navy is small. You see we use it for police purposes. We do not care for the sea. Our strength is in our population, which will soon be a billion. Thanks to you, we are equipped with all modern war-machinery. Send your navies. We will not notice them. Send your punitive expeditions, but first remember France. To land half a million soldiers on our shores would strain the resources of any of you. And our thousand millions would swallow them down in a mouthful. Send a million; send five millions, and we will swallow them down just as readily. Pouf! A mere nothing, a meagre morsel. Destroy, as you have threatened, you United States, the ten million coolies we have forced upon your shores— why, the amount scarcely equals half of our excess birth rate for a year."

So spoke Li Tang Fwung. The world was nonplussed, helpless, terrified. Truly had he spoken. There was no combating China's amazing birth rate. If her population was a billion, and was increasing twenty millions a year, in twenty-five years it would be a billion and a half—equal to the total population of the world in 1904. And nothing could be done. There was no way to dam up the over-spilling monstrous flood of life. War was futile. China laughed at a blockade of her coasts. She welcomed invasion. In her capacious maw was room for all the hosts of earth that could be hurled at her. And in the meantime her flood of yellow life poured out and on over Asia. China laughed and read in their magazines the learned lucubrations of the distracted Western scholars.

But there was one scholar China failed to reckon on—Jacobus Laningdale. Not that he was a scholar, except in the widest sense. Primarily, Jacobus Laningdale was a scientist, and, up to that time, a very obscure scientist, a professor employed in the laboratories of the Health Office of New York City. Jacobus Laningdale's head was very like any other head, but in that head was evolved an idea. Also, in that head was the wisdom to keep that idea secret. He did not write an article for the magazines. Instead, he asked for a vacation. On September 19, 1975, he arrived in Washington. It was evening, but he proceeded straight to the White House, for he had already arranged an audience with the President. He was closeted with President Moyer for three hours. What passed between them was not learned by the rest of the world until long after; in fact, at that time the world was not interested in Jacobus Laningdale. Next day the President called in his Cabinet. Jacobus Laningdale was present. The proceedings were kept secret. But that very afternoon Rufus Cowdery, Secretary of State, left Washington, and early the following morning sailed for England. The secret that he carried began to spread, but it spread only among the heads of Governments. Possibly half-a-dozen men in a nation were entrusted with the idea that had formed in Jacobus Laningdale's head. Following the spread of the secret, sprang up great activity in all the dockyards, arsenals, and navy-yards. The people of France and Austria became suspicious, but so sincere were their Governments' calls for confidence that they acquiesced in the unknown project that was afoot.

This was the time of the Great Truce. All countries pledged themselves solemnly not to go to war with any other country. The first definite action was the gradual mobilization of the armies of Russia, Germany, Austria, Italy, Greece, and Turkey. Then began the eastward movement. All railroads into Asia were glutted with troop trains. China was the objective, that was all that was known. A little later began the great sea movement. Expeditions of warships were launched from all countries. Fleet followed fleet, and all proceeded to the coast of China. The nations cleaned out their navy-yards. They sent their revenue cutters and dispatch boats and lighthouse tenders, and they sent their last antiquated cruisers and battleships. Not content with this, they impressed the merchant marine. The statistics show that 58,640 merchant steamers, equipped with searchlights and rapid-fire guns, were despatched by the various nations to China.

And China smiled and waited. On her land side, along her boundaries, were millions of the warriors of Europe. She mobilized five times as many millions of her militia and awaited the invasion. On her sea coasts she did the same. But China was puzzled. After all this enormous preparation, there was no invasion. She could not understand. Along the great Siberian frontier all was quiet. Along her coasts the towns and villages were not even shelled. Never, in the history of the world, had there been so mighty a gathering of war fleets. The fleets of all the world were there, and day and night millions of tons of battleships ploughed the brine of her coasts, and nothing happened. Nothing was attempted. Did they think to make her emerge from her shell? China smiled. Did they think to tire her out, or starve her out? China smiled again.

But on May 1, 1976, had the reader been in the imperial city of Peking, with its then population of eleven millions, he would have witnessed a curious sight. He would have seen the streets filled with the chattering yellow populace, every queued head tilted back, every slant eye turned skyward. And high up in the blue he would have beheld a tiny dot of black, which, because of its orderly evolutions, he would have identified as an airship. From this airship, as it curved its flight back and forth over the city, fell missiles—strange, harmless missiles, tubes of fragile glass that shattered into thousands of fragments on the streets and house-tops. But there was nothing deadly about these tubes of glass. Nothing happened. There were no explosions. It is true, three Chinese were killed by the tubes dropping on their heads from so enormous a height; but what were three Chinese against an excess birth rate of twenty millions? One tube struck perpendicularly in a fish-pond in a garden and was not broken. It was dragged ashore by the master of the house. He did not dare to open it, but, accompanied by his friends, and surrounded by an ever-increasing crowd, he carried the mysterious tube to the magistrate of the district. The latter was a brave man. With all eyes upon him, he shattered the tube with a blow from his brass-bowled pipe. Nothing happened. Of those who were very near, one or two thought they saw some mosquitoes fly out. That was all. The crowd set up a great laugh and dispersed.

As Peking was bombarded by glass tubes, so was all China. The tiny airships, dispatched from the warships, contained but two men each, and over all cities, towns, and villages they wheeled and curved, one man directing the ship, the other man throwing over the glass tubes.

Had the reader again been in Peking, six weeks later, he would have looked in vain for the eleven million inhabitants. Some few of them he would have found, a few hundred thousand, perhaps, their carcasses festering in the houses and in the deserted streets, and piled high on the abandoned death-waggons. But for the rest he would have had to seek along the highways and byways of the Empire. And not all would he have found fleeing from plague-stricken Peking, for behind them, by hundreds of thousands of unburied corpses by the wayside, he could have marked their flight. And as it was with Peking, so it was with all the cities, towns, and villages of the Empire. The plague smote them all. Nor was it one plague, nor two plagues; it was a score of plagues. Every virulent form of infectious death stalked through the land. Too late the Chinese government apprehended the meaning of the colossal preparations, the marshalling of the world-hosts, the flights of the tin airships, and the rain of the tubes of glass. The proclamations of the government were vain. They could not stop the eleven million plague-stricken wretches, fleeing from the one city of Peking to spread disease through all the land. The physicians and health officers died at their posts; and death, the all-conqueror, rode over the decrees of the Emperor and Li Tang Fwung. It rode over them as well, for Li Tang Fwung died in the second week, and the Emperor, hidden away in the Summer Palace, died in the fourth week.

Had there been one plague, China might have coped with it. But from a score of plagues no creature was immune. The man who escaped smallpox went down before scarlet fever. The man who was immune to yellow fever was carried away by cholera; and if he were immune to that, too, the Black Death, which was the bubonic plague, swept him away. For it was these bacteria, and germs, and microbes, and bacilli, cultured in the laboratories of the West, that had come down upon China in the rain of glass.

All organization vanished. The government crumbled away. Decrees and proclamations were useless when the men who made them and signed them one moment were dead the next. Nor could the maddened millions, spurred on to flight by death, pause to heed anything. They fled from the cities to infect the country, and wherever they fled they carried the plagues with them. The hot summer was on—Jacobus Laningdale had selected the time shrewdly—and the plague festered everywhere. Much is conjectured of what occurred, and much has been learned from the stories of the few survivors. The wretched creatures stormed across the Empire in many-millioned flight. The vast armies China had collected on her frontiers melted away. The farms were ravaged for food, and no more crops were planted, while the crops already in were left unattended and never came to harvest. The most remarkable thing, perhaps, was the flights. Many millions engaged in them, charging to the bounds of the Empire to be met and turned back by the gigantic armies of the West. The slaughter of the mad hosts on the boundaries was stupendous. Time and again the guarding line was drawn back twenty or thirty miles to escape the contagion of the multitudinous dead.

Once the plague broke through and seized upon the German and Austrian soldiers who were guarding the borders of Turkestan. Preparations had been made for such a happening, and though sixty thousand soldiers of Europe were carried off, the international corps of physicians isolated the contagion and dammed it back. It was during this struggle that it was suggested that a new plague-germ had originated, that in some way or other a sort of hybridization between plague-germs had taken place, producing a new and frightfully virulent germ. First suspected by Vomberg, who became infected with it and died, it was later isolated and studied by Stevens, Hazenfelt, Norman, and Landers.

Such was the unparalleled invasion of China. For that billion of people there was no hope. Pent in their vast and festering charnel-house, all organization and cohesion lost, they could do naught but die. They could not escape. As they were flung back from their land frontiers, so were they flung back from the sea. Seventy-five thousand vessels patrolled the coasts. By day their smoking funnels dimmed the sea-rim, and by night their flashing searchlights ploughed the dark and harrowed it for the tiniest escaping junk.

210

The attempts of the immense fleets of junks were pitiful. Not one ever got by the guarding sea-hounds. Modern war-machinery held back the disorganized mass of China, while the plagues did the work.

But old War was made a thing of laughter. Naught remained to him but patrol duty. China had laughed at war, and war she was getting, but it was ultra-modern war, twentieth century war, the war of the scientist and the laboratory, the war of Jacobus Laningdale. Hundred-ton guns were toys compared with the micro-organic projectiles hurled from the laboratories, the messengers of death, the destroying angels that stalked through the empire of a billion souls.

During all the summer and fall of 1976 China was an inferno. There was no eluding the microscopic projectiles that sought out the remotest hiding-places. The hundreds of millions of dead remained unburied and the germs multiplied themselves, and, toward the last, millions died daily of starvation. Besides, starvation weakened the victims and destroyed their natural defences against the plagues. Cannibalism, murder, and madness reigned. And so perished China.

Not until the following February, in the coldest weather, were the first expeditions made. These expeditions were small, composed of scientists and bodies of troops; but they entered China from every side. In spite of the most elaborate precautions against infection, numbers of soldiers and a few of the physicians were stricken. But the exploration went bravely on. They found China devastated, a howling wilderness through which wandered bands of wild dogs and desperate bandits who had survived. All survivors were put to death wherever found. And then began the great task, the sanitation of China. Five years and hundreds of millions of treasure were consumed, and then the world moved in—not in zones, as was the idea of Baron Albrecht, but heterogeneously, according to the democratic American programme. It was a vast and happy intermingling of nationalities that settled down in China in 1982 and the years that followed—a tremendous and successful experiment in cross-fertilization. We know to-day the splendid mechanical, intellectual, and art output that followed.

It was in 1987, the Great Truce having been dissolved, that the ancient quarrel between France and Germany over Alsace-Lorraine recrudesced. The war-cloud grew dark and threatening in April, and on April 17 the Convention of Copenhagen was called. The representatives of the nations of the world, being present, all nations solemnly pledged themselves never to use against one another the laboratory methods of warfare they had employed in the invasion of China.

—Excerpt from Walt Mervin's "*Certain Essays in History.*"

THE ENEMY OF ALL THE WORLD

It was Silas Bannerman who finally ran down that scientific wizard and arch-enemy of mankind, Emil Gluck. Gluck's confession, before he went to the electric chair, threw much light upon the series of mysterious events, many apparently unrelated, that so perturbed the world between the years 1933 and 1941. It was not until that remarkable document was made public that the world dreamed of there being any connection between the assassination of the King and Queen of Portugal and the murders of the New York City police officers. While the deeds of Emil Gluck were all that was abominable, we cannot but feel, to a certain extent, pity for the unfortunate, malformed, and maltreated genius. This side of his story has never been told before, and from his confession and from the great mass of evidence and the documents and records of the time we are able to construct a fairly accurate portrait of him, and to discern the factors and pressures that moulded him into the human monster he became and that drove him onward and downward along the fearful path he trod.

Emil Gluck was born in Syracuse, New York, in 1895. His father, Josephus Gluck, was a special policeman and night watchman, who, in the year 1900, died suddenly of pneumonia. The mother, a pretty, fragile creature, who, before her marriage, had been a milliner, grieved herself to death over the loss of her husband. This sensitiveness of the mother was the heritage that in the boy became morbid and horrible.

In 1901, the boy, Emil, then six years of age, went to live with his aunt, Mrs. Ann Bartell. She was his mother's sister, but in her breast was no kindly feeling for the sensitive, shrinking boy. Ann Bartell was a vain, shallow, and heartless woman. Also, she was cursed with poverty and burdened with a husband who was a lazy, erratic ne'er-do-well. Young Emil Gluck was not wanted, and Ann Bartell could be trusted to impress this fact sufficiently upon him. As an illustration of the treatment he received in that early, formative period, the following instance is given.

When he had been living in the Bartell home a little more than a year, he broke his leg. He sustained the injury through playing on the forbidden roof—as all boys have done and will continue to do to the end of time. The leg was broken in two places between the knee and thigh. Emil, helped by his frightened playmates, managed to drag himself to the front sidewalk, where he fainted. The children of the neighbourhood were afraid of the hard-featured shrew who presided over the Bartell house; but, summoning their resolution, they rang the bell and told Ann Bartell of the accident. She did not even look at the little lad who lay stricken on the sidewalk, but slammed the door and went back to her wash-tub. The time passed. A drizzle came on, and Emil Gluck, out of his faint, lay sobbing in the rain. The leg should have been set immediately. As it was, the inflammation rose rapidly and made a nasty case of it. At the end of two hours, the indignant women of the neighbourhood protested to Ann Bartell. This time she came out and looked at the lad. Also she kicked him in the side as he lay helpless at her feet, and she hysterically disowned him. He was not her child, she said, and recommended that the ambulance be called to take him to the city receiving hospital. Then she went back into the house.

It was a woman, Elizabeth Shepstone, who came along, learned the situation, and had the boy placed on a shutter. It was she who called the doctor, and who, brushing aside Ann Bartell, had the boy carried into the house. When the doctor arrived, Ann Bartell promptly warned him that she would not pay him for his services. For two months the little Emil lay in bed, the first month on his back without once being turned over; and he lay neglected and alone, save for the occasional visits of the unremunerated and over-worked physician. He had no toys, nothing with which to beguile the long and tedious hours. No kind word was spoken to him, no soothing hand laid upon his brow, no single touch or act of loving tenderness—naught but the reproaches and harshness of Ann Bartell, and the continually reiterated information that he was not wanted. And it can well be understood, in such environment, how there was generated in the lonely, neglected boy much of the bitterness and hostility for his kind that later was to express itself in deeds so frightful as to terrify the world.

It would seem strange that, from the hands of Ann Bartell, Emil Gluck should have received a college education; but the explanation is simple. Her ne'er-do-well husband, deserting her, made a strike in the Nevada goldfields, and returned to her a many-times millionaire. Ann Bartell hated the boy, and immediately she sent him to the Farristown Academy, a hundred miles away. Shy and sensitive, a lonely and misunderstood little soul, he was more lonely than ever at Farristown. He never came home, at vacation, and holidays, as the other boys did. Instead, he wandered about the deserted buildings and grounds, befriended and misunderstood by the servants and gardeners, reading much, it is remembered, spending his days in the fields or before the fire-place with his nose poked always in the pages of some book. It was at this time that he over-used his eyes and was compelled to take up the wearing of glasses, which same were so prominent in the photographs of him published in the newspapers in 1941.

He was a remarkable student. Application such as his would have taken him far; but he did not need application. A glance at a text meant mastery for him. The result was that he did an immense amount of collateral reading and acquired more in half a year than did the average student in half-a-dozen years. In 1909, barely fourteen years of age, he was ready—"more than ready" the headmaster of the academy said—to enter Yale or Harvard. His juvenility prevented him from entering those universities, and so, in 1909, we find him a freshman at historic Bowdoin College. In 1913 he graduated with highest honours, and immediately afterward followed Professor Bradlough to Berkeley, California. The one friend that Emil Gluck discovered in all his life was Professor Bradlough. The latter's weak lungs had led him to exchange Maine for California, the removal being facilitated by the offer of a professorship in the State University. Throughout the year 1914, Emil Gluck resided in Berkeley and took special scientific courses. Toward the end of that year two deaths changed his prospects and his relations with life. The death of Professor Bradlough took from him the one friend he was ever to know, and the death of Ann Bartell left him penniless. Hating the unfortunate lad to the last, she cut him off with one hundred dollars.

The following year, at twenty years of age, Emil Gluck was enrolled as an instructor of chemistry in the University of California. Here the years passed

215

quietly; he faithfully performed the drudgery that brought him his salary, and, a student always, he took half-a-dozen degrees. He was, among other things, a Doctor of Sociology, of Philosophy, and of Science, though he was known to the world, in later days, only as Professor Gluck.

He was twenty-seven years old when he first sprang into prominence in the newspapers through the publication of his book, *Sex and Progress*. The book remains to-day a milestone in the history and philosophy of marriage. It is a heavy tome of over seven hundred pages, painfully careful and accurate, and startlingly original. It was a book for scientists, and not one calculated to make a stir. But Gluck, in the last chapter, using barely three lines for it, mentioned the hypothetical desirability of trial marriages. At once the newspapers seized these three lines, "played them up yellow," as the slang was in those days, and set the whole world laughing at Emil Gluck, the bespectacled young professor of twenty-seven. Photographers snapped him, he was besieged by reporters, women's clubs throughout the land passed resolutions condemning him and his immoral theories; and on the floor of the California Assembly, while discussing the state appropriation to the University, a motion demanding the expulsion of Gluck was made under threat of withholding the appropriation—of course, none of his persecutors had read the book; the twisted newspaper version of only three lines of it was enough for them. Here began Emil Gluck's hatred for newspaper men. By them his serious and intrinsically valuable work of six years had been made a laughing-stock and a notoriety. To his dying day, and to their everlasting regret, he never forgave them.

It was the newspapers that were responsible for the next disaster that befell him. For the five years following the publication of his book he had remained silent, and silence for a lonely man is not good. One can conjecture sympathetically the awful solitude of Emil Gluck in that populous University; for he was without friends and without sympathy. His only recourse was books, and he went on reading and studying enormously. But in 1927 he accepted an invitation to appear before the Human Interest Society of Emeryville. He did not trust himself to speak, and as we write we have before us a copy of his learned paper. It is sober, scholarly, and scientific, and, it must also be added, conservative. But in one place he dealt with, and I quote his words, "the industrial and social revolution that is taking place in society." A reporter present seized upon the word "revolution," divorced it from the text, and wrote a garbled account that made Emil Gluck appear an anarchist. At once, "Professor Gluck, anarchist," flamed over the wires and was appropriately "featured" in all the newspapers in the land.

He had attempted to reply to the previous newspaper attack, but now he remained silent. Bitterness had already corroded his soul. The University faculty appealed to him to defend himself, but he sullenly declined, even refusing to enter in defence a copy of his paper to save himself from expulsion. He refused to resign, and was discharged from the University faculty. It must be added that political pressure had been put upon the University Regents and the President.

Persecuted, maligned, and misunderstood, the forlorn and lonely man made no attempt at retaliation. All his life he had been sinned against, and all his life he had sinned against no one. But his cup of bitterness was not yet full to overflowing. Having lost his position, and being without any income, he had to find work. His first place was at the Union Iron Works, in San Francisco, where he proved a most able draughtsman. It was here that he obtained his firsthand knowledge of battleships and their construction. But the reporters discovered him and featured him in his new vocation. He immediately resigned and found another place; but after the reporters had driven him away from half-a-dozen positions, he steeled himself to brazen out the newspaper persecution. This occurred when he started his electroplating establishment—in Oakland, on Telegraph Avenue. It was a small shop, employing three men and two boys. Gluck himself worked long hours. Night after night, as Policeman Carew testified on the stand, he did not leave the shop till one and two in the morning. It was during this period that he perfected the improved ignition device for gas-engines, the royalties from which ultimately made him wealthy.

He started his electroplating establishment early in the spring of 1928, and it was in the same year that he formed the disastrous love attachment for Irene Tackley. Now it is not to be imagined that an extraordinary creature such as Emil Gluck could be any other than an extraordinary lover. In addition to his genius, his loneliness, and his morbidness, it must be taken into consideration that he knew nothing about women. Whatever tides of desire flooded his being, he was unschooled in the conventional expression of them; while his excessive timidity was bound to make his love-making unusual. Irene Tackley was a rather pretty young woman, but shallow and light-headed. At the time she worked in a small candy store across the street from Gluck's shop. He used to come in and drink ice-cream sodas and lemon-squashes, and stare at her. It seems the girl did not care for him, and merely played with him. He was "queer," she said; and at another time she called him a crank when describing how he sat at the counter and peered at her through his spectacles, blushing and stammering when she took notice of him, and often leaving the shop in precipitate confusion.

Gluck made her the most amazing presents—a silver tea-service, a diamond ring, a set of furs, opera-glasses, a ponderous *History of the World* in many volumes, and a motor-cycle all silver-plated in his own shop. Enters now the girl's lover, putting his foot down, showing great anger, compelling her to return Gluck's strange assortment of presents. This man, William Sherbourne, was a gross and stolid creature, a heavy-jawed man of the working class who had become a successful building-contractor in a small way. Gluck did not understand. He tried to get an explanation, attempting to speak with the girl when she went home from work in the evening. She complained to Sherbourne, and one night he gave Gluck a beating. It was a very severe beating, for it is on the records of the Red Cross Emergency Hospital that Gluck was treated there that night and was unable to leave the hospital for a week.

Still Gluck did not understand. He continued to seek an explanation from the girl. In fear of Sherbourne, he applied to the Chief of Police for permission to carry a revolver, which permission was refused, the newspapers as usual playing it up sensationally. Then came the murder of Irene Tackley, six days before her contemplated marriage with Sherbourne. It was on a Saturday night. She had worked late in the candy store, departing after eleven o'clock with her week's wages in her purse. She rode on a San Pablo Avenue surface car to Thirty-fourth Street, where she alighted and started to walk the three blocks to her home. That was the last seen of her alive. Next morning she was found, strangled, in a vacant lot.

Emil Gluck was immediately arrested. Nothing that he could do could save him. He was convicted, not merely on circumstantial evidence, but on evidence "cooked up" by the Oakland police. There is no discussion but that a large portion of the evidence was manufactured. The testimony of Captain Shehan was the sheerest perjury, it being proved long afterward that on the night in question he had not only not been in the vicinity of the murder, but that he had been out of the city in a resort on the San Leandro Road. The unfortunate Gluck received life imprisonment in San Quentin, while the newspapers and the public held that it was a miscarriage of justice—that the death penalty should have been visited upon him.

Gluck entered San Quentin prison on April 17, 1929. He was then thirty-four years of age. And for three years and a half, much of the time in solitary confinement, he was left to meditate upon the injustice of man. It was during that period that his bitterness corroded home and he became a hater of all his kind. Three other things he did during the same period: he wrote his famous treatise, *Human Morals*, his remarkable brochure, *The Criminal Sane*, and he worked out his awful and monstrous scheme of revenge. It was an episode that had occurred in his electroplating establishment that suggested to him his unique weapon of revenge. As stated in his confession, he worked every detail out theoretically during his imprisonment, and was able, on his release, immediately to embark on his career of vengeance.

His release was sensational. Also it was miserably and criminally delayed by the soulless legal red tape then in vogue. On the night of February 1, 1932, Tim Haswell, a hold-up man, was shot during an attempted robbery by a citizen of Piedmont Heights. Tim Haswell lingered three days, during which time he not only confessed to the murder of Irene Tackley, but furnished conclusive proofs of the same. Bert Danniker, a convict dying of consumption in Folsom Prison, was implicated as accessory, and his confession followed. It is inconceivable to us of to-day—the bungling, dilatory processes of justice a generation ago. Emil Gluck was proved in February to be an innocent man, yet he was not released until the following October. For eight months, a greatly wronged man, he was compelled to undergo his unmerited punishment. This was not conducive to sweetness and light, and we can well imagine how he ate his soul with bitterness during those dreary eight months.

He came back to the world in the fall of 1932, as usual a "feature" topic in all the newspapers. The papers, instead of expressing heartfelt regret, continued their old sensational persecution. One paper did more—the *San Francisco Intelligencer*. John Hartwell, its editor, elaborated an ingenious theory that got around the confessions of the two criminals and went to show that Gluck was responsible, after all, for the murder of Irene Tackley. Hartwell died. And Sherbourne died too, while Policeman Phillipps was shot in the leg and discharged from the Oakland police force.

The murder of Hartwell was long a mystery. He was alone in his editorial office at the time. The reports of the revolver were heard by the office boy, who rushed in to find Hartwell expiring in his chair. What puzzled the police was the fact, not merely that he had been shot with his own revolver, but that the revolver had been exploded in the drawer of his desk. The bullets had torn through the front of the drawer and entered his body. The police scouted the theory of suicide, murder was dismissed as absurd, and the blame was thrown upon the Eureka Smokeless Cartridge Company. Spontaneous explosion was the police explanation, and the chemists of the cartridge company were well bullied at the inquest. But what the police did not know was that across the street, in the Mercer Building, Room 633, rented by Emil Gluck, had been occupied by Emil Gluck at the very moment Hartwell's revolver so mysteriously exploded.

At the time, no connection was made between Hartwell's death and the death of William Sherbourne. Sherbourne had continued to live in the home he had built for Irene Tackley, and one morning in January, 1933, he was found dead. Suicide was the verdict of the coroner's inquest, for he had been shot by his own revolver. The curious thing that happened that night was the shooting of Policeman Phillipps on the sidewalk in front of Sherbourne's house. The policeman crawled to a police telephone on the corner and rang up for an ambulance. He claimed that some one had shot him from behind in the leg. The leg in question was so badly shattered by three '38 calibre bullets that amputation was necessary. But when the police discovered that the damage had been done by his own revolver, a great laugh went up, and he was charged with having been drunk. In spite of his denial of having touched a drop, and of his persistent assertion that the revolver had been in his hip pocket and that he had not laid a finger to it, he was discharged from the force. Emil Gluck's confession, six years later, cleared the unfortunate policeman of disgrace, and he is alive to-day and in good health, the recipient of a handsome pension from the city.

Emil Gluck, having disposed of his immediate enemies, now sought a wider field, though his enmity for newspaper men and for the police remained always active. The royalties on his ignition device for gasolene-engines had mounted up while he lay in prison, and year by year the earning power of his invention increased. He was independent, able to travel wherever he willed over the earth and to glut his monstrous appetite for revenge. He had become a monomaniac and an anarchist—not a philosophic anarchist, merely, but a violent anarchist. Perhaps the word is misused, and he is better described as a nihilist, or an annihilist. It is known that he affiliated with none of the groups of terrorists. He operated wholly alone, but he created a thousandfold more terror and achieved a thousandfold more destruction than all the terrorist groups added together.

He signalized his departure from California by blowing up Fort Mason. In his confession he spoke of it as a little experiment—he was merely trying his hand. For eight years he wandered over the earth, a mysterious terror, destroying property to the tune of hundreds of millions of dollars, and destroying countless lives. One good result of his awful deeds was the destruction he wrought among the terrorists themselves. Every time he did anything the terrorists in the vicinity were gathered in by the police dragnet, and many of them were executed. Seventeen were executed at Rome alone, following the assassination of the Italian King.

Perhaps the most world-amazing achievement of his was the assassination of the King and Queen of Portugal. It was their wedding day. All possible precautions had been taken against the terrorists, and the way from the cathedral, through Lisbon's streets, was double-banked with troops, while a squad of two hundred mounted troopers surrounded the carriage. Suddenly the amazing thing happened. The automatic rifles of the troopers began to go off, as well as the rifles, in the immediate vicinity, of the double-banked infantry. In the excitement the muzzles of the exploding rifles were turned in all directions. The slaughter was terrible—horses, troops, spectators, and the King and Queen, were riddled with bullets. To complicate the affair, in different parts of the crowd behind the foot-soldiers, two terrorists had bombs explode on their persons. These bombs they had intended to throw if they got the opportunity. But who was to know this? The frightful havoc wrought by the bursting bombs but added to the confusion; it was considered part of the general attack.

One puzzling thing that could not be explained away was the conduct of the troopers with their exploding rifles. It seemed impossible that they should be in the plot, yet there were the hundreds their flying bullets had slain, including the King and Queen. On the other hand, more baffling than ever was the fact that seventy per cent. of the troopers themselves had been killed or wounded. Some explained this on the ground that the loyal foot-soldiers, witnessing the attack on the royal carriage, had opened fire on the traitors. Yet not one bit of evidence to verify this could be drawn from the survivors, though many were put to the torture. They contended stubbornly that they had not discharged their rifles at all, but that their rifles had discharged themselves. They were laughed at by the chemists, who held that, while it was just barely probable that a single cartridge, charged with the new smokeless powder, might spontaneously explode, it was beyond all probability and possibility for all the cartridges in a given area, so charged, spontaneously to explode. And so, in the end, no explanation of the amazing occurrence was reached. The general opinion of the rest of the world was that the whole affair was a blind panic of the feverish Latins, precipitated, it was true, by the bursting of two terrorist bombs; and in this connection was recalled the laughable encounter of long years before between the Russian fleet and the English fishing boats.

And Emil Gluck chuckled and went his way. He knew. But how was the world to know? He had stumbled upon the secret in his old electroplating shop on Telegraph Avenue in the city of Oakland. It happened, at that time, that a wireless telegraph station was established by the Thurston Power Company close to his shop. In a short time his electroplating vat was put out of order. The vat-wiring had many bad joints, and, on investigation, Gluck discovered minute welds at the joints in the wiring. These, by lowering the resistance, had caused an excessive current to pass through the solution, "boiling" it and spoiling the work. But what had caused the welds? was the question in Gluck's mind. His reasoning was simple. Before the establishment of the wireless station, the vat had worked well. Not until after the establishment of the wireless station had the vat been ruined. Therefore the wireless station had been the cause. But how? He quickly answered the question. If an electric discharge was capable of operating a coherer across three thousand miles of ocean, then, certainly, the electric discharges from the wireless station four hundred feet away could produce coherer effects on the bad joints in the vat-wiring.

Gluck thought no more about it at the time. He merely re-wired his vat and went on electroplating. But afterwards, in prison, he remembered the incident, and like a flash there came into his mind the full significance of it. He saw in it the silent, secret weapon with which to revenge himself on the world. His great discovery, which died with him, was control over the direction and scope of the electric discharge. At the time, this was the unsolved problem of wireless telegraphy—as it still is to-day—but Emil Gluck, in his prison cell, mastered it. And, when he was released, he applied it. It was fairly simple, given the directing power that was his, to introduce a spark into the powder-magazines of a fort, a battleship, or a revolver. And not alone could he thus explode powder at a distance, but he could ignite conflagrations. The great Boston fire was started by him—quite by accident, however, as he stated in his confession, adding that it was a pleasing accident and that he had never had any reason to regret it.

It was Emil Gluck that caused the terrible German-American War, with the loss of 800,000 lives and the consumption of almost incalculable treasure.

It will be remembered that in 1939, because of the Pickard incident, strained relations existed between the two countries. Germany, though aggrieved, was not anxious for war, and, as a peace token, sent the Crown Prince and seven battleships on a friendly visit to the United States. On the night of February 15, the seven warships lay at anchor in the Hudson opposite New York City. And on that night Emil Gluck, alone, with all his apparatus on board, was out in a launch. This launch, it was afterwards proved, was bought by him from the Ross Turner Company, while much of the apparatus he used that night had been purchased from the Columbia Electric Works. But this was not known at the time. All that was known was that the seven battleships blew up, one after another, at regular four-minute intervals. Ninety per cent. of the crews and officers, along with the Crown Prince, perished. Many years before, the American battleship *Maine* had been blown up in the harbour of Havana, and war with Spain had immediately followed—though there has always existed a reasonable doubt as to whether the explosion was due to conspiracy or accident. But accident could not explain the blowing up of the seven battleships on the Hudson at four-minute intervals. Germany believed that it had been done by a submarine, and immediately declared war. It was six months after Gluck's confession that she returned the Philippines and Hawaii to the United States.

In the meanwhile Emil Gluck, the malevolent wizard and arch-hater, travelled his whirlwind path of destruction. He left no traces. Scientifically thorough, he always cleaned up after himself. His method was to rent a room or a house, and secretly to install his apparatus—which apparatus, by the way, he so perfected and simplified that it occupied little space. After he had accomplished his purpose he carefully removed the apparatus. He bade fair to live out a long life of horrible crime.

The epidemic of shooting of New York City policemen was a remarkable affair. It became one of the horror mysteries of the time. In two short weeks over a hundred policemen were shot in the legs by their own revolvers. Inspector Jones did not solve the mystery, but it was his idea that finally outwitted Gluck. On his recommendation the policemen ceased carrying revolvers, and no more accidental shootings occurred.

It was in the early spring of 1940 that Gluck destroyed the Mare Island navy-yard. From a room in Vallejo he sent his electric discharges across the Vallejo Straits to Mare Island. He first played his flashes on the battleship *Maryland*. She lay at the dock of one of the mine-magazines. On her forward deck, on a huge temporary platform of timbers, were disposed over a hundred mines. These mines were for the defence of the Golden Gate. Any one of these mines was capable of destroying a dozen battleships, and there were over a hundred mines. The destruction was terrific, but it was only Gluck's overture. He played his flashes down the Mare Island shore, blowing up five torpedo boats, the torpedo station, and the great magazine at the eastern end of the island. Returning westward again, and scooping in occasional isolated magazines on the high ground back from the shore, he blew up three cruisers and the battleships *Oregon, Delaware, New Hampshire*, and *Florida*— the latter had just gone into dry-dock, and the magnificent dry-dock was destroyed along with her.

It was a frightful catastrophe, and a shiver of horror passed through the land. But it was nothing to what was to follow. In the late fall of that year Emil Gluck made a clean sweep of the Atlantic seaboard from Maine to Florida. Nothing escaped. Forts, mines, coast defences of all sorts, torpedo stations, magazines—everything went up. Three months afterward, in midwinter, he smote the north shore of the Mediterranean from Gibraltar to Greece in the same stupefying manner. A wail went up from the nations. It was clear that human agency was behind all this destruction, and it was equally clear, through Emil Gluck's impartiality, that the destruction was not the work of any particular nation. One thing was patent, namely, that whoever was the human behind it all, that human was a menace to the world. No nation was safe. There was no defence against this unknown and all-powerful foe. Warfare was futile—nay, not merely futile but itself the very essence of the peril. For a twelve-month the manufacture of powder ceased, and all soldiers and sailors were withdrawn from all fortifications and war vessels. And even a world-disarmament was seriously considered at the Convention of the Powers, held at The Hague at that time.

And then Silas Bannerman, a secret service agent of the United States, leaped into world-fame by arresting Emil Gluck. At first Bannerman was laughed at, but he had prepared his case well, and in a few weeks the most sceptical were convinced of Emil Gluck's guilt. The one thing, however, that Silas Bannerman never succeeded in explaining, even to his own satisfaction, was how first he came to connect Gluck with the atrocious crimes. It is true, Bannerman was in Vallejo, on secret government business, at the time of the destruction of Mare Island; and it is true that on the streets of Vallejo Emil Gluck was pointed out to him as a queer crank; but no impression was made at the time. It was not until afterward, when on a vacation in the Rocky Mountains and when reading the first published reports of the destruction along the Atlantic Coast, that suddenly Bannerman thought of Emil Gluck. And on the instant there flashed into his mind the connection between Gluck and the destruction. It was only an hypothesis, but it was sufficient. The great thing was the conception of the hypothesis, in itself an act of unconscious cerebration—a thing as unaccountable as the flashing, for instance, into Newton's mind of the principle of gravitation.

The rest was easy. Where was Gluck at the time of the destruction along the Atlantic sea-board? was the question that formed in Bannerman's mind. By his own request he was put upon the case. In no time he ascertained that Gluck had himself been up and down the Atlantic Coast in the late fall of 1940. Also he ascertained that Gluck had been in New York City during the epidemic of the shooting of police officers. Where was Gluck now? was Bannerman's next query. And, as if in answer, came the wholesale destruction along the Mediterranean. Gluck had sailed for Europe a month before—Bannerman knew that. It was not necessary for Bannerman to go to Europe. By means of cable messages and the co-operation of the European secret services, he traced Gluck's course along the Mediterranean and found that in every instance it coincided with the blowing up of coast defences and ships. Also, he learned that Gluck had just sailed on the Green Star liner *Plutonic* for the United States.

The case was complete in Bannerman's mind, though in the interval of waiting he worked up the details. In this he was ably assisted by George

Brown, an operator employed by the Wood's System of Wireless Telegraphy. When the *Plutonic* arrived off Sandy Hook she was boarded by Bannerman from a Government tug, and Emil Gluck was made a prisoner. The trial and the confession followed. In the confession Gluck professed regret only for one thing, namely, that he had taken his time. As he said, had he dreamed that he was ever to be discovered he would have worked more rapidly and accomplished a thousand times the destruction he did. His secret died with him, though it is now known that the French Government managed to get access to him and offered him a billion francs for his invention wherewith he was able to direct and closely to confine electric discharges. "What!" was Gluck's reply—"to sell to you that which would enable you to enslave and maltreat suffering Humanity?" And though the war departments of the nations have continued to experiment in their secret laboratories, they have so far failed to light upon the slightest trace of the secret. Emil Gluck was executed on December 4, 1941, and so died, at the age of forty-six, one of the world's most unfortunate geniuses, a man of tremendous intellect, but whose mighty powers, instead of making toward good, were so twisted and warped that he became the most amazing of criminals.

—Culled from Mr. A. G. Burnside's "Eccentricitics of Crime," by kind permission of the publishers, Messrs. Holiday and Whitsund.

THE DREAM OF DEBS

I awoke fully an hour before my customary time. This in itself was remarkable, and I lay very wide awake, pondering over it. Something was the matter, something was wrong—I knew not what. I was oppressed by a premonition of something terrible that had happened or was about to happen. But what was it? I strove to orient myself. I remembered that at the time of the Great Earthquake of 1906 many claimed they awakened some moments before the first shock and that during these moments they experienced strange feelings of dread. Was San Francisco again to be visited by earthquake?

I lay for a full minute, numbly expectant, but there occurred no reeling of walls nor shock and grind of falling masonry. All was quiet. That was it! The silence! No wonder I had been perturbed. The hum of the great live city was strangely absent. The surface cars passed along my street, at that time of day, on an average of one every three minutes; but in the ten succeeding minutes not a car passed. Perhaps it was a street-railway strike, was my thought; or perhaps there had been an accident and the power was shut off. But no, the silence was too profound. I heard no jar and rattle of waggon wheels, nor stamp of iron-shod hoofs straining up the steep cobble-stones.

Pressing the push-button beside my bed, I strove to hear the sound of the bell, though I well knew it was impossible for the sound to rise three stories to me even if the bell did ring. It rang all right, for a few minutes later Brown entered with the tray and morning paper. Though his features were impassive as ever, I noted a startled, apprehensive light in his eyes. I noted, also, that there was no cream on the tray.

"The Creamery did not deliver this morning," he explained; "nor did the bakery."

I glanced again at the tray. There were no fresh French rolls—only slices of stale graham bread from yesterday, the most detestable of bread so far as I was concerned.

"Nothing was delivered this morning, sir," Brown started to explain apologetically; but I interrupted him.

"The paper?"

"Yes, sir, it was delivered, but it was the only thing, and it is the last time, too. There won't be any paper to-morrow. The paper says so. Can I send out and get you some condensed milk?"

I shook my head, accepted the coffee black, and spread open the paper. The headlines explained everything—explained too much, in fact, for the lengths of pessimism to which the journal went were ridiculous. A general strike, it said, had been called all over the United States; and most foreboding anxieties were expressed concerning the provisioning of the great cities.

I read on hastily, skimming much and remembering much of labour troubles in the past. For a generation the general strike had been the dream of organized labour, which dream had arisen originally in the mind of Debs, one of the great labour leaders of thirty years before. I recollected that in my young college-settlement days I had even written an article on the subject for one of the magazines and that I had entitled it "The Dream of Debs." And I must confess that I had treated the idea very cavalierly and academically as a dream and nothing more. Time and the world had rolled on, Gompers was gone, the American Federation of Labour was gone, and gone was Debs with all his wild revolutionary ideas; but the dream had persisted, and here it was at last realized in fact. But I laughed, as I read, at the journal's gloomy outlook. I knew better. I had seen organized labour worsted in too many conflicts. It would be a matter only of days when the thing would be settled. This was a national strike, and it wouldn't take the Government long to break it.

I threw the paper down and proceeded to dress. It would certainly be interesting to be out in the streets of San Francisco when not a wheel was turning and the whole city was taking an enforced vacation.

"I beg your pardon, sir," Brown said, as he handed me my cigar-case, "but Mr. Harmmed has asked to see you before you go out."

"Send him in right away," I answered.

Harmmed was the butler. When he entered I could see he was labouring under controlled excitement. He came at once to the point.

"What shall I do, sir? There will be needed provisions, and the delivery drivers are on strike. And the electricity is shut off—I guess they're on strike, too."

"Are the shops open?" I asked.

"Only the small ones, sir. The retail clerks are out, and the big ones can't open; but the owners and their families are running the little ones themselves."

"Then take the machine," I said, "and go the rounds and make your purchases. Buy plenty of everything you need or may need. Get a box of candles—no, get half-a-dozen boxes. And, when you're done, tell Harrison to bring the machine around to the club for me—not later than eleven."

Harmmed shook his head gravely. "Mr. Harrison has struck along with the Chauffeurs' Union, and I don't know how to run the machine myself."

"Oh, ho, he has, has he?" said I. "Well, when next Mister Harrison happens around you tell him that he can look elsewhere for a position."

"Yes, sir."

"You don't happen to belong to a Butlers' Union, do you, Harmmed?"

"No, sir," was the answer. "And even if I did I'd not desert my employer in a crisis like this. No, sir, I would—"

"All right, thank you," I said. "Now you get ready to accompany me. I'll run the machine myself, and we'll lay in a stock of provisions to stand a siege."

It was a beautiful first of May, even as May days go. The sky was cloudless, there was no wind, and the air was warm—almost balmy. Many autos were out, but the owners were driving them themselves. The streets were crowded but quiet. The working class, dressed in its Sunday best, was out taking the air and observing the effects of the strike. It was all so unusual, and withal so peaceful, that I found myself enjoying it. My nerves were tingling with mild excitement. It was a sort of placid adventure. I passed Miss Chickering. She was at the helm of her little runabout. She swung around and came after me, catching me at the corner.

"Oh, Mr. Corf!" she hailed. "Do you know where I can buy candles? I've been to a dozen shops, and they're all sold out. It's dreadfully awful, isn't it?"

But her sparkling eyes gave the lie to her words. Like the rest of us, she was enjoying it hugely. Quite an adventure it was, getting those candles. It was not until we went across the city and down into the working-class quarter south of Market Street that we found small corner groceries that had not yet sold out. Miss Chickering thought one box was sufficient, but I persuaded her into taking four. My car was large, and I laid in a dozen boxes. There was no telling what delays might arise in the settlement of the strike. Also, I filled the car with sacks of flour, baking-powder, tinned goods, and all the ordinary necessaries of life suggested by Harmmed, who fussed around and clucked over the purchases like an anxious old hen.

The remarkable thing, that first day of the strike, was that no one really apprehended anything serious. The announcement of organized labour in the morning papers that it was prepared to stay out a month or three months was laughed at. And yet that very first day we might have guessed as much from the fact that the working class took practically no part in the great rush to buy provisions. Of course not. For weeks and months, craftily and secretly, the whole working class had been laying in private stocks of provisions. That was why we were permitted to go down and buy out the little groceries in the working-class neighbourhoods.

It was not until I arrived at the club that afternoon that I began to feel the first alarm. Everything was in confusion. There were no olives for the cocktails, and the service was by hitches and jerks. Most of the men were angry, and all were worried. A babel of voices greeted me as I entered. General Folsom, nursing his capacious paunch in a window-seat in the smoking-room was defending himself against half-a-dozen excited gentlemen who were demanding that he should do something.

231

"What can I do more than I have done?" he was saying. "There are no orders from Washington. If you gentlemen will get a wire through I'll do anything I am commanded to do. But I don't see what can be done. The first thing I did this morning, as soon as I learned of the strike, was to order in the troops from the Presidio—three thousand of them. They're guarding the banks, the Mint, the post office, and all the public buildings. There is no disorder whatever. The strikers are keeping the peace perfectly. You can't expect me to shoot them down as they walk along the streets with wives and children all in their best bib and tucker."

"I'd like to know what's happening on Wall Street," I heard Jimmy Wombold say as I passed along. I could imagine his anxiety, for I knew that he was deep in the big Consolidated-Western deal.

"Say, Corf," Atkinson bustled up to me, "is your machine running?"

"Yes," I answered, "but what's the matter with your own?"

"Broken down, and the garages are all closed. And my wife's somewhere around Truckee, I think, stalled on the overland. Can't get a wire to her for love or money. She should have arrived this evening. She may be starving. Lend me your machine."

"Can't get it across the bay," Halstead spoke up. "The ferries aren't running. But I tell you what you can do. There's Rollinson—oh, Rollinson, come here a moment. Atkinson wants to get a machine across the bay. His wife is stuck on the overland at Truckee. Can't you bring the *Lurlette* across from Tiburon and carry the machine over for him?"

The *Lurlette* was a two-hundred-ton, ocean-going schooner-yacht.

Rollinson shook his head. "You couldn't get a longshoreman to land the machine on board, even if I could get the *Lurlette* over, which I can't, for the crew are members of the Coast Seamen's Union, and they're on strike along with the rest."

"But my wife may be starving," I could hear Atkinson wailing as I moved on.

At the other end of the smoking-room I ran into a group of men bunched excitedly and angrily around Bertie Messener. And Bertie was stirring them up and prodding them in his cool, cynical way. Bertie didn't care about the strike. He didn't care much about anything. He was blasé—at least in all the clean things of life; the nasty things had no attraction for him. He was worth twenty millions, all of it in safe investments, and he had never done a tap of productive work in his life—inherited it all from his father and two uncles. He had been everywhere, seen everything, and done everything but get married, and this last in the face of the grim and determined attack of a few hundred ambitious mammas. For years he had been the greatest catch, and as yet he had avoided being caught. He was disgracefully eligible. On top of his wealth he was young, handsome, and, as I said before, clean. He was a great athlete, a young blond god that did everything perfectly and admirably with the solitary exception of matrimony. And he didn't care about anything, had no ambitions, no passions, no desire to do the very things he did so much better than other men.

"This is sedition!" one man in the group was crying. Another called it revolt and revolution, and another called it anarchy.

"I can't see it," Bertie said. "I have been out in the streets all morning. Perfect order reigns. I never saw a more law-abiding populace. There's no use calling it names. It's not any of those things. It's just what it claims to be, a general strike, and it's your turn to play, gentlemen."

"And we'll play all right!" cried Garfield, one of the traction millionaires. "We'll show this dirt where its place is—the beasts! Wait till the Government takes a hand."

"But where is the Government?" Bertie interposed. "It might as well be at the bottom of the sea so far as you're concerned. You don't know what's happening at Washington. You don't know whether you've got a Government or not."

"Don't you worry about that," Garfield blurted out.

"I assure you I'm not worrying," Bertie smiled languidly. "But it seems to me it's what you fellows are doing. Look in the glass, Garfield."

Garfield did not look, but had he looked he would have seen a very excited gentleman with rumpled, iron-grey hair, a flushed face, mouth sullen and vindictive, and eyes wildly gleaming.

"It's not right, I tell you," little Hanover said; and from his tone I was sure that he had already said it a number of times.

"Now that's going too far, Hanover," Bertie replied. "You fellows make me tired. You're all open-shop men. You've eroded my eardrums with your endless gabble for the open shop and the right of a man to work. You've harangued along those lines for years. Labour is doing nothing wrong in going out on this general strike. It is violating no law of God nor man. Don't you talk, Hanover. You've been ringing the changes too long on the God-given right to work . . . or not to work; you can't escape the corollary. It's a dirty little sordid scrap, that's all the whole thing is. You've got labour down and gouged it, and now labour's got you down and is gouging you, that's all, and you're squealing."

Every man in the group broke out in indignant denials that labour had ever been gouged.

"No, sir!" Garfield was shouting. "We've done the best for labour. Instead of gouging it, we've given it a chance to live. We've made work for it. Where would labour be if it hadn't been for us?"

"A whole lot better off," Bertie sneered. "You've got labour down and gouged it every time you got a chance, and you went out of your way to make chances."

"No! No!" were the cries.

"There was the teamsters' strike, right here in San Francisco," Bertie went on imperturbably. "The Employers' Association precipitated that strike. You know that. And you know I know it, too, for I've sat in these very rooms and heard the inside talk and news of the fight. First you precipitated the strike, then you bought the Mayor and the Chief of Police and broke the strike. A pretty spectacle, you philanthropists getting the teamsters down and gouging them.

234

"Hold on, I'm not through with you. It's only last year that the labour ticket of Colorado elected a governor. He was never seated. You know why. You know how your brother philanthropists and capitalists of Colorado worked it. It was a case of getting labour down and gouging it. You kept the president of the South-western Amalgamated Association of Miners in jail for three years on trumped-up murder charges, and with him out of the way you broke up the association. That was gouging labour, you'll admit. The third time the graduated income tax was declared unconstitutional was a gouge. So was the eight-hour Bill you killed in the last Congress.

"And of all unmitigated immoral gouges, your destruction of the closed-shop principle was the limit. You know how it was done. You bought out Farburg, the last president of the old American Federation of Labour. He was your creature—or the creature of all the trusts and employers' associations, which is the same thing. You precipitated the big closed-shop strike. Farburg betrayed that strike. You won, and the old American Federation of Labour crumbled to pieces. You fellows destroyed it, and by so doing undid yourselves; for right on top of it began the organization of the I.L.W.—the biggest and solidest organization of labour the United States has ever seen, and you are responsible for its existence and for the present general strike. You smashed all the old federations and drove labour into the I.L.W., and the I.L.W. called the general strike—still fighting for the closed shop. And then you have the effrontery to stand here face to face and tell me that you never got labour down and gouged it. Bah!"

This time there were no denials. Garfield broke out in self-defence—

"We've done nothing we were not compelled to do, if we were to win."

"I'm not saying anything about that," Bertie answered. "What I am complaining about is your squealing now that you're getting a taste of your own medicine. How many strikes have you won by starving labour into submission? Well, labour's worked out a scheme whereby to starve you into submission. It wants the closed shop, and, if it can get it by starving you, why, starve you shall."

"I notice that you have profited in the past by those very labour gouges you mention," insinuated Brentwood, one of the wiliest and most astute of our corporation lawyers. "The receiver is as bad as the thief," he sneered. "You had no hand in the gouging, but you took your whack out of the gouge."

"That is quite beside the question, Brentwood," Bertie drawled. "You're as bad as Hanover, intruding the moral element. I haven't said that anything is right or wrong. It's all a rotten game, I know; and my sole kick is that you fellows are squealing now that you're down and labour's taking a gouge out of you. Of course I've taken the profits from the gouging and, thanks to you, gentlemen, without having personally to do the dirty work. You did that for me—oh, believe me, not because I am more virtuous than you, but because my good father and his various brothers left me a lot of money with which to pay for the dirty work."

"If you mean to insinuate—" Brentwood began hotly.

"Hold on, don't get all-ruffled up," Bertie interposed insolently. "There's no use in playing hypocrites in this thieves' den. The high and lofty is all right for the newspapers, boys' clubs, and Sunday schools—that's part of the game; but for heaven's sake don't let's play it on one another. You know, and you know that I know just what jobbery was done in the building trades' strike last fall, who put up the money, who did the work, and who profited by it." (Brentwood flushed darkly.) "But we are all tarred with the same brush, and the best thing for us to do is to leave morality out of it. Again I repeat, play the game, play it to the last finish, but for goodness' sake don't squeal when you get hurt."

When I left the group Bertie was off on a new tack tormenting them with the more serious aspects of the situation, pointing out the shortage of supplies that was already making itself felt, and asking them what they were going to do about it. A little later I met him in the cloak-room, leaving, and gave him a lift home in my machine.

"It's a great stroke, this general strike," he said, as we bowled along through the crowded but orderly streets. "It's a smashing body-blow. Labour caught us napping and struck at our weakest place, the stomach. I'm going to get out of San Francisco, Corf. Take my advice and get out, too. Head for the country, anywhere. You'll have more chance. Buy up a stock of supplies and get into a tent or a cabin somewhere. Soon there'll be nothing but starvation in this city for such as we."

How correct Bertie Messener was I never dreamed. I decided that he was an alarmist. As for myself, I was content to remain and watch the fun. After I dropped him, instead of going directly home, I went on in a hunt for more food. To my surprise, I learned that the small groceries where I had bought in the morning were sold out. I extended my search to the Potrero, and by good luck managed to pick up another box of candles, two sacks of wheat flour, ten pounds of graham flour (which would do for the servants), a case of tinned corn, and two cases of tinned tomatoes. It did look as though there was going to be at least a temporary food shortage, and I hugged myself over the goodly stock of provisions I had laid in.

The next morning I had my coffee in bed as usual, and, more than the cream, I missed the daily paper. It was this absence of knowledge of what was going on in the world that I found the chief hardship. Down at the club there was little news. Rider had crossed from Oakland in his launch, and Halstead had been down to San Jose and back in his machine. They reported the same conditions in those places as in San Francisco. Everything was tied up by the strike. All grocery stocks had been bought out by the upper classes. And perfect order reigned. But what was happening over the rest of the country— in Chicago? New York? Washington? Most probably the same things that were happening with us, we concluded; but the fact that we did not know with absolute surety was irritating.

General Folsom had a bit of news. An attempt had been made to place army telegraphers in the telegraph offices, but the wires had been cut in every direction. This was, so far, the one unlawful act committed by labour, and that it was a concerted act he was fully convinced. He had communicated by wireless with the army post at Benicia, the telegraph lines were even then being patrolled by soldiers all the way to Sacramento. Once, for one short instant, they had got the Sacramento call, then the wires, somewhere, were cut again. General Folsom reasoned that similar attempts to open communication were being made by the authorities all the way across the continent, but he was non-committal as to whether or not he thought the attempt would succeed. What worried him was the wire-cutting; he could not but believe that it was an important part of the deep-laid labour conspiracy. Also, he regretted that the Government had not long since established its projected chain of wireless stations.

The days came and went, and for a while it was a humdrum time. Nothing happened. The edge of excitement had become blunted. The streets were not so crowded. The working class did not come uptown any more to see how we were taking the strike. And there were not so many automobiles running around. The repair-shops and garages were closed, and whenever a machine broke down it went out of commission. The clutch on mine broke, and neither love nor money could get it repaired. Like the rest, I was now walking. San Francisco lay dead, and we did not know what was happening over the rest of the country. But from the very fact that we did not know we could conclude only that the rest of the country lay as dead as San Francisco. From time to time the city was placarded with the proclamations of organized labour—these had been printed months before, and evidenced how thoroughly the I.L.W. had prepared for the strike. Every detail had been worked out long in advance. No violence had occurred as yet, with the exception of the shooting of a few wire-cutters by the soldiers, but the people of the slums were starving and growing ominously restless.

The business men, the millionaires, and the professional class held meetings and passed resolutions, but there was no way of making the proclamations public. They could not even get them printed. One result of these meetings, however, was that General Folsom was persuaded into taking military possession of the wholesale houses and of all the flour, grain, and food warehouses. It was high time, for suffering was becoming acute in the homes of the rich, and bread-lines were necessary. I knew that my servants were beginning to draw long faces, and it was amazing—the hole they made in my stock of provisions. In fact, as I afterward surmised, each servant was stealing from me and secreting a private stock of provisions for himself.

238

But with the formation of the bread-lines came new troubles. There was only so much of a food reserve in San Francisco, and at the best it could not last long. Organized labour, we knew, had its private supplies; nevertheless, the whole working class joined the bread-lines. As a result, the provisions General Folsom had taken possession of diminished with perilous rapidity. How were the soldiers to distinguish between a shabby middle-class man, a member of the I.L.W., or a slum dweller? The first and the last had to be fed, but the soldiers did not know all the I.L.W. men in the city, much less the wives and sons and daughters of the I.L.W. men. The employers helping, a few of the known union men were flung out of the bread-lines; but that amounted to nothing. To make matters worse, the Government tugs that had been hauling food from the army depots on Mare Island to Angel Island found no more food to haul. The soldiers now received their rations from the confiscated provisions, and they received them first.

The beginning of the end was in sight. Violence was beginning to show its face. Law and order were passing away, and passing away, I must confess, among the slum people and the upper classes. Organized labour still maintained perfect order. It could well afford to—it had plenty to eat. I remember the afternoon at the club when I caught Halstead and Brentwood whispering in a corner. They took me in on the venture. Brentwood's machine was still in running order, and they were going out cow-stealing. Halstead had a long butcher knife and a cleaver. We went out to the outskirts of the city. Here and there were cows grazing, but always they were guarded by their owners. We pursued our quest, following along the fringe of the city to the east, and on the hills near Hunter's Point we came upon a cow guarded by a little girl. There was also a young calf with the cow. We wasted no time on preliminaries. The little girl ran away screaming, while we slaughtered the cow. I omit the details, for they are not nice—we were unaccustomed to such work, and we bungled it.

But in the midst of it, working with the haste of fear, we heard cries, and we saw a number of men running toward us. We abandoned the spoils and took to our heels. To our surprise we were not pursued. Looking back, we saw the men hurriedly cutting up the cow. They had been on the same lay as ourselves. We argued that there was plenty for all, and ran back. The scene that followed beggars description. We fought and squabbled over the division like savages. Brentwood, I remember, was a perfect brute, snarling and snapping and threatening that murder would be done if we did not get our proper share.

And we were getting our share when there occurred a new irruption on the scene. This time it was the dreaded peace officers of the I.L.W. The little girl had brought them. They were armed with whips and clubs, and there were a score of them. The little girl danced up and down in anger, the tears streaming down her cheeks, crying: "Give it to 'em! Give it to 'em! That guy with the specs—he did it! Mash his face for him! Mash his face!" That guy with the specs was I, and I got my face mashed, too, though I had the presence of mind to take off my glasses at the first. My! but we did receive a trouncing as we scattered in all directions. Brentwood, Halstead, and I fled away for the machine. Brentwood's nose was bleeding, while Halstead's cheek was cut across with the scarlet slash of a black-snake whip.

And, lo, when the pursuit ceased and we had gained the machine, there, hiding behind it, was the frightened calf. Brentwood warned us to be cautious, and crept up on it like a wolf or tiger. Knife and cleaver had been left behind, but Brentwood still had his hands, and over and over on the ground he rolled with the poor little calf as he throttled it. We threw the carcass into the machine, covered it over with a robe, and started for home. But our misfortunes had only begun. We blew out a tyre. There was no way of fixing it, and twilight was coming on. We abandoned the machine, Brentwood pulling and staggering along in advance, the calf, covered by the robe, slung across his shoulders. We took turn about carrying that calf, and it nearly killed us. Also, we lost our way. And then, after hours of wandering and toil, we encountered a gang of hoodlums. They were not I.L.W. men, and I guess they were as hungry as we. At any rate, they got the calf and we got the thrashing. Brentwood raged like a madman the rest of the way home, and he looked like one, with his torn clothes, swollen nose, and blackened eyes.

There wasn't any more cow-stealing after that. General Folsom sent his troopers out and confiscated all the cows, and his troopers, aided by the militia, ate most of the meat. General Folsom was not to be blamed; it was his duty to maintain law and order, and he maintained it by means of the soldiers, wherefore he was compelled to feed them first of all.

It was about this time that the great panic occurred. The wealthy classes precipitated the flight, and then the slum people caught the contagion and stampeded wildly out of the city. General Folsom was pleased. It was estimated that at least 200,000 had deserted San Francisco, and by that much was his food problem solved. Well do I remember that day. In the morning I had eaten a crust of bread. Half of the afternoon I had stood in the bread-line; and after dark I returned home, tired and miserable, carrying a quart of rice and a slice of bacon. Brown met me at the door. His face was worn and terrified. All the servants had fled, he informed me. He alone remained. I was touched by his faithfulness and, when I learned that he had eaten nothing all day, I divided my food with him. We cooked half the rice and half the bacon, sharing it equally and reserving the other half for morning. I went to bed with my hunger, and tossed restlessly all night. In the morning I found Brown had deserted me, and, greater misfortune still, he had stolen what remained of the rice and bacon.

It was a gloomy handful of men that came together at the club that morning. There was no service at all. The last servant was gone. I noticed, too, that the silver was gone, and I learned where it had gone. The servants had not taken it, for the reason, I presume, that the club members got to it first. Their method of disposing of it was simple. Down south of Market Street, in the dwellings of the I.L.W., the housewives had given square meals in exchange for it. I went back to my house. Yes, my silver was gone—all but a massive pitcher. This I wrapped up and carried down south of Market Street.

I felt better after the meal, and returned to the club to learn if there was anything new in the situation. Hanover, Collins, and Dakon were just leaving. There was no one inside, they told me, and they invited me to come along with them. They were leaving the city, they said, on Dakon's horses, and there was a spare one for me. Dakon had four magnificent carriage horses that he wanted to save, and General Folsom had given him the tip that next morning all the horses that remained in the city were to be confiscated for food. There were not many horses left, for tens of thousands of them had been turned loose into the country when the hay and grain gave out during the first days. Birdall, I remember, who had great draying interests, had turned loose three hundred dray horses. At an average value of five hundred dollars, this had amounted to $150,000. He had hoped, at first, to recover most of the horses after the strike was over, but in the end he never recovered one of them. They were all eaten by the people that fled from San Francisco. For that matter, the killing of the army mules and horses for food had already begun.

Fortunately for Dakon, he had had a plentiful supply of hay and grain stored in his stable. We managed to raise four saddles, and we found the animals in good condition and spirited, withal unused to being ridden. I remembered the San Francisco of the great earthquake as we rode through the streets, but this San Francisco was vastly more pitiable. No cataclysm of nature had caused this, but, rather, the tyranny of the labour unions. We rode down past Union Square and through the theatre, hotel, and shopping districts. The streets were deserted. Here and there stood automobiles, abandoned where they had broken down or when the gasolene had given out. There was no sign of life, save for the occasional policemen and the soldiers guarding the banks and public buildings. Once we came upon an I.L.W. man pasting up the latest proclamation. We stopped to read. "We have maintained an orderly strike," it ran; "and we shall maintain order to the end. The end will come when our demands are satisfied, and our demands will be satisfied when we have starved our employers into submission, as we ourselves in the past have often been starved into submission."

"Messener's very words," Collins said. "And I, for one, am ready to submit, only they won't give me a chance to submit. I haven't had a full meal in an age. I wonder what horse-meat tastes like?"

We stopped to read another proclamation: "When we think our employers are ready to submit we shall open up the telegraphs and place the employers' associations of the United States in communication. But only messages relating to peace terms shall be permitted over the wires."

We rode on, crossed Market Street, and a little later were passing through the working-class district. Here the streets were not deserted. Leaning over the gates or standing in groups were the I.L.W. men. Happy, well-fed children were playing games, and stout housewives sat on the front steps gossiping. One and all cast amused glances at us. Little children ran after us, crying: "Hey, mister, ain't you hungry?" And one woman, nursing a child at her breast, called to Dakon: "Say, Fatty, I'll give you a meal for your skate—ham and potatoes, currant jelly, white bread, canned butter, and two cups of coffee."

"Have you noticed, the last few days," Hanover remarked to me, "that there's not been a stray dog in the streets?"

I had noticed, but I had not thought about it before. It was high time to leave the unfortunate city. We at last managed to connect with the San Bruno Road, along which we headed south. I had a country place near Menlo, and it was our objective. But soon we began to discover that the country was worse off and far more dangerous than the city. There the soldiers and the I.L.W. kept order; but the country had been turned over to anarchy. Two hundred thousand people had fled from San Francisco, and we had countless evidences that their flight had been like that of an army of locusts.

They had swept everything clean. There had been robbery and fighting. Here and there we passed bodies by the roadside and saw the blackened ruins of farm-houses. The fences were down, and the crops had been trampled by the feet of a multitude. All the vegetable patches had been rooted up by the famished hordes. All the chickens and farm animals had been slaughtered. This was true of all the main roads that led out of San Francisco. Here and there, away from the roads, farmers had held their own with shotguns and revolvers, and were still holding their own. They warned us away and refused to parley with us. And all the destruction and violence had been done by the slum-dwellers and the upper classes. The I.L.W. men, with plentiful food supplies, remained quietly in their homes in the cities.

Early in the ride we received concrete proof of how desperate was the situation. To the right of us we heard cries and rifle-shots. Bullets whistled dangerously near. There was a crashing in the underbrush; then a magnificent black truck-horse broke across the road in front of us and was gone. We had barely time to notice that he was bleeding and lame. He was followed by three soldiers. The chase went on among the trees on the left. We could hear the soldiers calling to one another. A fourth soldier limped out upon the road from the right, sat down on a boulder, and mopped the sweat from his face.

"Militia," Dakon whispered. "Deserters."

The man grinned up at us and asked for a match. In reply to Dakon's "What's the word?" he informed us that the militiamen were deserting. "No grub," he explained. "They're feedin' it all to the regulars." We also learned from him that the military prisoners had been released from Alcatraz Island because they could no longer be fed.

I shall never forget the next sight we encountered. We came upon it abruptly around a turn of the road. Overhead arched the trees. The sunshine was filtering down through the branches. Butterflies were fluttering by, and from the fields came the song of larks. And there it stood, a powerful touring car. About it and in it lay a number of corpses. It told its own tale. Its occupants, fleeing from the city, had been attacked and dragged down by a gang of slum dwellers—hoodlums. The thing had occurred within twenty-four hours. Freshly opened meat and fruit tins explained the reason for the attack. Dakon examined the bodies.

"I thought so," he reported. "I've ridden in that car. It was Perriton—the whole family. We've got to watch out for ourselves from now on."

"But we have no food with which to invite attack," I objected.

Dakon pointed to the horse I rode, and I understood.

244

Early in the day Dakon's horse had cast a shoe. The delicate hoof had split, and by noon the animal was limping. Dakon refused to ride it farther, and refused to desert it. So, on his solicitation, we went on. He would lead the horse and join us at my place. That was the last we saw of him; nor did we ever learn his end.

By one o'clock we arrived at the town of Menlo, or, rather, at the site of Menlo, for it was in ruins. Corpses lay everywhere. The business part of the town, as well as part of the residences, had been gutted by fire. Here and there a residence still held out; but there was no getting near them. When we approached too closely we were fired upon. We met a woman who was poking about in the smoking ruins of her cottage. The first attack, she told us had been on the stores, and as she talked we could picture that raging, roaring, hungry mob flinging itself on the handful of townspeople. Millionaires and paupers had fought side by side for the food, and then fought with one another after they got it. The town of Palo Alto and Stanford University had been sacked in similar fashion, we learned. Ahead of us lay a desolate, wasted land; and we thought we were wise in turning off to my place. It lay three miles to the west, snuggling among the first rolling swells of the foothills.

But as we rode along we saw that the devastation was not confined to the main roads. The van of the flight had kept to the roads, sacking the small towns as it went; while those that followed had scattered out and swept the whole countryside like a great broom. My place was built of concrete, masonry, and tiles, and so had escaped being burned, but it was gutted clean. We found the gardener's body in the windmill, littered around with empty shot-gun shells. He had put up a good fight. But no trace could we find of the two Italian labourers, nor of the house-keeper and her husband. Not a live thing remained. The calves, the colts, all the fancy poultry and thoroughbred stock, everything, was gone. The kitchen and the fireplaces, where the mob had cooked, were a mess, while many camp-fires outside bore witness to the large number that had fed and spent the night. What they had not eaten they had carried away. There was not a bite for us.

We spent the rest of the night vainly waiting for Dakon, and in the morning, with our revolvers, fought off half-a-dozen marauders. Then we killed one of Dakon's horses, hiding for the future what meat we did not immediately eat. In the afternoon Collins went out for a walk, but failed to return. This was the last straw to Hanover. He was for flight there and then, and I had great difficulty in persuading him to wait for daylight. As for myself, I was convinced that the end of the general strike was near, and I was resolved to return to San Francisco. So, in the morning, we parted company, Hanover heading south, fifty pounds of horse-meat strapped to his saddle, while I, similarly loaded, headed north. Little Hanover pulled through all right, and to the end of his life he will persist, I know, in boring everybody with the narrative of his subsequent adventures.

I got as far as Belmont, on the main road back, when I was robbed of my horse-meat by three militiamen. There was no change in the situation, they said, except that it was going from bad to worse. The I.L.W. had plenty of provisions hidden away and could last out for months. I managed to get as far as Baden, when my horse was taken away from me by a dozen men. Two of them were San Francisco policemen, and the remainder were regular soldiers. This was ominous. The situation was certainly extreme when the regulars were beginning to desert. When I continued my way on foot, they already had the fire started, and the last of Dakon's horses lay slaughtered on the ground.

As luck would have it, I sprained my ankle, and succeeded in getting no farther than South San Francisco. I lay there that night in an out-house, shivering with the cold and at the same time burning with fever. Two days I lay there, too sick to move, and on the third, reeling and giddy, supporting myself on an extemporized crutch, I tottered on toward San Francisco. I was weak as well, for it was the third day since food had passed my lips. It was a day of nightmare and torment. As in a dream I passed hundreds of regular soldiers drifting along in the opposite direction, and many policemen, with their families, organized in large groups for mutual protection.

As I entered the city I remembered the workman's house at which I had traded the silver pitcher, and in that direction my hunger drove me. Twilight was falling when I came to the place. I passed around by the alleyway and crawled up the black steps, on which I collapsed. I managed to reach out with the crutch and knock on the door. Then I must have fainted, for I came to in the kitchen, my face wet with water, and whisky being poured down my throat. I choked and spluttered and tried to talk. I began saying something about not having any more silver pitchers, but that I would make it up to them afterward if they would only give me something to eat. But the housewife interrupted me.

"Why, you poor man," she said, "haven't you heard? The strike was called off this afternoon. Of course we'll give you something to eat."

She bustled around, opening a tin of breakfast bacon and preparing to fry it.

"Let me have some now, please," I begged; and I ate the raw bacon on a slice of bread, while her husband explained that the demands of the I.L.W. had been granted. The wires had been opened up in the early afternoon, and everywhere the employers' associations had given in. There hadn't been any employers left in San Francisco, but General Folsom had spoken for them. The trains and steamers would start running in the morning, and so would everything else just as soon as system could be established.

And that was the end of the general strike. I never want to see another one. It was worse than a war. A general strike is a cruel and immoral thing, and the brain of man should be capable of running industry in a more rational way. Harrison is still my chauffeur. It was part of the conditions of the I.L.W. that all of its members should be reinstated in their old positions. Brown never came back, but the rest of the servants are with me. I hadn't the heart to discharge them—poor creatures, they were pretty hard-pressed when they deserted with the food and silver. And now I can't discharge them. They have all been unionized by the I.L.W. The tyranny of organized labour is getting beyond human endurance. Something must be done.

THE SEA-FARMER

"That wull be the doctor's launch," said Captain MacElrath.

The pilot grunted, while the skipper swept on with his glass from the launch to the strip of beach and to Kingston beyond, and then slowly across the entrance to Howth Head on the northern side.

"The tide's right, and we'll have you docked in two hours," the pilot vouchsafed, with an effort at cheeriness. "Ring's End Basin, is it?"

This time the skipper grunted.

"A dirty Dublin day."

Again the skipper grunted. He was weary with the night of wind in the Irish Channel behind him, the unbroken hours of which he had spent on the bridge. And he was weary with all the voyage behind him—two years and four months between home port and home port, eight hundred and fifty days by his log.

"Proper wunter weather," he answered, after a silence. "The town is undistinct. Ut wull be rainun' guid an' hearty for the day."

Captain MacElrath was a small man, just comfortably able to peep over the canvas dodger of the bridge. The pilot and third officer loomed above him, as did the man at the wheel, a bulky German, deserted from a warship, whom he had signed on in Rangoon. But his lack of inches made Captain MacElrath a no less able man. At least so the Company reckoned, and so would he have reckoned could he have had access to the carefully and minutely compiled record of him filed away in the office archives. But the Company had never given him a hint of its faith in him. It was not the way of the Company, for the Company went on the principle of never allowing an employee to think himself indispensable or even exceedingly useful; wherefore, while quick to censure, it never praised. What was Captain MacElrath, anyway, save a skipper, one skipper of the eighty-odd skippers that commanded the Company's eighty-odd freighters on all the highways and byways of the sea?

Beneath them, on the main deck, two Chinese stokers were carrying breakfast for'ard across the rusty iron plates that told their own grim story of weight and wash of sea. A sailor was taking down the life-line that stretched from the forecastle, past the hatches and cargo-winches, to the bridge-deck ladder.

"A rough voyage," suggested the pilot.

"Aye, she was fair smokin' ot times, but not thot I minded thot so much as the lossin' of time. I hate like onythun' tull loss time."

So saying, Captain MacElrath turned and glanced aft, aloft and alow, and the pilot, following his gaze, saw the mute but convincing explanation of that loss of time. The smoke-stack, buff-coloured underneath, was white with salt, while the whistle-pipe glittered crystalline in the random sunlight that broke for the instant through a cloud-rift. The port lifeboat was missing, its iron davits, twisted and wrenched, testifying to the mightiness of the blow that had been struck the old *Tryapsic*. The starboard davits were also empty. The shattered wreck of the lifeboat they had held lay on the fiddley beside the smashed engine-room skylight, which was covered by a tarpaulin. Below, to star-board, on the bridge deck, the pilot saw the crushed mess-room door, roughly bulkheaded against the pounding seas. Abreast of it, on the smokestack guys, and being taken down by the bos'n and a sailor, hung the huge square of rope netting which had failed to break those seas of their force.

"Twice afore I mentioned thot door tull the owners," said Captain MacElrath. "But they said ut would do. There was bug seas thot time. They was uncreditable bug. And thot buggest one dud the domage. Ut fair carried away the door an' laid ut flat on the mess table an' smashed out the chief's room. He was a but sore about ut."

"It must 'a' been a big un," the pilot remarked sympathetically.

"Aye, ut was thot. Thungs was lively for a but. Ut finished the mate. He was on the brudge wuth me, an' I told hum tull take a look tull the wedges o' number one hatch. She was takin' watter freely an' I was no sure o' number one. I dudna like the look o' ut, an' I was fuggerin' maybe tull heave to tull the marn, when she took ut over abaft the brudge. My word, she was a bug one. We got a but of ut ourselves on the brudge. I dudna miss the mate ot the first, what o' routin' out Chips an' bulkheadun' thot door an' stretchun' the tarpaulin over the sky-light. Then he was nowhere to be found. The men ot the wheel said as he seen hum goin' down the lodder just afore she hut us. We looked for'ard, we looked tull hus room, aye looked tull the engine-room, an' we looked along aft on the lower deck, and there he was, on both sides the cover to the steam-pipe runnun' tull the after-wunches."

The pilot ejaculated an oath of amazement and horror.

"Aye," the skipper went on wearily, "an' on both sides the steam-pipe uz well. I tell ye he was in two pieces, splut clean uz a herrin'. The sea must a-caught hum on the upper brudge deck, carried hum clean across the fiddley, an' banged hum head-on tull the pipe cover. It sheered through hum like so much butter, down atween the eyes, an' along the middle of hum, so that one leg an' arm was fast tull the one piece of hum, an' one leg an' arm fast tull the other piece of hum. I tull ye ut was fair grewsome. We putt hum together an' rolled hum in canvas uz we pulled hum out."

The pilot swore again.

"Oh, ut wasna onythun' tull greet about," Captain MacElrath assured him. "'Twas a guid ruddance. He was no a sailor, thot mate-fellow. He was only fut for a pugsty, an' a dom puir apology for thot same."

It is said that there are three kinds of Irish—Catholic, Protestant, and North-of-Ireland—and that the North-of-Ireland Irishman is a transplanted Scotchman. Captain MacElrath was a North-of-Ireland man, and, talking for much of the world like a Scotchman, nothing aroused his ire quicker than being mistaken for a Scotchman. Irish he stoutly was, and Irish he stoutly abided, though it was with a faint lip-lift of scorn that he mentioned mere South-of-Ireland men, or even Orange-men. Himself he was Presbyterian, while in his own community five men were all that ever mustered at a meeting in the Orange Men's Hall. His community was the Island McGill, where

250

seven thousand of his kind lived in such amity and sobriety that in the whole island there was but one policeman and never a public-house at all.

Captain MacElrath did not like the sea, and had never liked it. He wrung his livelihood from it, and that was all the sea was, the place where he worked, as the mill, the shop, and the counting-house were the places where other men worked. Romance never sang to him her siren song, and Adventure had never shouted in his sluggish blood. He lacked imagination. The wonders of the deep were without significance to him. Tornadoes, hurricanes, waterspouts, and tidal waves were so many obstacles to the way of a ship on the sea and of a master on the bridge—they were that to him, and nothing more. He had seen, and yet not seen, the many marvels and wonders of far lands. Under his eyelids burned the brazen glories of the tropic seas, or ached the bitter gales of the North Atlantic or far South Pacific; but his memory of them was of mess-room doors stove in, of decks awash and hatches threatened, of undue coal consumption, of long passages, and of fresh paint-work spoiled by unexpected squalls of rain.

"I know my buzz'ness," was the way he often put it, and beyond his business was all that he did not know, all that he had seen with the mortal eyes of him and yet that he never dreamed existed. That he knew his business his owners were convinced, or at forty he would not have held command of the *Tryapsic*, three thousand tons net register, with a cargo capacity of nine thousand tons and valued at fifty-thousand pounds.

He had taken up seafaring through no love of it, but because it had been his destiny, because he had been the second son of his father instead of the first. Island McGill was only so large, and the land could support but a certain definite proportion of those that dwelt upon it. The balance, and a large balance it was, was driven to the sea to seek its bread. It had been so for generations. The eldest sons took the farms from their fathers; to the other sons remained the sea and its salt-ploughing. So it was that Donald MacElrath, farmer's son and farm-boy himself, had shifted from the soil he loved to the sea he hated and which it was his destiny to farm. And farmed it he had, for twenty years, shrewd, cool-headed, sober, industrious, and thrifty, rising from ship's boy and forecastle hand to mate and master of sailing-ships and thence into steam, second officer, first, and master, from small command to larger, and at last to the bridge of the old *Tryapsic*—old, to be sure, but worth her fifty thousand pounds and still able to bear up in all seas, and weather her nine thousand tons of freight.

From the bridge of the *Tryapsic*, the high place he had gained in the competition of men, he stared at Dublin harbour opening out, at the town obscured by the dark sky of the dreary wind-driven day, and at the tangled tracery of spars and rigging of the harbour shipping. Back from twice around the world he was, and from interminable junketings up and down on far stretches, home-coming to the wife he had not seen in eight-and-twenty months, and to the child he had never seen and that was already walking and talking. He saw the watch below of stokers and trimmers bobbing out of the forecastle doors like rabbits from a warren and making their way aft over the rusty deck to the mustering of the port doctor. They were Chinese, with expressionless, Sphinx-like faces, and they walked in peculiar shambling fashion, dragging their feet as if the clumsy brogans were too heavy for their lean shanks.

He saw them and he did not see them, as he passed his hand beneath his visored cap and scratched reflectively his mop of sandy hair. For the scene before him was but the background in his brain for the vision of peace that was his—a vision that was his often during long nights on the bridge when the old *Tryapsic* wallowed on the vexed ocean floor, her decks awash, her rigging thrumming in the gale gusts or snow squalls or driving tropic rain. And the vision he saw was of farm and farm-house and straw-thatched outbuildings, of children playing in the sun, and the good wife at the door, of lowing kine, and clucking fowls, and the stamp of horses in the stable, of his father's farm next to him, with, beyond, the woodless, rolling land and the hedged fields, neat and orderly, extending to the crest of the smooth, soft hills. It was his vision and his dream, his Romance and Adventure, the goal of all his effort, the high reward for the salt-ploughing and the long, long furrows he ran up and down the whole world around in his farming of the sea.

In simple taste and homely inclination this much-travelled man was more simple and homely than the veriest yokel. Seventy-one years his father was, and had never slept a night out of his own bed in his own house on Island McGill. That was the life ideal, so Captain MacElrath considered, and he was prone to marvel that any man, not under compulsion, should leave a farm to go to sea. To this much-travelled man the whole world was as familiar as the village to the cobbler sitting in his shop. To Captain MacElrath the world was a village. In his mind's eye he saw its streets a thousand leagues long, aye, and longer; turnings that doubled earth's stormiest headlands or were the way to quiet inland ponds; cross-roads, taken one way, that led to flower-lands and summer seas, and that led the other way to bitter, ceaseless gales and the perilous bergs of the great west wind drift. And the cities, bright with lights, were as shops on these long streets—shops where business was transacted, where bunkers were replenished, cargoes taken or shifted, and orders received from the owners in London town to go elsewhere and beyond, ever along the long sea-lanes, seeking new cargoes here, carrying new cargoes there, running freights wherever shillings and pence beckoned and underwriters did not forbid. But it was all a weariness to contemplate, and, save that he wrung from it his bread, it was without profit under the sun.

The last good-bye to the wife had been at Cardiff, twenty-eight months before, when he sailed for Valparaiso with coals—nine thousand tons and down to his marks. From Valparaiso he had gone to Australia, light, a matter of six thousand miles on end with a stormy passage and running short of bunker coal. Coals again to Oregon, seven thousand miles, and nigh as many more with general cargo for Japan and China. Thence to Java, loading sugar for Marseilles, and back along the Mediterranean to the Black Sea, and on to Baltimore, down to her marks with crome ore, buffeted by hurricanes, short again of bunker coal and calling at Bermuda to replenish. Then a time charter, Norfolk, Virginia, loading mysterious contraband coal and sailing for South Africa under orders of the mysterious German supercargo put on board by the charterers. On to Madagascar, steaming four knots by the supercargo's orders, and the suspicion forming that the Russian fleet might want the coal. Confusion and delays, long waits at sea, international complications, the whole world excited over the old *Tryapsic* and her cargo of contraband, and then on to Japan and the naval port of Sassebo. Back to Australia, another time charter and general merchandise picked up at Sydney, Melbourne, and

Adelaide, and carried on to Mauritius, Lourenço Marques, Durban, Algoa Bay, and Cape Town. To Ceylon for orders, and from Ceylon to Rangoon to load rice for Rio Janeiro. Thence to Buenos Aires and loading maize for the United Kingdom or the Continent, stopping at St. Vincent, to receive orders to proceed to Dublin. Two years and four months, eight hundred and fifty days by the log, steaming up and down the thousand-league-long sea-lanes and back again to Dublin town. And he was well aweary.

A little tug had laid hold of the *Tryapsic*, and with clang and clatter and shouted command, with engines half-ahead, slow-speed, or half-astern, the battered old sea-tramp was nudged and nosed and shouldered through the dock-gates into Ring's End Basin. Lines were flung ashore, fore and aft, and a 'midship spring got out. Already a small group of the happy shore-staying folk had clustered on the dock.

"Ring off," Captain MacElrath commanded in his slow thick voice; and the third officer worked the lever of the engine-room telegraph.

"Gangway out!" called the second officer; and when this was accomplished, "That will do."

It was the last task of all, gangway out. "That will do" was the dismissal. The voyage was ended, and the crew shambled eagerly forward across the rusty decks to where their sea-bags were packed and ready for the shore. The taste of the land was strong in the men's mouths, and strong it was in the skipper's mouth as he muttered a gruff good day to the departing pilot, and himself went down to his cabin. Up the gangway were trooping the customs officers, the surveyor, the agent's clerk, and the stevedores. Quick work disposed of these and cleared his cabin, the agent waiting to take him to the office.

"Dud ye send word tull the wife?" had been his greeting to the clerk.

"Yes, a telegram, as soon as you were reported."

"She'll likely be comin' down on the marnin' train," the skipper had soliloquized, and gone inside to change his clothes and wash.

He took a last glance about the room and at two photographs on the wall, one of the wife the other of an infant—the child he had never seen.

He stepped out into the cabin, with its panelled walls of cedar and maple, and with its long table that seated ten, and at which he had eaten by himself through all the weary time. No laughter and clatter and wordy argument of the mess-room had been his. He had eaten silently, almost morosely, his silence emulated by the noiseless Asiatic who had served him. It came to him suddenly, the overwhelming realization of the loneliness of those two years and more. All his vexations and anxieties had been his own. He had shared them with no one. His two young officers were too young and flighty, the mate too stupid. There was no consulting with them. One tenant had shared the cabin with him, that tenant his responsibility. They had dined and supped together, walked the bridge together, and together they had bedded.

"Och!" he muttered to that grim companion, "I'm quit of you, an' wull quit . . . for a wee."

Ashore he passed the last of the seamen with their bags, and, at the agent's, with the usual delays, put through his ship business. When asked out by them to drink he took milk and soda.

"I am no teetotaler," he explained; "but for the life o' me I canna bide beer or whusky."

In the early afternoon, when he finished paying off his crew, he hurried to the private office where he had been told his wife was waiting.

His eyes were for her first, though the temptation was great to have more than a hurried glimpse of the child in the chair beside her. He held her off from him after the long embrace, and looked into her face long and steadily, drinking in every feature of it and wondering that he could mark no changes of time. A warm man, his wife thought him, though had the opinion of his officers been asked it would have been: a harsh man and a bitter one.

"Wull, Annie, how is ut wi' ye?" he queried, and drew her to him again.

And again he held her away from him, this wife of ten years and of whom he knew so little. She was almost a stranger—more a stranger than his Chinese steward, and certainly far more a stranger than his own officers whom he had seen every day, day and day, for eight hundred and fifty days.

255

Married ten years, and in that time he had been with her nine weeks—scarcely a honeymoon. Each time home had been a getting acquainted again with her. It was the fate of the men who went out to the salt-ploughing. Little they knew of their wives and less of their children. There was his chief engineer—old, near-sighted MacPherson—who told the story of returning home to be locked out of his house by his four-year kiddie that never had laid eyes on him before.

"An' thus 'ull be the loddie," the skipper said, reaching out a hesitant hand to the child's cheek.

But the boy drew away from him, sheltering against the mother's side.

"Och!" she cried, "and he doesna know his own father."

"Nor I hum. Heaven knows I could no a-picked hum out of a crowd, though he'll be havin' your nose I'm thunkun'."

"An' your own eyes, Donald. Look ut them. He's your own father, laddie. Kiss hum like the little mon ye are."

But the child drew closer to her, his expression of fear and distrust growing stronger, and when the father attempted to take him in his arms he threatened to cry.

The skipper straightened up, and to conceal the pang at his heart he drew out his watch and looked at it.

"Ut's time to go, Annie," he said. "Thot train 'ull be startun'."

He was silent on the train at first, divided between watching the wife with the child going to sleep in her arms and looking out of the window at the tilled fields and green unforested hills vague and indistinct in the driving drizzle that had set in. They had the compartment to themselves. When the boy slept she laid him out on the seat and wrapped him warmly. And when the health of relatives and friends had been inquired after, and the gossip of Island McGill narrated, along with the weather and the price of land and crops, there was little left to talk about save themselves, and Captain MacElrath took up the tale brought home for the good wife from all his world's-end wandering. But it was not a tale of marvels he told, nor of beautiful flower-lands nor mysterious Eastern cities.

"What like is Java?" she asked once.

"Full o' fever. Half the crew down wuth ut an' luttle work. Ut was quinine an' quinine the whole blessed time. Each marnun' 'twas quinine an' gin for all hands on an empty stomach. An' they who was no sick made ut out to be hovun' ut bad uz the rest."

Another time she asked about Newcastle.

"Coals an' coal-dust—thot's all. No a nice sutty. I lost two Chinks there, stokers the both of them. An' the owners paid a fine tull the Government of a hundred pounds each for them. 'We regret tull note,' they wrut me—I got the letter tull Oregon—'We regret tull note the loss o' two Chinese members o' yer crew ot Newcastle, an' we recommend greater carefulness un the future.' Greater carefulness! And I could no a-been more careful. The Chinks hod forty-five pounds each comun' tull them in wages, an' I was no a-thunkun' they 'ud run.

"But thot's their way—'we regret tull note,' 'we beg tull advise,' 'we recommend,' 'we canna understand'—an' the like o' thot. Domned cargo tank! An' they would thunk I could drive her like a *Lucania*, an' wi'out burnun' coals. There was thot propeller. I was after them a guid while for ut. The old one was iron, thuck on the edges, an' we couldna make our speed. An' the new one was bronze—nine hundred pounds ut cost, an' then wantun' their returns out o' ut, an' me wuth a bod passage an' lossin' time every day. 'We regret tull note your long passage from Voloparaiso tull Sydney wuth an average daily run o' only one hundred an' suxty-seven. We hod expected better results wuth the new propeller. You should a-made an average daily run o' two hundred and suxteen.'

"An' me on a wunter passage, blowin' a luvin' gale half the time, wuth hurricane force in atweenwhiles, an' hove to sux days, wuth engines stopped an' bunker coal runnun' short, an' me wuth a mate thot stupid he could no pass a shup's light ot night wi'out callun' me tull the brudge. I wrut an' told 'em so. An' then: 'Our nautical adviser suggests you kept too far south,' an' 'We are lookun' for better results from thot propeller.' Nautical adviser!—shore pilot! Ut was the regular latitude for a wunter passage from Voloparaiso tull Sydney.

"An' when I come un tull Auckland short o' coal, after lettun' her druft sux days wuth the fires out tull save the coal, an' wuth only twenty tons in my bunkers, I was thunkun' o' the lossin' o' time an' the expense, an' tull save the owners I took her un an' out wi'out pilotage. Pilotage was no compulsory. An' un Yokohama, who should I meet but Captun Robinson o' the *Dyapsic*. We got a-talkun' about ports an' places down Australia-way, an' first thing he says: 'Speakun' o' Auckland—of course, Captun, you was never un Auckland?' 'Yus,' I says, 'I was un there very recent.' 'Oh, ho,' he says, very angry-like, 'so you was the smart Aleck thot fetched me thot letter from the owners: "We note item of fufteen pounds for pilotage ot Auckland. A shup o' ours was un tull Auckland recently an' uncurred no such charge. We beg tull advise you thot we conseeder thus pilotage an onnecessary expense which should no be uncurred un the future."'

"But dud they say a word tull me for the fufteen pounds I saved tull them? No a word. They send a letter tull Captun Robinson for no savun' them the fufteen pounds, an' tull me: 'We note item of two guineas doctor's fee at Auckland for crew. Please explain thus onusual expunditure.' Ut was two o' the Chinks. I was thunkun' they hod beri-beri, an' thot was the why o' sendun' for the doctor. I buried the two of them ot sea not a week after. But ut was: 'Please explain thus onusual expunditure,' an' tull Captun Robinson, 'We beg tull advise you thot we conseeder thus pilotage an onnecessary expense.'

"Dudna I cable them from Newcastle, tellun' them the old tank was thot foul she needed dry-dock? Seven months out o' dry-dock, an' the West Coast the quickest place for foulun' un the world. But freights was up, an' they hod a charter o' coals for Portland. The *Arrata*, one o' the Woor Line, left port the same day uz us, bound for Portland, an' the old *Tryapsic* makun' sux knots, seven ot the best. An' ut was ot Comox, takun' un bunker coal, I got the letter from the owners. The boss humself hod signed ut, an' ot the bottom he wrut un hus own hond: 'The *Arrata* beat you by four an' a half days. Am dusappointed.' Dusappointed! When I had cabled them from Newcastle. When she drydocked ot Portland, there was whuskers on her a foot long, barnacles the size o' me fust, oysters like young sauce plates. Ut took them two days afterward tull clean the dock o' shells an' muck.

"An' there was the motter o' them fire-bars ot Newcastle. The firm ashore made them heavier than the engineer's speecifications, an' then forgot tull charge for the dufference. Ot the last moment, wuth me ashore gettun' me clearance, they come wuth the bill: 'Tull error on fire-bars, sux pounds.' They'd been tull the shup an' MacPherson hod O.K.'d ut. I said ut was strange an' would no pay. 'Then you are dootun' the chief engineer,' says they. 'I'm no dootun',' says I, 'but I canna see my way tull sign. Come wuth me tull the shup. The launch wull cost ye naught an' ut 'ull brung ye back. An' we wull see what MacPherson says.'

"But they would no come. Ot Portland I got the bill un a letter. I took no notice. Ot Hong-Kong I got a letter from the owners. The bill hod been sent tull them. I wrut them from Java explainun'. At Marseilles the owners wrut me: 'Tull extra work un engine-room, sux pounds. The engineer has O.K.'d ut, an' you have no O.K.'d ut. Are you dootun' the engineer's honesty?' I wrut an' told them I was no dootun' his honesty; thot the bill was for extra weight o' fire-bars; an' thot ut was O.K. Dud they pay ut? They no dud. They must unvestigate. An' some clerk un the office took sick, an' the bill was lost. An' there was more letters. I got letters from the owners an' the firm—'Tull error on fire-bars, sux pounds'—ot Baltimore, ot Delagoa Bay, ot Moji, ot Rangoon, ot Rio, an' ot Montevuddio. Ut uz no settled yut. I tell ye, Annie, the owners are hard tull please."

He communed with himself for a moment, and then muttered indignantly: "Tull error on fire-bars, sux pounds."

"Hov ye heard of Jamie?" his wife asked in the pause.

Captain MacElrath shook his head.

"He was washed off the poop wuth three seamen."

"Whereabouts?"

"Off the Horn. 'Twas on the *Thornsby*."

"They would be runnun' homeward bound?"

"Aye," she nodded. "We only got the word three days gone. His wife is greetin' like tull die."

"A good lod, Jamie," he commented, "but a stiff one ot carryun' on. I mind me when we was mates together un the *Albion*. An' so Jamie's gone."

Again a pause fell, to be broken by the wife.

"An' ye will no a-heard o' the *Bankshire*? MacDougall lost her in Magellan Straits. 'Twas only yesterday ut was in the paper."

"A cruel place, them Magellan Straits," he said. "Dudna thot domned mate-fellow nigh putt me ashore twice on the one passage through? He was a eediot, a lunatuc. I wouldna have hum on the brudge a munut. Comun' tull Narrow Reach, thuck weather, wuth snow squalls, me un the chart-room, dudna I guv hum the changed course? 'South-east-by-east,' I told hum. 'South-east-by-east, sir,' says he. Fufteen munuts after I comes on tull the brudge. 'Funny,' says thot mate-fellow, 'I'm no rememberun' ony islands un the mouth o' Narrow Reach. I took one look ot the islands an' yells, 'Putt your wheel hard a-starboard,' tull the mon ot the wheel. An' ye should a-seen the old *Tryapsic* turnun' the sharpest circle she ever turned. I waited for the snow tull clear, an' there was Narrow Reach, nice uz ye please, tull the east'ard an' the islands un the mouth o' False Bay tull the south'ard. 'What course was ye steerun'?' I says tull the mon ot the wheel. 'South-by-east, sir,' says he. I looked tull the mate-fellow. What could I say? I was thot wroth I could a-kult hum. Four points dufference. Five munuts more an' the old *Tryapsic* would a-been funushed.

"An' was ut no the same when we cleared the Straits tull the east'ard? Four hours would a-seen us guid an' clear. I was forty hours then on the brudge. I guv the mate his course, an' the bearun' o' the Askthar Light astern.

'Don't let her bear more tull the north'ard than west-by-north,' I said tull hum, 'an' ye wull be all right.' An' I went below an' turned un. But I couldna sleep for worryun'. After forty hours on the brudge, what was four hours more? I thought. An' for them four hours wull ye be lettun' the mate loss her on ye? 'No,' I says to myself. An' wuth thot I got up, hod a wash an' a cup o' coffee, an' went tull the brudge. I took one look ot the bearun' o' Askthar Light. 'Twas nor'west-by-west, and the old *Tryapsic* down on the shoals. He was a eediot, thot mate-fellow. Ye could look overside an' see the duscoloration of the watter. 'Twas a close call for the old *Tryapsic* I'm tellun' ye. Twice un thirty hours he'd a-hod her ashore uf ut hod no been for me."

Captain MacElrath fell to gazing at the sleeping child with mild wonder in his small blue eyes, and his wife sought to divert him from his woes.

"Ye remember Jummy MacCaul?" she asked. "Ye went tull school wuth hus two boys. Old Jummy MacCaul thot hoz the farm beyond Doctor Haythorn's place."

"Oh, aye, an' what o' hum? Uz he dead?"

"No, but he was after askun' your father, when he sailed last time for Voloparaiso, uf ye'd been there afore. An' when your father says no, then Jummy says, 'An' how wull he be knowun a' tull find hus way?' An' with thot your father says: 'Verry sumple ut uz, Jummy. Supposun' you was goin' tull the mainland tull a mon who luved un Belfast. Belfast uz a bug sutty, Jummy, an' how would ye be findun' your way?' 'By way o' me tongue,' says Jummy; 'I'd be askun' the folk I met.' 'I told ye ut was sumple,' says your father. 'Ut's the very same way my Donald finds the road tull Voloparaiso. He asks every shup he meets upon the sea tull ot last he meets wuth a shup thot's been tull Voloparaiso, an' the captun o' thot shup tells hum the way.' An' Jummy scratches hus head an' says he understands an' thot ut's a very sumple motter after all."

The skipper chuckled at the joke, and his tired blue eyes were merry for the moment.

"He was a thun chap, thot mate-fellow, oz thun oz you an' me putt together," he remarked after a time, a slight twinkle in his eye of appreciation of the bull. But the twinkle quickly disappeared and the blue eyes took on a bleak and wintry look. "What dud he do ot Voloparaiso but land sux hundred fathom o' chain cable an' take never a receipt from the lighter-mon. I was gettun' my clearance ot the time. When we got tull sea, I found he hod no receipt for the cable.

"'An' ye no took a receipt for ut?' says I.

"'No,' says he. 'Wasna ut goin' direct tull the agents?'

"'How long ha' ye been goin' tull sea,' says I, 'not tull be knowin' the mate's duty uz tull deluver no cargo wuthout receipt for same? An' on the West Coast ot thot. What's tull stop the lighter-mon from stealun' a few lengths o' ut?'

"An' ut come out uz I said. Sux hundred went over the side, but four hundred an' ninety-five was all the agents received. The lighter-mon swore ut was all he received from the mate—four hundred an' ninety-five fathom. I got a letter from the owners ot Portland. They no blamed the mate for ut, but me, an' me ashore ot the time on shup's buzz'ness. I could no be in the two places ot the one time. An' the letters from the owners an' the agents uz still comun' tull me.

"Thot mate-fellow was no a proper sailor, an' no a mon tull work for owners. Dudna he want tull break me wuth the Board of Trade for bein' below my marks? He said as much tull the bos'n. An' he told me tull my face homeward bound thot I'd been half an inch under my marks. 'Twas at Portland, loadun' cargo un fresh watter an' goin' tull Comox tull load bunker coal un salt watter. I tell ye, Annie, ut takes close fuggerin', an' I *was* half an inch under the load-line when the bunker coal was un. But I'm no tellun' any other body but you. An' thot mate-fellow untendun' tull report me tull the Board o' Trade, only for thot he saw fut tull be sliced un two pieces on the steam-pipe cover.

"He was a fool. After loadun' ot Portland I hod tull take on suxty tons o' coal tull last me tull Comox. The charges for lighterun' was heavy, an' no room ot the coal dock. A French barque was lyin' alongside the dock an' I spoke tull the captun, askun' hum what he would charge when work for the day was done, tull haul clear for a couple o' hours an' let me un. 'Twenty dollars,' said he. Ut was savun' money on lighters tull the owner, an' I gave ut tull hum. An' thot night, after dark, I hauled un an' took on the coal. Then I started tull go out un the stream an' drop anchor—under me own steam, of course.

"We hod tull go out stern first, an' somethun' went wrong wuth the reversun' gear. Old MacPherson said he could work ut by hond, but very slow ot thot. An' I said 'All right.' We started. The pilot was on board. The tide was ebbun' stuffly, an' right abreast an' a but below was a shup lyin' wuth a lighter on each side. I saw the shup's ridun' lights, but never a light on the lighters. Ut was close quarters to shuft a bug vessel onder steam, wuth MacPherson workun' the reversun' gear by hond. We hod to come close down upon the shup afore I could go ahead an' clear o' the shups on the dock-ends. An' we struck the lighter stern-on, just uz I rung tull MacPherson half ahead.

"'What was thot?' says the pilot, when we struck the lighter.

"'I dunna know,' says I, 'an' I'm wonderun'.'

"The pilot was no keen, ye see, tull hus job. I went on tull a guid place an' dropped anchor, an' ut would all a-been well but for thot domned eediot mate.

"'We smashed thot lighter,' says he, comun' up the lodder tull the brudge—an' the pilot stondun' there wuth his ears cocked tull hear.

"'What lighter?' says I.

"'Thot lighter alongside the shup,' says the mate.

"'I dudna see no lighter,' says I, and wuth thot I steps on hus fut guid an' hard.

"After the pilot was gone I says tull the mate: 'Uf you dunna know onythun', old mon, for Heaven's sake keep your mouth shut.'

"'But ye dud smash thot lighter, dudn't ye?' says he.

"'Uf we dud,' says I, 'ut's no your buzz'ness tull be tellun' the pilot—though, mind ye, I'm no admuttun' there was ony lighter.'

"An' next marnun', just uz I'm after dressun', the steward says, 'A mon tull see ye, sir.' 'Fetch hum un,' says I. An' un he come. 'Sut down,' says I. An' he sot down.

"He was the owner of the lighter, an' when he hod told hus story, I says, 'I dudna see ony lighter.'

"'What, mon?' says he. 'No see a two-hundred-ton lighter, bug oz a house, alongside thot shup?'

"'I was goin' by the shup's lights,' says I, 'an' I dudna touch the shup, thot I know.'

"'But ye dud touch the lighter,' says he. 'Ye smashed her. There's a thousand dollars' domage done, an' I'll see ye pay for ut.'

"'Look here, muster,' says I, 'when I'm shuftun' a shup ot night I follow the law, an' the law dustunctly says I must regulate me actions by the lights o' the shuppun'. Your lighter never hod no ridun' light, nor dud I look for ony lighter wuthout lights tull show ut.'

"'The mate says—' he beguns.

"'Domn the mate,' says I. 'Dud your lighter hov a ridun' light?'

"'No, ut dud not,' says he, 'but ut was a clear night wuth the moon a-showun'.'

"'Ye seem tull know your buzz'ness,' says I. 'But let me tell ye thot I know my buzz'ness uz well, an' thot I'm no a-lookun' for lighters wuthout lights. Uf ye thunk ye hov a case, go ahead. The steward will show ye out. Guid day.'

"An' thot was the end o' ut. But ut wull show ye what a puir fellow thot mate was. I call ut a blessun' for all masters thot he was sliced un two on thot steam-pipe cover. He had a pull un the office an' thot was the why he was kept on."

"The Wekley farm wull soon be for sale, so the agents be tellun' me," his wife remarked, slyly watching what effect her announcement would have upon him.

His eyes flashed eagerly on the instant, and he straightened up as might a man about to engage in some agreeable task. It was the farm of his vision, adjoining his father's, and her own people farmed not a mile away.

"We wull be buyun' ut," he said, "though we wull be no tellun' a soul of ut ontul ut's bought an' the money paid down. I've savun' consuderable these days, though pickun's uz no what they used to be, an' we hov a tidy nest-egg laid by. I wull see the father an' hove the money ready tull hus hond, so uf I'm ot sea he can buy whenever the land offers."

He rubbed the frosted moisture from the inside of the window and peered out at the pouring rain, through which he could discern nothing.

"When I was a young men I used tull be afeard thot the owners would guv me the sack. Stull afeard I am of the sack. But once thot farm is mine I wull no be afeard ony longer. Ut's a puir job thus sea-farmun'. Me managin' un all seas an' weather an' perils o' the deep a shup worth fufty thousand pounds, wuth cargoes ot times worth fufty thousand more—a hundred thousand pounds, half a million dollars uz the Yankees say, an' me wuth all the responsubility gettun' a screw o' twenty pounds a month. What mon ashore, managin' a buz'ness worth a hundred thousand pounds wull be gettun' uz small a screw uz twenty pounds? An' wuth such masters uz a captun serves— the owners, the underwriters, an' the Board o' Trade, all pullun' an wantun' dufferent thungs—the owners wantun' quick passages an' domn the rusk, the underwriters wantun' safe passages an' domn the delay, an' the Board o' Trade wantun' cautious passages an' caution always meanun' delay. Three dufferent masters, an' all three able an' wullun' to break ye uf ye don't serve their dufferent wushes."

He felt the train slackening speed, and peered again through the misty window. He stood up, buttoned his overcoat, turned up the collar, and awkwardly gathered the child, still asleep, in his arms.

"I wull see the father," he said, "an' hov the money ready tull hus hond so uf I'm ot sea when the land offers he wull no muss the chance tull buy. An' then the owners can guv me the sack uz soon uz they like. Ut will be all night un, an' I wull be wuth you, Annie, an' the sea can go tull hell."

Happiness was in both their faces at the prospect, and for a moment both saw the same vision of peace. Annie leaned toward him, and as the train stopped they kissed each other across the sleeping child.

SAMUEL

Margaret Henan would have been a striking figure under any circumstances, but never more so than when I first chanced upon her, a sack of grain of fully a hundredweight on her shoulder, as she walked with sure though tottering stride from the cart-tail to the stable, pausing for an instant to gather strength at the foot of the steep steps that led to the grain-bin. There were four of these steps, and she went up them, a step at a time, slowly, unwaveringly, and with so dogged certitude that it never entered my mind that her strength could fail her and let that hundred-weight sack fall from the lean and withered frame that wellnigh doubled under it. For she was patently an old woman, and it was her age that made me linger by the cart and watch.

Six times she went between the cart and the stable, each time with a full sack on her back, and beyond passing the time of day with me she took no notice of my presence. Then, the cart empty, she fumbled for matches and lighted a short clay pipe, pressing down the burning surface of the tobacco with a calloused and apparently nerveless thumb. The hands were noteworthy. They were large-knuckled, sinewy and malformed by labour, rimed with callouses, the nails blunt and broken, and with here and there cuts and bruises, healed and healing, such as are common to the hands of hard-working men. On the back were huge, upstanding veins, eloquent of age and toil. Looking at them, it was hard to believe that they were the hands of the woman who had once been the belle of Island McGill. This last, of course, I learned later. At the time I knew neither her history nor her identity.

She wore heavy man's brogans. Her legs were stockingless, and I had noticed when she walked that her bare feet were thrust into the crinkly, iron-like shoes that sloshed about her lean ankles at every step. Her figure, shapeless and waistless, was garbed in a rough man's shirt and in a ragged flannel petticoat that had once been red. But it was her face, wrinkled, withered and weather-beaten, surrounded by an aureole of unkempt and straggling wisps of greyish hair, that caught and held me. Neither drifted hair nor serried wrinkles could hide the splendid dome of a forehead, high and broad without verging in the slightest on the abnormal.

The sunken cheeks and pinched nose told little of the quality of the life that flickered behind those clear blue eyes of hers. Despite the minutiæ of wrinkle-work that somehow failed to weazen them, her eyes were clear as a girl's—clear, out-looking, and far-seeing, and with an open and unblinking steadfastness of gaze that was disconcerting. The remarkable thing was the distance between them. It is a lucky man or woman who has the width of an eye between, but with Margaret Henan the width between her eyes was fully that of an eye and a half. Yet so symmetrically moulded was her face that this remarkable feature produced no uncanny effect, and, for that matter, would have escaped the casual observer's notice. The mouth, shapeless and toothless, with down-turned corners and lips dry and parchment-like, nevertheless lacked the muscular slackness so usual with age. The lips might have been those of a mummy, save for that impression of rigid firmness they gave. Not that they were atrophied. On the contrary, they seemed tense and set with a muscular and spiritual determination. There, and in the eyes, was the secret of the certitude with which she carried the heavy sacks up the steep steps, with never a false step or overbalance, and emptied them in the grain-bin.

"You are an old woman to be working like this," I ventured.

She looked at me with that strange, unblinking gaze, and she thought and spoke with the slow deliberateness that characterized everything about her, as if well aware of an eternity that was hers and in which there was no need for haste. Again I was impressed by the enormous certitude of her. In this eternity that seemed so indubitably hers, there was time and to spare for safe-footing and stable equilibrium—for certitude, in short. No more in her spiritual life than in carrying the hundredweights of grain was there a possibility of a misstep or an overbalancing. The feeling produced in me was uncanny. Here was a human soul that, save for the most glimmering of contacts, was beyond the humanness of me. And the more I learned of Margaret Henan in the weeks that followed the more mysteriously remote she became. She was as alien as a far-journeyer from some other star, and no hint could she nor all the countryside give me of what forms of living, what heats of feeling, or rules of philosophic contemplation actuated her in all that she had been and was.

"I wull be suvunty-two come Guid Friday a fortnight," she said in reply to my question.

"But you are an old woman to be doing this man's work, and a strong man's work at that," I insisted.

Again she seemed to immerse herself in that atmosphere of contemplative eternity, and so strangely did it affect me that I should not have been surprised to have awaked a century or so later and found her just beginning to enunciate her reply—

"The work hoz tull be done, an' I am beholden tull no one."

"But have you no children, no family, relations?"

"Oh, aye, a-plenty o' them, but they no see fut tull be helpun' me."

She drew out her pipe for a moment, then added, with a nod of her head toward the house, "I luv' wuth meself."

I glanced at the house, straw-thatched and commodious, at the large stable, and at the large array of fields I knew must belong with the place.

"It is a big bit of land for you to farm by yourself."

"Oh, aye, a bug but, suvunty acres. Ut kept me old mon buzzy, along wuth a son an' a hired mon, tull say naught o' extra honds un the harvest an' a maid-servant un the house."

She clambered into the cart, gathered the reins in her hands, and quizzed me with her keen, shrewd eyes.

"Belike ye hail from over the watter—Ameruky, I'm meanun'?"

"Yes, I'm a Yankee," I answered.

"Ye wull no be findun' mony Island McGill folk stoppun' un Ameruky?"

"No; I don't remember ever meeting one, in the States."

She nodded her head.

"They are home-luvun' bodies, though I wull no be sayin' they are no fair-travelled. Yet they come home ot the last, them oz are no lost ot sea or kult by fevers an' such-like un foreign parts."

"Then your sons will have gone to sea and come home again?" I queried.

"Oh, aye, all savun' Samuel oz was drownded."

At the mention of Samuel I could have sworn to a strange light in her eyes, and it seemed to me, as by some telepathic flash, that I divined in her a tremendous wistfulness, an immense yearning. It seemed to me that here was the key to her inscrutableness, the clue that if followed properly would make all her strangeness plain. It came to me that here was a contact and that for the moment I was glimpsing into the soul of her. The question was tickling on my tongue, but she forestalled me.

She *tchk'd* to the horse, and with a "Guid day tull you, sir," drove off.

A simple, homely people are the folk of Island McGill, and I doubt if a more sober, thrifty, and industrious folk is to be found in all the world. Meeting them abroad—and to meet them abroad one must meet them on the sea, for a hybrid seafaring and farmer breed are they—one would never take them to be Irish. Irish they claim to be, speaking of the North of Ireland with pride and sneering at their Scottish brothers; yet Scotch they undoubtedly are, transplanted Scotch of long ago, it is true, but none the less Scotch, with a thousand traits, to say nothing of their tricks of speech and woolly utterance, which nothing less than their Scotch clannishness could have preserved to this late day.

A narrow loch, scarcely half a mile wide, separates Island McGill from the mainland of Ireland; and, once across this loch, one finds himself in an entirely different country. The Scotch impression is strong, and the people, to commence with, are Presbyterians. When it is considered that there is no public-house in all the island and that seven thousand souls dwell therein, some idea may be gained of the temperateness of the community. Wedded to old ways, public opinion and the ministers are powerful influences, while

270

fathers and mothers are revered and obeyed as in few other places in this modern world. Courting lasts never later than ten at night, and no girl walks out with her young man without her parents' knowledge and consent.

The young men go down to the sea and sow their wild oats in the wicked ports, returning periodically, between voyages, to live the old intensive morality, to court till ten o'clock, to sit under the minister each Sunday, and to listen at home to the same stern precepts that the elders preached to them from the time they were laddies. Much they learned of women in the ends of the earth, these seafaring sons, yet a canny wisdom was theirs and they never brought wives home with them. The one solitary exception to this had been the schoolmaster, who had been guilty of bringing a wife from half a mile the other side of the loch. For this he had never been forgiven, and he rested under a cloud for the remainder of his days. At his death the wife went back across the loch to her own people, and the blot on the escutcheon of Island McGill was erased. In the end the sailor-men married girls of their own homeland and settled down to become exemplars of all the virtues for which the island was noted.

Island McGill was without a history. She boasted none of the events that go to make history. There had never been any wearing of the green, any Fenian conspiracies, any land disturbances. There had been but one eviction, and that purely technical—a test case, and on advice of the tenant's lawyer. So Island McGill was without annals. History had passed her by. She paid her taxes, acknowledged her crowned rulers, and left the world alone; all she asked in return was that the world should leave her alone. The world was composed of two parts—Island McGill and the rest of it. And whatever was not Island McGill was outlandish and barbarian; and well she knew, for did not her seafaring sons bring home report of that world and its ungodly ways?

It was from the skipper of a Glasgow tramp, as passenger from Colombo to Rangoon, that I had first learned of the existence of Island McGill; and it was from him that I had carried the letter that gave me entrance to the house of Mrs. Ross, widow of a master mariner, with a daughter living with her and with two sons, master mariners themselves and out upon the sea. Mrs. Ross did not take in boarders, and it was Captain Ross's letter alone that had enabled me to get from her bed and board. In the evening, after my encounter with Margaret Henan, I questioned Mrs. Ross, and I knew on the instant that I had in truth stumbled upon mystery.

Like all Island McGill folk, as I was soon to discover, Mrs. Ross was at first averse to discussing Margaret Henan at all. Yet it was from her I learned that evening that Margaret Henan had once been one of the island belles. Herself the daughter of a well-to-do farmer, she had married Thomas Henan, equally well-to-do. Beyond the usual housewife's tasks she had never been accustomed to work. Unlike many of the island women, she had never lent a hand in the fields.

"But what of her children?" I asked.

"Two o' the sons, Jamie an' Timothy uz married an' be goun' tull sea. Thot bug house close tull the post office uz Jamie's. The daughters thot ha' no married be luvun' wuth them as dud marry. An' the rest be dead."

"The Samuels," Clara interpolated, with what I suspected was a giggle.

She was Mrs. Ross's daughter, a strapping young woman with handsome features and remarkably handsome black eyes.

"'Tuz naught to be smuckerun' ot," her mother reproved her.

"The Samuels?" I intervened. "I don't understand."

"Her four sons thot died."

"And were they all named Samuel?"

"Aye."

"Strange," I commented in the lagging silence.

"Very strange," Mrs. Ross affirmed, proceeding stolidly with the knitting of the woollen singlet on her knees—one of the countless under-garments that she interminably knitted for her skipper sons.

"And it was only the Samuels that died?" I queried, in further attempt.

"The others luved," was the answer. "A fine fomuly—no finer on the island. No better lods ever sailed out of Island McGill. The munuster held them up oz models tull pottern after. Nor was ever a whusper breathed again' the girls."

"But why is she left alone now in her old age?" I persisted. "Why don't her own flesh and blood look after her? Why does she live alone? Don't they ever go to see her or care for her?"

"Never a one un twenty years an' more now. She fetched ut on tull herself. She drove them from the house just oz she drove old Tom Henan, thot was her husband, tull hus death."

"Drink?" I ventured.

Mrs. Ross shook her head scornfully, as if drink was a weakness beneath the weakest of Island McGill.

A long pause followed, during which Mrs. Ross knitted stolidly on, only nodding permission when Clara's young man, mate on one of the Shire Line sailing ships, came to walk out with her. I studied the half-dozen ostrich eggs, hanging in the corner against the wall like a cluster of some monstrous fruit. On each shell were painted precipitous and impossible seas through which full-rigged ships foamed with a lack of perspective only equalled by their sharp technical perfection. On the mantelpiece stood two large pearl shells, obviously a pair, intricately carved by the patient hands of New Caledonian convicts. In the centre of the mantel was a stuffed bird-of-paradise, while about the room were scattered gorgeous shells from the southern seas, delicate sprays of coral sprouting from barnacled *pi-pi* shells and cased in glass, assegais from South Africa, stone axes from New Guinea, huge Alaskan tobacco-pouches beaded with heraldic totem designs, a boomerang from Australia, divers ships in glass bottles, a cannibal *kai-kai* bowl from the Marquesas, and fragile cabinets from China and the Indies and inlaid with mother-of-pearl and precious woods.

I gazed at this varied trove brought home by sailor sons, and pondered the mystery of Margaret Henan, who had driven her husband to his death and been forsaken by all her kin. It was not the drink. Then what was it?—some shocking cruelty? some amazing infidelity? or some fearful, old-world peasant-crime?

I broached my theories, but to all Mrs. Ross shook her head.

"Ut was no thot," she said. "Margaret was a guid wife an' a guid mother, an' I doubt she would harm a fly. She brought up her fomuly God-fearin' an' decent-minded. Her trouble was thot she took lunatic—turned eediot."

Mrs. Ross tapped significantly on her forehead to indicate a state of addlement.

"But I talked with her this afternoon," I objected, "and I found her a sensible woman—remarkably bright for one of her years."

"Aye, an' I'm grantun' all thot you say," she went on calmly. "But I am no referrun' tull thot. I am referrun' tull her wucked-headed an' vucious stubbornness. No more stubborn woman ever luv'd than Margaret Henan. Ut was all on account o' Samuel, which was the name o' her youngest an' they do say her favourut brother—hum oz died by hus own hond all through the munuster's mustake un no registerun' the new church ot Dublin. Ut was a lesson thot the name was musfortunate, but she would no take ut, an' there was talk when she called her first child Samuel—hum thot died o' the croup. An' wuth thot what does she do but call the next one Samuel, an' hum only three when he fell un tull the tub o' hot watter an' was plain cooked tull death. Ut all come, I tell you, o' her wucked-headed an' foolish stubbornness. For a Samuel she must hov; an' ut was the death of the four of her sons. After the first, dudna her own mother go down un the dirt tull her feet, a-beggun' an' pleadun' wuth her no tull name her next one Samuel? But she was no tull be turned from her purpose. Margaret Henan was always set on her ways, an' never more so thon on thot name Samuel.

"She was fair lunatuc on Samuel. Dudna her neighbours' an' all kuth an' kun savun' them thot luv'd un the house wuth her, get up an' walk out ot the christenun' of the second—hum thot was cooked? Thot they dud, an' ot the very moment the munuster asked what would the bairn's name be. 'Samuel,' says she; an' wuth thot they got up an' walked out an' left the house. An' ot the door dudna her Aunt Fannie, her mother's suster, turn an' say loud for all tull hear: 'What for wull she be wantun' tull murder the wee thing?' The munuster heard fine, an' dudna like ut, but, oz he told my Larry afterward, what could he do? Ut was the woman's wush, an' there was no law again' a mother callun' her child accordun' tull her wush.

"An' then was there no the third Samuel? An' when he was lost ot sea off the Cape, dudna she break all laws o' nature tull hov a fourth? She was forty-seven, I'm tellun' ye, an' she hod a child ot forty-seven. Thunk on ut! Ot forty-seven! Ut was fair scand'lous."

From Clara, next morning, I got the tale of Margaret Henan's favourite brother; and from here and there, in the week that followed, I pieced together the tragedy of Margaret Henan. Samuel Dundee had been the youngest of Margaret's four brothers, and, as Clara told me, she had well-nigh worshipped him. He was going to sea at the time, skipper of one of the sailing ships of the Bank Line, when he married Agnes Hewitt. She was described as a slender wisp of a girl, delicately featured and with a nervous organization of the supersensitive order. Theirs had been the first marriage in the "new" church, and after a two-weeks' honeymoon Samuel had kissed his bride good-bye and sailed in command of the *Loughbank*, a big four-masted barque.

And it was because of the "new" church that the minister's blunder occurred. Nor was it the blunder of the minister alone, as one of the elders later explained; for it was equally the blunder of the whole Presbytery of Coughleen, which included fifteen churches on Island McGill and the mainland. The old church, beyond repair, had been torn down and the new one built on the original foundation. Looking upon the foundation-stones as similar to a ship's keel, it never entered the minister's nor the Presbytery's head that the new church was legally any other than the old church.

"An' three couples was married the first week un the new church," Clara said. "First of all, Samuel Dundee an' Agnes Hewitt; the next day Albert Mahan an' Minnie Duncan; an' by the week-end Eddie Troy and Flo Mackintosh—all sailor-men, an' un sux weeks' time the last of them back tull their ships an' awa', an' no one o' them dreamin' of the wuckedness they'd been ot."

The Imp of the Perverse must have chuckled at the situation. All things favoured. The marriages had taken place in the first week of May, and it was not till three months later that the minister, as required by law, made his quarterly report to the civil authorities in Dublin. Promptly came back the announcement that his church had no legal existence, not being registered according to the law's demands. This was overcome by prompt registration; but the marriages were not to be so easily remedied. The three sailor husbands were away, and their wives, in short, were not their wives.

"But the munuster was no for alarmin' the bodies," said Clara. "He kept hus council an' bided hus time, waitun' for the lods tull be back from sea. Oz luck would have ut, he was away across the island tull a christenun' when Albert Mahan arrives home onexpected, hus shup just docked ot Dublin. Ut's nine o'clock ot night when the munuster, un hus sluppers an' dressun'-gown, gets the news. Up he jumps an' calls for horse an' saddle, an' awa' he goes like the wund for Albert Mahan's. Albert uz just goun' tull bed an' hoz one shoe off when the munuster arrives.

"'Come wuth me, the pair o' ye,' says he, breathless-like. 'What for, an' me dead weary an' goun' tull bed?' says Albert. 'Yull be lawful married,' says the munuster. Albert looks black an' says, 'Now, munuster, ye wull be jokun',' but tull humself, oz I've heard hum tell mony a time, he uz wonderun' thot the munuster should a-took tull whusky ot hus time o' life.

"'We be no married?' says Minnie. He shook his head. 'An' I om no Mussus Mahan?' 'No,' says he, 'ye are no Mussus Mahan. Ye are plain Muss Duncan.' 'But ye married 'us yoursel',' says she. 'I dud an' I dudna,' says he. An' wuth thot he tells them the whole upshot, an' Albert puts on hus shoe, an' they go wuth the munuster an' are married proper an' lawful, an' oz Albert Mahan says afterward mony's the time, "Tus no every mon thot hoz two weddun' nights on Island McGill."'

Six months later Eddie Troy came home and was promptly remarried. But Samuel Dundee was away on a three-years' voyage and his ship fell

276

overdue. Further to complicate the situation, a baby boy, past two years old, was waiting for him in the arms of his wife. The months passed, and the wife grew thin with worrying. "Ut's no meself I'm thunkun' on," she is reported to have said many times, "but ut's the puir fatherless bairn. Uf aught happened tull Samuel where wull the bairn stond?"

Lloyd's posted the *Loughbank* as missing, and the owners ceased the monthly remittance of Samuel's half-pay to his wife. It was the question of the child's legitimacy that preyed on her mind, and, when all hope of Samuel's return was abandoned, she drowned herself and the child in the loch. And here enters the greater tragedy. The *Loughbank* was not lost. By a series of sea disasters and delays too interminable to relate, she had made one of those long, unsighted passages such as occur once or twice in half a century. How the Imp must have held both his sides! Back from the sea came Samuel, and when they broke the news to him something else broke somewhere in his heart or head. Next morning they found him where he had tried to kill himself across the grave of his wife and child. Never in the history of Island McGill was there so fearful a death-bed. He spat in the minister's face and reviled him, and died blaspheming so terribly that those that tended on him did so with averted gaze and trembling hands.

And, in the face of all this, Margaret Henan named her first child Samuel.

How account for the woman's stubbornness? Or was it a morbid obsession that demanded a child of hers should be named Samuel? Her third child was a girl, named after herself, and the fourth was a boy again. Despite the strokes of fate that had already bereft her, and despite the loss of friends and relatives, she persisted in her resolve to name the child after her brother. She was shunned at church by those who had grown up with her. Her mother, after a final appeal, left her house with the warning that if the child were so named she would never speak to her again. And though the old lady lived thirty-odd years longer she kept her word. The minister agreed to christen the child any name but Samuel, and every other minister on Island McGill refused to christen it by the name she had chosen. There was talk on the part of Margaret Henan of going to law at the time, but in the end she carried the child to Belfast and there had it christened Samuel.

And then nothing happened. The whole island was confuted. The boy grew and prospered. The schoolmaster never ceased averring that it was the brightest lad he had ever seen. Samuel had a splendid constitution, a tremendous grip on life. To everybody's amazement he escaped the usual run of childish afflictions. Measles, whooping-cough and mumps knew him not. He was armour-clad against germs, immune to all disease. Headaches and earaches were things unknown. "Never so much oz a boil or a pumple," as one of the old bodies told me, ever marred his healthy skin. He broke school records in scholarship and athletics, and whipped every boy of his size or years on Island McGill.

It was a triumph for Margaret Henan. This paragon was hers, and it bore the cherished name. With the one exception of her mother, friends and relatives drifted back and acknowledged that they had been mistaken; though there were old crones who still abided by their opinion and who shook their heads ominously over their cups of tea. The boy was too wonderful to last. There was no escaping the curse of the name his mother had wickedly laid upon him. The young generation joined Margaret Henan in laughing at them, but the old crones continued to shake their heads.

Other children followed. Margaret Henan's fifth was a boy, whom she called Jamie, and in rapid succession followed three girls, Alice, Sara, and Nora, the boy Timothy, and two more girls, Florence and Katie. Katie was the last and eleventh, and Margaret Henan, at thirty-five, ceased from her exertions. She had done well by Island McGill and the Queen. Nine healthy children were hers. All prospered. It seemed her ill-luck had shot its bolt with the deaths of her first two. Nine lived, and one of them was named Samuel.

Jamie elected to follow the sea, though it was not so much a matter of election as compulsion, for the eldest sons on Island McGill remained on the land, while all other sons went to the salt-ploughing. Timothy followed Jamie, and by the time the latter had got his first command, a steamer in the Bay trade out of Cardiff, Timothy was mate of a big sailing ship. Samuel, however, did not take kindly to the soil. The farmer's life had no attraction for him. His brothers went to sea, not out of desire, but because it was the only way for them to gain their bread; and he, who had no need to go, envied them when, returned from far voyages, they sat by the kitchen fire, and told their bold tales of the wonderlands beyond the sea-rim.

Samuel became a teacher, much to his father's disgust, and even took extra certificates, going to Belfast for his examinations. When the old master retired, Samuel took over his school. Secretly, however, he studied navigation, and it was Margaret's delight when he sat by the kitchen fire, and, despite their master's tickets, tangled up his brothers in the theoretics of their profession. Tom Henan alone was outraged when Samuel, school teacher, gentleman, and heir to the Henan farm, shipped to sea before the mast. Margaret had an abiding faith in her son's star, and whatever he did she was sure was for the best. Like everything else connected with his glorious personality, there had never been known so swift a rise as in the case of Samuel. Barely with two years' sea experience before the mast, he was taken from the forecastle and made a provisional second mate. This occurred in a fever port on the West Coast, and the committee of skippers that examined him agreed that he knew more of the science of navigation than they had remembered or forgotten. Two years later he sailed from Liverpool, mate of the *Starry Grace*, with both master's and extra-master's tickets in his possession. And then it happened— the thing the old crones had been shaking their heads over for years.

It was told me by Gavin McNab, bos'n of the *Starry Grace* at the time, himself an Island McGill man.

"Wull do I remember ut," he said. "We was runnin' our Eastun' down, an' makun' heavy weather of ut. Oz fine a sailor-mon oz ever walked was Samuel Henan. I remember the look of hum wull thot last marnun', a-watch-un' them bug seas curlun' up astern, an' a-watchun' the old girl an' seeun' how she took them—the skupper down below an' drunkun' for days. Ut was ot seven thot Henan brought her up on tull the wund, not darun' tull run longer on thot fearful sea. Ot eight, after havun' breakfast, he turns un, an' a half hour after up comes the skupper, bleary-eyed an' shaky an' holdun' on tull the companion. Ut was fair smokun', I om tellun' ye, an' there he stood, blunkun' an' noddun' an' talkun' tull humsel'. 'Keep off,' says he ot last tull the mon ot the wheel. 'My God!' says the second mate, standun' beside hum.

The skupper never looks tull hum ot all, but keeps on mutterun" an' jabberun' tull humsel'. All of a suddent-like he straightens up an' throws hus head back, an' says: 'Put your wheel over, me mon—now domn ye! Are ye deef thot ye'll no be hearun' me?'

"Ut was a drunken mon's luck, for the *Starry Grace* wore off afore thot God-Almighty gale wuthout shuppun' a bucket o' watter, the second mate shoutun' orders an' the crew jumpun' like mod. An' wuth thot the skupper nods contented-like tull humself an' goes below after more whusky. Ut was plain murder o' the lives o' all of us, for ut was no the time for the buggest shup afloat tull be runnun'. Run? Never hov I seen the like! Ut was beyond all thunkun', an' me goun' tull sea, boy an' men, for forty year. I tell you ut was fair awesome.

"The face o' the second mate was white oz death, an' he stood ut alone for half an hour, when ut was too much for hum an' he went below an' called Samuel an' the third. Aye, a fine sailor-mon thot Samuel, but ut was too much for hum. He looked an' studied, and looked an' studied, but he could no see hus way. He durst na heave tull. She would ha' been sweeput o' all honds an' stucks an' everythung afore she could a-fetched up. There was naught tull do but keep on runnun'. An' uf ut worsened we were lost ony way, for soon or late that overtakun' sea was sure tull sweep us clear over poop an' all.

"Dud I say ut was a God-Almighty gale? Ut was worse nor thot. The devil himself must ha' hod a hond un the brewun' o' ut, ut was thot fearsome. I ha' looked on some sights, but I om no carun' tull look on the like o' thot again. No mon dared tull be un hus bunk. No, nor no mon on the decks. All honds of us stood on top the house an' held on an' watched. The three mates was on the poop, with two men ot the wheel, an' the only mon below was thot whusky-blighted captain snorun' drunk.

"An' then I see ut comun', a mile away, risun' above all the waves like an island un the sea—the buggest wave ever I looked upon. The three mates stood tulgether an' watched ut comun', a-prayun' like we thot she would no break un passun' us. But ut was no tull be. Ot the last, when she rose up like a mountain, curlun' above the stern an' blottun' out the sky, the mates scattered, the second an' third runnun' for the mizzen-shrouds an' climbun' up, but the first runnun' tull the wheel tull lend a hond. He was a brave men, thot Samuel Henan. He run straight un tull the face o' thot father o' all waves, no thunkun' on humself but thunkun' only o' the shup. The two men was lashed tull the wheel, but he would be ready tull hond un the case they was kult. An' then she took ut. We on the house could no see the poop for the thousand tons o' watter thot hod hut ut. Thot wave cleaned them out, took everythung along wuth ut—the two mates, climbun' up the mizzen-ruggun', Samuel Henan runnun' tull the wheel, the two men ot the wheel, aye, an' the wheel utself. We never saw aught o' them, for she broached tull what o' the wheel goun', an' two men o' us was drownded off the house, no tull mention the carpenter thot we pucked up ot the break o' the poop wuth every bone o' hus body broke tull he was like so much jelly."

And here enters the marvel of it, the miraculous wonder of that woman's heroic spirit. Margaret Henan was forty-seven when the news came home of the loss of Samuel; and it was not long after that the unbelievable rumour went around Island McGill. I say unbelievable. Island McGill would not believe. Doctor Hall pooh-pooh'd it. Everybody laughed at it as a good joke. They traced back the gossip to Sara Dack, servant to the Henans', and who alone lived with Margaret and her husband. But Sara Dack persisted in her assertion and was called a low-mouthed liar. One or two dared question Tom Henan himself, but beyond black looks and curses for their presumption they elicited nothing from him.

The rumour died down, and the island fell to discussing in all its ramifications the loss of the *Grenoble* in the China seas, with all her officers and half her crew born and married on Island McGill. But the rumour would not stay down. Sara Dack was louder in her assertions, the looks Tom Henan cast about him were blacker than ever, and Dr. Hall, after a visit to the Henan house, no longer pooh-pooh'd. Then Island McGill sat up, and there was a tremendous wagging of tongues. It was unnatural and ungodly. The like had never been heard. And when, as time passed, the truth of Sara Dack's utterances was manifest, the island folk decided, like the bos'n of the *Starry*

Grace, that only the devil could have had a hand in so untoward a happening. And the infatuated woman, so Sara Dack reported, insisted that it would be a boy. "Eleven bairns ha' I borne," she said; "sux o' them lossies an' five o' them loddies. An' sunce there be balance un all thungs, so wull there be balance wuth me. Sux o' one an' half a dozen o' the other—there uz the balance, an' oz sure oz the sun rises un the marnun', thot sure wull ut be a boy."

And boy it was, and a prodigy. Dr. Hall raved about its unblemished perfection and massive strength, and wrote a brochure on it for the Dublin Medical Society as the most interesting case of the sort in his long career. When Sara Dack gave the babe's unbelievable weight, Island McGill refused to believe and once again called her liar. But when Doctor Hall attested that he had himself weighed it and seen it tip that very notch, Island McGill held its breath and accepted whatever report Sara Dack made of the infant's progress or appetite. And once again Margaret Henan carried a babe to Belfast and had it christened *Samuel*.

"Oz good oz gold ut was," said Sara Dack to me.

Sara, at the time I met her, was a buxom, phlegmatic spinster of sixty, equipped with an experience so tragic and unusual that though her tongue ran on for decades its output would still be of imperishable interest to her cronies.

"Oz good oz good," said Sara Dack. "Ut never fretted. Sut ut down un the sun by the hour an' never a sound ut would make oz long oz ut was no hungered! An' thot strong! The grup o' uts honds was like a mon's. I mind me, when ut was but hours old, ut grupped me so mighty thot I fetched a scream I was thot frightened. Ut was the punk o' health. Ut slept an' ate, an' grew. Ut never bothered. Never a night's sleep ut lost tull no one, nor ever a munut's, an' thot wuth cuttin' uts teeth an' all. An' Margaret would dandle ut on her knee an' ask was there ever so fine a loddie un the three Kungdoms.

"The way ut grew! Ut was un keepun' wuth the way ut ate. Ot a year ut was the size o' a bairn of two. Ut was slow tull walk an' talk. Exceptun' for gurgly noises un uts throat an' for creepun' on all fours, ut dudna monage much un the walkun' an' talkun' line. But thot was tull be expected from the way ut grew. Ut all went tull growun' strong an' healthy. An' even old Tom Henan cheered up ot the might of ut an' said was there ever the like o' ut un the three Kungdoms. Ut was Doctor Hall thot first suspicioned, I mind me well, though ut was luttle I dreamt what he was up tull ot the time. I seehum holdun' thungs' un fronto' luttle Sammy's eyes, an' a-makun' noises, loud an' soft, an' far an' near, un luttle Sammy's ears. An' then I see Doctor Hall go away, wrunklun' hus eyebrows an' shakun' hus head like the bairn was ailun'. But he was no ailun', oz I could swear tull, me a-seeun' hum eat an' grow. But Doctor Hall no said a word tull Margaret an' I was no for guessun' the why he was sore puzzled.

"I mind me when luttle Sammy first spoke. He was two years old an' the size of a child o five, though he could no monage the walkun' yet but went around on all fours, happy an' contented-like an' makun' no trouble oz long oz he was fed promptly, which was onusual often. I was hangun' the wash on the line ot the time when out he comes, on all fours, hus bug head waggun' tull an' fro an' blunkun' un the sun. An' then, suddent, he talked. I was thot took a-back I near died o' fright, an' fine I knew ut then, the shakun' o' Doctor Hall's head. Talked? Never a bairn on Island McGill talked so loud an' tull such purpose. There was no mustakun' ut. I stood there all tremblun' an' shakun'. Little Sammy was brayun'. I tell you, sir, he was brayun' like an ass—just like thot,—loud an' long an' cheerful tull ut seemed hus lungs ud crack.

"He was a eediot—a great, awful, monster eediot. Ut was after he talked thot Doctor Hall told Margaret, but she would no believe. Ut would all come right, she said. Ut was growun' too fast for aught else. Guv ut time, said she, an' we would see. But old Tom Henan knew, an' he never held up hus head again. He could no abide the thung, an' would no brung humsel' tull touch ut, though I om no denyun' he was fair fascinated by ut. Mony the time, I see hum watchun' of ut around a corner, lookun' ot ut tull hus eyes fair bulged wuth the horror; an' when ut brayed old Tom ud stuck hus fungers tull hus ears an' look thot miserable I could a-puttied hum.

"An' bray ut could! Ut was the only thung ut could do besides eat an' grow. Whenever ut was hungry ut brayed, an' there was no stoppun' ut save wuth food. An' always of a marnun', when first ut crawled tull the kutchen-door an' blunked out ot the sun, ut brayed. An' ut was brayun' that brought about uts end.

"I mind me well. Ut was three years old an' oz bug oz a led o' ten. Old Tom hed been goun' from bed tull worse, ploughun' up an' down the fields an' talkun' an' mutterun' tull humself. On the marnun' o' the day I mind me, he was suttun' on the bench outside the kutchen, a-futtun' the handle tull a puck-axe. Unbeknown, the monster eediot crawled tull the door an' brayed after hus fashion ot the sun. I see old Tom start up an' look. An' there was the monster eediot, waggun' uts bug head an' blunkun' an' brayun' like the great bug ass ut was. Ut was too much for Tom. Somethun' went wrong wuth hum suddent-like. He jumped tull hus feet an' fetched the puck-handle down on the monster eediot's head. An' he hut ut again an' again like ut was a mod dog an' hum afeard o' ut. An' he went straight tull the stable an' hung humsel' tull a rafter. An' I was no for stoppun' on after such-like, an' I went tull stay along wuth me suster thot was married tull John Martin an' comfortable-off."

I sat on the bench by the kitchen door and regarded Margaret Henan, while with her callous thumb she pressed down the live fire of her pipe and gazed out across the twilight-sombred fields. It was the very bench Tom Henan had sat upon that last sanguinary day of life. And Margaret sat in the doorway where the monster, blinking at the sun, had so often wagged its head and brayed. We had been talking for an hour, she with that slow certitude of eternity that so befitted her; and, for the life of me, I could lay no finger on the motives that ran through the tangled warp and woof of her. Was she a martyr to Truth? Did she have it in her to worship at so abstract a shrine? Had she conceived Abstract Truth to be the one high goal of human endeavour on that day of long ago when she named her first-born Samuel? Or was hers the stubborn obstinacy of the ox? the fixity of purpose of the balky horse? the stolidity of the self-willed peasant-mind? Was it whim or fancy?—the one streak of lunacy in what was otherwise an eminently rational mind? Or, reverting, was hers the spirit of a Bruno? Was she convinced of the intellectual rightness of the stand she had taken? Was hers a steady, enlightened opposition to superstition? or—and a subtler thought—was she mastered by some vaster, profounder superstition, a fetish-worship of which the Alpha and the Omega was the cryptic Samuel?

"Wull ye be tellun' me," she said, "thot uf the second Samuel hod been named Larry thot he would no hov fell un the hot watter an' drownded? Atween you an' me, sir, an' ye are untellugent-lookun' tull the eye, would the name hov made ut onyways dufferent? Would the washun' no be done thot day uf he hod been Larry or Michael? Would hot watter no be hot, an' would hot watter no burn uf he hod hod ony other name but Samuel?"

I acknowledged the justice of her contention, and she went on.

"Do a wee but of a name change the plans o' God? Do the world run by hut or muss, an' be God a weak, shully-shallyun' creature thot ud alter the fate an' destiny o' thungs because the worm Margaret Henan seen fut tull name her bairn Samuel? There be my son Jamie. He wull no sign a Rooshan-Funn un hus crew because o' believun' thot Rooshan-Funns do be monajun' the wunds an' hov the makun' o' bod weather. Wull you be thunkun' so? Wull you be thunkun' thot God thot makes the wunds tull blow wull bend Hus head from on high tull lussen tull the word o' a greasy Rooshan-Funn un some dirty shup's fo'c'sle?"

I said no, certainly not; but she was not to be set aside from pressing home the point of her argument.

"Then wull you be thunkun' thot God thot directs the stars un their courses, an' tull whose mighty foot the world uz but a footstool, wull you be thunkun' thot He wull take a spite again' Margaret Henan an' send a bug wave off the Cape tull wash her son un tull eternity, all because she was for namun' hum Samuel?"

"But *why* Samuel?" I asked.

"An' thot I dinna know. I wantud ut so."

"But *why* did you want it so?"

"An' uz ut me thot would be answerun' a such-like question? Be there ony mon luvun' or dead thot can answer? Who can tell the *why* o' like? My

Jamie was fair daft on buttermilk, he would drunk ut tull, oz he said humself, hus back teeth was awash. But my Tumothy could no abide buttermilk. I like tull lussen tull the thunder growlun' an' roarun', an' rampajun'. My Katie could no abide the noise of ut, but must scream an' flutter an' go runnun' for the mudmost o' a feather-bed. Never yet hov I heard the answer tull the why o' like, God alone hoz thot answer. You an' me be mortal an' we canna know. Enough for us tull know what we like an' what we duslike. I *like*—thot uz the first word an' the last. An' behind thot like no men can go an' find the *why* o' ut. I *like* Samuel, an' I like ut well. Ut uz a sweet name, an' there be a rollun' wonder un the sound o' ut thot passes onderstandun'."

The twilight deepened, and in the silence I gazed upon that splendid dome of a forehead which time could not mar, at the width between the eyes, and at the eyes themselves—clear, out-looking, and wide-seeing. She rose to her feet with an air of dismissing me, saying—

"Ut wull be a dark walk home, an' there wull be more thon a sprunkle o' wet un the sky."

"Have you any regrets, Margaret Henan?" I asked, suddenly and without forethought.

She studied me a moment.

"Aye, thot I no ha' borne another son."

"And you would . . .?" I faltered.

"Aye, thot I would," she answered. "Ut would ha' been hus name."

I went down the dark road between the hawthorn hedges puzzling over the why of like, repeating *Samuel* to myself and aloud and listening to the rolling wonder in its sound that had charmed her soul and led her life in tragic places. *Samuel!* There was a rolling wonder in the sound. Aye, there was!

About Author

John Griffith London (born **John Griffith Chaney**; January 12, 1876 – November 22, 1916) was an American novelist, journalist, and social activist. A pioneer in the world of commercial magazine fiction, he was one of the first writers to become a worldwide celebrity and earn a large fortune from writing. He was also an innovator in the genre that would later become known as science fiction.

His most famous works include The Call of the Wild and White Fang, both set in the Klondike Gold Rush, as well as the short stories "To Build a Fire", "An Odyssey of the North", and "Love of Life". He also wrote about the South Pacific in stories such as "The Pearls of Parlay", and "The Heathen".

London was part of the radical literary group "The Crowd" in San Francisco and a passionate advocate of unionization, workers' rights, socialism, and eugenics. He wrote several works dealing with these topics, such as his dystopian novel The Iron Heel, his non-fiction exposé The People of the Abyss, The War of the Classes, and Before Adam.

Family

Jack London's mother, Flora Wellman, was the fifth and youngest child of Pennsylvania Canal builder Marshall Wellman and his first wife, Eleanor Garrett Jones. Marshall Wellman was descended from Thomas Wellman, an early Puritan settler in the Massachusetts Bay Colony. Flora left Ohio and moved to the Pacific coast when her father remarried after her mother died. In San Francisco, Flora worked as a music teacher and spiritualist, claiming to channel the spirit of a Sauk chief, Black Hawk.

Biographer Clarice Stasz and others believe London's father was astrologer William Chaney. Flora Wellman was living with Chaney in San Francisco when she became pregnant. Whether Wellman and Chaney were legally married is unknown. Stasz notes that in his memoirs, Chaney refers to London's mother Flora Wellman as having been his "wife"; he also cites an advertisement in which Flora called herself "Florence Wellman Chaney".

According to Flora Wellman's account, as recorded in the San Francisco Chronicle of June 4, 1875, Chaney demanded that she have an abortion. When she refused, he disclaimed responsibility for the child. In desperation, she shot herself. She was not seriously wounded, but she was temporarily deranged. After giving birth, Flora turned the baby over for care to Virginia Prentiss, an African-American woman and former slave. She was a major maternal figure throughout London's life. Late in 1876, Flora Wellman married John London, a partially disabled Civil War veteran, and brought her baby John, later known as Jack, to live with the newly married couple. The family moved around the San Francisco Bay Area before settling in Oakland, where London completed public grade school.

In 1897, when he was 21 and a student at the University of California, Berkeley, London searched for and read the newspaper accounts of his mother's suicide attempt and the name of his biological father. He wrote to William Chaney, then living in Chicago. Chaney responded that he could not be London's father because he was impotent; he casually asserted that London's mother had relations with other men and averred that she had slandered him when she said he insisted on an abortion. Chaney concluded by saying that he was more to be pitied than London. London was devastated by his father's letter; in the months following, he quit school at Berkeley and went to the Klondike during the gold rush boom.

Early life

London was born near Third and Brannan Streets in San Francisco. The house burned down in the fire after the 1906 San Francisco earthquake; the California Historical Society placed a plaque at the site in 1953. Although the family was working class, it was not as impoverished as London's later accounts claimed. London was largely self-educated.

In 1885, London found and read Ouida's long Victorian novel Signa. He credited this as the seed of his literary success. In 1886, he went to the Oakland Public Library and found a sympathetic librarian, Ina Coolbrith, who encouraged his learning. (She later became California's first poet laureate and an important figure in the San Francisco literary community).

In 1889, London began working 12 to 18 hours a day at Hickmott's Cannery. Seeking a way out, he borrowed money from his foster mother Virginia Prentiss, bought the sloop Razzle-Dazzle from an oyster pirate named French Frank, and became an oyster pirate himself. In his memoir, John Barleycorn, he claims also to have stolen French Frank's mistress Mamie. After a few months, his sloop became damaged beyond repair. London hired on as a member of the California Fish Patrol.

In 1893, he signed on to the sealing schooner Sophie Sutherland, bound for the coast of Japan. When he returned, the country was in the grip of the panic of '93 and Oakland was swept by labor unrest. After grueling jobs in a jute mill and a street-railway power plant, London joined Coxey's Army and began his career as a tramp. In 1894, he spent 30 days for vagrancy in the Erie County Penitentiary at Buffalo, New York. In The Road, he wrote:

> Man-handling was merely one of the very minor unprintable horrors of the Erie County Pen. I say 'unprintable'; and in justice I must also say undescribable. They were unthinkable to me until I saw them, and I was no spring chicken in the ways of the world and the awful abysses of human degradation. It would take a deep plummet to reach bottom in the Erie County Pen, and I do but skim lightly and facetiously the surface of things as I there saw them.
>
> — Jack London, The Road

After many experiences as a hobo and a sailor, he returned to Oakland and attended Oakland High School. He contributed a number of articles to the high school's magazine, The Aegis. His first published work was "Typhoon off the Coast of Japan", an account of his sailing experiences.

As a schoolboy, London often studied at Heinold's First and Last Chance Saloon, a port-side bar in Oakland. At 17, he confessed to the bar's owner, John Heinold, his desire to attend university and pursue a career as a writer. Heinold lent London tuition money to attend college.

London desperately wanted to attend the University of California, located in Berkeley. In 1896, after a summer of intense studying to pass certification exams, he was admitted. Financial circumstances forced him to leave in 1897 and he never graduated. No evidence has surfaced that he ever wrote for student publications while studying at Berkeley.

While at Berkeley, London continued to study and spend time at Heinold's saloon, where he was introduced to the sailors and adventurers who would influence his writing. In his autobiographical novel, John Barleycorn, London mentioned the pub's likeness seventeen times. Heinold's was the place where London met Alexander McLean, a captain known for his cruelty at sea. London based his protagonist Wolf Larsen, in the novel The Sea-Wolf, on McLean.

Heinold's First and Last Chance Saloon is now unofficially named Jack London's Rendezvous in his honor.

Gold rush and first success

On July 12, 1897, London (age 21) and his sister's husband Captain Shepard sailed to join the Klondike Gold Rush. This was the setting for some of his first successful stories. London's time in the harsh Klondike, however, was detrimental to his health. Like so many other men who were malnourished in the goldfields, London developed scurvy. His gums became swollen, leading to the loss of his four front teeth. A constant gnawing pain affected his hip and leg muscles, and his face was stricken with marks that always reminded him of the struggles he faced in the Klondike. Father William Judge, "The Saint of Dawson", had a facility in Dawson that provided shelter, food and any available medicine to London and others. His struggles there inspired London's short story, "To Build a Fire" (1902, revised in 1908), which many critics assess as his best.

His landlords in Dawson were mining engineers Marshall Latham Bond and Louis Whitford Bond, educated at Yale and Stanford, respectively. The brothers' father, Judge Hiram Bond, was a wealthy mining investor. The Bonds, especially Hiram, were active Republicans. Marshall Bond's diary mentions friendly sparring with London on political issues as a camp pastime.

London left Oakland with a social conscience and socialist leanings; he returned to become an activist for socialism. He concluded that his only hope of escaping the work "trap" was to get an education and "sell his brains". He saw his writing as a business, his ticket out of poverty, and, he hoped, a means of beating the wealthy at their own game. On returning to California in 1898, London began working to get published, a struggle described in his novel, Martin Eden (serialized in 1908, published in 1909). His first published story since high school was "To the Man On Trail", which has frequently been collected in anthologies. When The Overland Monthly offered him only five dollars for it—and was slow paying—London came close to abandoning his writing career. In his words, "literally and literarily I was saved" when The Black Cat accepted his story "A Thousand Deaths", and paid him $40—the "first money I ever received for a story".

London began his writing career just as new printing technologies enabled lower-cost production of magazines. This resulted in a boom in popular magazines aimed at a wide public audience and a strong market for short fiction. In 1900, he made $2,500 in writing, about $77,000 in today's currency. Among the works he sold to magazines was a short story known as either "Diable" (1902) or "Bâtard" (1904), two editions of the same basic story; London received $141.25 for this story on May 27, 1902. In the text, a cruel French Canadian brutalizes his dog, and the dog retaliates and kills the man. London told some of his critics that man's actions are the main cause of the behavior of their animals, and he would show this in another story, The Call of the Wild.

In early 1903, London sold The Call of the Wild to The Saturday Evening Post for $750, and the book rights to Macmillan for $2,000. Macmillan's promotional campaign propelled it to swift success.

While living at his rented villa on Lake Merritt in Oakland, California, London met poet George Sterling; in time they became best friends. In 1902, Sterling helped London find a home closer to his own in nearby Piedmont. In his letters London addressed Sterling as "Greek", owing to Sterling's aquiline nose and classical profile, and he signed them as "Wolf". London was later to depict Sterling as Russ Brissenden in his autobiographical novel Martin Eden (1910) and as Mark Hall in The Valley of the Moon (1913).

In later life London indulged his wide-ranging interests by accumulating a personal library of 15,000 volumes. He referred to his books as "the tools of my trade".

First marriage (1900–04)

London married Elizabeth "Bessie" Maddern on April 7, 1900, the same day The Son of the Wolf was published. Bess had been part of his circle of friends for a number of years. She was related to stage actresses Minnie Maddern Fiske and Emily Stevens. Stasz says, "Both acknowledged publicly that they were not marrying out of love, but from friendship and a belief that they would produce sturdy children." Kingman says, "they were comfortable together... Jack had made it clear to Bessie that he did not love her, but that he liked her enough to make a successful marriage."

London met Bessie through his friend at Oakland High School, Fred Jacobs; she was Fred's fiancée. Bessie, who tutored at Anderson's University Academy in Alameda California, tutored Jack in preparation for his entrance exams for the University of California at Berkeley in 1896. Jacobs was killed aboard the USAT Scandia in 1897, but Jack and Bessie continued their friendship, which included taking photos and developing the film together. This was the beginning of Jack's passion for photography.

During the marriage, London continued his friendship with Anna Strunsky, co-authoring The Kempton-Wace Letters, an epistolary novel contrasting two philosophies of love. Anna, writing "Dane Kempton's" letters, arguing for a romantic view of marriage, while London, writing "Herbert Wace's" letters, argued for a scientific view, based on Darwinism and eugenics. In the novel, his fictional character contrasted two women he had known.

London's pet name for Bess was "Mother-Girl" and Bess's for London was "Daddy-Boy". Their first child, Joan, was born on January 15, 1901, and their second, Bessie (later called Becky), on October 20, 1902. Both children were born in Piedmont, California. Here London wrote one of his most celebrated works, The Call of the Wild.

While London had pride in his children, the marriage was strained. Kingman says that by 1903 the couple were close to separation as they were "extremely incompatible". "Jack was still so kind and gentle with Bessie that when Cloudsley Johns was a house guest in February 1903 he didn't suspect a breakup of their marriage."

London reportedly complained to friends Joseph Noel and George Sterling:

> [Bessie] is devoted to purity. When I tell her morality is only evidence of low blood pressure, she hates me. She'd sell me and the children out for her damned purity. It's terrible. Every time I come back after being away from home for a night she won't let me be in the same room with her if she can help it.

Stasz writes that these were "code words for fear that was consorting with prostitutes and might bring home venereal disease."

On July 24, 1903, London told Bessie he was leaving and moved out. During 1904, London and Bess negotiated the terms of a divorce, and the decree was granted on November 11, 1904.

War correspondent (1904)

London accepted an assignment of the San Francisco Examiner to cover the Russo-Japanese War in early 1904, arriving in Yokohama on January 25, 1904. He was arrested by Japanese authorities in Shimonoseki, but released through the intervention of American ambassador Lloyd Griscom. After travelling to Korea, he was again arrested by Japanese authorities for straying too close to the border with Manchuria without official permission, and was sent back to Seoul. Released again, London was permitted to travel with the Imperial Japanese Army to the border, and to observe the Battle of the Yalu.

London asked William Randolph Hearst, the owner of the San Francisco Examiner, to be allowed to transfer to the Imperial Russian Army, where he felt that restrictions on his reporting and his movements would be less severe. However, before this could be arranged, he was arrested for a third time in four months, this time for assaulting his Japanese assistants, whom he accused of stealing the fodder for his horse. Released through the personal intervention of President Theodore Roosevelt, London departed the front in June 1904.

Bohemian Club

On August 18, 1904, London went with his close friend, the poet George Sterling, to "Summer High Jinks" at the Bohemian Grove. London was elected to honorary membership in the Bohemian Club and took part in many activities. Other noted members of the Bohemian Club during this time included Ambrose Bierce, Gelett Burgess, Allan Dunn, John Muir, Frank Norris, and Herman George Scheffauer.

Beginning in December 1914, London worked on The Acorn Planter, A California Forest Play, to be performed as one of the annual Grove Plays, but it was never selected. It was described as too difficult to set to music. London published The Acorn Planter in 1916.

Second marriage

After divorcing Maddern, London married Charmian Kittredge in 1905. London had been introduced to Kittredge in 1900 by her aunt Netta Eames, who was an editor at Overland Monthly magazine in San Francisco. The two met prior to his first marriage but became lovers years later after Jack and Bessie London visited Wake Robin, Netta Eames' Sonoma County resort, in 1903. London was injured when he fell from a buggy, and Netta arranged for Charmian to care for him. The two developed a friendship, as Charmian, Netta, her husband Roscoe, and London were politically aligned with socialist causes. At some point the relationship became romantic, and Jack divorced his wife to marry Charmian, who was five years his senior.

Biographer Russ Kingman called Charmian "Jack's soul-mate, always at his side, and a perfect match." Their time together included numerous trips, including a 1907 cruise on the yacht Snark to Hawaii and Australia. Many of London's stories are based on his visits to Hawaii, the last one for 10 months beginning in December 1915.

The couple also visited Goldfield, Nevada, in 1907, where they were guests of the Bond brothers, London's Dawson City landlords. The Bond brothers were working in Nevada as mining engineers.

London had contrasted the concepts of the "Mother Girl" and the "Mate Woman" in The Kempton-Wace Letters. His pet name for Bess had been "Mother-Girl;" his pet name for Charmian was "Mate-Woman."Charmian's aunt and foster mother, a disciple of Victoria Woodhull, had raised her without prudishness.Every biographer alludes to Charmian's uninhibited sexuality.

Joseph Noel calls the events from 1903 to 1905 "a domestic drama that would have intrigued the pen of an Ibsen.... London's had comedy relief in it and a sort of easy-going romance." In broad outline, London was restless in his first marriage, sought extramarital sexual affairs, and found, in Charmian Kittredge, not only a sexually active and adventurous partner, but his future life-companion. They attempted to have children; one child died at birth, and another pregnancy ended in a miscarriage.

In 1906, London published in Collier's magazine his eye-witness report of the San Francisco earthquake.

Beauty Ranch (1905–16)

In 1905, London purchased a 1,000 acres (4.0 km2) ranch in Glen Ellen, Sonoma County, California, on the eastern slope of Sonoma Mountain.He wrote: "Next to my wife, the ranch is the dearest thing in the world to me." He desperately wanted the ranch to become a successful business enterprise. Writing, always a commercial enterprise with London, now became even more a means to an end: "I write for no other purpose than to add to the beauty that now belongs to me. I write a book for no other reason than to add three or four hundred acres to my magnificent estate."

Stasz writes that London "had taken fully to heart the vision, expressed in his agrarian fiction, of the land as the closest earthly version of Eden ... he educated himself through the study of agricultural manuals and scientific tomes. He conceived of a system of ranching that today would be praised for its ecological wisdom." He was proud to own the first concrete silo in California, a circular piggery that he designed. He hoped to adapt the wisdom of Asian sustainable agriculture to the United States. He hired both Italian and Chinese stonemasons, whose distinctly different styles are obvious.

The ranch was an economic failure. Sympathetic observers such as Stasz treat his projects as potentially feasible, and ascribe their failure to bad luck or to being ahead of their time. Unsympathetic historians such as Kevin Starr suggest that he was a bad manager, distracted by other concerns and impaired by his alcoholism. Starr notes that London was absent from his ranch about six months a year between 1910 and 1916 and says, "He liked the show of managerial power, but not grinding attention to detail .... London's workers laughed at his efforts to play big-time rancher the operation a rich man's hobby."

London spent $80,000 ($2,280,000 in current value) to build a 15,000-square-foot (1,400 m2) stone mansion called Wolf House on the property. Just as the mansion was nearing completion, two weeks before the Londons planned to move in, it was destroyed by fire.

London's last visit to Hawaii, beginning in December 1915, lasted eight months. He met with Duke Kahanamoku, Prince Jonah Kūhiō Kalaniana'ole, Queen Lili'uokalani and many others, before returning to his ranch in July 1916. He was suffering from kidney failure, but he continued to work.

The ranch (abutting stone remnants of Wolf House) is now a National Historic Landmark and is protected in Jack London State Historic Park.

Animal activism

London witnessed animal cruelty in the training of circus animals, and his subsequent novels Jerry of the Islands and Michael, Brother of Jerry included a foreword entreating the public to become more informed about this practice. In 1918, the Massachusetts Society for the Prevention of Cruelty to Animals and the American Humane Education Society teamed up to create the Jack London Club, which sought to inform the public about cruelty to circus animals and encourage them to protest this establishment. Support from Club members led to a temporary cessation of trained animal acts at Ringling-Barnum and Bailey in 1925.

Death

London died November 22, 1916, in a sleeping porch in a cottage on his ranch. London had been a robust man but had suffered several serious illnesses, including scurvy in the Klondike. Additionally, during travels on the Snark, he and Charmian picked up unspecified tropical infections, and diseases, including yaws. At the time of his death, he suffered from dysentery, late-stage alcoholism, and uremia; he was in extreme pain and taking morphine.

London's ashes were buried on his property not far from the Wolf House. London's funeral took place on November 26, 1916, attended only by close friends, relatives, and workers of the property. In accordance with his wishes, he was cremated and buried next to some pioneer children, under a rock that belonged to the Wolf House. After Charmian's death in 1955, she was also cremated and then buried with her husband in the same spot that her husband chose. The grave is marked by a mossy boulder. The buildings and property were later preserved as Jack London State Historic Park, in Glen Ellen, California.

Suicide debate

Because he was using morphine, many older sources describe London's death as a suicide, and some still do. This conjecture appears to be a rumor, or speculation based on incidents in his fiction writings. His death certificate gives the cause as uremia, following acute renal colic.

The biographer Stasz writes, "Following London's death, for a number of reasons, a biographical myth developed in which he has been portrayed as an alcoholic womanizer who committed suicide. Recent scholarship based upon firsthand documents challenges this caricature." Most biographers, including Russ Kingman, now agree he died of uremia aggravated by an accidental morphine overdose.

London's fiction featured several suicides. In his autobiographical memoir John Barleycorn, he claims, as a youth, to have drunkenly stumbled overboard into the San Francisco Bay, "some maundering fancy of going out with the tide suddenly obsessed me". He said he drifted and nearly succeeded in drowning before sobering up and being rescued by fishermen. In the dénouement of The Little Lady of the Big House, the heroine, confronted by the pain of a mortal gunshot wound, undergoes a physician-assisted suicide by morphine. Also, in Martin Eden, the principal protagonist, who shares certain characteristics with London, drowns himself.

Plagiarism accusations

London was vulnerable to accusations of plagiarism, both because he was such a conspicuous, prolific, and successful writer and because of his methods of working. He wrote in a letter to Elwyn Hoffman, "expression, you see—with me—is far easier than invention." He purchased plots and novels from the young Sinclair Lewis and used incidents from newspaper clippings as writing material.

In July 1901, two pieces of fiction appeared within the same month: London's "Moon-Face", in the San Francisco Argonaut, and Frank Norris' "The Passing of Cock-eye Blacklock", in Century Magazine. Newspapers showed the similarities between the stories, which London said were "quite different in manner of treatment, patently the same in foundation and motive." London explained both writers based their stories on the same newspaper account. A year later, it was discovered that Charles Forrest McLean had published a fictional story also based on the same incident.

Egerton Ryerson Young claimed The Call of the Wild (1903) was taken from Young's book My Dogs in the Northland (1902). London acknowledged using it as a source and claimed to have written a letter to Young thanking him.

In 1906, the New York World published "deadly parallel" columns showing eighteen passages from London's short story "Love of Life" side by side with similar passages from a nonfiction article by Augustus Biddle and J. K. Macdonald, titled "Lost in the Land of the Midnight Sun". London noted the World did not accuse him of "plagiarism", but only of "identity of time and situation", to which he defiantly "pled guilty".

The most serious charge of plagiarism was based on London's "The Bishop's Vision", Chapter 7 of his novel The Iron Heel (1908). The chapter is nearly identical to an ironic essay that Frank Harris published in 1901, titled "The Bishop of London and Public Morality". Harris was incensed and suggested he should receive 1/60th of the royalties from The Iron Heel, the disputed material constituting about that fraction of the whole novel. London insisted he had clipped a reprint of the article, which had appeared in an American newspaper, and believed it to be a genuine speech delivered by the Bishop of London.

Views

Atheism

London was an atheist. He is quoted as saying, "I believe that when I am dead, I am dead. I believe that with my death I am just as much obliterated as the last mosquito you and I squashed."

Socialism

London wrote from a socialist viewpoint, which is evident in his novel The Iron Heel. Neither a theorist nor an intellectual socialist, London's socialism grew out of his life experience. As London explained in his essay, "How I Became a Socialist", his views were influenced by his experience with people at the bottom of the social pit. His optimism and individualism faded, and he vowed never to do more hard physical work than necessary. He wrote that his individualism was hammered out of him, and he was politically reborn. He often closed his letters "Yours for the Revolution."

London joined the Socialist Labor Party in April 1896. In the same year, the San Francisco Chronicle published a story about the twenty-year-old London's giving nightly speeches in Oakland's City Hall Park, an activity he was arrested for a year later. In 1901, he left the Socialist Labor Party and joined the new Socialist Party of America. He ran unsuccessfully as the high-profile Socialist candidate for mayor of Oakland in 1901 (receiving 245 votes) and 1905 (improving to 981 votes), toured the country lecturing on socialism in 1906, and published two collections of essays about socialism: The War of the Classes (1905) and Revolution, and other Essays (1906).

Stasz notes that "London regarded the Wobblies as a welcome addition to the Socialist cause, although he never joined them in going so far as to recommend sabotage." Stasz mentions a personal meeting between London and Big Bill Haywood in 1912.

In his late (1913) book The Cruise of the Snark, London writes about appeals to him for membership of the Snark's crew from office workers and other "toilers" who longed for escape from the cities, and of being cheated by workmen.

In his Glen Ellen ranch years, London felt some ambivalence toward socialism and complained about the "inefficient Italian labourers" in his employ. In 1916, he resigned from the Glen Ellen chapter of the Socialist Party, but stated emphatically he did so "because of its lack of fire and fight, and its loss of emphasis on the class struggle." In an unflattering portrait of London's ranch days, California cultural historian Kevin Starr refers to this period as "post-socialist" and says "... by 1911 ... London was more bored by the class struggle than he cared to admit."

Race

London shared common concerns among many European Americans in California about Asian immigration, described as "the yellow peril"; he used the latter term as the title of a 1904 essay. This theme was also the subject of a story he wrote in 1910 called "The Unparalleled Invasion". Presented as an historical essay set in the future, the story narrates events between 1976 and 1987, in which China, with an ever-increasing population, is taking over and colonizing its neighbors with the intention of taking over the entire Earth. The western nations respond with biological warfare and bombard China with dozens of the most infectious diseases. On his fears about China, he admits, "it must be taken into consideration that the above postulate is itself a product of Western race-egotism, urged by our belief in our own righteousness and fostered by a faith in ourselves which may be as erroneous as are most fond race fancies."

By contrast, many of London's short stories are notable for their empathetic portrayal of Mexican ("The Mexican"), Asian ("The Chinago"), and Hawaiian ("Koolau the Leper") characters. London's war correspondence from the Russo-Japanese War, as well as his unfinished novel Cherry, show he admired much about Japanese customs and capabilities. London's writings have been popular among the Japanese, who believe he portrayed them positively.

In "Koolau the Leper", London describes Koolau, who is a Hawaiian leper—and thus a very different sort of "superman" than Martin Eden—and who fights off an entire cavalry troop to elude capture, as "indomitable spiritually—a ... magnificent rebel". This character is based on Hawaiian leper Kaluaikoolau, who in 1893 revolted and resisted capture from forces of the Provisional Government of Hawaii in the Kalalau Valley.

An amateur boxer and avid boxing fan, London reported on the 1910 Johnson–Jeffries fight, in which the black boxer Jack Johnson vanquished Jim Jeffries, known as the "Great White Hope". In 1908, London had reported on an earlier fight of Johnson's, contrasting the black boxer's coolness and intellectual style, with the apelike appearance and fighting style of his Canadian opponent, Tommy Burns:

> [What won] on Saturday was bigness, coolness, quickness, cleverness, and vast physical superiority ... Because a white man wishes a white man to win, this should not prevent him from giving absolute credit to the best man, even when that best man was black. All hail to Johnson. ... superb. He was impregnable ... as inaccessible as Mont Blanc.

Those who defend London against charges of racism cite the letter he wrote to the Japanese-American Commercial Weekly in 1913:

> In reply to yours of August 16, 1913. First of all, I should say by stopping the stupid newspaper from always fomenting race prejudice. This of course, being impossible, I would say, next, by educating the people of Japan so that they will be too intelligently tolerant to respond to any call to race prejudice. And, finally, by realizing, in industry and

303

government, of socialism—which last word is merely a word that stands for the actual application of in the affairs of men of the theory of the Brotherhood of Man.

In the meantime the nations and races are only unruly boys who have not yet grown to the stature of men. So we must expect them to do unruly and boisterous things at times. And, just as boys grow up, so the races of mankind will grow up and laugh when they look back upon their childish quarrels.

In 1996, after the City of Whitehorse, Yukon, renamed a street in honor of London, protests over London's alleged racism forced the city to change the name of "Jack London Boulevard"[failed verification] back to "Two-mile Hill".

Eugenics

London supported eugenics, including forced sterilization of criminals or those deemed feeble minded. His novel Before Adam(1906–07) has been described as having pro-eugenic themes.

London wrote to Frederick H. Robinson of the periodical Medical Review of Reviews, stating, "I believe the future belongs to eugenics, and will be determined by the practice of eugenics."

Works

Short stories

Western writer and historian Dale L. Walker writes:

London's true métier was the short story ... London's true genius lay in the short form, 7,500 words and under, where the flood of images in his teeming brain and the innate power of his narrative gift were at once constrained and freed. His stories that run longer than the magic 7,500 generally—but certainly not always—could have benefited from self-editing.

London's "strength of utterance" is at its height in his stories, and they are painstakingly well-constructed. "To Build a Fire" is the best known of all his stories. Set in the harsh Klondike, it recounts the haphazard trek of a new arrival who has ignored an old-timer's warning about the risks of traveling alone. Falling through the ice into a creek in seventy-five-below weather, the unnamed man is keenly aware that survival depends on his untested skills at quickly building a fire to dry his clothes and warm his extremities. After publishing a tame version of this story—with a sunny outcome—in The Youth's Companion in 1902, London offered a second, more severe take on the man's predicament in The Century Magazine in 1908. Reading both provides an illustration of London's growth and maturation as a writer. As Labor (1994) observes: "To compare the two versions is itself an instructive lesson in what distinguished a great work of literary art from a good children's story."

Other stories from the Klondike period include: "All Gold Canyon", about a battle between a gold prospector and a claim jumper; "The Law of Life", about an aging American Indian man abandoned by his tribe and left to die; "Love of Life", about a trek by a prospector across the Canadian tundra; "To the Man on Trail," which tells the story of a prospector fleeing the Mounted Police in a sled race, and raises the question of the contrast between written law and morality; and "An Odyssey of the North," which raises questions of conditional morality, and paints a sympathetic portrait of a man of mixed White and Aleut ancestry.

London was a boxing fan and an avid amateur boxer. "A Piece of Steak" is a tale about a match between older and younger boxers. It contrasts the differing experiences of youth and age but also raises the social question of the treatment of aging workers. "The Mexican" combines boxing with a social theme, as a young Mexican endures an unfair fight and ethnic prejudice to earn money with which to aid the revolution.

Several of London's stories would today be classified as science fiction. "The Unparalleled Invasion" describes germ warfare against China; "Goliath" is about an irresistible energy weapon; "The Shadow and the Flash" is a tale about two brothers who take different routes to achieving invisibility; "A

Relic of the Pliocene" is a tall tale about an encounter of a modern-day man with a mammoth. "The Red One" is a late story from a period when London was intrigued by the theories of the psychiatrist and writer Jung. It tells of an island tribe held in thrall by an extraterrestrial object.

Some nineteen original collections of short stories were published during London's brief life or shortly after his death. There have been several posthumous anthologies drawn from this pool of stories. Many of these stories were located in the Klondike and the Pacific. A collection of Jack London's San Francisco Stories was published in October 2010 by Sydney Samizdat Press.

Novels

London's most famous novels are The Call of the Wild, White Fang, The Sea-Wolf, The Iron Heel, and Martin Eden.

In a letter dated December 27, 1901, London's Macmillan publisher George Platt Brett, Sr., said "he believed Jack's fiction represented 'the very best kind of work' done in America."

Critic Maxwell Geismar called The Call of the Wild "a beautiful prose poem"; editor Franklin Walker said that it "belongs on a shelf with Walden and Huckleberry Finn"; and novelist E.L. Doctorow called it "a mordant parable ... his masterpiece."

The historian Dale L. Walker commented:

> Jack London was an uncomfortable novelist, that form too long for his natural impatience and the quickness of his mind. His novels, even the best of them, are hugely flawed.

Some critics have said that his novels are episodic and resemble linked short stories. Dale L. Walker writes:

> The Star Rover, that magnificent experiment, is actually a series of short stories connected by a unifying device ... Smoke Bellew is a series of stories bound together in a novel-like form by their reappearing

protagonist, Kit Bellew; and John Barleycorn ... is a synoptic series of short episodes.

Ambrose Bierce said of The Sea-Wolf that "the great thing—and it is among the greatest of things—is that tremendous creation, Wolf Larsen ... the hewing out and setting up of such a figure is enough for a man to do in one lifetime. "However, he noted, "The love element, with its absurd suppressions, and impossible proprieties, is awful."

The Iron Heel is an example of a dystopian novel that anticipates and influenced George Orwell's Nineteen Eighty-Four. London's socialist politics are explicitly on display here. The Iron Heel meets the contemporary definition of soft science fiction. The Star Rover (1915) is also science fiction.

Apocrypha

Jack London Credo

London's literary executor, Irving Shepard, quoted a Jack London Credo in an introduction to a 1956 collection of London stories:

> I would rather be ashes than dust!

> I would rather that my spark should burn out in a brilliant blaze than it should be stifled by dry-rot.

> I would rather be a superb meteor, every atom of me in magnificent glow, than a sleepy and permanent planet.

> The function of man is to live, not to exist.

> I shall not waste my days in trying to prolong them.

> I shall use my time.

The biographer Stasz notes that the passage "has many marks of London's style" but the only line that could be safely attributed to London was the first. The words Shepard quoted were from a story in the San Francisco Bulletin, December 2, 1916, by journalist Ernest J. Hopkins, who visited the ranch just weeks before London's death. Stasz notes, "Even more so than today journalists' quotes were unreliable or even sheer inventions," and says no direct source in London's writings has been found. However, at least one line, according to Stasz, is authentic, being referenced by London and written in his own hand in the autograph book of Australian suffragette Vida Goldstein:

> Dear Miss Goldstein:–
>
> Seven years ago I wrote you that I'd rather be ashes than dust. I still subscribe to that sentiment.
>
> Sincerely yours,
>
> Jack London
>
> Jan. 13, 1909

In his short story "By The Turtles of Tasman", a character, defending her "ne'er-do-well grasshopperish father" to her "antlike uncle", says: "... my father has been a king. He has lived .... Have you lived merely to live? Are you afraid to die? I'd rather sing one wild song and burst my heart with it, than live a thousand years watching my digestion and being afraid of the wet. When you are dust, my father will be ashes."

"The Scab"

A short diatribe on "The Scab" is often quoted within the U.S. labor movement and frequently attributed to London. It opens:

> After God had finished the rattlesnake, the toad, and the vampire, he had some awful substance left with which he made a scab. A scab is a two-legged animal with a corkscrew soul, a water brain, a combination backbone of jelly and glue. Where others have hearts, he carries a tumor of rotten principles. When a scab comes down the street, men turn their backs and Angels weep in Heaven, and the Devil shuts the gates of hell to keep him out....

In 1913 and 1914, a number of newspapers printed the first three sentences with varying terms used instead of "scab", such as "knocker","stool pigeon"or "scandal monger"

This passage as given above was the subject of a 1974 Supreme Court case, Letter Carriers v. Austin, in which Justice Thurgood Marshall referred to it as "a well-known piece of trade union literature, generally attributed to author Jack London". A union newsletter had published a "list of scabs," which was granted to be factual and therefore not libelous, but then went on to quote the passage as the "definition of a scab". The case turned on the question of whether the "definition" was defamatory. The court ruled that "Jack London's... 'definition of a scab' is merely rhetorical hyperbole, a lusty and imaginative expression of the contempt felt by union members towards those who refuse to join", and as such was not libelous and was protected under the First Amendment.

Despite being frequently attributed to London, the passage does not appear at all in the extensive collection of his writings at Sonoma State University's website. However, in his book The War of the Classes he published a 1903 speech entitled "The Scab", which gave a much more balanced view of the topic:

> The laborer who gives more time or strength or skill for the same wage than another, or equal time or strength or skill for a less wage, is a scab. The generousness on his part is hurtful to his fellow-laborers, for it compels them to an equal generousness which is not to their liking, and which gives them less of food and shelter. But a word may be said for the scab. Just as his act makes his rivals compulsorily generous, so do they, by fortune of birth and training, make compulsory his act of generousness.
>
> [...]
>
> Nobody desires to scab, to give most for least. The ambition of every individual is quite the opposite, to give least for most; and, as a result, living in a tooth-and-nail society, battle royal is waged by the ambitious individuals. But in its most salient aspect, that of the struggle over the division of the joint product, it is no longer a battle between individuals, but between groups of individuals. Capital and labor apply

themselves to raw material, make something useful out of it, add to its value, and then proceed to quarrel over the division of the added value. Neither cares to give most for least. Each is intent on giving less than the other and on receiving more.

Legacy and honors

Mount London, also known as Boundary Peak 100, on the Alaska-British Columbia boundary, in the Boundary Ranges of the Coast Mountains of British Columbia, is named for him.

Jack London Square on the waterfront of Oakland, California was named for him.

He was honored by the United States Postal Service with a 25¢ Great Americans series postage stamp released on January 11, 1986.

Jack London Lake (Russian), a mountain lake located in the upper reaches of the Kolyma River in Yagodninsky district of Magadan Oblast.

Fictional portrayals of London include Michael O'Shea in the 1943 film Jack London, Jeff East in the 1980 film Klondike Fever, Aaron Ashmore in the Murdoch Mysteries episode "Murdoch of the Klondike" from 2012, and Johnny Simmons in the 2014 miniseries Klondike. (Source: Wikipedia)

NOTABLE WORKS

NOVELS

The Cruise of the Dazzler (1902)

A Daughter of the Snows (1902)

The Call of the Wild (1903)

The Kempton-Wace Letters (1903) (published anonymously, co-authored with Anna Strunsky)

The Sea-Wolf (1904)

The Game (1905)

White Fang (1906)

Before Adam (1907)

The Iron Heel (1908)

Martin Eden (1909)

Burning Daylight (1910)

Adventure (1911)

The Scarlet Plague (1912)

A Son of the Sun (1912)

The Abysmal Brute (1913)

The Valley of the Moon (1913)

The Mutiny of the Elsinore (1914)

The Star Rover (1915) (published in England as The Jacket)

The Little Lady of the Big House (1916)

Jerry of the Islands (1917)

Michael, Brother of Jerry (1917)

Hearts of Three (1920) (novelization of a script by Charles Goddard)

The Assassination Bureau, Ltd (1963) (left half-finished, completed by Robert L. Fish)

SHORT STORIES

"An Old Soldier's Story" (1894)

"Who Believes in Ghosts!" (1895)

"And 'FRISCO Kid Came Back" (1895)

"Night's Swim In Yeddo Bay" (1895)

"One More Unfortunate" (1895)

"Sakaicho, Hona Asi And Hakadaki" (1895)

"A Klondike Christmas" (1897)

"Mahatma's Little Joke" (1897)

"O Haru" (1897)

"Plague Ship" (1897)

"The Strange Experience Of A Misogynist" (1897)

"Two Gold Bricks" (1897)

"The Devil's Dice Box" (1898)

"A Dream Image" (1898)

"The Test: A Clondyke Wooing" (1898)

"To the Man on Trail" (1898)

"In a Far Country" (1899)

"The King of Mazy May" (1899)

"The End Of The Chapter" (1899)

"The Grilling Of Loren Ellery" (1899)

"The Handsome Cabin Boy" (1899)

"In The Time Of Prince Charley" (1899)

"Old Baldy" (1899)

"The Men of Forty Mile" (1899)

"Pluck and Pertinacity" (1899)

"The Rejuvenation of Major Rathbone" (1899)

"The White Silence" (1899)

"A Thousand Deaths" (1899)

"Wisdom of the Trail" (1899)

"An Odyssey of the North" (1900)

"The Son of the Wolf" (1900)

"Even unto Death" (1900)

"The Man with the Gash" (1900)

"A Lesson in Heraldry" (1900)

"A Northland Miracle" (1900)

"Proper "GIRLIE"" (1900)

"Thanksgiving on Slav Creek" (1900)

"Their Alcove" (1900)

"Housekeeping in the Klondike" (1900)

"Dutch Courage" (1900)

"Where the Trail Forks" (1900)

"Hyperborean Brew" (1901)

"A Relic of the Pliocene" (1901)

"The Lost Poacher" (1901)

"The God of His Fathers" (1901)

""FRISCO Kid's" Story" (1901)

"The Law of Life" (1901)

"The Minions of Midas" (1901)

"In the Forests of the North" (1902)

"The "Fuzziness" of Hoockla-Heen" (1902)

"The Story of Keesh" (1902)

"Keesh, Son of Keesh" (1902)

"Nam-Bok, the Unveracious" (1902)

"Li Wan the Fair" (1902)

"Lost Face"

"Master of Mystery" (1902)

"The Sunlanders" (1902)

"The Death of Ligoun" (1902)

"Moon-Face" (1902)

"Diable—A Dog" (1902), renamed Bâtard in 1904

"To Build a Fire" (1902, revised 1908)

"The League of the Old Men" (1902)

"The Dominant Primordial Beast" (1903)

"The One Thousand Dozen" (1903)

"The Marriage of Lit-lit" (1903)

"The Shadow and the Flash" (1903)

"The Leopard Man's Story" (1903)

"Negore the Coward" (1904)

"All Gold Cañon" (1905)

"Love of Life" (1905)

"The Sun-Dog Trail" (1905)

"The Apostate" (1906)

"Up the Slide" (1906)

"Planchette" (1906)

"Brown Wolf" (1906)

"Make Westing" (1907)

"Chased by the Trail" (1907)

"Trust" (1908)

"A Curious Fragment" (1908)

"Aloha Oe" (1908)

"That Spot" (1908)

"The Enemy of All the World" (1908)

"The House of Mapuhi" (1909)

"Good-by, Jack" (1909)

"The Sea-Farmer" (1912)

"The Feathers of the Sun" (1912)

"The Prodigal Father" (1912)

"Samuel" (1913)

"The Sea-Gangsters" (1913)

"The Strength of the Strong" (1914)

"Told in the Drooling Ward" (1914)

"The Hussy" (1916)

"Like Argus of the Ancient Times" (1917)

"Jerry of the Islands" (1917)

"The Red One" (1918)

"Shin-Bones" (1918)

"The Bones of Kahekili" (1919)

SHORT STORY COLLECTIONS

Son of the Wolf (1900)

Chris Farrington, Able Seaman (1901)

The God of His Fathers & Other Stories (1901)

Children of the Frost (1902)

The Faith of Men and Other Stories (1904)

Tales of the Fish Patrol (1906)

Moon-Face and Other Stories (1906)

Love of Life and Other Stories (1907)

Lost Face (1910)

South Sea Tales (1911)

When God Laughs and Other Stories (1911)

The House of Pride & Other Tales of Hawaii (1912)

Smoke Bellew (1912)

A Son of the Sun (1912)

The Night Born (1913)

The Strength of the Strong (1914)

The Turtles of Tasman (1916)

The Human Drift (1917)

The Red One (1918)

On the Makaloa Mat (1919)

Dutch Courage and Other Stories (1922)

AUTOBIOGRAPHICAL MEMOIRS

The Road (1907)

The Cruise of the Snark (1911)

John Barleycorn (1913)

NON-FICTION AND ESSAYS

Through the Rapids on the Way to the Klondike (1899)

From Dawson to the Sea (1899)

<u>POETRY</u>

A Heart (1899)

Abalone Song (1913)

And Some Night (1914)

Ballade of the False Lover (1914)

Cupid's Deal (1913)

Daybreak (1901)

Effusion (1901)

George Sterling (1913)

Gold (1915)

He Chortled with Glee (1899)

He Never Tried Again (1912)

His Trip to Hades (1913)

Homeland (1914)

Hors de Saison (1913)

If I Were God (1899)

In a Year (1901)

In and Out (1911)

Je Vis en Espoir (1897)

Memory (1913)

Moods (1913)

My Confession (1912)

My Little Palmist (1914)

Of Man of the Future (1915)

Oh You Everybody's Girl (19)

On the Face of the Earth You are the One (1915)

Rainbows End (1914)

Republican Rallying Song (1916)

Sonnet (1901)

The Gift of God (1905)

The Klondyker's Dream (1914)

The Lover's Liturgy (1913)

The Mammon Worshippers (1911)

The Republican Battle-Hymn (1905)

The Return of Ulysses (1915)

The Sea Sprite and the Shooting Star (1916)

The Socialist's Dream (1912)

The Song of the Flames (1903)

The Way of War (1906)

The Worker and the Tramp (1911)

Tick! Tick! Tick! (1915)

Too Late (1912)

Weasel Thieves (1913)

When All the World Shouted my Name (1905)

Where the Rainbow Fell (1902)

Your Kiss (1914)

PLAYS

Theft (1910)

Daughters of the Rich: A One Act Play (1915)

The Acorn Planter: A California Forest Play (1916)

CPSIA information can be obtained
at www.ICGtesting.com
Printed in the USA
LVHW042300050920
665177LV00005B/659